DORR TO

3 134

D1047964

"An e   e
fans of   is
an absolute must read! *Emergency Deep* is compelling in
its relevance to today's headlines, superbly written with
characters, technology, plot suspense, and combat of the
very highest order."

—Joe Buff, author of *Straits of Power* and *Tidal Rip*

Terminal Run

"[DiMercurio] augments his many high-tech underwater
battles with vivid flashbacks, steamy sex scenes, and even
flourishes of wit."   —*Publishers Weekly*

Threat Vector

"Michael DiMercurio plunges you into the world of undersea warfare with stunning technical accuracy, the best
and brightest heroes, and a deadly look at the future."

—C. A. Mobley, author of *Code of Conflict*

Piranha Firing Point

"If dueling with torpedoes is your idea of a good time,
you'll love it."   —*The Sunday Star-Times* (Auckland)

continued . . .

Barracuda Final Bearing

"Terrific. . . . The fighting really goes into high gear."
—*San Francisco Examiner*

"A stunningly effective technopolitical thriller . . . a dandy, hell-and-high-water yarn."   —*Kirkus Reviews*

"Impressive. . . . Those who thrill to the blip of sonar and the thud of torpedoes will relish this deepwater dive."
—*Publishers Weekly*

Phoenix Sub Zero

"Moves at a breakneck pace."
—Larry Bond, bestselling author of *Combat*

"A master of submarine technology, rivaling Tom Clancy. . . . [An] exciting story from first page to last."
—*Publishers Weekly*

"A good, suspenseful, and spine-tingling read . . . exhilarating."   —The Associated Press

"Powerful . . . rousing . . . for Tom Clancy fans."
—*Kirkus Reviews*

Attack of the Seawolf

"Thrilling, fast-paced, action-packed . . . not to be missed."

—The Associated Press

"As much fun as *The Hunt for Red October,* both as a chase and a catalogue of the Navy's goodies."

—*Arizona Daily Star*

"Superb storytelling . . . suspenseful action. . . . Michael DiMercurio, a former submarine officer, delivers a taut yarn at flank speed." —*The Virginian-Pilot*

"Nail-biting excitement . . . a must for technothriller fans." —*Publishers Weekly*

"Gobs of exciting submarine warfare . . . with a supervillain who gives new meaning to the word 'torture.' "

—*Kirkus Reviews*

Voyage of the Devilfish

"Those who liked *The Hunt for Red October* will love this book." —*Library Journal*

"Cat-and-mouse games in the waters beneath the Arctic ice cap . . . building to a page-turning, nuclear-tipped climax." —*Publishers Weekly*

"Authentic . . . fresh . . . tense . . . a chillingly realistic firsthand feel." —*Kirkus Reviews*

EMERGENCY DEEP

Michael DiMercurio

AN ONYX BOOK

ONYX
Published by New American Library, a division of
Penguin Group (USA) Inc., 375 Hudson Street,
New York, New York 10014, USA
Penguin Group (Canada), 10 Alcorn Avenue, Toronto,
Ontario M4V 3B2, Canada (a division of Pearson Penguin Canada Inc.)
Penguin Books Ltd., 80 Strand, London WC2R 0RL, England
Penguin Ireland, 25 St. Stephen's Green, Dublin 2,
Ireland (a division of Penguin Books Ltd.)
Penguin Group (Australia), 250 Camberwell Road, Camberwell, Victoria 3124,
Australia (a division of Pearson Australia Group Pty. Ltd.)
Penguin Books India Pvt. Ltd., 11 Community Centre, Panchsheel Park,
New Delhi - 110 017, India
Penguin Group (NZ), Cnr Airborne and Rosedale Roads, Albany,
Auckland 1310, New Zealand (a division of Pearson New Zealand Ltd.)
Penguin Books (South Africa) (Pty.) Ltd., 24 Sturdee Avenue,
Rosebank, Johannesburg 2196, South Africa

Penguin Books Ltd., Registered Offices:
80 Strand, London WC2R 0RL, England

First published by Onyx, an imprint of New American Library,
a division of Penguin Group (USA) Inc.

First Printing, December 2004
10 9 8 7 6 5 4 3 2 1

In Memory of Robert Lee Carter, Jr. (1965–2002)

"Not taken away,
just taken ahead."

Rock on, Mr. President.

Our Vision

To be the keystone of a U.S. Intelligence Community that is pre-eminent in the world, known for both the high quality of our work and the excellence of our people.

Our Mission

We support the President, the National Security Council, and all who make and execute U.S. national security policy by (1) providing accurate, evidence-based, comprehensive, and timely foreign intelligence related to national security, and (2) conducting counterintelligence activities, special activities, and other functions related to foreign intelligence and national security as directed by the President.

Our Core Beliefs and Values

We shall provide (1) intelligence that adds substantial value to the management of crises, the conduct of war, and the development of policy, and (2) objectivity in the substance of intelligence, and a deep commitment to the customer in its form and timing.

—Vision, Mission, and Values of the Central Intelligence Agency

The U.S. Submarine Force will remain the world's pre-eminent Submarine Force. We will aggressively incorporate new and innovative technologies to maintain dominance throughout the maritime battlespace. We will promote the multiple capabilities of submarines and develop tactics to support national objectives through battlespace preparation, sea control, supporting the land battle, and strategic deterrence. We will fill the role of the Joint Commander's stealthy, full-spectrum expeditionary platform.

—Vision of the U.S. Submarine Force

Emergency Deep U.S. Submarine Force term for an emergency dive from periscope depth to 150 feet, which is deep enough that the top of the sail will avoid the bottom of a supertanker, but shallow enough that the ship can recover from flooding caused by a collision.

"Emergency deep" is called by the officer of the deck on the periscope when sighting a close surface ship. A submarine hull is built to withstand pressure and cannot absorb the puncture force of a collision, and could easily flood and sink if rammed. Upon the call of "emergency deep," the ship control party performs "immediate actions" without further orders. The diving officer orders full speed, the chief of the watch floods depth control tanks, the planesmen dive the ship to a ten degree "down bubble" and pull out at 150 feet.

The immediate actions for an emergency deep are also taken if the officer of the deck shouts any sudden expletive at periscope depth, because *"oh shit"* is the functional equivalent of "emergency deep."

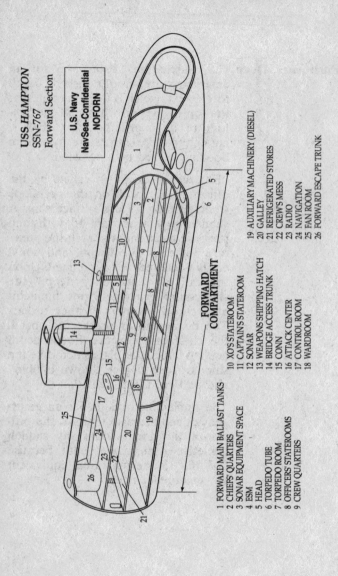

USS HAMPTON
SSN-767
Forward Section

U.S. Navy
NavSea-Confidential
NOFORN

FORWARD
COMPARTMENT

1 FORWARD MAIN BALLAST TANKS
2 CHIEFS' QUARTERS
3 SONAR EQUIPMENT SPACE
4 ESM
5 HEAD
6 TORPEDO TUBE
7 TORPEDO ROOM
8 OFFICERS' STATEROOMS
9 CREW QUARTERS
10 XO'S STATEROOM
11 CAPTAIN'S STATEROOM
12 SONAR
13 WEAPONS SHIPPING HATCH
14 BRIDGE ACCESS TRUNK
15 CONN
16 ATTACK CENTER
17 CONTROL ROOM
18 WARDROOM
19 AUXILIARY MACHINERY (DIESEL)
20 GALLEY
21 REFRIGERATED STORES
22 CREW'S MESS
23 RADIO
24 NAVIGATION
25 FAN ROOM
26 FORWARD ESCAPE TRUNK

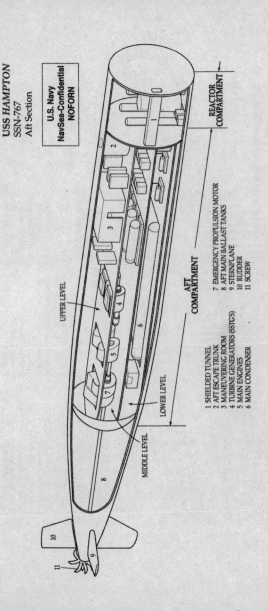

USS HAMPTON
SSN-767
Aft Section

U.S. Navy
NavSea-Confidential
NOFORN

REACTOR
COMPARTMENT

AFT
COMPARTMENT

UPPER LEVEL

MIDDLE LEVEL

LOWER LEVEL

1 SHIELDED TUNNEL
2 AFT ESCAPE TRUNK
3 MANEUVERING ROOM
4 TURBINE GENERATORS (SSTGS)
5 MAIN ENGINES
6 MAIN CONDENSER
7 EMERGENCY PROPULSION MOTOR
8 AFT MAIN BALLAST TANKS
9 STERNPLANE
10 RUDDER
11 SCREW

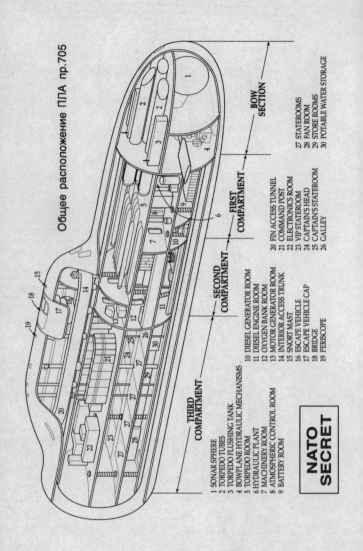

Общее расположение ППА пр. 705

BOW SECTION

FIRST COMPARTMENT

SECOND COMPARTMENT

THIRD COMPARTMENT

1 SONAR SPHERE
2 TORPEDO TUBES
3 TORPEDO FLUSHING TANK
4 BOWPLANE HYDRAULIC MECHANISMS
5 TORPEDO ROOM
6 HYDRAULIC PLANT
7 MACHINERY ROOM
8 ATMOSPHERIC CONTROL ROOM
9 BATTERY ROOM

10 DIESEL GENERATOR ROOM
11 DIESEL ENGINE ROOM
12 OXYGEN BANK ROOM
13 MOTOR GENERATOR ROOM
14 INTERIOR ACCESS TRUNK
15 SNORT MAST
16 ESCAPE VEHICLE
17 ESCAPE VEHICLE CAP
18 BRIDGE
19 PERISCOPE

20 FIN ACCESS TUNNEL
21 COMMAND POST
22 ELECTRONICS ROOM
23 VIP STATEROOM
24 CAPTAIN'S HEAD
25 CAPTAIN'S STATEROOM
26 GALLEY

27 STATEROOMS
28 FAN ROOM
29 STORE ROOMS
30 POTABLE WATER STORAGE

NATO SECRET

Общее расположение ПЛА пр.705

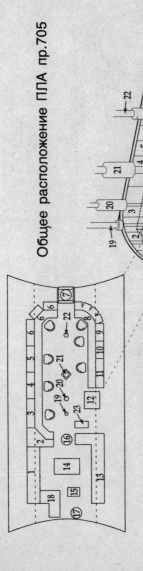

1 SONAR AND FIRECONTROL CABINETS
2 REACTOR PLANT CONTROL
3 TEMPERATURE MONITORING
4 STEAM PLANT CONTROL
5 AUTOMATIC VALVE CONTROL
6 SHIP CONTROL AND BALLAST PANEL
  (PANIC PANEL ABOVE)
7 VERTICAL ACCESSWAY CUBICLE
8 FIRECONTROL PANEL
9 RADIO

10 ELECTRONIC
   COUNTERMEASURES PANEL
11 SONAR
12 NAVIGATION CONTROL
13 NAVIGATION ELECTRONICS
14 400-CYCLE GENERATORS
15 GYROS AND INERTIAL
   NAVIGATION CONTROL
16 INERTIAL NAVIGATION
   BINNACLE

17 ACCESS TO LOWER LEVEL
18 REACTOR CONTROL ELECTRONICS
19 ESM MAST
20 RADAR MAST
21 MULTIFREQUENCY ANTENNA MAST
22 PERISCOPE MAST
23 VERTICAL DISPLAY

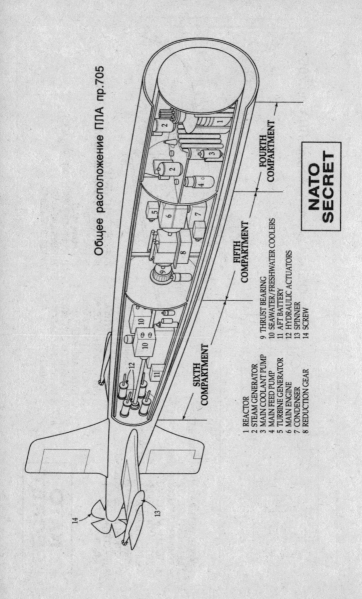

Общее расположение ПЛА пр.705

NATO
SECRET

SIXTH COMPARTMENT

FIFTH COMPARTMENT

FOURTH COMPARTMENT

1 REACTOR
2 STEAM GENERATOR
3 MAIN COOLANT PUMP
4 MAIN FEED PUMP
5 TURBINE GENERATOR
6 MAIN ENGINE
7 CONDENSER
8 REDUCTION GEAR
9 THRUST BEARING
10 SEAWATER/FRESHWATER COOLERS
11 AFT BATTERY
12 HYDRAULIC ACTUATORS
13 SPINNER
14 SCREW

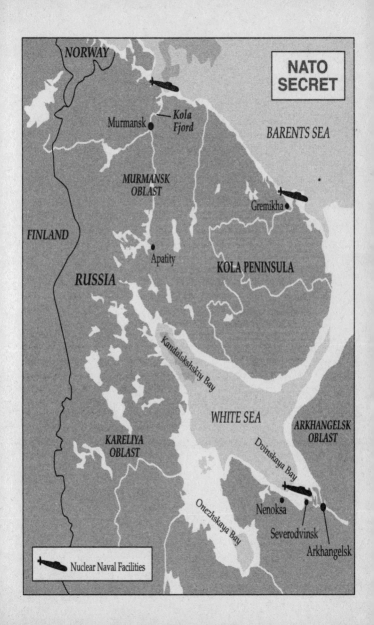

PROLOGUE

The observation court's impeccably maintained shrubbery cast stark shadows across the moonlit cobblestone deck and the granite balustrade overlooking the cliff. Below, in the valley formed by the flow of the Severn River, the grounds of the United States Naval Academy filled half the horizon. Buildings made of forbidding tall granite walls and aged green copper roofs were crowded together on the waterfront estate, each one a seemingly invincible fortress. The vast central building, Bancroft Hall, spread out over acres, the eight wings of the world's biggest dormitory enclosing a tall rotunda and a thousand-foot-long mess hall. To the left, the wide playing fields were deserted, some illuminated by stadium lights, others dark. In the boat basin, dozens of lonely sailboats creaked against their moorings. Off to the right the academic buildings stood in rigid formation, their architecture more modern with their straight vertical slab sides, missing the snarling gargoyles and sculpted warship prows and carved shields of Bancroft Hall, yet still immediately recognizable as daughters of the nineteenth-century structure. Behind the academic row the majestic chapel stood watch, its needlelike spire reaching up to pierce the starry summer sky, its massive bronze doors engraved with intricate detail, its stained glass visibly ornate even in the moonlight. Beneath its marble floor, Captain John Paul Jones lay quiet in his tomb, his massive sarcophagus guarded by three graceful black marble dolphins.

From the observation court, Bancroft Hall was dark except for a few lit windows, but at its front entrance the glaring floodlights lit the wide brick courtyard formed by the first four wings. A central flight of steps and gracefully curving dual ramps led up to the rotunda entrance, where heavy granite columns guarded the three-story-tall brass doors. Two large-bore cannons faced each other at the entrance to the court, just beyond the menacing face of the Indian figurehead taken from the battleship *Delaware,* nicknamed Tecumseh decades in the past. In another five hours, the courtyard would be filled with a thousand midshipmen, marching in formation up the ramps to the war-cadence drumbeats of a brass band playing in front of the steps, but at just after two in the morning of the July Monday, the courtyard was cemetery quiet, the only sound a humid summer sea breeze rustling the leaves of the trees beyond the walls of the second wing.

Tecumseh's eyes glared steadfastly toward the front windows of the fourth wing, to the right of the central doors of the rotunda. Across the sand-colored bricks of the court and up the steps, beyond the granite columns and through the brass doors, the inside of the rotunda lay, its interior silent as a cathedral. The domed ceiling rose fifty feet above the marble floor. A circular mural was painted above the huge doors depicting a desperate sea battle, the battleship wounded and heeling far over as it fired its massive guns against a bitter enemy, flames spreading across the water, explosions rising from the pounding waves, grimacing sailors and officers bleeding and fighting and dying. To the right and left, cast-iron rails of the upper decks of the third and fourth wing overlooked the domed space. Straight ahead, marble steps rose two stories to the immense hushed interior of Memorial Hall, where the names of the graduates who had fallen in battle were engraved in gold below a giant blue flag. The flag's faded white lettering could be read from far below on the floor of the rotunda, the block letters speaking from centuries past, spelling the words of the ancient command, DON'T GIVE UP THE SHIP.

Through the double doors to the right, the fourth wing's five-hundred-foot-long main shaft passageway was as wide as a freeway. Down a flight of steps the blue ceramic tile of the bulkheads changed to a drab brown, the space brightly lit even in the middle of the night. At the far end, the passageway turned a corner and narrowed, only ten feet separating the walls on either side. A hundred feet down this passageway was an intersection, and to the right, the back shaft passageway extended toward Tecumseh Court.

Four doors down on the left was a typical midshipman's room, identical to a thousand others, except for the brass plaque bolted to the wall beside the door. The plaque framed a portrait of a young man wearing a starched high-collar dress white uniform with a rugged face and haunted piercing eyes. The lettering of the plaque was a dedication to the man in the portrait, Commander Howard Gilmore, a Naval Academy graduate and captain of the World War II submarine *Growler*. In a sudden air ambush, Gilmore had been shot and wounded on the conning tower. If the crew had taken the time to get him down the hatch, the submarine would have been doomed. In that split second Gilmore made the decision that earned him the Medal of Honor and this room's dedication plaque—he ordered his second-in-command to crash-dive the submarine without him, shouting down the executive officer's protest with a terse order to save the ship: *"Take her down!"* The USS *Growler* submerged and her crew survived, but Howard Gilmore was never seen again. After his death, newly reporting midshipmen to the Naval Academy were all required to memorize the story of that day at sea and Gilmore's example of honor in battle.

To the right of Gilmore's plaque, the midshipman room's door was shut. On the other side of it, the overhead lights were off but the rays of the full moon shone through the venetian blinds, the slanted bars of light illuminating the frowning face of the youth sitting silently at the desk. Across the desk in the shadows, another midshipman sat in silence. The two had been midshipmen for only seventeen days, but the odds did not favor their remaining midshipmen another seventeen.

The summer training period had begun on Induction Day in late June. The name given to freshman summer training, Plebe Summer, was deceptive. It had a Club Med ring to it, the words in the shiny Annapolis catalog filling young hearts with visions of a quaint summer spent sailing and going to orientation sessions on a college campus by the bay. Far to the north, at a former fort called West Point, Army cadets sweated through training labeled 'Beast Barracks,' a name much closer to the truth, but still far from describing the experience. During the summer, the thousand new midshipmen—the plebes—suffered a harsh probation period that combined the physical rigors of Marine Corps boot camp with the psychological trials of a Nazi prisoner-of-war camp.

The midshipman sitting in the moonlight was the tallest plebe in November Company's second platoon, third squad. His physique was wiry, his high school double varsity letters in track and tennis the result of natural speed and lightning-quick reflexes. His pale complexion and denim-blue eyes were visible below his shorn scalp, which had once been covered with fine blond hair. He tapped the end of a mechanical pencil on his blotter, thinking about the two full-ride Ivy League academic scholarships he'd turned down to come to this place. The name tag on the uniform hanging neatly in the closet behind him read VORNADO, a name he shared with the fighter pilot and admiral who had inspired him to come here, and whom he was about to disappoint.

The midshipman sitting in the shadows across from Peter Vornado shook his head in frustration. Midshipman Fourth Class Burke Kinnaird Dillinger stood almost a head shorter than Vornado, but had a weight lifter's build with every muscle defined, his shoulders broad, his neck thicker than Vornado's thigh, his biceps bulging. He had reported with a thick mane of wavy hair black as diesel oil, the only sign it had once been there the five-o'clock shadow on his skull. His cold gray-blue eyes glared dangerously from under thick black eyebrows as he frowned across the desk. On Induction Day, Vornado had learned that his roommate was also the son of a flag officer, but while Admiral Vornado had commanded an aircraft carrier battle group, General Dillinger had worked in the dark corners of the Defense Intelligence Agency. Not that it mattered, Vornado thought, since they would be certain to be processed out of the Academy within days.

The silence was eventually broken by Vornado's baritone murmur. "We'd better think about this one last time, B.K. We do this thing, we stand a good chance of getting caught. And if we don't, we'll be asked about it. If we lie, we'll be kicked out for violating the honor code. If we confess, we'll be kicked out for a major conduct offense. Either way we're screwed. And either way it'll be damned hard to explain at home, and we won't even be able to get into the local community college. I want revenge as much as you do, but not if it costs me this much."

"We went over this," Dillinger said, a tone of annoyance in his smooth tenor voice. "We're at a decision point. We only have two possible futures. In one, that son of a bitch Whitehead and his classmates get the message not to fuck with us. He lays off our case and we go on to graduate. But if we do nothing, Whitehead hazes us right out the door. From the first day he was on us, and every day it's gotten worse. After what that bastard did tonight, I can't control myself anymore. If we don't do this, we'd better face the fact that we'll never see the end of Plebe Summer. That's not something I want to explain back home. So you tell me, Vornado. What choice do we have?"

Vornado nodded. On Induction Day, minutes after they had left their hair on the barber shop floor and traded civilian clothes for ill-fitting crackerjack white cotton uniforms, Midshipman First Class Whitehead had swaggered in front of their ragged formation. Whitehead was a gaunt senior—a firstie—wearing a perfectly starched tropical white uniform with black shoulderboards and a splash of ribbons over his left breast pocket. There was a stark and seemingly intentional contrast between his tailored and starched white uniform and the plebes' shapeless coveralls. He wore a brimmed midshipman's cap over perfectly trimmed black hair. Around his waist was a black leather swordbelt and an officer's sword in its gilt scabbard. He kept one hand on the handle, as if he would unsheath it at any moment and slice off the head of one of the offending plebes. He wore a constant expression of barely controlled anger, his eyes wide enough to see white above and below his dull brown irises. In the first moments of Whitehead's command of the squad, he had introduced himself by putting his face two inches from Vornado's. His brown eyes drilled into Vornado's from under the shiny black brim of his spotless white hat, making Vornado feel naked in his ridiculous blue-banded sailor's cap. After glaring silently at Vornado for a long moment, Whitehead erupted into a fog-horn scream that pierced Vornado's ears, tiny droplets of spit flying into Vornado's eyes.

"Hey, fuckface! Listen up! You are unworthy pond scum!

*You are lower than whaleshit at the bottom of the ocean!
You will not last one month at my Naval Academy!"*

Vornado had gulped and kept his eyes straight ahead,
trying to stare calmly through the firstie to the wall beyond
him, trying to ignore the older midshipman's hot breath on
his face. The screaming continued for a miserable five minutes, but finally Whitehead moved down the row, stopping
in front of his second target, Midshipman Dillinger. Vornado listened with his eyes rigidly straight ahead as
Whitehead made fun of Dillinger's name and screamed that
he too would soon be leaving the Academy.

When Whitehead finally finished, he marched the squad
outside. Vornado assumed they were on the way to be issued their gear, but instead found himself marched into
McDonough Hall, one of the cavernous gyms, where a boxing ring waited. Whitehead paired up the squad, all of them
evenly matched in height and weight except for Vornado
and Dillinger. Vornado glanced at Dillinger's football line-
man's body and wondered how long it would take for him
to get knocked out. Whitehead's mismatch seemed meant
to get Vornado killed, an assault by proxy. The two hadn't
even exchanged a word of greeting before they were required to fight each other. Vornado pulled off his crackerjack pants and tunic, his required gym gear uniform
beneath, and climbed hesitantly into the ring at Whitehead's insistence, his heart pounding in sudden terror as he
saw the flexing muscles of the heavier plebe. Vornado had
never boxed in his life, and his last fistfight had been in
third grade. He strapped on the flimsy old leather headgear,
wondering how much protection it would offer against the
kind of punch Dillinger could throw.

He gulped as Whitehead rang the bell. Dillinger charged
straight across the canvas, his speed remarkable for his bull-
ish build. His immediate jackhammer jab sailed toward
Vornado's face. For an instant Vornado felt himself freeze
in fear, but without conscious thought his body ducked and
danced backward, his right arm tensing and lashing out at
the compact opponent. The punch connected, Vornado's
right fist landing hard on Dillinger's ear. The force of his
own punch threw Vornado hard into the ropes and spun
Dillinger half to his right. Vornado bounced off the ropes,
his momentum sending him back toward Dillinger, who

fired a second jab that Vornado evaded. Dillinger, infuriated by Vornado's punch, attacked viciously while Vornado backpedaled. Dillinger lashed out with a right, missing as Vornado stepped aside and jabbed back. But then Dillinger faked left and moved right. A blurry fist the size of a truck came from nowhere and smashed into Vornado's face, snapping his head back. Blood spurted furiously from his nose, splattering sickeningly on the canvas. There was no pain at first, just the shock of being moved across the ring in an instant by sheer force, but the explosion of blood distracted Dillinger long enough that Vornado was able to connect with a left cross to Dillinger's eye, and the punch knocked Dillinger into the corner and opened a cut that spewed dark blood over half of his face. Dillinger's expression registered surprise and rage for a moment before he started across the ring for revenge. Halfway there the bell rang as Whitehead stopped the fight, screaming at Dillinger and Vornado to freeze and stand at attention. The pain arrived then, making Vornado dizzy, his nose throbbing in agony, the ring and the staring faces of his classmates spinning slowly around him. He and Dillinger stood stupidly bleeding and hyperventilating. Whitehead shook his head in disgust and waved disparagingly at them.

"Usually drawing blood in the ring earns you an A, but not for these lame second-generation pussies. Take a long look at the 'blood brothers,' gentlemen. You won't be seeing them for long, because they'll be quitting as soon as the Commandant accepts resignations in week three, and if they don't they'll wish they had. And do you know why? Because they haven't earned the right to be here, that's why."

Whitehead ordered in the next pair and shouted at them to fight instead of cavort across a dance floor as Vornado and Dillinger had. Vornado broke his rigid attention long enough to glance at Dillinger, who glared back with a dark smoldering anger, but Vornado knew the fury wasn't for him but for their firstie.

Three hours later, after equipment issue, Whitehead marched the squad back to the zero deck of Bancroft Hall and assigned them their rooms. "You've got the Gilmore room, Vornado. Maybe some of his character will rub off on you, but somehow I doubt it." Vornado entered the spartan room and dropped his new seabag. The door opened and his boxing opponent walked in. He looked around and nodded cautiously in greeting.

"Peter Vornado, Norfolk, Virginia," Vornado said, extending his hand. "Nice fight. You scared the hell out of me."

A smile lit up the shorter plebe's face for just an instant as he clamped Vornado's hand in a tight grip. "B.K. Dillinger, McLean, Virginia. Thanks, but I just pretended you were Whitehead. Who would think a skinny guy like you could throw a punch like that?" Dillinger rubbed his eyebrow, the butterfly bandage fresh after the squad had waited outside the boxing complex's Misery Hall for the medic to examine him.

In the next days they had exchanged few words, their attention taken by the constant pace of Plebe Summer, the minutes stretched into hours by Whitehead's relentless hazing. It had not been enough for the firstie to shout insults at the two roommates in front of their squad, or to direct his fury at them every day. He carefully planned his brand of torture around the Academy's already miserable routine. The main fixture of the summer's training was the "come-around." In a come-around the plebes would "hit a bulk-head" by standing at rigid attention against the wall, "braced up" with their necks shoved into their chests, while Whitehead shouted abuse and made them recite their memorized "rates" of information they were required to know, testing their minds like no high school final exam ever had.

"Sir, there are one hundred forty-three days till Navy beats the hell out of Army, one hundred sixty-two days until Christmas leave, three hundred and thirty-three days till Second Class Ring Dance, and three hundred and thirty-seven days until First Class graduation. Sir, the menu for noon meal is hamburgers with cheese, onions and assorted condiments, potato puffs, baked beans, ice cream, iced tea with lemon wedges, and milk. What time is it—sir, I am greatly embarrassed and deeply humiliated that due to unforeseen circumstances beyond my control, the inner workings and hidden mechanisms of my chronometer are in such inaccord with the great sidereal movement with which time is generally reckoned that I cannot with any degree of accuracy state the correct time, sir, but without fear of being too greatly in error, I will state that it is about four minutes, three seconds, and eleven ticks past three bells, sir."

There was an absurd amount to memorize—the names and hometowns of the hundred plebe midshipmen in their company, the POW code of conduct, all twenty-seven verses of the four-page-long poem "The Laws of the Navy," eight boat hails, six dozen professional engineering terms and their definitions, ship-handling commands, how to bring about a square-rigger sailing vessel, Morse code, the coaches and captains of every sport, twelve Navy fight songs, the history of a hundred monuments and buildings on the grounds, the latitude and longitude of Annapolis, the number of bricks in Tecumseh Court, the scores of every Navy bowl game, fifty naval sayings, the heads of the academic departments, the officers of the professional development departments, and detailed knowledge of three front-page newspaper articles and three sports-page articles from that day's *Washington Post*. Each day the requirements multiplied.

But it wasn't just that they had to memorize a telephone book of information. They had to spit it out with Whitehead screaming in their faces at a come-around or at the meal table. At the table Whitehead called on Vornado and Dillinger constantly. The rule was "three chews and a swallow" before the plebe would have to belt out the answer to whatever Whitehead asked. Vornado had barely eaten in the last weeks, his weight dropping, his face becoming gaunt and hollow. Dillinger had lost weight even faster, his T-shirts and coverall pants hanging on him.

While the meal interrogations and come-arounds were severe, it was the special come-arounds Whitehead conducted for Dillinger and Vornado that were making them the most miserable, each one a new torture. In Whitehead's special come-arounds he kept them from the rest of the squad, double-timing them up four flights of stairs to an empty fourth-deck room. While Whitehead walked, they were required to "chop" down the center of the passageways, which meant they had to run with their chins braced, their eyes straight ahead, and turn by "squaring the corner," pivoting while shouting "Go Navy, sir!" or "Beat Army, sir!" Once in the room, Whitehead would hammer away at them to resign. When they refused, he would make them hold their rifles straight out from their bodies, arms parallel to the deck, until their arms shook and their skin was slick with sweat. Or he would make them hang from the top of the tall room door, their hands bleeding from the door's sharp metal plates. While their muscles shook from the strain, Whitehead would scream in their faces that they were useless, that they had cheated the admissions process, that they had no place at the Naval Academy.

In the hours of Whitehead's special come-arounds, the thought rose in Vornado's mind that perhaps he should quit, but then he saw his father's face and heard his father's voice as the naval officer ran down the gangway of the gigantic aircraft carrier and scooped young Vornado's six-year-old body into his arms after a long deployment. It was the happy memories that made Whitehead vanish for a few merciful seconds. Vornado tried to keep his mind away from the painful memories—his mother's long sickness when Vornado was a second grader and her death during the hot summer before third grade, the battle lost to the cancer that turned a beautiful, energetic woman into a sad wraith. Vornado's father had struggled to balance his sea-going career with raising Vornado and his little sister, calling in Vornado's unmarried aunt to live with them, an emergency wartime measure that had become permanent. Vornado's father had never remarried. He claimed there was no time between being a father to his children and to the men of the fighter squadron he commanded. The older Vornado's long deployments were the worst, but when he would return home, the family was happy. Vornado's sister, Diana, had gone through a dark time when their mother died. Vornado had stepped in to help her then, and it was her letters to him now that were helping him. That and the long letters from his father, explaining things about the Navy that Vornado had never known, telling him stories from his own experience at Annapolis. Two years before, Vornado's father had been awarded his third star, and duty had taken him back to sea. Vornado was worried about Diana with the old man deployed and him locked down during Plebe Summer. But there was little he could do except write her letters during the few moments he was allowed as free time.

In Vornado's letters to his sister, he never mentioned

Whitehead or his special come-arounds. Tonight's special Whitehead come-around had been dramatically worse than the ones before. The empty fourth-deck room was equipped with a telephone. The room's window was open to the wide copper roof deck, a large cardboard shipping box outside the window a few feet from the edge overlooking a seventy-foot drop to the courtyard below. Dillinger was ordered to wait outside, braced at attention against the bulkhead. Vornado stood at attention while Whitehead ordered him to pick up the phone, dial his father, and announce he would quit the Academy. Vornado responded with the closest expression a plebe could come to refusing a firstie's order, by barking out, "Beat Army, sir!" Whitehead ordered him to climb out the window. Vornado obeyed, feeling like an idiot standing at attention under the stars of the hot July night. Whitehead ordered him to look down to the courtyard below. While he was on the fourth deck, the building had a ground floor—the "zero deck"—and two subbasements, making the ledge seven stories high. Vornado looked over the edge, a terrible vertigo turning his stomach. With an effort of will he came back to attention. Whitehead ordered him to climb into the box. With a sense of unreality Vornado complied, knowing he was making a terrible mistake. Whitehead pushed Vornado down and shut the box lid. Three more times Whitehead ordered Vornado to quit, and three times Vornado refused. He felt the box spinning left, then right, a loud scraping noise vibrating beneath Vornado's body as Whitehead pushed the box four feet to the edge of the roof. Vornado could barely believe it when he felt Whitehead tipping the box. He leaned hard into the opposite box wall, his heart hammering in fear.

Whitehead's voice became quiet for the first time since Vornado had met him. He whispered from outside the box that distressed plebes sometimes came to this part of the fourth deck and jumped out the window, ending their problems with Plebe Summer and avoiding the shame of quitting or being kicked out, and that Whitehead's classmates waited below to grab the box so the Commandant's investigation would reveal that Vornado was a suicide victim. After a pause, he gave Vornado one final order to quit.

Vornado couldn't find his voice. In the panic of the moment he wondered what Dillinger would do, and realized

that his volatile roommate would just get out of the box and
smash his fist into Whitehead's face. No, Dillinger would
never have gotten into the box in the first place. As Vornado
completed the thought, the box suddenly tilted. *Whitehead
was really doing this.* The box tipped and began a sickening
freefall. Vornado's stomach rose up in terror, his mind spinning in fury and helpless fright. The box slowly tumbled in
its flight until it was upside down. Vornado shut his eyes.
For horrifying endless seconds the box fell.

The box's motion suddenly stopped, the impact sudden
but soft. The box was upside down, its lid opening and
dumping Vornado onto a bare mattress on the room's floor.
He stared incredulously at the room around him, thinking
in a stupor that instead of landing on the courtyard far
below, he had fallen *into* the room. Vornado felt himself
vomiting, but nothing came up, because he hadn't eaten in
two days from Whitehead's hazing at the meal table. The
dry heaves continued for three more convulsions, Vornado's eyes clamped shut against the tears of fear and rage
erupting against his will. He could feel himself shaking, and
realized that he was about to get up and throw a punch
at Whitehead.

Vornado's father's voice spoke from a distance in his
mind, telling him that this was what Whitehead was hoping
for, an assault by a plebe on a firstie less than three weeks
into Plebe Summer. That was how Whitehead would get
Vornado discharged, because there could be no extenuating
circumstances. The senior officers would believe that a
plebe who would attack his firstie in the stress of Plebe
Summer would certainly crack in battle, and Whitehead
would have won. If Vornado could just keep himself from
throwing that punch, there was nothing more Whitehead
could do to him. With that thought Vornado regained control of himself. He rose to his feet, his body still trembling.
He came to a rigid, braced attention, and shouted in his
baritone voice, "Beat Army, sir!"

Whitehead's expression was murderous anger. "You
weak, bony pussy," he said in disgust. "Get in the passageway and hit a bulkhead."

Vornado jogged from the room, stopped at the wall, did
an about-face, and came to a braced attention while
Whitehead called Dillinger into the room. As he waited,

he wondered if Whitehead were about to do the same thing to Dillinger. Eventually Dillinger emerged, his face red and his uniform soaked in sweat, his eyes dark and unreadable. They had been marched back to their rooms. Vornado had been tempted to ask Dillinger what Whitehead had done to him, but Dillinger's expression had warned him off. Neither did Vornado volunteer anything about his experience.

That had been five hours ago, and neither plebe had been able to sleep. Two hours after taps, they left their beds and sat at their desks, both deep in thought. Vornado tapped his pencil on the blotter, still weighing their options as he stared out the window.

Across the desk Burke Dillinger bit his lip, waiting for his roommate to make a decision. It was amazing how much the tall, self-assured Vornado reminded him of his older brother. There was just something about being the oldest that seemed to make all the difference in life. How easy it must be, Dillinger thought, to sail through life with that innate confidence. His brother and Vornado just seemed to have that natural certainty that when they gave an order that it would be followed immediately. Neither had any of the doubts or worries that Dillinger struggled with every day.

It had been two years since his life had been turned upside down by his father's stunning admission at the dinner table. For Dillinger's entire life, he had known his father to be a salesman for General Dynamics, a gigantic defense contractor. The old man would be gone for months at a time, working on sales projects. Then between the salad and the steak one night, his father announced that he had been promoted. He now had three stars. Dillinger had looked up quizzically at his father, who went on to announce that he was taking over as Deputy Director of the Defense Intelligence Agency at the Pentagon, and that he was now a lieutenant general. It took the younger Dillinger some time to realize that his father had been an Army officer all along, but had been a field agent for the obscure intelligence agency, and now that he would be a headquarters man, he could drop his cover story. A cover story that had made him a liar.

The elder Dillinger had been a West Point grad, with an office downstairs with his diplomas and his Bronze Star, but there was also an honorable discharge certificate framed on the wall, along with General Dynamics sales awards, photos of his father in a suit and tie shaking hands with customers, and binders filled with sales data. As Dillinger had dropped his fork to the plate, all he could think was that his own father, while preaching West Point's code of "Duty, Honor, Country," had lived a damned lie. Dillinger couldn't shake a sense of betrayal. The only thing that had helped was being chided by his accomplished older brother, Matt, who had insisted he get a hold of himself and move on.

Dillinger had never excelled at school, as Matt had, but he had thrown himself into sports, finding success where his brother hadn't. He knew he would not gain entry to an Ivy League school, and even if he did, there would be no competing with Matt, who was bound for Harvard Law after his graduation this academic year. Dillinger had decided to apply to Annapolis out of defiance to his father, who had never missed an Army-Navy game in thirty years and who had always lost his voice the day after every game from cheering for his beloved Army team. And yet, going to a service academy was also a salute to the old man, an attempt to wear the uniform to emulate him, or perhaps to distinguish himself from his bookish older brother. And while he was going to the Naval Academy, he would enter the Marine Corps and become an infantryman as his father had been. Or a Navy SEAL, a commando. The day the letter had come awarding him an appointment to Annapolis had been his happiest. But the recent developments with Whitehead meant Dillinger would be coming home a miserable failure less than a month after leaving for the Academy. Dillinger bit his lip in frustration at Vornado's indecision, thinking he would have to do this alone.

"I don't know about you," Dillinger announced. "But if I'm going to get thrown out of here, I want it to be for kicking Midshipman First Class Whitehead's ass. I'm going down fighting with no regrets. And I'm doing this with you or without you. You've got about thirty seconds to decide before I leave the room."

Vornado looked up suddenly. "Give me the details, B.K. How do we do this?"

Dillinger bent down and opened the desk's built-in safe, the only privacy a plebe had. He pulled out a roll of duct tape, a zipper bag filled with long plastic cable ties, two black ski caps, and two pairs of black sweat gear. Vornado stared at the pile.

"We put on the black gear and take Whitehead out to the river. Let him swim with his hands and feet tied up, the bastard."

Vornado shook his head. "River's too far. It means carrying him a quarter mile, either through Bancroft Hall or out in the yard. And his room's right on T-Court. I've got a better idea." Vornado laid out his plan, and Dillinger nodded.

"By the way," Vornado whispered while he put on the black sweatshirt and pulled the balaclava ski mask down over his face. "Where'd you get all this stuff?"

"I called my father last weekend. I told him what I needed and he sent it in a care package."

"You tell him what we were doing?"

"No, but I think he has an idea."

Vornado swallowed hard as he realized what he was about to do. "Ready?" Vornado asked.

Dillinger nodded as he stood. He walked up to Vornado with his fists held straight out from his body. At first Vornado stared at him, but then saw what Dillinger wanted. As if they were about to start a boxing match, Vornado balled up his fists and punched both of Dillinger's. Dillinger grinned and turned toward the door and opened it.

The passageway was brightly lit by the overhead fluorescent fixtures. The clock loudly ticked over a minute, now showing the time to be half past two. They hurried down the passageway in a fast walk. It was the first time they had been in a passageway without chopping down the center in a brace and squaring corners. Whitehead's room was all the way down the hall toward Tecumseh Court, the three-man first classmen's room with the corner view of the wide expanse of brick between the wings. Just outside his door were the double doors to the court, their use restricted to the upperclassmen. Whitehead would be alone in the room, since only a few firsties manned the Plebe Detail. Outside Whitehead's door Vornado glanced at Dillinger through the ski mask, only his roommate's eyes visible in the small eyeholes. Dillinger's glance was steady and intense. Vornado nodded, and they pushed Whitehead's door slowly open.

For a moment they stood in the room, the door silently shutting behind them. It was strange to be in the room of the midshipman who had tortured them so relentlessly for the past three weeks. His sword and swordbelt were lying across a desk chair. A freshly drycleaned tropical white uniform hung outside the closet, fully rigged with shoulderboards and ribbons. His freshly polished white shoes lay on top of a page of newspaper on the desk. The room was perfect other than that small amount of clutter and the rumpled blanket of Whitehead's bed. Whitehead lay on the sheet in his boxer shorts and white T-shirt, snoring softly in the predawn darkness.

Dillinger handed Vornado a cable tie and took one for himself. Vornado carefully moved Whitehead's arm so that his wrists were together, then wrapped them with the cable tie. The hasp of the tie made a slight buzzing sound as Vornado tightened it up, but Whitehead didn't stir. Vornado looked over at Dillinger, who had pulled the covers off Whitehead's ankles and tightened a cable tie on his ankles. The next part was tougher, because odds were that Whitehead would wake up and struggle. Before they left their own room they had pulled off the correct lengths of duct tape so the tape wouldn't make a ripping noise as they unwound it. Vornado took the shorter length and carefully and gently placed it over Whitehead's mouth and wrapped it back over his lower ears to the back of his head, then slowly turned his head so he could get the tape around the other side. When he finished, Whitehead twitched but didn't wake up. Dillinger had pulled a longer length of duct tape off his black sweatpants and wrapped one end around Whitehead's wrists and then circled his waist. They would have to lift him off the bed to finish this part, and odds were this would be when he woke up.

Dillinger lifted Whitehead up from the mattress. He made a noise and his body kicked suddenly. Whitehead's eyes came open and widened in panic, and he tried to get up. Vornado pinned Whitehead's shoulders and Dillinger grabbed his legs, but the thin firstie writhed in fury. Vornado began to regret the idea, now seeing that Whitehead would be too strong for the two of them to abduct from the hall by themselves. Suddenly Dillinger cocked his fist and smashed it into Whitehead's stomach and immediately

Whitehead stopped struggling and collapsed in a fetal position on the bed, coughing into the duct tape binding his mouth. Quickly, while Whitehead had the wind knocked out of him, Vornado lifted him enough to finish wrapping the duct tape around his waist and arms, immobilizing his upper body.

Without a word the two plebes grabbed their squad leader and carried him out of the room door, down the hall, and through the upperclass-only doors to Tecumseh Court. Whitehead recovered from the body punch enough to begin struggling as they carried him, but it slowed them down only slightly. With his wrists tied to his waist and his ankles tied together, all he could do was bend and twist. Vornado felt naked in the harsh floodlights of the court. Surely the watchstanders in the main office next to the rotunda would see them and run out to stop them. They hurried across the court until they reached the snarling Indian figurehead statue of Tecumseh, Dillinger pushing Whitehead into the tall marble base of the monument. Dillinger produced the roll of duct tape while Vornado forced Whitehead to stand straight. Dillinger made half a dozen rapid laps of the statue, tying Whitehead to it with the duct tape. The unrolling duct tape made loud rasping noises in the quiet courtyard as it unwound. Whitehead's eyes stared at them in impotent fury. He made muffled sounds from his mouth, the duct tape gagging him. Dillinger made the final wrap around the firstie, making his head fast to the marble obelisk, the tape passing across Whitehead's eyes.

When they were finished, Dillinger stood back for a moment, then produced a permanent-ink marker and wrote the word on Whitehead's forehead that Whitehead had taunted them with for the last weeks: PUSSY.

Vornado was about to turn to run back to the fourth wing's upperclass doors when Dillinger wound up with his fist and fired a punch at Whitehead's forehead. Whitehead's skull smashed into the hard marble surface with a sickening crunch. The firstie's body relaxed and he hung limply from the duct tape.

"Jesus, B.K., what the hell did you do that for?" Vornado hissed, pulling Dillinger away. Dillinger cradled his hand in pain, cursing quietly. Vornado dragged Dillinger away from Tecumseh toward the hall. The plebes broke into a sprint toward the upperclass doors. They hurried down the passageway past Whitehead's door and to the safety of their room. The door shut behind them as they stripped off the black sweats and pulled their regulation gym gear back on. Vornado felt a mixture of elation and fear, with a pang of regret as he remembered the sound of Whitehead's skull smacking the marble.

"What about this stuff?" Vornado puffed.

"Back in the safe for now," Dillinger said. "I saved the box it came in. I'll mail it to my brother during tomorrow's free period."

"What if they investigate?" Vornado whispered from under his covers, his body slick with sweat.

"Let them," Dillinger whispered back, the anger clear even in his whisper. "They ask me what I was doing, I'll tell them the truth. I was deep in sleep, dreaming."

Vornado shut his eyes, but knew there would be no sleep for him the rest of the night. Twenty minutes later, he could hear the sound of Dillinger snoring from across the room.

The plebes of November Company, second platoon, third squad, formed up outside Midshipman Whitehead's room for morning 0615 come-around, as usual. There was no sign of Whitehead. Vornado braced against the bulkhead, waiting. Several minutes passed with no sign of a firstie. Vornado glanced across the passageway, finding Dillinger, who stood impassively at attention, his face betraying nothing. After ten minutes of waiting, the two-striper company subcommander, Midshipman Lieutenant Adcock, walked slowly up.

For a minute he stood in front of the squad, sleepily tucking in his shirt and wrapping his sword belt around his waist. When he finished he looked up with a serious expression and spoke in a low voice.

"Gentlemen, Mr. Whitehead has been taken to Hospital Point. He's in serious condition with a head injury. Somebody apparently pulled a recon raid and tied him up to Tecumseh. The Commandant will be conducting an investigation. A new squad leader will be here later today. If you thought Mr. Whitehead was tough, you'd better prepare yourself for Mr. Kaminsky. Mr. Kaminsky will be the brigade commander when the academic year starts."

Vornado stared straight ahead in his braced attention. The word *investigation* sent a shiver down his spine. And the fact that the new squad leader would be the number one midshipman at the Academy made his stomach suddenly sour.

The door of the room that had been Whitehead's opened slowly. Midshipman First Class Kaminsky stood in the doorway.

"Come on in," he said to Vornado in a deep, authoritative, but quiet voice. Vornado jogged into the room and came to attention on the other side of the door. Kaminsky reached behind him to shut it. "Carry on and sit down," he said, motioning to the desk where Whitehead's white shoes had been last night.

"Aye-aye, sir!" Vornado barked, pulling the chair back and sitting on the front three inches of it, his upper body at rigid attention.

"I said carry on, Mr. Vornado. Relax," Kaminsky said. Vornado relaxed his posture, glancing up at Kaminsky and seeing him for the first time, the tall firstie previously a blur in his peripheral vision. Kaminsky had shaved his large head. His shoulders bulged from his tropical white uniform, his biceps crowding the shirtsleeves. *A power lifter,* Vornado thought. *He should get along well with Dillinger, at least until he finds out what we did.*

Kaminsky stood away from the desk, looking out the window at the sun-drenched Tecumseh Court.

"I suppose you realize why we're here," Kaminsky said, still staring out at the courtyard, a tone of weariness in his voice. "I'm not just the first set brigade commander; I'm the brigade Honor Committee chairman."

Vornado tried not to gulp in guilt, but felt his heart racing as Kaminsky turned to face him. Kaminsky looked at him for a moment, his eyes on Vornado's name tag. He turned back to the window and drummed his fingers on the windowsill.

"Mr. Vornado, just so we know what we're talking about here, I want you to recite the honor code."

"Aye-aye, sir," Vornado said, coming back to attention in his seat. " 'A midshipman will not lie, cheat, or steal, nor tolerate those who do,' sir."

"Fine. You can relax. Let me tell you how I got to be involved in the Honor Committee," he said slowly. "It was plebe year. I got called in by my company officer, who told me I had been reported for an honor offense. With an honor violation, there's no warning. If they find you guilty, you're separated from the naval service that very day. That was bad enough, but the alleged honor offense was that I took a quart of milk from the mess hall." Kaminsky slowly moved across the room and sat down at the desk across from Vornado. "Now, we take milk from the mess hall all the time. The firsties did it, so did the second class, the youngsters, and if there was any milk left, the plebes. No one had ever considered it an honor offense. It didn't even occur to anyone. But somehow it occurred to the man who turned me in. Ridiculous or not, they had to conduct a full investigation. It took a week of meetings to get through all the procedures, and of course I was found not guilty. But during it all, I guess the Commandant got a sense of who I was, and I was ordered to be the company honor rep. It wasn't long till I was a regimental striper. If I hadn't been put up for the honor offense, odds are today I'd just be a one-striper, keeping my head down and trying to graduate. Funny how things worked out."

Vornado said nothing, not sure if Kaminsky expected him to say anything. The older midshipman paused, glancing down at the table.

"Later on, I eventually found out who had accused me of the honor offense." Kaminsky laughed without smiling. "Fred Whitehead."

Vornado stared at the firstie, his mouth open.

"Funny thing," Kaminsky said, standing again and wandering back to the window. "During our Plebe Summer Whitehead was almost run off by our firstie, Smokin' Joe Kraft. Mr. Kraft had it in for Whitehead. Three special come-arounds every day, laps and push-ups and flaming fits. Whitehead was the squad's shit screen." Kaminsky looked over. "Kind of like you and Dillinger were."

Vornado swallowed, wondering if Kaminsky's past tense meant anything ominous.

"Mr. Kraft was convinced that Whitehead didn't belong here. I saw all the stuff Kraft pulled on Whitehead, and I felt sorry for him. When Whitehead survived all the harassment and made it to the end of Plebe Summer, I figured Whitehead had bested a firstie asshole. And then Whitehead pulled the honor violation trick. I saw it then— Mr. Kraft had been right all along. He had looked into Whitehead's character and seen something no one else could see."

Kaminsky turned and returned to his seat at the desk, his eyes staring into Vornado's. "Another funny thing, Mr. Vornado. Mr. Kraft was the son of a three-star admiral. He never made a big deal of it, but all of his classmates did. They'd pile on Whitehead, screaming at him that if the son of a three-star admiral wanted him out, he should pack his trash and resign."

Vornado exhaled, his throat suddenly tight.

"You're the son of an admiral too, aren't you?" Kaminsky kept staring at Vornado's eyes.

"Sir, yes sir," Vornado said.

Kaminsky found something on his desk, a remote control to his huge stereo. He stared down at the buttons on it, then began to turn it in his hands.

"Mr. Vornado, I'm going to ask you a direct question and I want you to give me a direct answer," Kaminsky said. "Bear in mind that you are on your honor."

Vornado gulped, knowing his protruding Adam's apple had just jumped. Kaminsky had to know his every thought. "Aye-aye, sir."

"Did you participate in the recon raid that injured Mr. Whitehead?"

Vornado exhaled, knowing this moment would come. He also knew there was no way he could look Kaminsky in the eye and lie about this.

"Sir, ye—"

Suddenly the stereo boomed, making Vornado jump half out of his seat, the music blasting into the room from the large speakers. As suddenly as the music started, it stopped, plunging the room into pin-drop quiet.

"Sorry about that," Kaminsky said as he looked down at the remote control. "This thing's a little touchy. I'll ask you again, Mr. Vornado. Did you pull the recon raid that got Whitehead hurt?"

"Sir, yes, I—"

Again the bass thrum of the music screeched from the

stereo system, the music playing longer this time. After twenty seconds of driving beat, Kaminsky shut off the stereo again.

"Let's see if we can get this straight," Kaminsky said, his head nodding to an imaginary beat, as if he were dancing to the music, the motion comical, as if he were deliberately trying to rob the moment of its seriousness. "Mr. Vornado." Kaminsky blatantly pointed his remote control at the stereo, his finger poised over the play button. "Did you participate in the recon raid that got Mr. Whitehead hurt?"

Vornado looked into Kaminsky's eyes, a dawning understanding finally arriving. "Sir, no, sir. I slept through the night. I learned about it at morning come-around."

Kaminsky nodded seriously, as if he were a professor who had just made an obscure point clear to a slow pupil.

"That's what I thought," he said, finding a pen and scribbling something into an open file on his desk. "Thank you, Mr. Vornado. You can return to your room. If you would, send in Mr. Dillinger."

His heart hammering, Vornado bolted to his feet at attention and barked, "Aye-aye, sir." He braced up, jogged to the door, opened it on the latch, then chopped to the center of the passageway, where he pivoted ninety degrees to the right while shouting, "Go Navy, sir!" He chopped down to the Gilmore room with his chin shoved into his chest until he reached the passageway door of his room. He pivoted again, shouting "Beat Army, sir!" and pushed open the door.

Inside the room with Dillinger were four upperclassmen, all of them in working khaki uniforms, which looked strange, since every upperclassman had worn only tropical white uniforms the entire summer. Vornado came to attention, braced up, and sounded off, yelling, "Midshipman Vornado, Fourth Class, sir!"

One of the upperclassman grinned from his perch on the desk. "Relax, asshole," he said. Vornado released his brace, and saw that the upperclassman was a junior, a second classman. The other khaki-clad midshipmen also wore the insignia of second classmen, a gold anchor on each collar. Two of them came up to him, close enough to scream in his face. Vornado tensed, wondering what new torture awaited, but one second classman put his hand on Vornado's shoulder, and the other grabbed his right hand and pumped it in a warm handshake. The second classmen were grinning. As if from a distance, he could hear their words: "Good job, Mr. Vornado . . . excellent work . . . Twenty-third Company evidently has a plebe class with some balls for once."

Vornado stared at them, then remembered that Kaminsky wanted to see Dillinger. Just as he was opening his mouth to speak, the door opened and Kaminsky appeared.

"Attention on deck!" Vornado shouted, sounding off as he had before. Dillinger also jumped to his feet, sounding off and bracing at attention.

Kaminsky took in the situation and shook his head in mock disgust, shaking the second classmen's hands.

"Get the fuck out of here, you guys. You're contaminating plebe indoctrination."

"Oh, come on, you got our backs, Vic," one of the khaki-uniformed midshipmen said. "We were just telling young Vornado and Dillinger here some Whitehead stories. Just so they know the whole Academy isn't a bunch of Whiteheads."

"Yeah, yeah, yeah," Kaminsky said, as if he were a weary father shepherding unruly children. "Go on, get out of here. And don't come back till the academic year starts or you're going to read about it."

"Oh, the brigade commander speaks," another of the juniors said sarcastically, making a sloppy salute. "Yessir, mister six striper, *sir*."

When the last second classman left, Kaminsky looked over at Dillinger. "Mr. Dillinger, I want to see you in my room, please."

When he was alone in the room, Vornado paced the floor, wondering what was going to happen, his head spinning from his interview with Kaminsky and seeing the mob of second classmen. Finally he heard the sound of Dillinger chopping down the passageway, his distant, "Go Navy, sir!" and the closer "Beat Army, sir!" as he squared the last corner and came through the room door.

Vornado looked at him, trying to read his face. Dillinger's face was frozen in dismayed shock. Vornado's heart sank. Kaminsky must have blamed the whole thing on Dillinger. But as he watched, Dillinger broke into a sudden grin, his face lighting up, his previous expression an attempt to play a trick on his roommate. Vornado stared at him.

"Well? What the hell happened?"

Dillinger shrugged. "He asked me if I did it, and I told him the truth. I slept like a baby last night. He nodded as if he completely believed me. He wrote something down and sent me to the room."

"So that's it? We're off the hook?"

Dillinger nodded, still grinning. He walked over, holding out both fists boxer style, the same way he had before they'd taken out Whitehead. Vornado banged his fists against Dillinger's. Dillinger moaned in pain, gripping his right fist. Vornado stared down at it, the bruise from Dillinger's punch to Whitehead's forehead making his knuckles a blotchy red and purple. Vornado stared at the bruise.

"Kaminsky see that?"

Dillinger nodded. "I banged it on the desk a few days ago. Hurry up; we'll be late for come-around."

Vornado nodded. Almost as if he were dreaming, he turned and walked to the window and looked out at the grounds of the Academy, seeing Tecumseh and the double cannons at the entrance to T-Court. For the first time since he had reported here, he had the feeling that this place was somehow his, that he belonged here after all. He looked out at the bricks of Tecumseh Court and thought about his father walking across those bricks years ago, and saw himself walking across them as an upperclassman.

Tecumseh glared back at him, his perpetual stare unchanged by the events of the night and the morning afterward. Vornado smiled and put his sailor's cap on, latched open the door, and sprinted behind Dillinger into the passageway with his chin braced into his chest, pivoting as he squared the corner.

"Go Navy, sir!" he shouted.

Twenty Years Later

PART 1:

▼

Stolen Arrows

1

The undersides of the waves forty feet above his head shimmered as they reflected the silver moonlight to the deep. He shivered despite the warmth of the water in the tropical marina. His pulse rushed in his ears; he was puffing through his single air bottle too fast and his hand shook as he raised his watch for the fifth time in two minutes.

Burke Dillinger shut his eyes and went over the plan for the hundredth time, thinking of the thousand things that could go wrong. It was eight minutes past three in the morning on Friday, the fifth of July. If Buffalo Patterson were right, just about everyone within a mile radius was snoring through an alcohol-induced haze from the previous evening's Independence Day celebrations. In one minute Dillinger would push off the bottom and penetrate the waves. He looked over at the place where he would be in ten minutes, but it was too dark at the bottom of the slip. He wondered if the contact lenses made it difficult to see, but he had been promised that would not be the case, even though they were flat black, and even though they covered the whites of his eyes as well as his irises. Before he had donned the closed-circuit scuba gear, the black waterproof face makeup and full-eyeball black contact lenses made his mirror reflection eerily grotesque. His mouth tasted coppery and bitter, but it wasn't clear if that was from the pre-operation nerves or his dental blackout makeup that made his previously white teeth become coal black.

The dim watch face clicked over to 3:09 A.M. He gently rose from the bottom of the slip and shut his eyes as he pulled off his diving mask and strapped it to his upper right arm, where it wouldn't reflect the light from a pier floodlight and alert the sentry. When his face rose above the water he opened his eyes. Directly in front of him was the prize, but he ignored it as he searched the dimness of the seaside of the Fort Lauderdale pier. His eyes were night adjusted, but he couldn't see anything moving. He glanced quickly over his right shoulder toward the breakwater, his seaman's eye measuring the narrow width of the channel entrance between the breakwater and the boats of the marina. As he thought of his destination he shivered again, his nerves jangling in excitement or fear or both. He turned back toward the pier, but there was still no motion. He allowed himself the luxury of a long glance at the object of the mission.

She lay there in the Florida moonlight, as seductive and beautiful as a new bride. Her hull stretched far to the right, where her smooth bullet-nosed bow pointed toward the breakwater. The cylinder of her body extended gracefully aft to where he floated, where it smoothly curved down to the water's surface, the warm waves licking the roundness of her flank. Further aft, her rudder protruded suddenly from the waves, seeming disembodied by the separation of the black water of the slip from the rest of the hull. To the right, up forward, the ship's superstructure, her sail, rose from the cylinder of her hull, a stark upward-pointing wing. The radio antenna was bumped out of the sail, and two periscopes were raised aft of the crow's nest of the sail cockpit, the bridge.

The nuclear fast attack submarine was tied to the pier with doubled-up lines, the crew having considerately tied her up with her bow outward bound, in the tiny yacht basin, with no patroling Coast Guard cutter, no rubber dinghy port watch, no perceptible security at all except the heavily guarded inner and outer marina fence, two armed sentries on the pier, and an antiterrorist sniper up in the lookout's cubbyhole of the sail. At least he hoped there were no other security measures—and since he was responsible as the leader of the submarine expert team, he had assured Buffalo that there would be only the two pier sentries and the sniper. Fortunately he had been correct, and aside from the two 9mm semiautomatic pistols of the sentries and the M-16 automatic rifle of the sniper, nothing stood between Dillinger and this glorious vessel. She was the Los Angeles–class submarine *Albany,* hull number SSN-754, complete with ten vertical-launch conventional land-attack

Tomahawk cruise missiles, two dozen of the world-class Mark 48 ADCAP torpedoes, and the jackpot, the two vertical-launch Tomahawk TLAM-N nuclear-tipped land-attack cruise missiles. Their warheads were small, but they were *hydrogen bombs*—small but extremely effective, and able to get to all those hard-to-reach places. Dillinger looked impatiently at his watch again—what seemed like five minutes had been barely thirty-seven seconds.

Finally the watch face clicked to 3:10. Dillinger imagined he saw a slight movement from the pier on the left. A flash of light came from the upper body of one of the sentries, and he fell with a barely audible thump. A second burst of light came from the left and the second sentry collapsed to the concrete. The operation—finally—was under way. Dillinger took a deep breath and swam quickly to the stern, where the hull met the waves in a gentle slope. Three of Buffalo Patterson's men had already climbed up on the hull. One of them, Meathook Allman, turned and reached for Dillinger and pulled him up on the slippery surface of the hull, the antisonar foam coating making it seem like he had stepped onto the back of a whale.

"Radio on," Meathook hissed at him. In the panic of the moment Dillinger had forgotten to insert the radio earphone and boom microphone under his black wet-suit hood as soon as he got on deck. He ran forward in a crouch toward the sail as he clumsily fiddled with the radio earpiece and positioned his boom microphone. At first he wasn't sure the special-frequency low-power EHF radio worked until he heard Buffalo mutter the word *two*, for the second phase of the invasion.

As Dillinger ran, his hand brushed against the pistol holster on his left hip. Buffalo's words rang in his ears—*If you have to unholster your piece, the mission is a failure, and if the mission fails, you're dead.* Dillinger kept running until his footfalls hit the locked operations compartment hatch under his feet. The antiterrorist procedures that had called for the deck hatch to be locked would make invading the submarine much harder. The only way into the vessel would be from inside the sail, down the vertical tunnel, but that was guarded by the ship's sniper who lay protected up in the bridge cockpit. His next steps carried him to the shear-sided sail, which used to have steel ladder rungs welded onto its flank for use in climbing to the bridge from the deck. The ladder rungs were long gone, the shipyard workers grinding them off in the wake of the antiterrorist warnings of the recent past. The ship's crew used a portable chain ladder tossed down from the bridge cockpit, and so would Buffalo's troops.

Lanky Meathook Allman crouched down and threw a rubber-covered aluminum grappling hook to the top of the sail, trying to aim for the radio antenna pole. When the first two tries missed, Dillinger was sure the sail sentry would call out or shoot. Or someone on a party boat in the yacht marina would dial 911 and report them as they stood there helplessly in the shadow of the superstructure. Dillinger's heart hammered in his tight chest as he forced his body against the warm metal of the sail. Finally the third attempt worked and the line wound around the raised radio mast. Meathook calmly pulled on special gloves, glanced around him, then climbed the line, his legs horizontal as he gracefully hand-over-handed himself twenty-five feet to the top of the sail. Dillinger stared in awe of the man's upper-body strength, which made his ascent look so easy Dillinger felt like attempting it.

The chain ladder came down on the starboard side of the sail, the sea side, barely two minutes after Meathook left the deck. The sniper on the top of the sail must not have heard a thing, the watchstander obviously not expecting a man to arrive unannounced, a man impolite enough to shove a Taser in his face and pull the trigger. Two of Buffalo's men went up while Dillinger steadied the ladder; then another held the ladder from below as Dillinger made his way up. He threw his leg over the coaming of the bridge and landed on the grating of the cockpit. He glanced aft to where the sniper would be collapsed from the attack, but he couldn't see anything. In the dark Dillinger put his feet into the open upper tunnel hatchway below him and found the ladder rungs of the vertical tunnel. He slowly lowered himself down five rungs of the tunnel ladder, struggling with the bulk of his scuba air bottle, when the light of a red-lamped flashlight below came on and illuminated the narrow space.

"It's locked," Meathook said over the radio.

"Let me try," Dillinger said, the voice-activated radio transmitting his smooth tenor when he spoke, then clicking off. Meathook and his partner, Cowpie Kipling, made room for him to crouch down over the access tunnel's lower hatch. They were probably right, he thought, but they were the muscle and he was the technical expert, and it was possible they were improperly operating the hatch ring. *Righty tighty, lefty loosey,* Dillinger thought as he squatted over the hatch and rotated the ring counterclockwise. It turned ten degrees and stopped. He tried it three times, then sighed. Dillinger had been right about this too—the antiterrorist procedures now called for locked hatches in foreign ports and domestic liberty ports. That was why the submarine's crew had required so few sentries on the pier, because they had made the submarine a hermetically sealed steel fortress. The average terrorist group would be stopped by the locked hatch. The average invasion force might employ an acetylene torch and an hour of work to get into the submarine. But Buffalo Patterson's men were hardly average, and this mission could not wait an hour.

Dillinger muttered, "Locked," and climbed back up the ladder ten rungs. Buffalo's voice on the radio said, "Three." Their man stationed in the bridge cockpit, Beergut Barnes, lowered a heavy watertight tool bag. A second one came down while the men at the lower hatch were working with tools from the first bag. Dillinger shined his red flashlight on the lower hatch as the two terrorists produced a small battery-operated air compressor and inflated a circular rubber device around the hatch. When they were finished, it looked like a kid's blow-up pool had been inflated, but the bottom of it was the hatch itself.

"Air on," Dillinger heard in his earpiece. He inserted his regulator as the men pulled a large bottle out of the second tool bag. It looked like a Thermos bottle the diameter of · a golf bag, but only half as tall. Meathook opened the lid and he and Cowpie carefully poured a clear liquid into the hatch-pool. Immediately it began boiling furiously, and a cold vapor cloud filled the tunnel, the fog so thick that visibility shrank to less than a foot. The men didn't stop but kept pouring the liquid over the hatch until the bottle was empty and the pool was half-filled, though still boiling violently. The men put the bottle aside and waited in the fog-shrouded tunnel until the remaining liquid boiled away, leaving only a frost-covered icy hatch. A large mallet appeared in Meathook's hand. He swung it in an arc over his head and smashed it into the hatch, which exploded with a resounding *boom* into a thousand shards that collapsed into the ship through the hatchway, the falling hatch sucking the fog out of the tunnel. Dillinger jumped at the sudden noise—their break-in had all the subtlety of a train wreck.

"Nothing like liquid nitrogen to break through HY-80 steel," Meathook said as he put the mallet away. "Eighty thousand psi strength at room temperature, *zero* at minus one-ninety Fahrenheit."

"Radio silence, asshole," Buffalo commanded. Dillinger stared into the gaping hole where the four-hundred-pound steel hatch had once been, and where now there was bright white fluorescent light pouring up into the mist of the tunnel. "Four," Buffalo said, and Meathook launched his skinny legs down the hatch, his body vanishing down the ladder, his pistol in his hand as he stepped onto the wreckage-littered deck. Cowpie was next, then Dillinger. As soon as he put his feet on an open spot on the deck he spit out his regulator, hoping he would have enough air left for the next phase of the operation. He waited with his body tense against the bulkhead as more of Buffalo's men came pouring in the hatch, a dozen of them coming out of the water while Meathook had been pouring liquid nitrogen on the hatch. Five of Dillinger's submarine technicians would be emerging from the slip and heading toward the sail right after the last of Buffalo's men.

"Five," Buffalo said, and Dillinger headed aft toward the control room with Meathook. At nearly half past three in the morning, no one had investigated the cacophonous crash from the collapse of the hatch in the upper-level passageway. The sound-mounted deckplates, which were so adept at minimizing the noise of clomping boots, must have muffled the sound of falling steel. That was the last thought Dillinger could remember before he came face-to-face with a two-hundred-pound, six-foot-tall duty chief, whose eyes grew wide as he froze and stared at the black-faced scuba-gear-wearing invasion force. Dillinger stopped breathing as panic rose in his throat. He watched as Cowpie casually raised his Taser and fired down the passageway. Two electrodes sailed toward the chief and hit his chest. Twenty-six watts of electromuscular disruption dropped him to the deck with a dull thud, his head bouncing twice. He lay on the floor convulsing, his eyes blinking and his mouth open. Meathook advanced to stand over him and produced two cable ties, wrapping one around his ankles and the other around his wrists, then stepped over him.

"Let's go," Meathook said in Dillinger's ear. Dillinger followed Meathook, stepping over the unmoving form of the duty chief, and into the control room, which was deserted. The duty officer and messenger of the watch must be on the middle level, perhaps in the crew's mess or taking a quick nap between security tours of the ship and the pier.

Remembering his procedures, Dillinger hurried to the port side of the control room and found the electrical panel aft of the port-side wraparound ballast-control panel. He opened the gray cover, snapped open ten circuit breakers, and unscrewed ten fuses. He pocketed the fuses and shut the panel door. The ten circuits of the ship's alarms and communication systems had just been disabled. Short of digging in a spare-parts bin for more fuses, no watchstander happening on their half-completed invasion would be able to sound an alarm. There was no need to worry about the ship's radio circuits—the radio equipment was complicated, temperamental, and locked behind a combination-controlled door. Besides, soon there would be no radiomen anyway.

Dillinger nodded to Meathook, and the two hurried aft to the fan room. Dillinger half expected the door to be locked, but it was unsecured. He rotated the four heavy metal latches and pulled the door of the chamber open, the suction of the air-handler circulation fan making it hard to move the door. From this one chamber the size of a closet all the air that circulated throughout the ship passed, the fan powered by a fifty-horsepower motor. If Dillinger's instructions had been followed, the upper-bridge-access trunk hatch would have been shut when Buffalo ordered phase five to begin. That meant that all the air circulating through the closed environment of the ship was coming from and returning to this air chamber.

"Air on, mask on," Dillinger said into his boom mike while Meathook reached into his tool bag. He clamped the regulator into his mouth, pulled his diver's mask off his upper arm, and strapped it over his wet-suit hood. Meat-hook unstrapped a tool bag and withdrew three oblong grenades, each the size of a two-liter soda bottle, armed them, set their timers for ten seconds, pulled their pins, and tossed them into the air chamber. Dillinger shut the chamber door and latched the four hatch dogs. Three muffled bangs sounded from the fan room. Dillinger waved Meat-hook forward, back to the control room, where they would spend the next ten minutes waiting.

During those ten minutes, the fan room pumped fentanyl opiate-derivative gas throughout the sealed vessel. Anyone sleeping wouldn't wake up, and anyone standing would collapse to the deck. The effects of the gas would last at least a half hour, long enough for Buffalo's men to cable-tie wrists and ankles together and duct-tape mouths.

Dillinger stepped up the periscope stand and put his face to the periscope, as well as he could through the diver's mask. It wasn't nearly as good as an observation with his eye on the lens, but he could see a small circle of light from the periscope. He rotated the instrument and trained the view down to the pier. The bodies of the sentries had been concealed by Buffalo's second wave, and were nowhere to be seen. There were no police or military vehicles approaching from the north, and nothing from the south. No one was visibly moving in the boats of the marina. So far they had apparently done their jobs without being detected.

Buffalo Patterson tapped Dillinger on the shoulder. Dillinger stepped away so the beefy cell leader could look out the periscope. Buffalo looked like he'd stepped off a two-hundred-horsepower Harley and crashed into a biker bar, his wet-suit sleeves raggedly cut off to expose a dozen tattoos on each massive shoulder, his arms seemingly as big around as telephone poles. Buffalo's head was shaved, and he wore a blond handlebar mustache over yellowed and uneven teeth. Of course, at that moment the man's arms, teeth, mustache, head, and eyeballs were all uniformly flat black, making him look like a nightmare. Dillinger glanced at his watch. It had been eleven minutes since the gas grenades had exploded. "Buffalo, it's time," Dillinger said.

"Cowpie, take out your regulator," Buffalo ordered.

Cowpie blinked and gingerly removed his regulator and took an experimental breath. Dillinger had questioned Buffalo's plan for testing the atmosphere, but Buffalo had insisted that it was practical and quick, and that if Cowpie hit the deck, they'd wait five minutes and try again. Cowpie just nodded and removed his mask. The air was good. "Six," Buffalo ordered, and left the control room through the forward passageway.

Dillinger pulled off his mask and dropped his regulator, then unstrapped the scuba bottle and buoyancy-compensator rig, feeling a hundred pounds lighter. He took a shallow breath. The air smelled odd, the almond scent of the breath of someone who had been drinking all night. But there was no eye irritation. Dillinger found his creepy reflection in a Plexiglas status board and stared at himself for a moment. He was thirty-eight years old and would have looked much younger except for his thick salt-and-pepper hair that had grown prematurely gray. He stood slightly taller than medium height, with a medium build after losing much of the muscular bulk he'd had twenty years before. He had cold and penetrating wolflike gray-blue eyes, pronounced cheekbones, clear and slightly olive-toned skin, a curved nose, and full lips, his jaw still as square as when he had been a plebe. At least, that was his normal appearance—the reflection in the plastic was of a man with hair so dark it could have been soaked in crankcase oil, skin blacker than a coal miner's, with black gums and blacker teeth, and the grimmest feature of all—eyes that were completely black from his lower lashes to his eyelids. He opened his eyes wide, reached toward his face with a black hand, and pinched the left contact lens out of his eye. The odd feeling of the slick polymer material coming off the surface of his eye made him wince. In his hand was a contact lens that was almost two inches wide, and which had taken nearly twenty minutes to insert. He flicked the odd lens to the deck and pulled out the right one, then checked his reflection again. It was still gruesome, but at least the whites of his eyes had returned to normal, the cold gray-blue irises staring back at him. He glanced at the reflection again, his black hair making him look younger than when it was its normal gray-streaked color.

He blinked and turned from the bulkhead. When he did,

he saw five members of his team arrive in the control room, now that the bridge trunk upper hatch was reopened. Steve Flood was Dillinger's right-hand man, a tall, slim, perpetually smiling New Jersey bachelor who customarily wore pointy-toed cowboy boots and an oval metal belt buckle, and who had an eighties haircut brushed back on his scalp. Dillinger motioned Flood to take the periscope watch.

"How'd it go, Skip?" Flood asked, his voice muffled from the Type 18 periscope optic module.

"Nominal. Had to use LIN on the hatch."

"I saw. Did the liquid nitrogen damage the hatch seating surface?"

"Don't think so," Dillinger said, checking his watch nervously. "But we'll see if the ship leaks at depth."

"Upper tunnel hatch should hold as the pressure boundary. Lower hatch is just for looks anyway. Any resistance coming in?"

"Had to splash the duty chief."

Buffalo Patterson returned to the room from the forward passageway. He looked at Dillinger as he spoke into his boom mike: "How close are we?"

Dillinger barked into his microphone, "Patty, report your status."

Patrick Schluss was a twenty-six-year-old, heavyset, prematurely balding man with a pockmarked face, who ironically had the heaviest facial and body hair Dillinger had ever seen. The high-spirited youth was an engineering genius, and would get the ship's propulsion systems online so they could move under their own power. Helping Schluss would be the other three members of Dillinger's crew, the hardest part of the operation taking place in the engineroom.

Schluss's baritone voice came over the circuit. "Skip, propulsion is on the emergency propulsion motor. Battery's on the low side. We're clear to cut the ship loose."

"Good job, Patty," Dillinger replied. "Buffalo, I relieve you," he said, glancing at the muscle-bound leader as he took over. "Gentlemen, phase seven." Dillinger clapped Flood on the shoulder and found binoculars hanging in a cubbyhole.

"Good luck, Skip," Flood called.

Dillinger walked forward to the control room exit. He

climbed up the tunnel ladder to the bridge cockpit and lowered the grating back down over the hatch to form a level surface to stand on. He blinked again, his eyes irritated from removing the contacts, and did a deliberate naked eye examination of the slip, the breakwater, the yacht basin, the pier on the port side, and the cruise ship piers in the distance. They were still alone, bathed in the dim light of the marina floodlights. He hoisted the binoculars to his face and checked the basin exit channel, looking for patrol craft. He scanned the basin, looking at each yacht, but their decks were deserted and their interior lights were off. He tasted the air for a moment. There was no wind. The moonlight had dimmed as the night clouded up. The current in the slip should be minimal. High tide was in twenty minutes. Dillinger had memorized the chart and pored over photographs and videos of the yacht basin. He was ready.

"Status of the line charges," Dillinger breathed into his boom mike. Buffalo's men had wrapped Semtex RDX/PETN moldable plastic explosive ropes with pager-activated blasting caps around the four doubled-up lines and the three thick shore-power cables. If they had used too little plastic Semtex, they would have to cut the sub loose or shoot the lines. If they had used too much, the entire town would wake up from the detonation. The explosives, though they violated the operation's stealth, would allow them to leave the pier with no one required to man the submarine's deck to toss off the lines, someone in a suspicious wet suit who could be shot at or recognized. Still, the noise could alert the yachtsmen and the harbormaster. Dillinger shook his head and prayed the yachtsmen had imbibed heavily.

"All charges armed," Buffalo said over the circuit.

Dillinger unzipped his wet suit, reached into an internal pocket, and withdrew a plastic package the size of a cigarette box. He unwrapped the three layers of waterproofing and produced the object, a small flip-open cell phone.

"Here we go," Dillinger said. "Merc, you up?"

"Stationed and ready," the calm voice of young Matt Mercury-Pryce intoned. "Merc" was a tall youngster with wavy sand-colored hair, a brainy athlete who was a serious, driven worker during the day and drank to excess at night, and tended to blow his money on women, sports cars, and ski trips, but was famous for his icy calm no matter the situation. He was a natural mariner and one of the best seamen Dillinger had ever known. The ship was in good hands with the boy at the controls.

"Good man, Merc," Dillinger said. "Lower the outboard, train to zero nine zero."

Dillinger flipped open the cell phone and turned it on. When the readout panel came on, he clicked a speed-dial number from the menu. A short beeping tone sounded, and he punched the nine button three times, then hung up and returned the phone to his chest pocket. Buffalo had said there would be a fifteen-second delay.

"Skip," Merc's voice called. "Outboard's down and trained to zero nine zero."

Before Dillinger could reply the Semtex charges on the lines and the shorepower cables exploded with a sharp thump. It seemed loud in the silence of the wee hours. Dillinger frowned, wondering how many dozens of yachtsmen they had just awakened, but Buffalo had insisted the noise was unavoidable. Dillinger looked over the side of the bridge down to the deck. All the lines were hanging limply from the deck cleats. There was no sign of the shore-power cables. The ship was floating free in the slip.

"Merc, start the outboard," Dillinger ordered. Now that the ship was free of the pier, the thruster located forty feet ahead of the rudder would pull the ship's tail into the slip. As Dillinger watched, the rudder aft moved slowly away from the pier, the ship rotating counterclockwise. Dillinger watched the bow, hoping the maneuver wouldn't damage the fragile fiberglass of the sonar dome, but the hull seemed to be fading away from the pier wall. When the gap between the stern and the pier opened to twenty feet, Dillinger spoke into his microphone: "Stop the outboard, right full rudder, back one-third."

"Outboard off, rudder's right full, revs for back one-third," Merc replied.

Dillinger craned his neck over the bridge coaming to watch the rudder turn as he backed up the submarine. There were only fifty yards of clearance before he would smash the screw into the yacht club bulkhead.

"All stop, ahead two-thirds, maintain right full rudder."

"Roger, ahead two-thirds," Merc replied.

The ship froze in the slip as the ahead revolutions of the screw stopped her rearward momentum. Dillinger held his breath as the ship slowly surged forward. The rudder would need to bite into the water flow soon or the ship would crash into the pier bulkhead. Dillinger watched the motion of the vessel as it picked up speed, ready to order Merc to back full revolutions if the rudder failed to turn the bow, but as the ship approached within half a shiplength of the pier, the rudder bit in and the bow turned. The ship was making way at bare steerageway out of the slip. And still there had been no one to stop them.

Dillinger watched as the bow began to line up with the channel that paralleled the long, rocky breakwater, the finger of land that pointed due east.

"Merc, rudder amidships, steady as she goes."

"Rudder amidships, steady zero nine one."

"Roger, Merc. Train the outboard to zero zero zero."

"Training the outboard to zero zero zero," Merc replied. "Outboard trained to triple zero."

"Raise the outboard, Merc."

The channel slowly approached the dark submarine. The end of the breakwater drew abreast of the sail. The water here was rougher, making the buoys toss in the slow swells of the Atlantic. The water depth was increasing steeply, falling off at the close continental shelf, making their escape easy—had they stolen the ship from Norfolk, there would have been a ten-hour flank-speed run to the hundred-fathom curve, but from Port Everglades they could dive inside twenty minutes, assuming the reactor got online.

"Merc, slow to ahead one-third." They would need to conserve the battery or it wouldn't last until the reactor took over.

"One-third, roger."

Dillinger put the binoculars to his face and scanned the channel ahead, but they were alone in the sea. He noticed that his stomach had settled, probably thanks to the ship's moving away from the danger of being caught. As the breakwater's end faded astern, he took one glance back at the yacht basin, which was still quiet as a cemetery, and called down to Merc.

"Cleared the breakwater, Merc. Put Meathook at the helm and get me a sounding."

"Roger, Skip. Meathook's got the wheel."

"Meathook, you read?"

"I read you, Skipper, and I've got the wheel. Steering zero nine one, ahead one-third."

"Let's go; ten minutes to the dive point."

The deck crew bent over the hatch, where they muscled a large package up on the deck—one of the deliveries the second wave had made while Dillinger had been in the fan room. This last chore, to be done on deck before the ship submerged, would be the most suspicious thing they had done so far, but it could not be avoided. Dillinger glanced aft as the deck crew unpacked the package. The noise of a large compressor roared from the aft deck as the inflatable pontoon boat grew and slowly took shape. When it was finished, it was thirty feet long and eight feet wide, its sides formed by the two-foot-diameter cylindrical cells that formed a closed oval. The bottom was sturdy reinforced rubber. Buffalo had stated that it could hold a hundred prone men without shipping any water. They needed to put on the pontoon raft only the thirty or so members of the crew who had been sleeping in the berthing spaces—the rest had been ashore on liberty. It didn't matter if the authorities were alerted to the hogtied crew floating on the pontoon. The alarm would sound as soon as the seventy ashore crew members returned to an empty pier.

He craned his neck to look aft, and noticed the bucket brigade of Buffalo's muscular troops handing bodies up from the forward escape hatch and manhandling them into the pontoon boat. Finally the word came from Buffalo: "All crew members loaded on the pontoon, Skip."

"You check out the spaces to make sure we didn't miss anyone?"

"That's done. We're going below."

As Dillinger watched, the hatch shut as the deck crew went below.

"Last man down," Buffalo reported. "Get this tub underwater."

"Patty, what's the status of the reactor?"

"Normal full-power lineup," Schluss said. "Skipper, request to shift propulsion to the main engines."

"Meathook, all stop. Patty, shift propulsion. Merc, prepare to dive."

A string of acknowledgments came in on Dillinger's headphones. He hurriedly rigged the bridge for dive. One of Buffalo's men came up to the hatchway and took the grating below, then the windshield, the compass alidade, and the bridge communication box. He examined the interior of the cockpit for anything he'd left behind, and tucked the flashlight into his pocket. Still crouching down, he pulled up the fiberglass clamshells that formed a canopy over the hole of the bridge cockpit, making the sail's upper surface smooth. He shoved his legs into the hatchway and lowered himself until he could reach up and pull the hatch shut. He spun the operating ring and watched the hatch dogs engage on the seating surface, then tightened it hard, since it was the pressure boundary with the lower hatch out of commission. He climbed down the vertical tunnel past the ruined lower hatch and continued down the ladder to the deckplates. One of Buffalo's crew had cleaned up the metal wreckage.

"Boss, propulsion is shifted, recommend ahead standard."

"Meathook, all ahead standard."

He hurried into the control room, where Meathook sat at the right seat of the ship control panel, which resembled a 747 cockpit with left and right seats, a central console, a vertical instrument readout display in front of the seats, and an inclined instrument readout that rose to the overhead. To the left was the wraparound ballast-control panel with its control seat. Behind the central console was another empty seat. Merc stood on the conn platform with his face pressed to the periscope optics module, walking in slow circles as he performed a surface search.

"Skipper, we're ready," Merc reported.

"Sounding?"

"Eight-four fathoms."

"Merc, take her down."

Fifteen tense minutes later the ship leveled off four hundred feet below the surface and sped up on the run out of Port Everglades. Dillinger let out a deep breath. They had done it, he thought. In the dead of night, in less than two hours, he and his team had hijacked a nuclear submarine.

"I'm going to wash this blackface off and find coveralls,"

Dillinger said, a smile breaking out on his face. "Steve, take over here. Nothing faster than eighteen knots on course east. Merc, get one of Buffalo's men to relieve you and get out the Atlantic charts and plot our inertial nav position. And get the Cape of Good Hope, Persian Gulf, and Red Sea charts out and plot the thousand-mile range circle around Tel Aviv. Get Buffalo working on blowing all the classified safes open. And make sure Lionel is gainfully employed working on the nuke cruise missiles. Tell him to figure out how to insert the targeting instructions, and see if there are any interlocks we'll have to break through. He's got forty-eight hours. Make sure he doesn't sleep until that's done."

Dillinger walked out of the control room and found the door to the captain's stateroom. He shut it behind him and breathed a deep sigh of relief. They were safe here, deep underwater. He checked his diving watch—it was 0448. In an hour the relieving duty section would come to the marina, yawning after a night of liberty, only to find their submarine gone. Odds were the pontoon boat would not be discovered until later, after sunrise. Either way, by zero six hundred all hell would break loose all the way to the Pentagon and the White House.

Not since taking out that bastard Whitehead had anything felt better than the warm shower water in the captain's head as he washed off the black makeup and the sweat of fear. When he returned to the control room, wearing the ship's captain's coveralls and too-large black sneakers, the gathered crew broke into applause. Buffalo Patterson smirked as he pulled the last necessity from the watertight tool bag—six bottles of Dom Pérignon and twenty bubble-wrapped long-stemmed glasses. Corks flew in the control room of the USS *Albany* as the successful invasion force clinked glasses and drank the champagne.

"A toast to the package we're delivering to Tel Aviv," Buffalo growled, his glass held to the overhead.

The crowd drank to the toast, except for Dillinger. But a few moments later, Dillinger grinned as he downed his second glass. *We did it,* he thought.

2
_____

The pine-scented forest breeze blew his hair off his forehead as he called the audible in his crouch behind the center. His voice was a deep baritone with a ring of unquestioned authority as he shouted the final sequence: "Forty-six, seventy-seven, hut-hut-*hut*!"

The snap landed the football in his hands and he faded backward toward the goalposts, his eyes flickering between his running back and the incoming linebacker, the latter a formidable problem and barreling in like the 4:05 freight. He cocked the ball and launched it in a perfect downfield spiral, not to the location of the running back, but to where he would be a second and a half in the future when the ball fell in its curving arc. He saw the ball descend, spinning tightly, toward the receiver's outstretched arms, the secondary wildly lunging for the ball and missing. That was all he remembered before the momentum of the linebacker knocked the wind from his chest and slammed him down into the soft carpet of the thick grass, the defender bouncing on him.

He looked up as the linebacker's long brunette hair cascaded over his throat and forehead, and her smiling face looked at him for a half second before her full red lips reached out for his, her tongue finding his as she ground her thin hips into him, at once seductive and subtle. He looked up into her emerald-green eyes, which shifted from his left eye to his right.

"Hi," she said breathlessly. "Look at you, sexy; you look like the day you graduated from the Academy." She ran her fingers through his hair, then sat up on his hips and laughed. "I'm the envy of all the girls."

"You're not so bad yourself," Peter Vornado said, his usual commanding baritone becoming a soft bedroom voice. He looked at Rachel, amazed that this slim body had given birth to their three children, more amazed that a face so lovely could belong to a woman who loved him. Despite sixteen years, it still seemed like a dream, an unearned lottery win. And best of all, she seemed to feel the same way about him.

"Touchdown!" the eight-year-old voice of his son cried in triumph from far downfield.

"No way! Foul! Offensive pass interference, Dad!" his twelve-going-on-nineteen-year-old daughter cried.

"Isn't this supposed to be touch football?" Vornado asked his wife, smiling at her, glad that she was back to being the woman he'd kissed at the altar rather than the gloomy and pessimistic one he'd known lately.

"If I'm not mistaken, I am touching you, aren't I?" She smiled, her smooth white teeth an invitation, her hips bucking on his again, reminding him of the promise of the moment the children were asleep.

"Indeed you are." Vornado grinned at her.

She leaned closer and kissed him again, her hunger clear in the way her mouth moved, but the kiss so quick that he wondered if it had happened at all. She was still smiling when two feet galloped to a halt near them.

"Ew, gross, you two!" the voice of Vornado's daughter Marla interrupted. Vornado sat up on his elbows and looked up at the slim, graceful young lady who just yesterday was a little girl, but now dressed like a fashion model and moved like a woman. She stood over them, crinkling her nose but smiling. A puffing boy ran up and took in the scene in disgust. Peter Junior was wiry and smaller than his peers, but a motivated and mirthful scholar and athlete. For once he agreed with his sister and said, "Yeah, gross." He spiked the ball on Vornado's chest, making him sit up in surprise and pain.

"Excuse me." Vornado winked at Rachel. "I have no choice but to kick his ass." He got to his feet and watched as the boy ran off. Vornado stood two inches taller than six feet, his thirty-eight-year-old body thin yet muscled from years of marathons and cross-country bicycling. A wave of fine dirty-blond hair cascaded over his forehead. He had clear denim-blue eyes, strong bone structure with

defined cheekbones, and a straight jawline. His skin was
fair and tended to burn even on winter days. From a distance he could pass for a man in his mid-twenties, and only
close examination would yield clues to his age, such as the
wrinkled crow's-feet at his eyes and the slightly windburned
skin of his cheeks and forehead, but the signs of age
seemed to add to his natural air of authority, as if he had
been an oldest brother or ran a Wall Street corporation.

Vornado took off in a lightning fast sprint toward the
goal line, catching up and wrapping an arm around his son
and taking him to the grass. He tickled the boy, his laughter
musical. When Peter begged for mercy, Vornado let him
go and stood up. He glanced at the grassy clearing in the
dense pine forest, marveling at the peace and beauty and
silence.

Suddenly the silence was pierced by a sound that didn't
belong there. At first Vornado thought he had imagined it,
the sound fading away as suddenly as it had come. But a
moment later it was back, a flapping, chopping, vibrating
noise. It grew louder, growing into the droning of powerful
jet engines and the roaring bass throb of helicopter rotors.
He looked at Rachel, whose face had fallen into a grim
frown. Vornado felt a sudden tenseness, a flash of nerves,
and a tightening of his chest. He tried to shake off the
feeling, reassuring himself it must be a search-and-rescue
craft or a firefighting helicopter. The noise grew louder still
until he could feel the powerful rotors rattling his chest.
Finally the mammoth aircraft became visible as it came in
low over the pine treetops. There was no doubt that the
helicopter would try to land in the clearing, but its rotor
circle was so large that it seemed it would chop down the
closest trees. There was an odd augmenting of the rotor
sounds. Vornado glanced to the side to see something even
stranger than a helicopter landing in his backyard.

"Dad! Dad, look!" his son shouted, pointing and jumping
up and down.

On either side of the approaching chopper were smaller
black Apache attack helicopters, each bristling with guns
and missiles, hovering above the trees, guarding the larger
machine as it slowly descended toward the grassy field.
Vornado recognized the huge gray helicopter as an SH-60B

Seahawk, its logo a star set into a circle with three stripes on either side, with large black block letters spelling U.S. NAVY.

The Seahawk's landing gear touched the earth in midfield, the craft's rotors slowing to idle, the trees of the forest bending in the blast of the machine's rotor wash, the grass rippling in protest. Vornado squinted into the sun at the hovering escort attack choppers as the three Nomex coverall–clad crewmen emerged from the Seahawk's aft sliding door. Two of the crewmen carried MAC-10 machine pistols in their hands and wore utility belts loaded with grenades. The third, the ranking crewman, had a holstered 9-mm on his belt, with one hand on the holster like a state trooper approaching a dangerous traffic stop. The three men stood on the field, the one with the holstered piece glaring at Vornado, the other two scanning the field in suspicion. The lead crewman glanced at something in his hand, then walked slowly toward Vornado. As he grew close Vornado could see the man had been looking at a photograph. A photograph of Peter Vornado.

The lead crewman was a tall, powerfully built man in his thirties with a flattop haircut, a menacing look on his jowly face. The man shouted over the roar of the rotor blast with a gravelly, no-nonsense voice.

"Peter Vornado?"

Vornado nodded. "Who are you?"

The man's coveralls had no name or insignia on them. He produced a leather identification wallet with a U.S. Navy ID card and flashed it in front of Vornado's eyes.

"Lieutenant Commander Alex Detmer," he said.

"You from squadron or HQ?"

"ONI," Detmer said laconically. "Office of Naval Intelligence."

"What's all this?" Vornado asked, his head motioning to include the Seahawk and the hovering Apaches.

"It's an emergency, Commander. You're coming with us."

Vornado's jaw clenched in frustration. Detmer's face held a deadly serious expression, his men carried heavy automatic weapons, and the Navy seagoing aircraft was guarded by heavily armed attack helicopters. He tried to remember if he'd ever heard of Army attack aircraft guarding a Navy helicopter and couldn't think of a single time. There was definitely something seriously wrong.

"Can you tell me what it's about?" Vornado asked, glancing at his children, who stared in awe at the Seahawk and the menacing Apaches. Rachel's wary eyes were fixed on the automatic pistols of the men surrounding her husband.

"Negative, sir. Our orders are to give you ten minutes to pack and accompany you while you do."

Vornado's headache started then, a small ache behind his eyes that moved toward his temples and throbbed its way to the back of his skull.

"Let's go," Vornado said. He walked toward the house, pulling Rachel close to him as he strode ahead of Detmer. One of the men stayed behind to guard the Seahawk. The second followed behind Detmer.

"You're going with them?" she asked in a low voice.

He nodded. "Do I have a choice?"

"They didn't tell you what's going on, did they?"

"No."

"You could call Smokin' Joe. At least make sure he knows about it."

Vornado thought a moment, wondering what it would mean if Joe Kraft didn't know this was happening. He nodded agreement.

"That damned machine is going to wake the baby," Rachel complained.

"At least if she's awake I can say good-bye to her."

The baby monitor on the waistband of Rachel's jeans suddenly lit up, the two-year-old crying in panic at the noise.

"Peter, keep them out of the house with those guns," she said as they approached the back deck of the log house. She went inside while he spoke to Detmer, who nodded at his subordinate. Detmer followed Vornado into the house while the guard stayed on the deck.

Vornado hurried to the first-floor office of the cabin and loaded his computer into his briefcase. He jogged upstairs into the bathroom, found the Advil bottle, and put four of the liquid-filled gel caps into his mouth and bit them hard. The foul-tasting medicine filled his mouth, and he swallowed it and the gel caps without water, hoping that this time it would stop the pounding headache. He blinked several times, forcing himself to ignore the pain, tossed toiletries into a shaving kit, and threw clothing into a small black leather bag. He hadn't brought uniforms with him on the vacation, so wherever they were going they'd have to accept him wearing jeans, hiking boots, and a golf shirt. He pulled on a worn brown bomber jacket, traded his plastic sports watch for the blue-faced Rolex Submariner, then glanced surreptitiously toward the door of the bedroom and grabbed the cordless handset of the cabin's phone. He stood by the window away from the door and looked out at the Seahawk idling impatiently in the clearing while he punched buttons on the cordless handset, the number memorized.

The female voice on the phone was cold and impersonal. "ComSubRon Eight, Lieutenant Monroe, this is a nonsecure line, may I help you, sir?"

"Melissa, put Kraft on the phone," Vornado ordered with a hard, businesslike edge to his deep voice.

Her voice softened. "Yes, sir. Please hold for the commodore."

Detmer stepped into the room. Vornado wondered if he would try to stop the phone call, but he just stood there and glared at Vornado. It only took ten seconds for the senior officer to come to the phone.

"Hello, Peter," the older man said, a growling cigar-smoke-and-bourbon voice that could fill a room. "I take it you have some visitors there."

"They're here all right, Commodore. Is this coming from you? You couldn't call me? Or just send a car?"

"Security's too tight and there's no time." The older man's voice was flat and brisk, the usual jolly tone missing. "Get going, Peter. You'll be briefed. Good hunting." The connection clicked as the commodore hung up. Vornado stared stupefied at the phone, thinking about the last time he'd heard the boss use that phrase.

Rachel walked into the room, an expression of loss and worry lining her face. In her arms was Erin, a twenty-two-month-old with platinum-blond hair and sapphire-blue eyes, but who otherwise had the same beautiful features as her mother. The baby smiled delightedly at him.

"Da-da!" she said, throwing her arms out for Vornado.

He took her, the toddler's body warm from her midafternoon nap. Vornado cursed to himself. The last thing on earth he wanted to do was leave his family and the cabin. Whatever it was Kraft wanted, it wouldn't be pleasant.

Detmer, who had withdrawn to the hallway, spoke up. "Sir? It's time."

"Daddy read?" baby Erin asked, her young voice and experimental pronunciation melting his heart. She loved the box of books he had bought for her early in the week, and would spend all day snuggled in his lap while he read to her if he would let her. He looked into her upraised little face and smiled without conviction.

"Daddy's got to go to work, honey," he told her gently.

"No, Daddy, no work," she protested. Vornado glanced at Rachel, who still looked worried and anxious.

"Marla," Vornado called. His daughter was just outside the bedroom, as was Peter Junior, both of them staring at him. "Take Erin down and give her a snack. Peter, help your sister." He kissed Erin and put her in Marla's arms, despite the baby's attempt to cling to him. Dismissed, the children filed out of the room and stepped heavily down the steps, the baby still babbling.

"Peter," Rachel said, "what do you think this is?"

"I'm not sure," Vornado said. If Commodore Kraft had to pull him off vacation in this big a hurry, with all the talent he had at his fingertips, then it meant deep trouble. For an instant Vornado wondered if his family would be safe, but he suppressed the thought. "It could be nothing," he lied. "One of those crazy exercises."

Rachel looked out the window at the hovering Apaches and the huge Seahawk, then looked back at him. Her voice trembled as she replied, "Yeah, an exercise."

"Sir?" Detmer said, his tone becoming much less friendly. "Walk with me to the aircraft immediately or I'm authorized to drag you."

Vornado ignored him and kissed his wife. She kissed him back, then hugged him. He broke away and took the bag as he left the room. She followed him to the foyer. The kids stood by the door. Vornado kissed them all, the headache still throbbing in his temples.

" 'Bye, babe," he said to Rachel, seeing her liquid eyes staring up at him. "Peter, take care of things. You've got the watch," he said to his son as he squeezed his shoulder. "Marla, I love you, honey. Listen to your mother. 'Bye, Erin." He leaned over to kiss the littlest Vornado, who planted a wet kiss on his lips and smiled at him.

"Bye-bye work, Daddy," she said, her usual farewell when he left on business.

Vornado grabbed his gear and ducked out the door, hating good-byes, and hurried with Detmer to the chopper, his armed subordinates joining them, their machine pistols pointed warily to the sky. Vornado approached the roaring Seahawk and stepped through the door, the crewmen following. It took a moment for Vornado's eyes to adjust to the dim interior. He found a canvas seat and strapped himself in and glanced out the port window. As Detmer's last crewman climbed aboard, Vornado could see through the gap in the starboard door Rachel sprinting toward the chopper.

"Hold it," Vornado shouted, tapping Detmer's shoulder. He leaned out the half-closed aircraft door as she ran breathlessly to the helicopter. "What's the matter?"

"You forgot this," she said, her face still beautiful even as she frowned in worry. She held up a gold Saint Christopher's medal and put it around his neck, then kissed him. "Please be careful," she said over the roar of the rotors. "And don't take that off—I have a really bad feeling about all this."

"Don't worry; it'll be okay, honey, but thanks," Vornado said, tucking the medal under his T-shirt, the hair on the back of his neck sticking up. He felt a hand pull him back into the aircraft and the door rolled shut.

The jet engines throttled up, the airframe shook, and the fuselage tilted steeply forward as the chopper lifted off. The field fell away from the window and the tops of the trees slowly moved under them, the valley fading below as the chopper accelerated until the pine trees of the mountains sped by impossibly fast. The Seahawk hugged the treetops of the rolling terrain, as if the pilot expected to be fired upon at any moment. Slightly behind them the port-side Apache flew, the vicious machine seeming ready to go to war at any second. Vornado wondered if the emergency that had pulled him out of the Shenandoah Valley cabin was so bad that the pilots had to act as if they were streaking over a war zone. Vornado's stomach jumped as the chopper rose suddenly, then sank as it followed the contour of the Virginia countryside. Whatever this was, it had shaken the brass.

"Mr. Detmer," Vornado shouted to the intelligence spook. "Where are we going?"

"Atlantic Ocean off the Virginia Capes, about a hundred and sixty nautical miles east of Hampton Roads," Detmer said. "You'll need to put on this safety harness."

Vornado nodded, putting on the heavy canvas harness, then leaned back against the bulkhead, his eyes shut. The headache pounded between his temples, but at least it wasn't the skull crusher he'd had when the Seahawk first arrived.

After an hour the chopper's engine tone changed, the rotors throttling down, then back up, then down again. Vornado opened his eyes and looked out the window. The Apache was still there, but there was no scenery other than a stretch of deep blue ocean all the way to the horizon. The waves slowly and steadily grew closer until the aircraft was only a few hundred feet over the surface. They began to slow until the ocean below was barely moving, the waves alarmingly close. Vornado could see a black shape outside the window. It was just as he had suspected.

Detmer slid the helicopter's door open. The bright sunlight glared off the Atlantic and into the chopper. The slight chop of the waves was about a hundred feet beneath the helicopter's airframe. The roar of the rotors came blasting into the cabin. Just below the window was a surfaced nuclear submarine floating with no wake. The top of the sail could be seen, with the cockpit manned by two officers. A periscope protruded from the sail. Behind it a radio mast was raised. On the cylindrical deck, a crew of life-jacketed men waited.

"Commander, put this lifejacket on over your harness!"

Vornado strapped on the bulky kapok lifejacket. As he did, Detmer attached Vornado's luggage to the cable and lowered it to the submarine below, then raised the cable back up and fastened it to Vornado's harness.

"Ready, Commander?"

Vornado nodded as Detmer motioned him to the door.

"Good luck!" Detmer called, clapping Vornado on the shoulder. "And good hunting!"

Vornado waved and pushed himself out of the door, the cable lowering him into space. He seemed to hang there for a long time, until eventually he was grabbed by the deck crew and his boots hit the hull of the submarine. The leader of the crew, a lieutenant with the name tag LOGAN, smiled at him as he unfastened the cable from Vornado's harness.

"Welcome back, Captain," he said.

3

Commander Peter Vornado nodded at the two men on top of the sail, the crow's-feet at his eyes crinkling. "Good to be back, Mr. Logan, but I'd just as soon you guys waited at the pier for me next time the ship gets under way." Vornado frowned. "Any chance you know what the hell's going on?"

"We were hoping you could tell us, Skipper," Logan said. "Better hurry below, sir. XO wants us back deep on the flank run ASAP."

Vornado ducked down the forward escape trunk. The world of the glaring sun and deep blue Atlantic vanished, the electric smell of the ship suddenly overwhelming him. It was a unique aroma of lube oil, diesel exhaust, cooking grease, and ozone, the smell focusing his mind on the dangerous business at hand. The dim escape trunk extended twelve feet down into the bowels of the ship. Vornado's feet hit the deck of the middle-level crew's mess. As his feet hit the deck, a PA-system speaker boomed over his head, making the announcement that the submarine USS *Hampton*'s commanding officer had just come aboard: "*Hampton,* arriving!"

Vornado hurried up the ladder to the upper level and into the control room. This small space, filled with cables, valves, panels, consoles, and displays, was more familiar to him than his own house. He had grown up in control rooms like this one, he thought, the room as comfortable as the pulpit to a preacher or a fighter's cockpit to its pilot. It was in this place that he fulfilled his potential, where he had become who he was. In the center of the room was a stainless-steel railed and elevated periscope stand, the conn, where the officer of the deck presided over his watch.

A voice from the back of the room shouted, "Captain's in control!"

One of the periscopes was raised, and an officer stood with his face pressed to the optics module. A second officer stood on the periscope stand with him, a tall, wiry man, slightly shorter than Vornado, with an affable tanned face, the stubble on his square jaw forming the beginning of a beard, his brown eyes penetrating and intelligent though somewhat world-weary, his black hair showing traces of gray. His blue coveralls also had gold dolphins, his collar insignia gold oak leaves, the name tag reading WILLEY. When Vornado approached him, his eyes crinkled into an expression of genuine appreciation, with a touch of a wink, as if he and Vornado were fellow conspirators.

"Good to have you back, sir," he said in a Southern drawl, a mixture of east Texas and west Louisiana. He reached out, and Vornado shook his hand.

"Thanks, XO," Vornado said, using the universal Navy nickname for the ship's second-in-command, the executive officer.

Logan announced to the room, "Last man down, bridge rigged for dive by Master Chief Matthews and checked by Lieutenant Farragut."

Vornado raised an eyebrow at Willey and asked him quietly, "Base course and speed?"

"One four five," the XO drawled. "Flank speed." He nodded seriously when Vornado looked surprised.

"Off'sa'deck," Vornado said to the OOD, "take the ship back deep at flank speed and return to base course. Catch up with your point of intended motion. I'll be debriefing the XO in my stateroom."

The officer at the periscope pulled his face from the instrument just long enough to say, "Deep and flank, aye, sir." He put his face back on the scope and barked out, "Diving officer, submerge the ship to five four six feet, steep angle. Helm, all ahead two-thirds."

The deck tilted downward as Vornado climbed carefully aft to his stateroom with Willey following.

"The captain has left control," the navigation electronics technician announced. Vornado shut the door of his stateroom.

Behind him, in the forward section of the control room,

Officer of the Deck Holmes continued scanning with the periscope until the ship was too deep to see any light from the surface above. He lowered the scope, then leaned over the diving officer's chair and snapped his fingers three times. "Pay up, pal," he said. The diving officer reached into his pocket, withdrew a twenty-dollar bill, and handed it over his shoulder.

"You were right, Nav," the diving officer said. "Captain acted like he gets lowered from a helicopter to the ship in midtransit every day."

"I told you. He's cool as seawater at test depth. The man's a machine."

In his stateroom, Vornado grabbed the edge of his fold-down desk as the hull inclined further downward in their steep dive. He grabbed a uniform out of the cubbyhole closet and pulled off his civilian clothes, hopping on one foot on the steep deck of the descending submarine.

As he was zipping up his coveralls, a loud rolling creak sounded from the overhead, rising to a crescendo and ending in a bang. Vornado smirked, thinking how the newer hands just reporting aboard would duck at the frightening sound. After a decade at sea, Vornado knew it was just the hull compressing as it adjusted to the higher ocean pressure of the deep. Beneath his feet, the deck began to tremble as the ship came up to flank speed, finally level at their cruising depth.

He emerged from the head in his uniform, feeling almost normal. As he pulled on socks and his rubber-soled submarine combat boots he looked around at the ten-by-ten stateroom. It was tidy, with the bed stowed and the small café table and seats erected in its place. A small fold-down table was lowered, his captain's chair in front of it. On the bulkhead there were three pictures—one of the USS *Hampton* taken from a helicopter with Vornado on the bridge, one of Vornado with Rachel and the two older children before Erin was born, and a portrait of Erin taken a few months ago. Vornado's bags were placed carefully by the door to the head. Vornado waved Willey to a seat at the table while he pushed up the fold-down desk and plopped down in the captain's chair.

"So, XO. What the hell is going on?"

Willey narrowed his eyes at Vornado. "Hell, Skipper, I

have no idea. This morning we were on holiday routine. I was out getting the oil changed in the truck, and when I pulled into the driveway there's a squadron staff truck with an armed shore patrol petty officer. They tell me to drop everything, and when I get to the pier, turns out squadron had been on the boat with the duty section starting the reactor at eight in the morning. They'd disconnected the pier phones and quarantined the ship, with all cell phones confiscated, including mine. By the time they got to me the reactor was online, shore power was disconnected, and the lines were singled up. The rest of the crew was brought in with cars driven by armed squadron staffers. Everywhere there's guns, guns, guns. I get to the ship and Commodore Smokin' Joe Kraft himself is on the afterdeck, and even he's wearing a goddamned sidearm like the rest of them. He tells me to take the boat out without you. I ask him what's going on, and he says I'll rendezvous with you at the hundred-fathom curve, and that you'll tell me."

Vornado tapped his platinum Academy ring on the arm of his chair, as he did when deep in thought. He looked up at Willey. "It must have been tough on you and the crew, going to sea without the captain on board."

Willey raised his eyebrows. "Why, no, sir, it was actually one of the smoothest underways we've ever had."

Vornado's jaw dropped, until he realized Willey was baiting him. "Fuck you, XO," he said, and Willey burst into explosive laughter.

"So Kraft left an op order?"

"Yes, sir," Willey said. "Made me sign for it and lock it up in my safe, but it's sealed until you call for it." Willey disappeared through the door to the head, then returned with an envelope.

"What were the other boats on the pier doing?" Vornado asked as he opened the package. "Were they getting ready to shove off?"

"Oh, yeah. The whole force was tossing over lines and getting under way."

"What about the *Tucson*?" Vornado asked. *Tucson* was their fierce competitor on the pier, with a swashbuckling captain—a lifelong friend of Vornado's—and one of the most advanced submarines in the squadron, with the latest FY05 sonar upgrade—only *Tucson* and *Hampton* had the upgrade so far, making their sonar as sensitive as the *Seawolf* and *Virginia* platforms.

"*Tucson*'s two days into a two-week battery replacement. She ain't goin' nowhere. There's no way to speed that one up."

Vornado nodded, looking down at two slim copies of a bound numbered-copy operation order, labeled TOP SECRET STOLEN ARROWS, the last two words the operation's codeword that classified the order higher than top secret.

Vornado handed one of the orders to Willey and broke the seal on the second, then read in silence. After reading for fifteen long minutes, he looked up at Willey, who was staring at him in disbelief. Vornado swallowed hard. Willey shook his head, finally coming up with the only two words he could express in this situation: "Holy shit."

Vornado nodded and looked back down at the op order. A terrorist commando group had made off with a U.S. attack submarine and was sneaking it to within nuclear cruise missile range of Tel Aviv. They could only go two ways—to the Mediterranean or to the Indian Ocean approaches to the Saudi peninsula. Most of the submarine force was scrambling across the Atlantic to the Mediterranean entrance at the Strait of Gibraltar, with the *Hampton* ordered to guard the more distant—and less probable—intercept point, at the entrance to the Indian Ocean at Africa's Cape of Good Hope. The op order's rules of engagement were chilling—they were to intercept the *Albany,* then shoot to kill.

Vornado wandered out of the stateroom to control and leaned over the chart table, measuring their course and speed toward the southern Atlantic. He glanced at his Rolex, which showed the hour approaching 1600. It was hard to believe he was here deep under the sea when he had begun the day with the children and his wife, eating pancakes at the remote log cabin. It seemed like a lifetime ago.

4

Day eighteen began in the featureless darkness of the deep ocean. Where there had been nothing but dark water near its freezing point six hundred feet beneath the waves, something came into being, an elliptically shaped hard substance that divided the water, the sea flowing over the ellipsoid that gradually became a cylinder made of steel. The cylinder kept coming, foot by foot, until a vertical fin sailed by, an unadorned tower pointing to the surface far above. The fin faded away as the cylinder continued moving past, until finally the cylinder tapered slowly to a point. Vertical and horizontal stabilizers sailed by, then a seven-bladed screw rotating slowly and stirring up the water in the thing's wake. For several minutes after the beast's passage the water churned in agitation, then calmed. Several minutes after the monstrosity of steel and fiberglass had swept past, it was as if it had never existed, and the dark sea continued on to the perpetuity of endless time.

Within the bowels of the cylinder, in its forward compartment's upper level, in the captain's stateroom, Commander Peter Vornado toweled off after his morning shower. He pulled on his at-sea uniform of coveralls and sneakers, stood deep in thought for a moment, then reached into a cubbyhole and found something hanging on one of the hooks inside—a gold chain with a medal hanging from it. He ran his fingers over the Saint Christopher's medal, the vision of his wife's worried face in front of him as he leaned out the helicopter's door. He could still hear her voice ringing in his ears: *Please be careful. And don't take that off— I have a really bad feeling about all this.* He lifted the medal up, put it around his neck, and tucked it under his T-shirt.

He squinted at his face in his stateroom mirror. For the past week he had grown his beard, but was dismayed to see that it had come in completely gray. It looked odd with his blond hair and blue eyes and fair complexion, and made him look twenty years older. He took his razor, lathered up, and shaved it off. After he dried his face he frowned into the mirror again, realizing that he still looked much older than last week. Perhaps it was the stress of this mission, he thought. He hadn't been sleeping well and the headaches were getting worse. Vornado promised himself he'd see a doctor as soon as he got back to Virginia Beach.

Vornado left the stateroom and walked into the control room. Lieutenant Commander Mark Holmes stood the watch on the conn. Vornado waved at him and leaned over the aft port chart table. They had been at the Cape Town intercept position for ten days. Vornado had ordered the ship to execute a bow-tie pattern, driving northeast for twenty miles, then turning south for five miles, west for twenty miles, south again for five miles, then returning to the northeast for another twenty-mile leg, their passage tracing the bow-tie pattern. The maneuver kept their sonar gear out of the water disturbed by their passage, their movement through the sea helping the sonar processors screen out own-ship noise, and at no time did *Hampton* put the "threat vector"—the direction from which *Albany* was expected to approach—in the baffles where broadband sonar would be blind. Behind them the ship trailed the thin wire–towed linear array, a long sonar transducer set on a half-mile-long cable, the unit in undisturbed water far from the noise of the mother ship, listening into slices of the sea and tuned precisely to hear the particular tonals emitted by 688-class submarines.

Vornado spoke quietly to the morning's officer of the deck and junior officer of the deck, navigator Mark Holmes and main propulsion assistant Mike Logan. He leaned over the sonar repeater console, then walked into the sonar room, where Chief Bradley stood the watch with one of his more junior men. Vornado lifted his palms, as if to ask, "Anything?" and Bradley shook his head solemnly, his lips pursed.

B. K. Dillinger pocketed three Cuban Montecristo cigars from the stash the *Albany*'s captain had kept in his safe and stepped into the control room. He was the last one to enter. The entire crew was there, except for the watchstanders in the engineering spaces and a few of Buffalo's men in the torpedo room. Steve Flood handed him a set of headphones. Dillinger adjusted the boom microphone and checked the circuit. The brass chronometer showed it to be just after 1400 GMT.

"Lionel," Dillinger said to his young weapons expert, "make torpedo tubes one and two ready in all respects and open outer doors."

Lionel Tonelle acknowledged from the weapon control panel. The youngster had come up with an innovative way to approach the Cape of Good Hope choke point, where Patty Schluss had insisted the U.S. Navy would have an ambush submarine waiting for them. Dillinger had planned to add five days to the trip and take the cape extremely wide to avoid Patty's submarine, but Lionel had proposed a solution that had made storming the cape possible. The kid proposed that they take the data from one of the Mark 48 torpedoes and import it into the BQQ-5E active sonar suite. The torpedo's sonar in passive listen-only mode would sail twenty miles ahead of them and listen for the acoustic signs of an ambush sub. The plan was perfect, because using a torpedo as an "offboard sensor" meant they would detect an enemy sub before it detected them.

And a lurking American sub at the cape, when it heard an incoming torpedo, would go absolutely ape and take extreme evasive action by turning and running away at maximum speed. A waiting sub at slow speed would be nearly silent, but a running sub at flank speed would be loud as a train wreck. Dillinger would switch the torpedo from a scout to a weapon, and the Mark 48 would chase down their opponent and kill it. Even if it ran out of fuel too soon to put down the ambush sub, the torpedo would do its job of flushing out a bad guy, and Dillinger could target it with a salvo of fresh weapons at his leisure. There would be a bonus for Lionel when this was all over, Dillinger thought.

"Tubes one and two ready in all respects, Skipper, with doors one and two open."

"Good, Lionel. Apply torpedo power to unit one. Select presets and read them out."

"Powering up one." Lionel went through the list of torpedo presets, programming the weapon to cruise at slow speed in a spiral search pattern at the optimum depth for listening for a submerged contact—about seven hundred feet—and most important of all, the ceiling setting inserted at 150 feet so that the torpedo would ignore shallow contacts. An accidental torpedo hit that took down a merchant ship in the crowded shipping lanes of the Cape of Good Hope would be a disaster, a large finger pointing at them. They'd never make it to the Persian Gulf if that happened.

"Everybody ready? Lionel, shoot tube one on programmed bearing."

Lionel operated the panel, hitting the standby key, then the fire key. The deck jumped as a violent booming roar slammed Dillinger's ears. The high-pressure air that loaded the water tank that made the water push out the ton-and-a-half weapon would unload the tank by ventilating the high pressure back into the ship—wonderful for avoiding making air bubbles outside the hull, but brutal to sensitive eardrums.

Flood had put on headphones in sonar. He gave a thumbs-up sign. "Weapon's good."

Dillinger nodded. It wouldn't do to have his own torpedo circle around and kill him. Dillinger stepped into sonar and looked over Lionel's shoulder. The display was updating, getting data from the torpedo wire. It looked somewhat like a radar screen, the data freshening in a circular pattern, but instead of the screen forming a God's-eye view like a radar did, the center of the display looked horizontally in the direction of travel. A bright dot to the right meant a detect to the right of the unit's travel, and similarly a dot at six o'clock meant a detect deeper than the unit's flight trajectory. Back at the firecontrol consoles, the combat control system was reeling off the distance and bearing to the torpedo, estimating its position from own-ship based on its search speed. If Lionel detected something at this panel, Merc would know where the torpedo was at the detect point. That would allow them to plot the target's bearing and range to the point that it was heard.

There was nothing to do but wait. Dillinger unwrapped a Montecristo and lit it, the mellow smoke forming a cloud around him. In another hour he would launch a second scout torpedo so it would be ten miles ahead of them when the first torpedo ran out of fuel and sank. Dillinger unfolded the small jump seat on the conn and sat down and puffed the cigar. Steve Flood joined him.

"Well, Steve," Dillinger said, blowing a smoke ring. "If someone's out there waiting to ambush us, they're going to get a nasty surprise."

"Skip," Lionel interrupted. "We've got a definite detect. Look at the Q-five screen." To someone who didn't know him, Lionel's voice sounded as normal as if he were announcing dinner being served, but Dillinger knew his weapons expert. Lionel was anxious, excited, and unsure of himself.

Dillinger hurried into the sonar room and leaned over Lionel's high-backed seat. As the torpedo spiraled through its travel, dots on one side of the display's crosshairs lit the screen, then moved on to the next quadrant as the previous quadrant's dots faded out, almost like a radar screen display. Dillinger watched as the display lit up three quadrants, the final sweep of data yielding a bright collection of dots, the dots coalescing together into a bright stain on the display. Dillinger bit his lip, waiting for the next corkscrew turn of the torpedo. The detection blip showed up again, even more clearly.

"That's it," Dillinger said. "You can switch the torpedo to attack mode?"

"Absolutely, Skipper."

Peter Vornado shut the door to his stateroom after his latest impatient trip to the chart table and sonar repeater in control. He sank into his command chair, his mind returning to the most ominous thing about the mission—the fact that the admirals at headquarters didn't share his optimism, as shown by the EAM they'd sent. "EAM" stood for emergency action message. At the midpoint of their trip, they had been summoned to periscope depth by ocean-penetrating extremely low frequency radio—an oddball system that took tremendous power and radio tower farms the size of villages, and which took twenty minutes to transmit a single character, but was effective at recalling a deep submarine to periscope depth to get an urgent message from the rapid-transmitting satellites overhead. The periscope depth excursion obtained an EAM that had chilled Vornado, an order he never thought he'd read—the order to employ the RUR-5 Delta SUBROC antisubmarine rockets with nuclear warhead depth charges against the *Albany* in the event he thought the ship was in danger.

No nuclear release order had ever been transmitted to a submarine captain in the entire history of nuclear weapons. The two recently loaded SUBROCs had been labeled by Vornado himself as useless, because they couldn't be used in the heat of battle against an enemy sub without coming to periscope depth to request nuclear release permission and the endless wait for permission to be granted, the president himself required to agree on the use of a nuke. But there the permission was, lying on the message printout page, allowing Vornado to make the call, and ordering him to nuke the *Albany* if the battle got hairy. This was even more serious than he had thought.

The new SUBROCs differed from their ancestors, which had been dumb ballistic rockets that deployed a depth bomb much too close to the launching ship. They had been Cold War suicide weapons. The new RUR-5 Deltas were essentially Block V Tomahawk cruise missiles that flew out a hundred or more miles and popped the W-44 nuclear depth charge on the head of the enemy, or close enough. As long as the enemy was within a twenty-mile radius of the relatively small ten-kiloton blast, his hull would be cut to ribbons. Of course, the use of a nuke was still a tough call, because a nuclear explosion would "blue out" an entire sector of the compass from the trillions of bubbles released into the deep ocean. It would take days to be able to hear a sonar noise in that area of the blast. An enemy just outside the blast zone could take advantage of a blue-out to escape the area and return to ambush the launching sub.

The SUBROCs had been loaded during Vornado's vacation, during the same weapons offload that had pulled off all their Mod 6 Mark 48 torpedoes and replaced them with the more reliable and older Mod 5 units, the explanation given that the Mod 6 units had a flaw that they could be lured away from their targets by noise countermeasures, while the older Mod 5s were more relentless in following targets, at the cost of a knot of top speed and a mile or two of range.

Vornado's thoughts were interrupted by the sound that doubled his heart rate—the clicking of the 1MC speakers, which should never have been used during the rig for ultraquiet, and the stressed voice of the officer of the deck, shouting the most frightening words a submariner could hear:

"Torpedo in the water! Torpedo in the water!"

5

Vornado shot to his feet so fast his chair crashed back into the bulkhead. He pulled the stateroom door open and flew into the control room. All he'd heard about fear this intense was true. He had become so aware of everything around him that time seemed to expand. Although he was hurtling into the control room, it seemed to move toward him infinitely slowly. The officer of the deck's face was contorted in fear, his eyes wide, his hands shaking. Vornado could see the broadband sonar display from five feet away, his eyes zeroing in on the bright vertical trace to the northwest.

When the officer of the deck, Mark Holmes, saw him, he turned and tried to spit out the words of his briefing, but it seemed to take forever: "Captain, sonar holds a Mark 48 ADCAP torpedo in the water, inbound from bearing three three two. I'm turning the ship to run from the torpedo at flank speed and my intention is to fire three torpedoes down the bearing line—"

Vornado was about to nod his head in agreement, but as a tenth of a second slowly passed, something seemed terribly wrong. In a flash he saw a mental image, then lost it. He blinked in disorientation, wondering if the adrenaline making his heart pound were interfering with his judgment, or if his headaches could be the sign of something seriously amiss with his brain, but then the flash happened again, brighter and longer this time. This time it lingered, and wrapped in the ball of light in Vornado's mind was an image, a vision of a toothless shark wearing a blindfold. Vornado did a double take, doubting what he'd perceived, but when he tried to reexamine it, the vision vaporized, leaving him wondering if this were something coming from

his own intuition and thought processes or from completely
outside himself.

The standard procedure when detecting a torpedo in the
water was to run like hell, with the machinery making a
thousand times more noise at maximum speed than they
were making now. But if this torpedo couldn't attack them,
running would just alert whoever had launched the offending weapon. A blind toothless shark, Vornado thought.

"Hold it, hold it, hold it," Vornado said, OOD Mark
Holmes's eyes growing huge in disbelief. All around him
the room was chaotic as watchstanders ran into the room
to man battlestations, the immediate action for a call of
torpedo in the water. "Helm, steer course west," Vornado
barked. He checked the engine order telegraph—the arrow
was still pointing to all ahead one-third, since Holmes
hadn't yet ordered the ship to speed up to flank.

"Captain has the conn," Holmes said, the captain's orders to the helmsman automatically transferring control of
the ship's motion to the captain and relieving Holmes of
the duty.

Vornado snapped on a headset and hurriedly adjusted
the boom microphone as he took in the broadband sonar
display. "Sonar, Captain," Vornado said into his mike.
"Report torpedo turn count." If sonar were following procedure rather than giving in to panic, they would be checking the pulsing from the torpedo's counterrotating screws
to see what speed it was going. The Mark 48 had three
departure speeds and only one attack velocity—if it were
barreling in at fifty-eight knots, it would have detected the
Hampton, but if it were poking along at twenty-eight knots,
it was just on its way to a search point and hadn't sniffed
out their presence.

"Captain, Sonar." His earphones crackled. "We think the
weapon is inbound at its slow speed setting."

Vornado exhaled in relief. "Attention in the firecontrol
party," he announced on his headset. "The torpedo is a
shot in the dark, meant to provoke a reaction from a sub
unknown to the firing ship. It's moving at its slow speed.
That means that it has not yet detected us. We still have
time to get out of its search cone before it gets in range.
My intention is drive off the torpedo's track at a right angle
to the torpedo's course, so our hull will not bounce back

an upshifted or downshifted frequency if the torpedo goes active. We will speed up slightly, to move off the torpedo's track, but not so fast that we will make noise and alert the weapon. We'll keep watching it and continue monitoring all sonar data coming from the northwest. Carry on. Coordinator, input a speed of twenty-eight knots into the firecontrol system for the torpedo."

"Coordinator, aye," Willey said from his spot in front of the attack center's firecontrol consoles. During battlestations the XO became the firecontrol coordinator, or just "coordinator," and was in charge of the target's "solution," that magical package of unknown data—range, speed, and course—that had to be calculated and inferred using passive sonar bearing-only data. With sonar that just listened instead of pinged active, only the direction to the target was known, but with the power of the computer and the tricks of planar geometry, the target's motion could be determined by maneuvering the ship and seeing how the target's bearings changed.

As Vornado ordered the ship to the southwest, perpendicular to the torpedo's motion, he had an odd feeling of certainty, as if he were remembering this rather than experiencing it for the first time. The first throb of the headache arrived just after that thought, taking his optimism with it.

"Weapon switching to active search mode, Skipper," Lionel reported. "Weapon has sped up to fifty-eight knots! Unit is homing."

"You got anything on own-ship's sensors, Steve?" Dillinger called to Flood.

"I've got a tiny spoke in the 688-class turbine generator harmonic frequency. Towed array likely beam bearing at one eight five, sending it to firecontrol as Sierra One."

Dillinger rushed to the control room. His men were there, waiting.

Vornado waited, staring at the pos two display, waiting for the *Albany* to come inside their range of detection while the crew watched the weapon to make sure it hadn't detected them yet.

"Conn, Sonar"—Chief Bradley clicked in—"new narrowband sonar contact held on the towed array, bearing either zero two zero or zero eight zero, designate Sierra Seven. Contact is a submerged warship, Los Angeles class."

The room broke out into a restrained cheer, which was understandable given the tension of the engagement. The battle had just broken their way, with them detecting *Albany* before she heard them. Vornado smiled to himself as he tapped the glass of the sonar display panel. The FY05 sonar upgrade had served them well. He wondered what this would be like if both ships had the same upgraded equipment. A pulse of pain flared behind Vornado's right eye, making him shut his eyes. With an effort he opened them, remembering his crew was watching him.

"Attention in the firecontrol party," Vornado said, his voice deep and authoritative. "Designate new sonar contact Master One. My intentions are to maneuver the ship to get two target motion analysis legs on Master One, get a firing solution, and launch a horizontal salvo of Mark 48 ADCAP torpedoes ASAP. Coordinator, get a curve. Carry on."

A "curve" was half the data needed to determine the target's distance, course, and speed.

"Get a curve, Coordinator, aye." Willey's voice had a happy ring to it, which was rare.

Vornado waited, supervising the firecontrol team and watching the pos two panel, manned by young Lieutenant Carl Howden, Farragut's damage control officer. Less than two minutes later Willey was ready to maneuver the ship.

"Captain, we have a curve."

Vornado ordered the ship to the southeast. "Sonar, Captain, maneuvering. Coordinator, once we're steady on the new course, get a curve, and hurry so we can turn back away from the torpedo."

"Get a curve, aye."

Vornado bit the inside of his lip, trying not to show how tense and nervous he felt about maneuvering across the torpedo's path. He had to take the risk, or they couldn't fire on the *Albany*. Still, it was like putting his head into the mouth of an untrained lion.

"Captain," Willey announced in triumph, "we have a firing solution."

"Firing point procedures," Vornado said to the team. He

was about to open his mouth for the next order when Chief Bradley's panicked voice suddenly interrupted.

"Conn, Sonar, torpedo has sped up to attack velocity. I've got an active sonar pulse from the torpedo!"

Time suddenly seemed to explode into slow motion again as a burst of adrenaline and pure fear slammed into Vornado's central nervous system. He tried to take a deep breath and force himself to think before reacting on instinct, but the part of his mind that was most rational seemed far distant, and all his training screamed in his mind for him to run. He fought the panic for the next tenth of a second, but his rational side, frightened as it was, agreed with his fears. It was definitely time to run.

"Helm, all ahead flank! Dive, make your depth eleven hundred feet!" Vornado's orders were loud and deliberate, betraying none of the adrenaline pulsing through his bloodstream, but there was no sense shouting orders the watchstanders couldn't understand. He grabbed the 7MC microphone from the overhead cradle and clicked the mike. "Maneuvering, Captain, *cavitate*!" Normally the engineering watchstanders would accelerate slowly to avoid making vapor bubbles on the surface of the screw, vapor bubbles that would collapse and shriek out into the water the unmistakable sound of a submarine speeding up, but this was no time for stealth. Stealth went out the window twelve seconds ago, when the torpedo detected them and switched to fast-attack mode.

"OOD, status of signal ejectors?"

"Forward loaded with active countermeasure, aft with passive."

"Launch the forward and aft signal ejectors." The active countermeasure would leave the signal ejector and float in the sea, where it would begin putting out loud frequency tonals that matched a 688-class submarine going flank speed. If pinged on by an active torpedo sonar, it would emit a sonar tone at an upshifted or downshifted frequency so that the unit would sound like the echo from a moving submarine. The active countermeasure almost always fooled an incoming torpedo, but only temporarily, because smart torpedoes like the Mark 48 would circle around and go into "reattack" mode, and restart the search after being diverted by a countermeasure. The passive unit would emit a large cloud of dense bubbles, enough to confuse an active sonar by returning a large ping echo. Together with the active evasion device, odds favored the torpedo being confused, at least for a few minutes.

The deck began to tremble from the flank speed bell. At first the vibrations were gentle and subtle, but a minute later the entire ship was shaking as if it were strapped to an old-fashioned exercise-belt machine. Vornado grabbed a handrail at the conn, his knuckles white, the trembling of the ship a calming feeling, as if the vibration signaled his brain that the ship was running from danger as fast as it could.

"Attention in the firecontrol party, while we're evading, we're resuming the attack." Shooting torpedoes at flank speed was a risk, Vornado thought, because the weapon emerging from the canted tube could break in half from the force of the seawater flow, and could detonate just outside the hull, but this was war. "I intend to launch weapons despite our speed. Firing point procedures, tubes one and two, horizontal salvo, Master One, two degree offset, one-minute interval."

Vornado's principal watchstanders would report their readiness one by one. As he waited, his awareness expanded to envelop the ship and the sea around him, wary of anything that would prevent him from firing on the *Albany*.

"Ship ready," Holmes said.

"Weapon ready," Weapons Officer Mario Marchese called.

"Solution ready," Willey said.

"Tube one, shoot on generated bearing," Vornado ordered.

"Set," Howden said, sending his final firecontrol solution to Master One to Marchese's panel.

"Stand by," Marchese announced, hitting the fixed function key that told the weapon to prepare for engine start.

"Shoot!" Vornado ordered.

"Fire!" Marchese said, hitting the fire function key.

There was a tenth of a second's swishing sound in the ship, followed by a sudden bang that grew into a half-second of roaring noise, the sound slamming through Vornado's chest and smashing his eardrums. For all the fury of the noise, it wasn't the sound of the torpedo launch but the result of the water-round-torpedo tank venting the high pressure torpedo-firing air back into the interior of the ship. It was a satisfying noise, the same calming feeling obtained from firing a heavy handgun.

"Conn, Sonar, own-ship's unit, normal launch."

Maybe it was the air-pressure spike from the torpedo launch or the stress of the moment, but for whatever reason, the headache stopped being something Vornado suffered in the background, but became searingly painful as it bloomed at the top of his head. He reached into his pocket, but there were no Advil capsules.

"Coming up on one minute, Captain," Holmes reported.

"Tube two," Vornado said, feeling distant from himself, "shoot on generated bearing."

The pain spread from the top of Vornado's skull to the region over his ears, becoming fiercer by the second.

"Set." Howden's voice sounded as if it were coming from a tunnel.

"Stand by." Marchese's voice was even more distorted.

Vornado grabbed the railing of the periscope stand with his other hand to steady himself just before the room seemed to tilt to port.

"Captain?" Willey said, his voice worried.

"Shoot," Vornado remembered, his hand rising to his forehead, his eyes shut against the pain.

"Fire," Marchese said, just before the second earsplitting boom sounded in the ship, the deckplates seeming to jump from the fury of the torpedo launch.

"Conn, Sonar, second own-ship's unit, normal launch."

"Sonar, Captain," Vornado said, knowing he had something important to say, but the pain spreading to his temples made him forget. "Goddammit, XO, get a messenger to grab five Advils from my stateroom, now."

Willey grabbed the phonetalker standing next to him and sent him aft. He disappeared into Vornado's sea cabin.

"Captain, Sonar, yes?"

"Skipper," Willey said, his hand cupping his boom mike so he could speak confidentially to Vornado, "you look white as a ghost."

"I'm okay," Vornado said, the effort of talking sending ripples of intense pain from his jaw to his temples. Suddenly his eye sockets seemed to clamp down on his eyeballs as the headache intensified. The pain had grown to a level

he had never experienced. The one he'd felt as the Seahawk landed was nothing compared to this. He had to function, he thought, or the ship could be lost. The messenger
skidded to a halt in front of the conn with the Advil caplets
and a cup of water. Vornado popped all five at once, biting
them hard and swallowing the liquid, then accepting the
water from the frightened kid and gulping it down. He took
a deep breath. If anything the pain was becoming worse, a
sudden lightning bolt flashing in his vision. He blinked, trying to look normal.

"Rough range to the incoming torpedo?" Vornado
asked, hoping the pain didn't register in his voice.

B. K. Dillinger took the first smooth puffs of his second
Montecristo as he leaned against the cool metal of the number two periscope, waiting for Lionel to report that the
torpedo had lost the wire connection, the first indication
that the unit no longer existed but had detonated. The
panel indication would happen a few seconds before the
shock wave of the explosion reached them.

But instead of the victory announcement, Lionel turned
to look at him, an expression of anger on his features.
"Skipper, we lost the torpedo."

"What do you mean?" Dillinger shot back.

"My panel's showing wire guide continuity but I've lost
the homing annunciator and speed indicator. It was out
there for seventy minutes, but we have it running deep at
maximum speed. I think it ran out of fuel."

"God*dammit* to fucking hell, Lionel!" Dillinger roared
in sudden fury, ripping off his headset and hurling it into
the navigation equipment across the room. The only sound
in the room was the shattering of the plastic earpiece and
the rain of plastic onto the deck.

"Conn, Sonar, incoming torpedo." Chief Bradley paused.
Vornado bit his lip, waiting for more bad news. "Incoming
torpedo has shut down!"

"Yeah!" Marchese shouted, his fist in the air. Howden
reached up and slapped Logan's hand at the firecontrol
console.

"Ran out of fuel." Willey grinned at Vornado. "In the

water too long. Now those bastards can see how it feels to be on the business end of a Mark 48 ADCAP."

Vornado had to stop their all-out noisy run from the torpedo. If he could get the ship silent, fast, the *Albany* might not be able to find them in time to get off another shot.

"Helm, all stop," Vornado said. "Left one degree rudder, steady course west. Sonar, Captain, maneuvering to the west and slowing. Maneuvering, Captain, downshift reactor recirculation pumps to superslow." Vornado glanced at Willey, who was smiling until he saw Vornado's face, and then the lines of worry returned to his expression.

"Sir, recommend SUBROC launch," Willey said. "We need to nuke the bastard before he gets off another shot. The next one could be luckier."

Vornado bit the inside of his lip, his headache pounding and interfering with his ability to think. With a conscious effort he reasoned with himself, thinking that with a torpedo he would be able to confirm a kill, but after an underwater nuclear detonation caused a billion bubbles to fill the water, the sonar blue-out could mask the noise of the *Albany* if she survived. And if the enemy launched from behind the curtain of a blue-out, the incoming torpedo wouldn't be detectable until it was on them. But something nagged at him, even though the battle was going *Hampton*'s way.

"Conn, Sonar, own-ship's first-fired unit going active."

"Very well, Sonar." Vornado glanced at the weapon-control console, where the first indications of the torpedoes detecting the target would arrive. He looked at the XO. "We don't need to use the nukes, XO. The Mark 48s have him."

"Conn, Sonar, own-ship's second-fired unit going active."

"Sir, I still recommend we nuke him. We can't let this guy have a chance."

"Wait on the launch, but spin up VLS tubes eleven and twelve. Just in case, XO." Vertical launch system tubes eleven and twelve were loaded with the new SUBROC nuclear-tipped depth charges.

A slow grin spread across Willey's face. "Spin up VLS eleven and twelve, aye, sir. It'll be a pleasure."

*   *   *

"Skipper," Steve Flood called from the sonar room, "I've got a transient noise from the target. I have to take a guess, but I'd say it's a torpedo launch."

Dillinger bit his lip, wanting to smash something. What a damned stupid way to lose this battle. What the hell did he think he was doing, vectoring in a torpedo that was almost out of gas? He should have launched another one, but it would have taken an hour or longer to get to the same point in the sea as the torpedo that shut down. He had to force himself to concentrate on how to turn this around. As he began to form options for a counterattack, Flood called out their death sentence:

"Skipper, second torpedo launch. Weapons are loud. They could be in high-speed transit, and that's forty-five knots."

"Do we have the target?"

"Still on narrowband," Flood said. "Good broadband to the torpedo launch point. It's not great, Skipper, but it's a good enough solution to shoot. At least if we send out some weapons, the target may break off his attack."

B. K. Dillinger made a decision. He would launch a salvo of weapons down the bearing to the target and either steer them in flight or send them to the vicinity of the torpedo launches from the target. If nothing else, torpedoes would scare the target submarine—they had proved that when their first torpedo had gone active, and the enemy had run at flank speed to evade it and made more noise than a freight train. The battle was only temporarily in the enemy's favor. Dillinger and the *Albany* were about to turn this around.

"Gentlemen, don't worry about a miss; we'll fire one and two, cut the wires, and launch three and four and keep the wires on weapons three and four to steer them if we can, based on what the target does." If only they could hear the bastard, Dillinger thought, but when he heard these four weapons coming for him, he'd run scared. "After we shoot, we'll drive off the launch point at flank and then execute an under-ice evasion tactic." Flood stared at him with his mouth open, but there was no time to argue. "Shoot one and two."

Merc locked in the solution to the submarine target and sent it to Flood at the weapon-control panel.

"Set," Merc said.

"Stand by," Flood said. "Firing one."

The deckplates trembled as the booming roar of the torpedo tube launch reverberated in the ship. Dillinger yawned to clear his tortured eardrums, his attention locked on the position two panel.

"Set for two," Merc said.

"Stand by and firing two." Flood hit the fixed function key, and the second torpedo launch sounded in the room.

"Cut the wires and shut doors to one and two," Dillinger said. "Open door to three and four."

Flood operated the panel. Dillinger cursed to himself at the time delay to reset the tube doors.

"Set," Merc said.

"Fire three," Flood said. The torpedo launch boomed again.

"Set for four."

Flood fired the fourth torpedo.

"Drain tubes one and two and have Meathook and Beergut ram two new weapons into one and two. When they're ready I'll send Lionel down to connect the wires and shut the breech doors. Buffalo," Dillinger said to Patterson, who sat at the helmsman's station. "All ahead flank. Left ten degrees rudder, steady course east."

Buffalo grabbed the engine order telegraph knob and clicked it to FLANK. He turned the wheel and watched the rudder display on the ship control console, positioning it to left ten degrees.

The deckplates began to vibrate as the ship accelerated.

"You want Pat to cavitate?" Flood asked anxiously.

"No," Dillinger said. "Let's get away from where we launched and get off the torpedo tracks quietly before the incoming Mark 48s go active. Until they start pinging, they're blind."

Dillinger waited, watching the speed indicator on the ship-control console as the *Albany* sped up from five knots to ten, then fifteen, then twenty and beyond. The rail of the periscope stand rattled as the ship came up to its maximum speed at thirty-four knots. Dillinger pursed his lips, cursing the older submarine's slow top speed. He watched the second hand of the chronometer slowly circle the clock face. One minute had passed since they leveled out at thirty-four knots.

"Torpedoes should have been pinging active by now, Skip," Flood said, frowning.

Dillinger grabbed the 7MC micorphone from the overhead and shouted into it, "Pat, shut the throttles and group scram the reactor! Use residual steam to answer all back two-thirds!" He dropped the microphone, the unit bouncing on the deck, suspended by its coiled cord.

"Buffalo, ring up all back two-thirds. Watch the speed indicator and tell me when it shows two knots. Meanwhile, right one degree rudder, steady course one nine zero so we're pointed toward the incoming torpedoes."

Dillinger hurried to the ballast-control panel and threw himself down in the chair. He glanced at the ship-control panel, wondering if Pat had enough steam to slow the ship down from its flank speed run before boiling the steam generators dry. The bell of the engine order telegraph answered his thoughts, the needle from maneuvering changing from back two-thirds to all stop while the speed indicator still read four knots. Patty had run out of steam in the boilers and had to shut the astern throttles or risk damaging the shutdown reactor plant.

With the reactor scrammed and most of the electrical load centers turned off, the ship would become extremely quiet. As soon as the ship's forward momentum slowed from the friction of the water, the combination of not moving—and not upshifting or downshifting a sonar active pulse—and having minimal own-ship-generated noise from turning off all the rotating equipment would make them essentially invisible, both to the incoming torpedo sonars and to the ambushing submarine. But it also made them vulnerable if one of the torpedoes did find them, since they had no ability to speed up, and it would take ten or twelve minutes to bring the reactor back to the power range.

"Speed, two knots," Buffalo said. "I'm on one six zero."

Dillinger concentrated on his panel to engage the hovering system computer. He glanced at the ship's digital depth indicator, which read 556 feet. He selected 560 feet on the hovering computer with a zero rise rate and waited for the ship to slow down to zero knots.

A sudden high-pitched rising whistle sounded in the room, the screech lowering in pitch and then steadily rising again, the cycle starting over. Flood's face darkened as he looked at Dillinger. "Torpedoes are at their enable points, Skipper, and going active."

"Speed zero," Buffalo called.

"Ring up all stop," Dillinger said as he engaged the hovering system in automatic, waiting to see if it would take over the ship's depth control. Speed and depth were correct, but if the ship were heavy or light, the computer would not take over, and if the ship were unbalanced it would also reject the automatic command. Dillinger held his breath, hoping the ship was balanced.

While he waited, a second torpedo active sonar joined the first, the two units screaming their rising siren notes. Dillinger felt a shiver rise up his spine. Fear would be a factor now, he knew, for all of them, but with the ship hiding in plain view, there would be no mistakes to make. They would play possum at this depth, motionless, quiet as a hole in the ocean, and the torpedoes would not see them, their processors rejecting zero-speed objects to screen out the noise of reflected particles in the water, and reacting only to upshifted or downshifted frequency echoes that resulted from target speed, much like a predator's eyes are only able to react to the motion of its prey.

It was an odd tactic, but since he knew the programming of the torpedoes, he knew they would not see him if he froze. The torpedoes' rejection of echoes at the same frequency as the outgoing pulse would keep them from detonating on unmoving countermeasures, but would allow Dillinger to hide the ship—that is, unless the firing ship had reprogrammed that little feature. There was no time to deal with that, Dillinger thought. All he could do now was hope the under-ice tactic would work.

The hovering system computer accepted the input and took over depth control. Dillinger stood up from the panel, an expression of relief on his face.

"Now we wait," he said, brushing sweat off his forehead. The room had grown hot and stuffy since Pat Schluss had shut down the reactor, the loss of the plant taking with it the air-conditioning systems and the seawater cooling systems. The tremendous heat of the steam plant inside this canned atmosphere would warm the entire submarine with 100-percent-humidity air. It was already at least ninety-five degrees in the control room. Back aft the temperature would already have climbed to over 120.

Dillinger's armpits melted into sweat as he stepped over to the conn platform. The firecontrol systems would remain online, their cooling systems fed from forward auxiliary seawater and their power supplies coming from the vital bus, but before long the temperature in the room would begin to affect them. Dillinger watched the tracks of the torpedoes on the geographic plot selected on position one. Each second the computer updated the positions of the two spade shapes coming in toward the central diamond that symbolized the *Albany,* each torpedo's track shown as a ruler-straight line as they streaked in from their launch points.

Dillinger bit his lip as the weapons sailed in, closer and closer.

Chief Bradley suddenly shouted in Vornado's ear: "Conn, Sonar, torpedo in the water! Bearing three five seven!"

"Dammit," Vornado cursed, concentrating on the geographic plot.

"Conn, Sonar, second torpedo in the water, three five six. No, now we have three. Conn, Sonar, four torpedoes in the water! Recommend evading to the south!"

Vornado's temples throbbed in severe pain. He had the dim thought that the headaches were somehow connected to fear and stress, but it didn't matter. The pain spread to the base of his skull and forward to his eye sockets. He tried to breathe, but the headache was a nail in his forehead, and his vision was becoming blurry.

"Conn, Sonar, first torpedo in the water is at high speed and has gone active!"

"XO, get the corpsman up here," Vornado said through his teeth, suddenly angry at the pain, the thought that it could cost him the battle and the ship itself filling him with fury.

Willey sent the messenger aft, then looked at Vornado.

"I recommend cavitating flank and running south, sir," he said.

All Vornado could think about was the SUBROC missile. The ship was suddenly in grave danger, and the mission was in jeopardy. His orders demanded that he fire the nuke in the event the battle turned and the ship was in danger.

"No, XO," Vornado ordered, dim thoughts registering that this was it, that this was the day his heart would stop beating. The thought winked out as a stabbing pain flashed through his temples, a sudden dizziness turning the room to starboard. For an instant Vornado felt as though the attack center consoles were far downhill from him, despite Willey's straight posture. Vornado could hear the faint sound of a torpedo sonar with its rising and falling siren sound from the starboard side.

"Captain?" Willey said, an odd expression contorting his face.

There was only one thing he could do, Vornado thought.

"Attention in the firecontrol party," Vornado said, his voice too loud. "I intend to point toward the incoming torpedoes and emergency blow to the surface. We'll resubmerge vertically to SUBROC missile firing depth and fire tubes eleven and twelve, and if we're lucky the Mark 48s won't climb above a hundred-foot ceiling. If we get away with the tactic, Master One should be gone for good. Helm, right full rudder, all ahead full. Chief of the Watch, emergency blow the forward group!"

The wailing tones of the torpedo sonars screamed outside the hull, the loud sonar systems never quieting, their sharktooth sound-wave pattern allowing them to transmit and receive sonar at the same time. The noise grew louder and louder, growing to an ear-piercing howl. On the firecontrol display the spades got closer to the diamond in the center, the spade tracks taking them to the west of the *Albany*. Dillinger held his breath, and then something amazing happened—the sonar sounds from the torpedoes downshifted, like a train whistle's pitch sinking as it swept by. The first Mark 48 ADCAP torpedo had just sailed right by them, less than a mile away to the west. As Dillinger waited, the second torpedo blew past them, this one closer, perhaps only a half mile away.

Flood's face, pale and sweat soaked, suddenly broke into an expression of gleeful relief. "You did it, Skipper! They went right by!"

"Don't celebrate yet, Steve. Let's see if the target steers them. What's happening with our units?"

In the rush to avoid the incoming torpedoes, Dillinger had neglected to watch the four he'd launched.

"Units one and two are enabled and doing an active snake search. Three and four are still on the run to enable."

Dillinger nodded. Somewhere to the south the hunter-killer submarine that had tried to ambush him was now running from *Albany*'s fierce ADCAP torpedoes. He pulled a fresh cigar from his coverall pocket. "How's it feel, shit-head?" he mumbled to the firecontrol display.

"Excuse me, Skip?" Matt Mercury-Pryce said.

"Talking to the target, Merc," Dillinger said with a grin as he lit the cigar and settled in for the wait. If these torpedoes connected, the battle was won, and he and *Albany* could continue on toward the Tomahawk firing point.

"Emergency blow forward, aye, sir," the chief of the watch said from his ballast-control panel, but glancing doubtfully over his shoulder at Vornado. Vornado did his best to return a confident look, but the pain was starting to crowd out all rational thought.

The chief of the watch pulled down the interlock knob on the large stainless-steel lever that pointed downward, then rotated the lever from straight down to straight up. Immediately a violent roar shook the control room, the flow noise from the ultra–high pressure air banks in the forward ballast tanks emptying their contents into the tanks and blowing out the water into the sea through the open louvers at the bottom of the tanks. *Hampton* had just become a hundred tons lighter, and within moments would be bound for the surface, no earthly force able to keep her underwater. The digital depth gauge began clicking off the depth as the ship began to rise from eleven hundred feet. The deck began to inch upward from the buoyancy in the bow, the deck inclining drastically with each ticking second.

"Chief of the Watch, emergency blow the aft group,"

Vornado ordered through the fog of his headache, a detached part of him realizing that the fog was real. The control room was filling with a cold, dense fog from the pinhole leaks of the high-pressure air actuation system. Visibility in the room shrank until he could barely see Willey standing in front of him. Vornado grabbed the periscope stand railing as the deck tilted upward past fifteen degrees, the uphill slope of the deck angling upward even more as the ship rose.

"Emergency blow aft, aye, sir," the chief said as he stood and reached for the second stainless-steel lever and rotated it up to the overhead.

If the noise had been loud before, it was deafening now. The fog in the room was so thick that Vornado could no longer see the attack center consoles, and he could barely make out the gauges on the ship-control panel. A sudden wave of dizziness hit him, perhaps made worse by the disorienting lack of a visible deck or overhead or bulkheads. He held on harder to the railing, vertigo punching him in the stomach.

"Depth, five hundred, up angle forty degrees, sir!" the diving officer shouted.

"Secure the blow," Vornado croaked, even his voice affected by his illness. "Maintain angle less than fifty degrees."

"Depth three hundred!"

"All stop!" Vornado called.

"Surfacing!" the diving officer called.

The angle suddenly came off the deck, the righting of the ship catapulting Vornado into the forward railing and the diving officer's seat. His ears rang, his jaw ached, and his temples throbbed. He tried to open his eyes, seeing the fog in the room with his right eye, but black nothingness from the left. The pain came in waves, each one making him more nauseous than the one before. He tried to turn his head when he felt his stomach convulsing, the vomit spewing out of him, half onto the deck and half on his coveralls, but in the storm of pain he no longer cared.

He could hear Willey's voice as though from a hundred miles away coming down a tunnel.

"Skipper? Cap'n? *Captain!*"

Vornado suddenly realized his grasp on consciousness

was weakening. He grabbed the periscope pole and looked up at Willey. "XO, take the conn. Vertical dive to missile firing depth. Launch the SUBROCs at Master One. Nuke the son of a bitch." Vornado coughed hard, then vomited a second time. He struggled to get his orders out. "Shoot what's left of the torpedo room at this bastard and fight the ship as best you can. And . . ." Vornadao swallowed hard, knowing the next order would sound strange. "Call my wife." He shut his eyes hard against the pain, knowing Willey was staring at him.

Vornado's eyes were open, but he couldn't see the control room. Another wave of nausea overtook him and his stomach contracted and he vomited again, and when it ended he realized he was soaked in sweat. He could feel wetness on his cheeks, from the pain and the vomiting, he thought. The world seemed to rotate around him and he was floating. For a long time he floated, disembodied, the pain receding, and there was nothing but gray fog.

Through the turning grayness he could hear voices, an odd jumble of sounds, each overlapping and interrupting the others. Some he knew, some seemed barely recognizable.

This is Commander Willey. I have the conn; Lieutenant Commander Holmes retains the deck.

He's in bad shape, XO . . . medical evacuation helicoper . . .

Vertical dive complete, vents shut, depth seven zero feet.

Beautiful boat, Peter. Congratulations on getting command.

You are worthless pond scum, Vornado, Midshipman Whitehead screamed.

VLS eleven ready, Mario Marchese announced.

It's a beautiful baby girl, the doctor said.

Fire, George Willey said.

Be careful out there, Rachel said.

A banging noise thumped.

VLS eleven launch, and engine ignition SUBROC unit one, Marchese said.

Don't leave, Dad, Marla's voice said.

VLS twelve ready.

Daddy, no work, Erin's small voice said.

Fire. Another banging sound.

VLS twelve launch, engine ignition SUBROC unit two.

Weapons Officer, make tubes one and two ready in all respects.

I have a bad feeling about this, honey, Rachel said. For an instant her face floated in front of him, and then she disappeared into the grayness.

The noises faded and the pain lessened, and for a time there was nothing but the fog.

B. K. Dillinger's hair was plastered to his scalp with sweat. The room was much hotter than he'd expected from the heat of the reactor and the loss of all air-conditioning. The firecontrol computers had crashed, and Lionel had resuscitated them in tape drive mode. The loss of the swift hard disk was frustrating. All four displays now could only show a primitive line-of-sight torpedo targeting mode, and the computer was shockingly slow. Dillinger pondered restarting the reactor just to get firecontrol back, but fought the impulse. At least sonar was still functional.

"We've lost the Q-five," Steve Flood called from sonar. Dillinger spun to look into the sonar room, and saw that all the consoles had gone black. The sonar system was dead.

"And that's it for firecontrol," Lionel said as the attack center consoles winked out. "It's too hot for the electronics, Skip."

Dillinger nodded. "Do you think the weapons got their steer commands before firecontrol shutdown?" He had ordered the weapons to climb above the layer depth after Flood had heard a roaring noise to the south, the bearing of the target. Dillinger had wondered if the son of a bitch had emergency surfaced, which would get him above the sonar-reflecting thermal-layer depth with the bonus of putting a huge cloud of bubbles in the water that could distract the Mark 48s.

"The weapons got the steer command," Lionel said. "They definitely climbed above the layer."

The sound of a torpedo sonar sounded in the room, shrieking in from the port side. Dillinger waited, holding his breath, until the sonar sound dropped and the sound faded to the starboard side. It was the sixth time in twenty minutes a torpedo had whizzed by.

"They're still in reattack mode," Flood said.

The Mark 48s would circle back to the target point looking for the target if they got a hint of a target detection.
They could probably get an active return from the *Albany*'s
hull, but the lack of a Doppler shift was confusing them.
They were blind against a stationary target.

"How long till they run out of fuel?"

"Twenty minutes, a half hour," Flood said.

Dillinger nodded. The room was as quiet as a tomb without the air-handling fans and the whine of the electronics.
It was almost disturbing how quiet it was. The silence was
interrupted by an ominous sound, a faint splash from directly overhead.

"What was that?" Flood asked.

"Sonobuoy dropped from an aircraft?" Dillinger asked.

"Too big," Flood said, his eyes wide. "Shit, that may
have been an air-launched torpedo or a depth charge."

"Just sit tight," Dillinger said. "If it is a torpedo, it will
be as useless as the Mark 48s."

A second faint splashing noise sounded from overhead.

"What the hell is that?" Flood said.

Dillinger opened his mouth to speak when the shock
wave of an explosion hit the hull.

"Conn, Sonar, torpedo in the water, bearing two seven
zero."

"Dammit," Willey said. "Sonar, Conn, is it above layer?
Distant or close aboard?"

"Conn, Sonar, above layer and distant. Second torpedo,
bearing two nine zero, above layer, second unit much
louder."

Willey's voice was hoarse as he shouted. "Helm, all
ahead flank! Dive, make your depth eleven hundred feet,
forty-degree down angle. Helm, right five degrees rudder,
steady course zero eight zero." He grabbed the 7MC microphone from the overhead. "Maneuvering, XO, cavitate!"

The deck plunged as the ship sped up and dived below
the layer. Willey watched the digital depth gauge click off
the depth as the deckplates beneath his feet inclined further
down, the deck becoming steep as a staircase.

The hull creaked loudly as the ship dived deeper. The
deckplates began to tremble with the power of the flank

bell as the speed needle climbed above twenty knots and beyond. The sound of the torpedo sonar could be heard from astern, the sound faint at first, but growing louder. The deck flattened as they pulled out nearly a quarter mile deep. A second torpedo sonar sounded in the room, the two units now wailing up and down, the eerie noise sounding like two fire engines behind them.

The seconds clicked on, the torpedoes getting louder.

"Conn, Sonar, torpedoes close aboard, inside one thousand yards." Chief Bradley's voice was icily calm, as if he realized there was nothing they could do to stop the incoming death machines.

Willey bit his lip. The emergency-blow tactic might work again, but there was nothing in the high-pressure air banks. All the air had been expended in the first emergency-blow maneuver. If he could lose the torpedoes in the thermal layer, they might still escape.

"Dive, make your depth three hundred feet, five-degree up angle on the ship."

The diving officer acknowledged, but the torpedo sonars were even louder. They would be here any second. The digital depth gauge unwound until it read three hundred feet, the diving officer taking the five-degree angle off the ship.

A bead of sweat slowly ran down Willey's face into his eye. He wiped it away and ordered, "Dive, make your depth one hundred feet, very flat angle on the ship." Willey glanced down at Vornado lying motionless on the deck, wondering what he would have ordered if he were conscious. "We'll penetrate the layer slowly. At some point the torpedo sonar signals will reflect off the bottom of the thermal layer and they'll lose our signal. They may even go deep again in reattack."

The sonars wailed even louder behind them. Willey watched the depth indicator, knowing the layer depth to be about 240 feet. Once they climbed above it, the physics of sound would alter dramatically, and with luck, the torpedo sonar echoes would bounce off the bottom of the layer and they wouldn't hear the *Hampton*.

"One hundred feet, sir!" the diving officer shouted.

"All stop!" Willey ordered.

The room froze. For an instant the torpedo sonars receded as the units sped on ahead. While the crew waited, a loud explosion sounded from the northwest.

"SUBROC detonation," Holmes said.

A moment later the second explosion sound came.

"Got him," Willey said.

Just then the sound of a torpedo sonar came blasting into the room from the bow.

"They found us," Holmes said, grimacing in anger, helplessness, and fear.

Willey took a deep breath, wondering how long it would take to die when the torpedoes detonated, and whether it would be the explosion or the flooding that would kill him. Willey swallowed hard—he didn't want to drown, he thought. Much better to be blown to bits in an instant. The torpedo sonar wailed louder and louder, the unit closer than a shiplength.

The sound of the explosion was deafening.

6

Executive Officer George Willey opened his eyes, amazed that the control room was intact. The deck didn't shake and the ship didn't heel over. The lights remained on and the air handlers kept humming. The firecontrol displays were steady. The sound of the second torpedo coming in could be heard, its sonar squealing into the sea, having followed them above the layer, and then the second explosion came, this one even louder. And like the first detonation, nothing happened to the ship.

"Dive, make your depth one five zero feet," Willey ordered. "Maneuvering, Conn, shift main coolant pumps to slow speed. Sonar, XO, we're coming to periscope depth."

Willey kneeled down in front of Captain Vornado, whom he had propped into the conn jump seat. He was clammy and unconscious. The corpsman leaned over him on the other side, holding his head up and his eyelid open while he shined a flashlight into Vornado's eye.

"What's wrong with him?"

"I can't be sure, sir," the chief corpsman said. "But it's serious. We need a medical evacuation ASAP."

Willey turned to Holmes, who was now second-in-command. "OOD, what do you think happened with the Mark 48 torpedoes?"

Holmes shook his head. "I think they were both duds, XO. Warheads detonated but there was no power. They must have blown apart on less than full high-explosive charges."

Willey nodded.

"Conn, Sonar," Chief Bradley's voice came over the circuit. "There's something wrong. The SUBROCs detonated, but I don't have a blue-out."

Willey blinked. "Say again, Sonar. What do you mean, you don't have a blue-out?"

"We just had two nuclear detonations to the north. I shouldn't be able to hear anything for a ninety-degree sector, but I've got biologics and normal ocean noise all around the azimuth."

Willey's eyes grew wide. If there were no indication of a nuclear explosion, it meant the SUBROCs could have been duds as well. Which meant that Master One, the *Albany,* was still out there.

"Conn, Sonar, we have Master One on narrowband to the north."

"Oh, shit," Willey said. "Weapons Officer, shut the outer doors to tubes one and two and open outer doors for tubes three and four. Make Mark 48 units three and four ready in all respects."

"Conn, Sonar, we have broadband on Master One and something else."

"What, Sonar?" Willey asked, his mind rushing ahead to fire two more weapons at the *Albany*.

"It . . . Sir, it sounds like a voice."

The booming roar of the second SUBROC detonation took a few seconds to quiet down. When it did, the control room returned to its unnaturally quiet state. B. K. Dillinger sat heavily on the jump seat aft of the periscope stand and wiped the sweat out of his eyes. The terrorist mission of the *Albany* was over.

"Well, that's it," he said. He stood and pulled the 1MC shipwide announcing system mike from the overhead cradle. He clicked it and spoke, his voice echoing in every compartment on every level. "Gentlemen, this is your captain speaking. We put up a damned good fight. We may have won it if the other side hadn't used the nukes. It's time to forget all that and shift gears. I want everyone focused on a safe transit back to Norfolk. Stand by for crew augmentation. Carry on." He put the microphone back in the cradle and picked up the 7MC microphone that dangled from its cord to the deck.

Ten minutes later the reactor was restarted, sonar was reinitialized, and cold air poured out of the ventilation ducts.

"Captain, UQC is lined up."

Dillinger nodded and scanned the op order Flood handed him. He picked up the UQC microphone, which patched his voice into the active sonar system. He spoke slowly and distinctly into it, his voice projecting miles from the bow's sonar sphere, his voice bouncing off the ocean floor and echoing back into the speaker on the console.

"Charlie . . . delta . . . four . . . echo," he said slowly. "Charlie delta four echo, this is lima mike eight fox." He repeated the call five times, then waited, then repeated the call. When there was no answer, he called five more times, then began reading the coded message into the UQC microphone.

"What do you mean, a voice?" Willey asked.

"I can make out the phrase 'charlie delta four echo.' I'll pipe it into the conn."

Willey stared at the console as he heard the human voice coming over the speaker.

"Charlie delta four echo, over."

Vornado suddenly spoke up from the deck, his eyes still shut. "B.K., what are you doing out here?"

"Commo, what is that?" Willey asked the communications officer, Lieutenant Junior Grade Mikey Selles. Selles ran aft to the passageway toward the radio room. He came back in ten seconds, his face pale.

"Sir, charlie delta four echo is our call sign for today. Master One is calling us on the underwater telephone."

"B.K.?" Vornado said, smiling in his half sleep. "Dillinger, is that you?"

Selles handed the codebook to Lieutenant Commander Holmes, who nodded and looked up at Willey.

"It decodes, XO," Holmes said. "It reads, 'terminate exercise and initiate secure UHF communication, Commander Dillinger, acting CO, USS *Albany*, sends.' "

Willey glared at Holmes. " 'Terminate exercise'? Acting commanding officer? What the hell?"

"It fits, XO," Selles said. "The dud Mark 48s? The SUB-ROCs that made a big bang but didn't blue out? They reloaded our whole torpedo room with Mark 48 ADCAP Mod Fives and unloaded the Mod Sixes when the captain was away. But those weapons weren't Mod Fives; they were *exercise* shots."

"I'll be goddamned," Willey cursed. "Fucking squadron. We were out here for a fucking exercise."

The South African National Defense Force Sea King helicopter approached the rendezvous point at maximum speed, then slowed as the conning towers of the two submarines came into view, the two American attack subs floating motionless within two shiplengths of each other. On the deck of one, a crew of lifejacket-clad men waved. On their deck a basket stretcher waited, a prone man wrapped in blankets strapped in. The pilot brought the aircraft over the aft deck of the submarine. The rear door of the Sea King opened and the cable dropped to the deck.

On the deck of the USS *Hampton* a man kneeled over the prone naval officer, looking into his face to see if Vornado's open eyes would register recognition. Finally Vornado blinked and looked up at the officer. He frowned, his eyes glassy.

"B.K.? Is it really you?" Vornado's voice was a harsh whisper.

"It's me, Peter," Burke Dillinger said, his hand on Vornado's sleeve. "How you doin', buddy?"

"B.K., watch out," Vornado croaked, his eyes wide. "They stole the *Albany*. They'll shoot at you."

"I know, Peter," Dillinger said. "It was an exercise. I was in command of the *Albany*. We had orders from ComSubLant. Trying to see if we had a weakness in our defenses. You did a great job fighting us, by the way."

Vornado nodded, frowning. "So you'll watch out? For the *Albany*, B.K.? I don't want them to shoot you down too."

Dillinger nodded solemnly, patting his friend's shoulder. "I'll watch out, Peter. You let these guys take care of you, okay?"

"Another helicopter," Vornado said, glancing up at the Sea King, which was hovering overhead and lowering a hoisting cable to the deck crew. "Tell Rachel I'm still wearing it. Will you tell her?"

Dillinger nodded, wondering what Vornado meant, but memorizing the message in case it made sense to Rachel Vornado. "I'll tell her, Peter. Get well."

"Sir, we have to hoist him now!" the deck chief called.

Dillinger nodded. He looked down at Vornado to say good-bye and saw that Vornado's fists were held out from his body. Dillinger put on a brave smile, balled up his fists and gently knocked them into Vornado's, then stood back.

At the signal from the deck chief, the helicopter winched in the stretcher. The massive chopper turned and shut its rear door, then tilted steeply forward, its rotor circle biting into the air as it accelerated away.

PART 2:

▼

Terminal

7

Four hours before dawn, a small private jet lifted off a runway of a suburban airport outside of Cape Town, South Africa, bound for Newark Liberty International. The sole passenger sat bundled in blankets and shivered despite the heat inside the aircraft. Two South African National Defense Force nurses tended him, checking his intravenous feed bottles and making occasional notes in his medical file. A hemisphere away, two central nervous system cancer specialists at New York's Memorial Sloan-Kettering Cancer Center had been notified that there was a new patient being flown in.

The patient slept uneasily and talked in his sleep. At one point he whispered the word *Albany,* then shivered quietly.

A half hour later, dawn's light moved over central Asia and chased away the blackness, except over northern Russia, where a damp cold overcast lingered over half the continent. The cloud cover ran from just east of Moscow northwest to the White Sea and the Barents, becoming dense thunderheads over Russia's Kola Peninsula, not far east of the Norwegian and Finlandian borders. The only significant civilization on the peninsula was centered around the town of Murmansk, which occupied the eastern bank of the Kola Fjord.

The decaying town had seen better days, its modern history commencing in the Second World War when it was a receiving terminal for Allied convoys, provided they could brave the winter ice of the Barents Sea. In the last half of the twentieth century, the arms race with the West had put Murmansk at the center of the activity, the village and the towns downstream becoming shipbuilding sites for the Soviet Union's nuclear submarine construction programs. Two decades ago that frantic effort dramatically slowed, and the shipbuilding facilities and the submarine bases were left to decay. At government-owned property all along the Murmansk Fjord and along the coastline of the Kola Peninsula, abandoned hulks of nuclear submarines rotted and rusted, waiting to be scrapped or decontaminated. With the end of an era, Murmansk attempted to reinvent itself as an arctic seaport and hub of commerce, but with nonexistent manufacturing in the northern provinces, the commercial efforts of the town fathers had failed, and the city's once busy waterfront became a rusting ghost town. The railroad tracks that led from the Murmansk Fjord factories south to Moscow were crumbling, only one of them suitable to allow a freight train to pass safely.

At the waterfront, next to the ancient tank farm and docks of the Murmansk Oil Company, an oblong abandoned building extended ten meters over the water of the fjord. Decades before, it had been called the Red Army Equipment Terminal. Here, tons of lend-lease trucks and cannons and ammunition had arrived from the convoys that formed up in Nova Scotia to resupply Stalin's armies during the Great Patriotic War. Half a century later, the building had fallen into severe disrepair. A fire had gutted the structure in the 1990s and the few tenants had left, leaving a rotting, toxic interior. It would cost millions to demolish properly, the structure filled with hazardous lead paint and asbestos, so it was left to the elements. It was an unremarkable squat brick box, with broken-out windows—most of the upper row blackened with scorching above them from the fire. The roof was uneven and half-collapsed in the landward section. A passerby would never give the burned out building a second glance.

However, if taken inside the building, it would be like leaving grimy 1920s Soviet Russia and stepping into a modern cleanroom factory. The white of the high-bay manufacturing facility was illuminated by bright spotlights. The factory was oblong, its axis perpendicular to the flow of the fjord. It was thirty-five meters wide and three hundred long, its ceiling forty meters above the floor. Overhead, a huge gleaming steel bridge crane glided by on twelve railroad wheels to the fjord end of the building. A man named Leonov Kaznikov had bought the facility for next to nothing. His younger, more technical brother, Sergei, had stealthily

built a building within a building, erecting sturdy block
walls and steel girders on the inside and hollowing out the
floor so that the manufacturing deck was almost thirty meters below the outside's grade level, and twenty meters
below the fjord's high-tide level. Since it had become operational, the workers had renamed the facility, always calling
it "the Terminal," and always using a tone of respect for
the incredible engineering feat of its dual nature.

But if the building itself were spectacular, it was nothing
compared to the product inside. The cylinder being worked
on was about ten meters in diameter, a three-meter-long
cylindrical band of metal. It was covered with white plastic
and set on gleaming platforms, and on the inside, workers
in cleanroom suits worked on it. Five meters away, another
ten-meter-diameter cylinder was placed, its central axis—
like the first—in line with the long axis of the building.
Although it was hard to discern with the protective layers
of shrink-wrapped white plastic, each can was double-
walled, the separation between the inner and outer cylinder
about a half meter.

The huge bridge crane silently whooshed by to the left,
its hook holding a heavy box of equipment and taking it
to the eastern landward end of the building. Down the long
axis of the factory, the cylinders were perfectly aligned.
The cylinder diameters were identical for most of the floor,
although at the east building end they began to taper
slightly. A photograph taken from here of the cylinders on
the floor would remind the observer of a sectioned tuna,
with the tuna steaks still lying on their sides. But the shape
below was no tuna.

Another shipment was scheduled to arrive today. The
shipment was a cylinder of metal, but unlike the spotless
shiny modules in the building's interior, this load would be
a rusting, stinking mess, perhaps half filled with mud and
sand, or even infested with rats. It had been shipped in by
barge, the barge pushed by a tugboat that had come down
the fjord after yesterday's sunset, and arrived at the west
end of the Terminal a few hours after midnight. The building's fjord end could open up to admit the barge, the Terminal crew winching in the barge until it was completely
inside the protected terminal interior. From the other side
of the fjord, no one would see the spotless cleanroom man-

ufacturing facility—the barge docking room was as decayed as the building exterior, and there was a special locker room for the men to pass from the barge unloading sector to the cleanroom side.

There was also a twelve-meter-long section of the Terminal inland of the barge unloading facility where the barge's load would be prepared to enter the spotless cleanroom facility. The load would be steam-cleaned and sand-blasted, its exterior prepped for the special coating that would seal the steel outside surface, and a second coating system applied to the inner titanium metal. The loads that were to be delivered this month would also need to be decontaminated from intense radioactivity. These sections would go to a special lead-and-polymer-lined section of the Terminal for further work. When the cylinder was ready, large doors would roll to the side to permit the can to roll into the cleanroom, where it would join the other cylinders for the work being done in the Terminal.

The sprawling office complex campus was nestled deep in the forested northern Virginia suburb of McLean on the west bank of the Potomac River, on an estate once owned by relatives of Confederate general Robert E. Lee, in a town that had been absorbed into McLean in 1910. The original estate had been located, before being annexed, in a town called Langley, and was still called that by the 23,000 people who worked there despite the fact that Langley did not exist on any maps. This odd fact suited the purpose of the complex, as it belonged to an organization that would prefer to remain anonymous. The main building was a cast-concrete structure built in the shape of a U facing what had once been a grassy quad, but three decades after it had been built, the quad grew a new steel-and-glass building and a globe-shaped auditorium that could seat seven thousand, which the employees called The Bubble. While the campus could belong to any Fortune 500 company as its corporate headquarters, this complex had the tightest security in the United States. At the inner security gate, two armed guards patrolled while a third checked identification of those requesting entry. The cast-brass sign on the guardshack was new, and would never have been hung in the old days, but these were different times. The sign read in large polished block letters, CENTRAL INTELLI-GENCE AGENCY.

Deep inside the offices of Science and Technology's National Photographic Interpretation Center, a naval intelligence photographic interpretation expert pored over the intelligence harvest from the Terminal.

"Good God in heaven," he breathed. *"The Alfa's back."*

8

"I can get out on my own," Peter Vornado said, ignoring Rachel's concerned expression. After three unsuccessful tries, he sank back into the Town Car's rear seat, exhausted. The orderly gently pulled him out of the car and lifted him into the wheelchair. Vornado looked around, more aware of the weather than anyone he knew, the result of weather being a submariner's luxury. It was a beautiful cloudless August Thursday on Manhattan's Upper East Side, hot and blessedly free of oppressive humidity. Birds called from the trees lining the entrance to the tall building, and colorful flowers bloomed in lush plantings on either side of the doors. Vornado was rolled through the doorway and taken to the elevator. After the bright sunlight, the air-conditioned interior of Memorial Sloan-Kettering Cancer Center seemed gloomy.

For the last four days Vornado had come to this building for tests—CAT scans and PET scans mostly, but there had also been needles, bloodwork, X-rays, and even camera borescopes inserted into his nose and mouth. And through it all the crushing headaches ebbed and flowed, with a seizure shaking him violently on the third day. His vision, which had returned since the *Hampton* medical evacuation, once again became blurry and spotted, and when he woke this morning he was nearly blind on the left side. All these machines and doctors and tests would merely confirm what Vornado already knew—he had a brain tumor, and the only question was whether it was malignant or benign. The senior staff doctor had insisted on waiting until the complete battery of test results was in before announcing the prognosis.

Vornado waited with Rachel in the examination room

while they took his vital signs and asked after his vision. He was wheeled into the senior doctor's office. Dr. Peppinger was a slight, cheerful, and energetic older New Yorker with short salt-and-pepper hair, a starched shirt, and a tie under his white lab jacket. He sat at his cherry desk in an elegant room with its walls covered with wood-framed diplomas and framed family photos, with one wall taken up by the wide plate-glass view of the East River. Peppinger stood behind his desk and scanned through Vornado's files, then sat down heavily and looked up, his eyebrows high in an expression of empathy.

"Peter, Rachel, I'm sorry. I need you to prepare yourselves for some difficult news."

Vornado's headache, which had been buzzing in the background, suddenly pulsed in his temples. He frowned, a hand to his eyebrows.

"You have a brain tumor, Peter. It's fairly large, a bit larger than a golf ball, on your left side. We call it a glioblastoma. I've prepared a package of information for you and Rachel to review, but what you need to know up front is that this tumor had spread its cells to the far corners of your brain from its first days, and it's in an advanced stage now."

Vornado blinked, staring at the doctor and trying to understand the words through the pain of the headache. When he found his voice, it was hoarse. "What do we do now?"

"We need to go in on an urgent basis and 'debulk' the tumor."

"Brain surgery," Vornado said, blowing his lips out. "Don't you need to take a biopsy or a needle test or something first?"

Peppinger shook his head. "No, Peter. Glioblastomas are malignant, and your tumor is in stage four. In your situation we don't talk about 'removing' the tumor, but just getting most of the mass of it out of your braincase to take the pressure off the vital centers of your brain, so that your vision and speech and thought patterns won't be unduly affected. You can think of the growth as sort of a spider with a central mass and legs that reach out into several areas of the brain. Even if we were able to remove everything we could see, we'd never get all the cells, and leaving even a few behind will regenerate the tumor. The surgery is a quality-of-life issue."

Rachel spoke for the first time, her voice quiet with a slight tremble. "Doctor, is there a cure? Radiation and chemotherapy?"

Peppinger shook his head. "I'm sorry; there is no cure. Glioblastomas are one of the most aggressive cancers. We will be recommending a fairly intense course of both radiation and chemotherapy, again, to preserve some of Peter's end-stage quality of life. There are some new chemotherapy formulas we're using now that will avoid some of the burdensome side effects, but I have to tell you, it will still be severe."

"But with the radiation and chemo, he wouldn't go into remission?" Rachel asked.

"I'm sorry; the chances of that are almost nil, Rachel. After surgery we'll be fighting for every day."

"How much time?" Vornado asked, his voice normal again. He glanced at Rachel, worried that it seemed she wasn't grasping that he had just been given a death sentence.

Peppinger nodded, knowing the question would come. "Based on your excellent health before you got the tumor and your age, Peter, with the surgery, radiation, and chemotherapy we can confidently predict survival for six to eight weeks."

Vornado sat back hard in the wheelchair. "Jesus, I thought you'd say a year or two or three. You're giving me *two months*?"

Peppinger nodded again. "I'm afraid so, Peter."

"And yet I have to have brain surgery, chemo, and radiation to last sixty days. How long will I last if I do nothing?"

Peppinger wasn't surprised by the question. "Between two and three weeks. You would have more seizures, and it's likely your problems with blindness would become worse. You'd probably also lose your ability to speak, and large-muscle motor function—simple body movement— would become difficult very soon. You'd be in a coma not long after. It's completely up to you, but the treatment strategy will give you more meaningful time to spend with your family. Your quality of life will be much improved and prolonged over the nontreatment scenario. It won't be easy, but we have new approaches to pain reduction that will allow you to keep your lucidity. We believe in treating the pain as aggressively as we treat the disease, Peter. Under the surgery-radiation-chemotherapy regime, the time you have left will allow you to interact with your family and friends. And you can help Rachel plan for her future."

Vornado looked at Rachel. Her earlier denial was gone. Her eyes had filled with moisture but the tears had not yet spilled out of them. Vornado thought about his limited options. Part of him wanted to avoid the treatment. He hated lying on hospital beds and being surrounded by people working on him, like a helpless ship in a drydock. He'd rather go back to the house and sit in his leather club chair in his study and fade away without the medical sideshow. But Rachel's expression changed his heart. And when he thought of the children, the decision was made. Even if it meant surviving in excruciating pain, he needed every day he could get to be with the kids. Perhaps, he thought, he could pack a lifetime of fatherhood into sixty days. He wondered how the children would think about him, and whether the older two would tell little Erin about him, since she would be too young to remember much. A vision rolled in his mind of Marla and Peter Junior in their twenties with a teenage Erin, talking about him a decade after his death, and that was the thought that made him put his head in his hands and hide his eyes, the tears streaking down his cheeks anyway. It was worse when Rachel hurried to him and hugged him, and he could feel her body shaking as she sobbed.

"I'll leave you two alone," Peppinger said, rising from his chair. "You don't have to decide now. Come back on Monday and we'll discuss it some more and make treatment arrangements. You can check out with the front desk when you're ready." Peppinger squeezed Vornado's shoulder on his way out of the office.

Vornado struggled for composure, finally managing to sit up and put on a brave warface for Rachel. He stroked her hair and wiped her tears from her face.

"It'll be okay, honey," he said, his hoarse voice trembling. "When was the last time I was home for two months? It'll be like a vacation."

All his adult life Vornado had defined himself by what he did. Like his father before him, Vornado had been career Navy. He had risen to the top of the pyramid and had been one of the few to screen for commanding officer, and had had the good fortune to be named as one of the top captains in the submarine force. For the last year, being a submarine captain was who he was. And now that was permanently over. And the odd thing about it was that he didn't care. He had loved the submarine force and his career, but now that he faced death by cancer, his feelings of loss all centered around leaving behind Rachel and the kids. If he could just have his health back, he thought, he wouldn't care if he swept floors for a living. He just wanted to live and be a husband and father, and now all he had was sixty days.

"We need to talk to the children," he heard himself say to Rachel. She nodded, and they checked out at the front desk, left the building and returned to the Town Car to go to the hotel. The kids were waiting there with Rachel's sister, Ann. Vornado dreaded giving them the news, imagining how they would react. They knew something was seriously wrong, but they certainly didn't expect their father to be gone in a few weeks. Vornado thought about the timing as the doors opened to the wide sidewalk and the wheelchair stopped while they waited for the car. He wouldn't make it to his seventeenth wedding anniversary the first week of November. And he'd had his last Thanksgiving and Christmas with the children. He shook his head, thinking of how miserable they would be over the holidays. And then there was the matter of money and what would happen to Rachel.

When the orderly shut the car's door, Vornado looked at Rachel. "I want you to remarry," he heard himself say, shocked that the words had come out, and not knowing why he had said that, or why now. Rachel shut her eyes and dissolved into tears, her face on his shoulder. He reached up to touch her face, and when he did, his hands shook. The car pulled away from the hospital and headed south.

* * *

Twelve floors above the sidewalk, Dr. Peppinger watched from his eastward wall of windows as the Vornados' car pulled out into traffic. The phone was pressed to his ear as he paged Dr. Friedman at Duke University Comprehensive Cancer Center. His phone rang a few minutes later.

"Allan," Peppinger said. "I think I have a candidate for the vaccine clinical trial. Healthy thirty-eight-year-old male, no complications. I'd personally like to see him in the program. I'll send you his file if you can get back to me today." He listened for a few minutes. "I'll e-mail it right now."

Peppinger put the phone down, then dialed his assistant. "Diane, please e-mail Peter Vornado's file to Dr. Friedman at Duke."

After an appointment like Vornado's, it helped to stand at the window and look out at the skyline. He hadn't told Vornado about the Duke trials. The vaccine clinical trials were in their infancy, and the program took only a few people a year, and the last time he'd talked to Allan, the program was fully booked. Even if Vornado did get in, odds were that he would have no more hope on the vaccine treatment than on the radiation and chemotherapy, but perhaps his trial results could contribute to the glioblastoma body of research. Perhaps something could be gained from all these premature brain tumor deaths, Peppinger thought. It would be nice, someday, if he could give some measure of hope to the parade of young men and women who came through this office and received the same news Peter Vornado had.

Peppinger sat back down in his chair, fantasizing for a few minutes what it would be like to have a different career. He thought of Vornado and what it must have been like being the captain of a nuclear submarine. That would be a career, Peppinger thought. When Vornado recovered from surgery, Peppinger decided, he might ask him about it.

9

Victor Kaminsky walked rapidly down the hall to Hank Lewis's office inside the new administration building. It felt strange to wear a suit after the last year in the field. Kaminsky had been a CIA Clandestine Service officer for ten years, after graduating from the Naval Academy and serving in the Marines. Most of his fieldwork had been spent in Russia working for the Russian Directorate until two years ago, when he had been asked to join Hank Lewis's Anti-Proliferation Task Force. Today's meeting was about a new assignment.

Kaminsky was broad shouldered, six feet tall, and built solidly. In the last half decade of his forty-two years he had gained twenty unwanted pounds, but he was told that he wore the extra weight well. Some said that it made him seem more intimidating. Kaminsky had the lined and weathered face of a laborer, with a shaved head that made him seem even tougher than his build would suggest. His dull blue eyes were intelligent and piercing, but when he wanted to he could wear a blank expression that made him seem harmless, nondescript and slow.

Kaminsky was led into Lewis's new office. He smiled and shook the boss's hand. Lewis was a tall man with an affable but commanding face, impeccably dressed in a well-cut gray suit with a red patterned tie, gleaming shoes, and a short, groomed haircut. Lewis smiled back and clapped Kaminsky on the shoulder.

"Good to see you, Vic. Have I got a deal for you."

Kaminsky nodded. "When do I leave?"

Lewis smiled. "Within the hour. I've got a car for you and a plane waiting. Your first stop is Gdánsk, Poland, where you'll update your welding qualifications with titanium, and you'll get reacquainted with diesel engines and hydraulic systems. You're going to be a hull mechanic."

"How long will I be gone this time?"

"About six weeks," Lewis lied.

Kaminsky laughed, the time frame their running joke. The first time Lewis had sent Kaminsky on a six-week assignment, he had returned over a year later.

"Where to after Poland?"

"Northern Russia."

Lewis's office was an SCIF, a special compartmented information facility, where he could speak freely without fear of electronic surveillance. He pulled a remote keyboard from under the table and signed into the computer, then started a PowerPoint slide show. The first slide was a map of the northern Russian Kola Peninsula, with the city of Murmansk inland with a north-running river, the Kola Fjord, on its western boundary.

"Murmansk," Lewis said. "There's a private factory on the bank of the Kola Fjord."

An aerial photo of the Terminal appeared.

"Piece-of-shit factory if you ask me," Kaminsky sneered.

"Here it is close-up." Lewis clicked the next slide, showing the Terminal from the ground. It still looked shabby. "And here's the inside." The next slide showed the interior, with the sparkling white painted bridge crane hoisting a plastic-sheathed cylindrical module in place in line with others on the gleaming white clean-room floor. Kaminsky stood and examined the photograph, his face close to the screen. He whistled.

"That's quite an assembly room."

"We don't know much about this, but what we do know raises questions. They call this facility the Terminal, and it was bought as a derelict building by the Kaznikov organized crime family."

"Kaznikov," Kaminsky said, thinking.

"They're an offshoot of the Dianov Moscow Mafiya. Second cousins. The Kaznikov younger generation are the ones involved in this operation. The older brother, Leonov, is the commercial and criminal brain. He's also the salesman between the two of them. The younger brother, Sergei, is the technical genius who had the idea to rebuild the Termi-

nal and the ability to do it undetected. This factory was a
rotting, decayed building about to collapse, but the Kaznikovs rebuilt it and spent a few years refurbishing the inside
with some extremely expensive stuff. After that they began
receiving deliveries in covered barges, and what caught our
eye is that the barges can float half into the building and
get offloaded away from eyes in the sky."

"So you need someone on the inside to see what's up?"

"No. We know what's going on. They're building a submarine using discarded Russian Navy parts. They have a
contract with Moscow to decommission and scrap these
submarine parts, but instead of scrapping them, they're rebuilding them. It would take an enormous investment, but
apparently they have the cash to do this. It's for export
sale."

"Terrorists?"

"We thought so at first." The screen flashed the face of
a tough-looking older man, of Spanish descent, with swar-
thy skin and dark features. His small eyes were framed by
large square wire-framed glasses. "This is a Colombian
drug lord named Orlando Suarto. He was the guy who used
the Russian Mafiya to help him build that submarine deep
inside the Colombian mountains." The picture changed to
show the interior of a warehouse, with large red-painted
metal cylinders filling it.

"I remember. A diesel submarine that would be used to
run drugs. Kind of hard to catch."

"Exactly. It's a lucky thing we caught wind of it when
we did."

"But they had this sub in a warehouse in Bogotá in the
high mountains. How did that make sense?"

"They had the materials and the craftsmen in the city.
The sub was small, only thirty meters long with a hull diameter of only three and a half meters. They built it in modules small enough for each to fit on a truck—with the
narrow hull diameter, it could be driven on the roads. The
heaviest module was the engineroom, and it was built on a
heavy crawler trailer. The plan was to finish each module,
then ship the modules to a large boathouse on the Carib-
bean coast where Suarto had a marina. They'd be assembled in the boathouse in a homemade drydock under a
roof, away from prying satellite eyes. Had construction con-

tinued, this thing could have smuggled two hundred tons of cocaine at a time. Enough that the first trip would pay for the sub's construction two dozen times over. If this sub had been completed, there would be almost nothing we could have done about it."

"Which must be why we compromised our intelligence sources to bust Suarto before he could finish the sub."

"We didn't know anything about it. Neither did DEA. Apparently the Russians Suarto brought in to build this thing talked too much and blew the operation's cover. Once his operation was exposed, Suarto went underground for a while, but never gave up on the idea of a submarine to smuggle drugs. He decided to look elsewhere for a submarine. He turned to the Russians again, since they had proved reliable and fast on the first one, but this time he would avoid his initial mistake and build the sub in Russia."

"Go on."

"The Kaznikovs bought the Terminal, rebuilt it, and obtained these old pieces of Russian submarines. To jump ahead, the Russian Mafiya proposed that Suarto buy a nuke sub, and he was impressed. The cost is much higher, but a nuke can carry that much more 'product' and evade detection better—it would be a thousand times quieter than the diesel boat Suarto started off building."

"So what's my part in this?"

"You'll be installing things deliberately altered so they won't work. We aim to delay this submarine. Perhaps indefinitely. Take a look at this." The next image on the screen showed a bundle of cylindrical shapes moved across the cleanroom floor by the sparkling white bridge crane. The moving image stopped, and a photograph of six gleaming metal cylinders froze on the screen. "The Science and Technology folks say these are torpedo tubes. The original six tube holes were plated over with steel, just to make the hull watertight. But now the hull plates have been removed, and all six tubes with all their door-opening machinery and torpedo-loading gear are being installed."

Kaminsky looked at the photograph, the significance lost on him. "So? Maybe Suarto wants this sub to survive an encounter with a Coast Guard cutter."

"No." Lewis shook his head. "A weapons system is incompatible with the idea of a drug runner. It would take up most of the space that would have been devoted to cocaine. And a drug sub wouldn't shoot its way out of an encounter; it would just fade away silently and come back two nights later. Stealth is the ultimate weapon for Suarto, not firepower. No, torpedo tubes mean something else."

The display changed to show a rugged Arabian face of indeterminate age, perhaps as young as thirty-five or as old as forty-five. He had a goatee that was clipped to a point on either side of his chin, giving the man a devilish appearance. His eyes were dark and intense, and he had a hawkish nose and thin lips. Even with his face relaxed, his expression seemed fierce.

"Meet Abdas al-Sattar," Lewis said. "Until last month Abdas was second-in-command of the Egyptian extremist Islamic movement Ahel al Beit, which means 'family of the prophet.' This is the café where the leader of Ahel al Beit ate breakfast after morning prayers."

The image on the screen was a scorched crater surrounded by blackened rubble.

"Abdas blew his boss to Allah and then blamed the CIA. A very effective way to take over a terrorist organization. Abdas wanted Ahel al Beit to take a more aggressive role in its interactions with Israel. He wants to nuke Tel Aviv. That's why his trip to Murmansk last month rang alarm bells at Langley. If he's visiting with the Kaznikovs, he may be trying to outbid Suarto for this submarine."

"What good would torpedoes do against Israel?"

"Not much," Lewis said. "But these torpedo tubes can launch cruise missiles. Nuclear-tipped cruise missiles. With this submarine and a couple of nuclear cruise missiles, Abdas al-Sattar can erase Tel Aviv from the map, and stopping him would be difficult at best. At our request, the Navy just did a realistic blind exercise to test whether a rogue sub could evade their forces and get within firing range of Tel Aviv. Short of using tactical antisubmarine nuclear weapons, it looks nearly impossible to stop a mission like this in the short time it would take from the moment the sub is in operation to the time it's in firing range of Israel."

"Sir, this thing is just an old rusty nuke from the Russian scrap pile. How bad could it be?"

"That's the subject of your next briefing on the plane

with the Science and Technology Directorate. Apparently the particulars of this submarine are a concern. They say it's a Russian supersub with a long history of striking fear into the hearts of the Navy's admirals." Lewis turned off the display and stood. "There's a jet waiting for you at Dulles. A Science and Technology briefer will give you the rest on the plane."

Kaminsky sighed. "An intercontinental flight with a science geek. Thanks, boss."

10

Orlando Suarto stood at the broad front window of his oak-paneled fourth-floor study and looked at the panoramic view down the valley where the dust of the approaching vehicle rose in the clear air of the early morning. He sipped coffee from a small china cup, the steam of it rising into his nostrils.

"The scoundrel is almost here," Suarto said quietly to his chief lieutenant, Filip Valdez.

Suarto was of medium height and balding, with a ring of gray-white hair running from temple to temple. His brown eyes were magnified by the large square lenses of steel-rimmed glasses that had gone out of fashion three decades before. He dressed casually in a golf shirt and jeans with deck shoes. He stood in a slight slouch, and his face had begun to sag two decades ago. Suarto may not have been an imposing figure, but his energy and animated forceful-ness could fill a stadium, and these qualities in combination with his ruthless business vision had made him rich.

Suarto watched the huge bus labor up the winding road from the valley floor far below. The phone call from Kazni-kov reported that another customer wanted to buy the sub-marine nearing completion in the Terminal. Kaznikov, of course, had refused to allow someone to outbid Suarto, explaining that he and Suarto had a long history. But Kaz-nikov complained that the new customer was willing to tri-ple the sale price, and that the operation was overbudget, so a higher price was attractive. Still, Kaznikov said, he had refused, but under intense pressure, had agreed to call Su-arto and ask if he would meet the other customer. The man, Kaznikov insisted, was persuasive, and would make it worth the Colombian's time. Kaznikov assured Suarto that a second submarine could be delivered sixteen months after the decision, so that its schedule would not be dependent on the final fitting out of the first ship. There were parts aplenty on the Kola coast for more submarines, should Suarto find himself in need of a sister ship.

Suarto tried not to let his fury rise to the surface. He had suffered through too much to allow this idea to take a backseat to a buyer with a bigger wallet, to allow his vision to wait another year and a half for delivery. But there was one way to stop this miserable situation. If Suarto met the new customer, he would make it clear that taking the submarine would cost the yield of sixteen voyages, the minimum usage of the vessel at one trip a month for the duration of the building program. There was no way anyone could meet that price, Suarto knew, and so this new customer would walk away disappointed.

Or perhaps he wouldn't walk away at all. If this new buyer were tempting Kaznikov too much, Suarto would solve the problem by putting a bullet between the customer's eyes. The submarine would be safe from Kaznikov's temptation. And the best way to ventilate the new customer's skull was to meet with him on Suarto's turf. Suarto had asked about the buyer. Kaznikov wouldn't divulge the details until Suarto agreed to the meeting. Suarto gave his consent, but only on the condition that the meeting would be held at his mountain estate. Even after Suarto's promise, Kaznikov had few details. The new customer's name was Abdas al-Sattar, an Egyptian leader of a group called Ahel al Beit, a sworn enemy of Israel. Kaznikov couldn't say what his plans were for the submarine, but assumed it was to use the vessel as a warship.

When Suarto attempted to expedite the meeting, he had been told by Kaznikov that the Egyptian preferred the meeting to be in Europe. Suarto had refused, insisting that Abdas come to Bogotá. The meeting venue was eventually settled, but would be delayed a month. The Egyptian, according to Kaznikov, was afraid of air travel and insisted on traveling there in his yacht, a yacht big enough to carry his own bus, a converted long-distance, full-size bus. Suarto watched the huge bus climb the mountain road to the estate house, shaking his head at the odd Egyptian. Who would draw attention to himself with such a conveyance? It had to be twelve feet wide and sixty feet long. The bus drew up to the portico below Suarto's front-facing study windows. He turned from the window toward the large double doors of the study to greet his visitor. He made eye contact with Valdez, who nodded with one hand patting his Glock holster. Suarto opened his desk drawer, where the fully loaded MAC-10 machine pistol waited. He hoisted it, breathing in its oiled machinery smell, hearing the satisfying sound of the safety clicking off before he replaced it in the drawer.

Suarto waited, knowing that while he did the Egyptian was being frisked and passed through a metal detector below. Finally the man arrived at the door. Suarto looked him in the eye, taking in the leader of the Ahel al Beit. Abdas stood a head taller than Valdez, tall enough that he was forced to duck to enter the room. He strode in, his long white cape trailing on the floor. He was dressed in traditional Arab headgear, with a black headband, a white silk robe, and a white belt. The robe sparkled in the light, as if it had diamond fragments sewn into the fabric. Abdas had a long, lean face, with high cheekbones, penetrating dark eyes, a hooked nose, and a goatee that was cut strangely so that it pointed toward his ears in twin horns. Suarto couldn't decide if the face was handsome or frightening. It seemed to depend on the man's expression. As he moved across the thick carpeting and extended his hand, his face curved into a warm mask of pleasure, as if he were greeting a lifelong friend.

"Lord Suarto, it is my privilege to meet you at last," al-Sattar said in accented English, his voice perhaps the deepest commanding baritone Suarto had ever heard. His handshake was dry and strong, a politician's handshake, with his left hand gripping Suarto's wrist. Suarto turned on his own brand of charm, welcoming the Egyptian to Bogotá and asking him to sit. The pleasantries took an hour, after which Suarto took al-Sattar to the huge dining hall for a long meal. The visitor heartily ate small portions, appearing to enjoy them, although refusing the wine and whiskey. When the meal ended, Suarto invited al-Sattar back to the study, wondering when the man would get to business. After another half hour passed, it became clear to Suarto that Abdas was waiting for him to come to the point.

Suarto dived in. "I understand you would outbid me to buy the submarine nearing completion in the Terminal."

Abdas smiled, nodding. "I would, Señor Suarto. I have immediate need for such a vessel. I would pay you its entire cost to compensate you for the delay in making a second submarine."

Suarto shook his head. "I'm afraid that is simply not possible, sir. I have been working on this concept for seven long years, and the payoff of this submarine is twenty times its sale price, and I doubt you would want to pay such a fee. Kaznikov can build you the second unit, but I must insist on taking delivery of this ship."

Suarto glanced quickly at Valdez, who stood away from the two men in the leather couches. Valdez's hand moved toward his weapon just slightly. Abdas nodded amicably, as if Suarto had agreed instead of refused.

"Could I convince you by doubling my initial offer? I'm prepared to pay you right now, in gold that I have transported on the bus."

Suarto shook his head. "Thank you, but I must insist. I am very sorry, Abdas, but I need the first ship. I appreciate your generous offer, but it is simply not something I could do."

For the next fifteen minutes, Abdas calmly explained his situation and his reasons for wanting the sub before his plea ended. Suarto and Valdez watched the Egyptian, who then calmly drank his coffee, smiled, and stood, extending his hand.

"All I could ask was to be heard out, and you have heard me, Señor Suarto. I thank you for your gracious hospitality. I will take my leave of you now, and wish you the best of luck with the submarine."

Suarto was surprised that al-Sattar would let the matter go so easily, but stranger things had happened. A momentary thought came to him—to kill the man anyway—but he decided to take him at face value. There had been no deception in the man's expression. He walked al-Sattar to the first floor, where a gathering of Egyptians were in deep discussion with a half dozen of Suarto's men.

"What's the problem?" Valdez asked.

"The bus has broken down," al-Sattar's aide admitted.

"The long trip up the mountain overheated the engine. It will have to be towed back down the mountain."

Abdas turned to Suarto. "Señor Suarto, I am greatly embarrassed that this has happened. We will wait in the bus until we can find a suitable wrecker. I deeply regret that it seems stuck in front of your mansion."

Suarto waved his hand in a generous sweep. "Please, take my cars back to your yacht. I will have them driven back here when you are finished with them. You can use the Land Cruisers to haul your luggage. I will see to the repair of your bus and I'll ocean-ship it back to you so you won't be delayed."

Abdas seemed touched by Suarto's generosity. "Sir, please allow me to pay you for the trouble. It is much too kind of you to do all that."

"It is no trouble, Abdas. I must insist."

It took another twenty minutes, but finally al-Sattar agreed to take a convoy of Suarto's Mercedes S600s to the yacht landing. The door shut behind Abdas al-Sattar as he continued to wave at his Colombian host. For ten minutes the cars drove down the winding road, the mountaintop estate still in view far above, the shining blue bus parked directly in front of the huge stone mansion. All during the drive, Abdas's eyes never left the bus. As the Mercedes wove its way down the road, he thought about the three tons of Semtex plastic explosive packed into the bus, filling its baggage compartment and packed into every cabinet, table, wall, and ceiling surface. The entire bus was practically made of explosives, which had made for a frightening trip to Suarto's mansion.

"Holy One?" his aide asked.

Abdas nodded. The aide punched ten numbers into his cell phone. As Abdas watched, the bus and the mansion disappeared in an orange fireball, a mushroom cloud rising three hundred feet into the air before the shock wave pounded the car as it traveled toward the valley below. The booming roar continued for several minutes, finally dying down as the huge cloud of smoke rose from the spot where the stone mansion had once been. Abdas wished he could watch until the smoke cleared, so that he could verify that none of the huge mansion still stood, and that Suarto was dead, but time was short.

"How long to the airport?" he asked.

"An hour at this time of day," his aide replied.

"Have the jets started in twenty minutes," Abdas ordered. We need to be out of Colombian airspace as soon as possible. Suarto had powerful friends."

"Yes, Holy One," the aide replied, the cell phone at his ear.

Abdas al-Sattar sat back in the plush leather seat and shut his eyes, a smile coming to his face. The submarine was now officially his.

"Call Kaznikov," he ordered, his eyes shut. "Get a progress report on the torpedo tubes."

The car drove down the mountain, the next curve putting the smoke at the mountaintop out of sight. As they rounded a corner, three fire trucks came the other way, climbing the mountain, their sirens wailing and their lights flashing. Abdas opened an eye to watch them, and muttered, "You're too late."

An hour later al-Sattar's private jet lifted off from the Bogotá runway and climbed off to the northeast, headed for Murmansk.

11

Victor Kaminsky walked through the security door of the cargo building across the tarmac to the gigantic Polar Air 747 cargo jet. A crewman of the jet walked under the fuselage, inspecting the nose gear. Kaminsky walked toward the jet, several hundred feet from the airside of the building. The pilot glanced up from his preflight inspection.

"Are you Danalov?" he asked, his voice a shout over the loud jet engines.

Danalov was Kaminsky's cover identity. He nodded.

"Let me check your passport," the pilot said. Kaminsky pulled it out of the back pocket of his jeans. The pilot nodded. "Please board, Mr. Danalov."

"Are we ready to go?" Kaminsky asked.

"Ten minutes. There's one more passenger."

Kaminsky waved and climbed the stairway to the jet's door, his duffel bag strapped to his shoulder, a laptop briefcase in his other hand. Kaminsky stepped into the vast cargo bay, which was empty. As his eyes adjusted to the relative gloom of the interior, the cargo master waved him up the steep stairs to the upper deck. The laminate-paneled passageway had staterooms opening off it and led forward to a seating area and a galley. The flight engineer poked his head out of the cockpit and motioned him to one of the wide seats. The plane was cool after the sweltering August heat of the tarmac. Kaminsky settled into a window seat on the right side, stuffing his bag under the seat in front of him and opening his laptop on the tray table.

"Viktor Danalov?" the young female voice asked. Kaminsky looked up to see a stunning brunette in the aisle. He stood, having to duck his head at the low overhead. He took the woman's extended hand. He hadn't expected the briefing officer from the Directorate of Science and Technology to be a woman. "I'm Tina," she said. "Tina Rancourt, S and T. I'll be making the trip with you."

"Pleased to meet you," Kaminsky stuttered. She unpacked her briefcase, put her laptop in the seat pocket in front of the aisle seat, then strapped in beside Kaminsky.

The noise in the cabin suddenly changed when the main deck access hatch was shut. The plane began to move forward, turning tightly to the taxiway to runway zero three. The cargo master's voice came over the intercom, giving the usual pretakeoff safety briefing. Within five minutes the big jet shuddered at the end of the runway as the engines came to full power. It rolled slowly at first, then gathered speed and angled steeply upward midway down the runway and climbed to the northeast. The wheels made a loud grinding noise as they retracted, the flap motors equally loud as the plane reached the midpoint of its climb out of northern Virginia.

Once airborne, Kaminsky could speak freely to Rancourt without fear of someone picking up their voices from the vibrations of the windows. Rancourt opened her notebook computer on Kaminsky's tray table, and began her briefing as soon as her notebook booted up. She turned the notebook display slightly so he could also see the screen. As she leaned over, Kaminsky could smell just a trace of a scent, perhaps her shampoo. He bit his lip, realizing he had neglected an important part of his life, his mind wandering to what his controller, Vanya, would be like, and if their field relationship would be platonic.

"What did Hank Lewis tell you about this op?" Rancourt asked.

Kaminsky took fewer than ten sentences to describe Hank's cryptic briefing, concluding with Hank's description of the submarine as a Russian supersub.

"Good," she said. "He didn't exaggerate. The nature of the submarine being built at the Terminal is tremendously important. They could have opted to build any other submarine, and we would have watched complacently. But not this sub." She clicked the first slide of the PowerPoint presentation. The words *Zolotaya Ruba* flashed on the screen. "Is this term familiar to you?"

Kaminsky shook his head. Rancourt clicked the next slide. The words *Golden Fish* flashed below the Russian phrase. She hit the next slide, which added the word *Lira*. The next click added the phrase *Project 705*. Then the next, which read, *NATO Code Name: Alfa.*

"I don't recognize any of that."

"We didn't expect you to," Rancourt said. "These are Russian references to the submarine being resurrected in the Terminal."

She clicked the slide to show a picture of the Terminal from high overhead, the shabby building seeming near collapse. The slide changed itself to a ground view, and then showed the interior of the clean-room assembly area, the tuna-can slices of metal being joined together one by one, beginning at the bow. As Kaminsky watched the screen, the clean-room factory area faded to white, only the submarine sections remaining in the picture. A computer animation began, bringing all the sections of the submarine together and making the white plastic covering of each section melt away to show a flat black–painted surface. A superstructure—a long, gently curved fin—appeared on top of the cylinder, and the bow became rounded and the stern pointed, the horizontal and vertical stabilizers appearing. The animation continued, the background of white becoming the blueness of the sea, the top surface of the hull shimmering in wave reflections. A mast came out of the fin, extending toward the surface. Kaminsky tapped his chin, a habit when deep in thought. He glanced at Tina Rancourt, who sipped a Coke while the animation finished.

"Project 705, the Alfa submarine, was one of the oddest military projects in the history of warfare," Rancourt began. "This one Russian project set the entire military defense plans of the 1970s on their ear, and altered how we fought the Cold War for two decades after that. This submarine changed history, and had the potential to alter the outcome of the Cold War."

"Oh, come on," Kaminsky scoffed. "It's just a submarine that shoots torpedoes and can sink ships. How special could it have been?"

"Just listen," Rancourt said. "Let me take you back to 1955, ten years after World War Two ended." The screen faded to black, then began to roll film from the mid-fifties, showing Main Street America, bloated and curvaceous automobiles, women in long dresses and pearls and beehive hairstyles, white tract houses with picket fences, men in suits and hats, smoking pipes. A moving image of President Eisenhower appeared, playing a peaceful round of golf.

"Let's remember that the war was won by America dropping two nuclear weapons on an adversary, striking fear into the hearts of any country that would oppose us after that." The screen flashed up the film of the Hiroshima atomic bomb detonating, then the Nagasaki explosion, then continued to show various nuclear test explosion films. As she spoke, mushroom clouds bloomed on the display screen. "We always think of ourselves as being benevolent and fair. The rest of the world didn't share that opinion, particularly the Soviets in the 1950s." Rancourt clicked the mouse, the films fading to black and a new image appearing, a U.S. aircraft carrier steaming at high speed, with a deck full of Korean War–era fighter jets. As Kaminsky watched, one of the jets took off from the deck and climbed skyward.

"Remember, this was before the invention of the intercontinental ballistic missile and the surveillance satellite. The way America would deliver nuclear bombs back then was either with long-range bombers . . ." Rancourt paused as an image of a B-47 bomber streaked into view and roared into the sky, all six jet engines and the underbelly rocket-assist engine spouting black smoke. The screen image showed an aircraft carrier's jet fighter-bomber streaking off the deck and turning as it climbed. "Or with smaller jets flying off aircraft carriers. The Soviet Air Force was far less worried about bombers than aircraft carriers. Do you think that makes sense?"

The screen view changed to show a Soviet supersonic interceptor jet with a red star painted on its silver tail, banking hard right and climbing, its wings bristling with air-to-air missiles.

Kaminsky tapped his chin. "I wouldn't have come to that conclusion. But if you say so, I guess it's true. I'd imagine the answer is that the Russians probably thought their radar defenses were adequate and could catch incoming bombers. They figured interceptors like the one you're showing could take on the bomber fleet."

"Good, that's a big part of it." Rancourt nodded. "But I'm surprised you're not thinking like a spy."

Kaminsky bit his lip. "Okay, my second answer is that Air Force bases are usually near cities or at least small towns. When a bomber takes off, it rattles the windows of the neighbors, so a Russian agent could just make a phone call and say a B-52 bomber wing just departed."

"Exactly. The Soviets had agents on the ground near every U.S. Air Force base, even the top-secret Dreamland. Every time a bomber took off, Moscow knew about it, and would put their interceptor squadrons on high alert. The bombers made much of their trips at high altitude, and whether they were right or wrong, the Russian Air Force was convinced they could shoot American bombers down before they could do much damage. The Soviet Politburo believed its Air Force generals. That left the U.S. Navy jets flying off carriers."

The image on the display showed the underside of a fighter's fuselage looking aft as the aircraft rolled down an aircraft-carrier deck, the steam of the catapult wafting away in the wind of the carrier's passage, the nonskid-painted deck flashing by in a blur of speed under the jet. Suddenly the deck vanished, replaced by close blue waves; then the view of the deck returned as the ship shrank quickly in the distance while the airplane climbed. The image continued, the aircraft carrier growing small in the camera's view, the companion ships of the task force coming into view, steaming in parallel with the carrier, their wakes ruler straight and extending to the horizon.

"It was the aircraft carrier that rattled the Russians. Think about this—before surveillance satellites, a seagoing task force would sail from the U.S. coast and disappear, particularly in bad weather, and if it were at sea for months, it was possible that no one would know where it was. The Soviet KGB 'agents' at sea were on fishing trawlers pretending to fish but actually spying on U.S. Navy bases, but a fast carrier battle group could leave them in the dust. A swift-moving carrier task force with all those nuclear bomb delivery planes would vanish until the very moment it came into aircraft range of Russian targets."

The image of the seagoing task force faded, replaced with the same camera aspect showing terrain flashing past the underbelly of the airplane in a blur of supersonic motion.

Mountains and canyon walls flew past for a moment, then the buildings of a city, impossibly close under the airplane's wings. "And U.S. Navy jets flying off aircraft carriers could carry huge hydrogen bombs into Russian airspace, flying below radar detection the entire way in and getting past Russian defenses, all the way to the Kremlin. In Russian nightmares, the sneak attack didn't come from the U.S. Air Force; it came special delivery from the U.S. Navy."

The display changed to show Moscow at night, the windows of the buildings of the Kremlin lit brightly, a light snow falling.

"In the early Cold War, the lights burned well into the wee hours every night at the Defense Ministry as they tried to find an antidote to the U.S. aircraft carrier."

"I had no idea," Kaminsky said. "Now that you put it that way, I can see why they were scared. You should teach history."

Rancourt didn't acknowledge the compliment, still all business. A film of a decorated Soviet general lecturing a room of senior Russian officers flashed on the screen.

"Anyway, the Soviet Defense Ministry gave orders to the Russian Navy that its new emergency mission was to come up with a way to intercept and sink an American aircraft carrier with almost zero notice, before the carrier's fighter-bombers could get within nuclear striking range of Moscow."

"Why wouldn't they just send their own fighter-bomber toward the carrier with a nuke and drop it off? Boom. No more aircraft carrier."

"Spoken like an Armed Services Committee senator."

"Did you just call me dumb?"

Rancourt laughed for the first time. "Sorry, but what would seem an obvious solution is not a solution at all. U.S. Navy fighter pilots are trained—they're the best in the world—at dogfighting. The task force fleet ships and the carrier herself put out more air search radar waves than you can imagine. If a seagull approaches an aircraft carrier, the admiral of the task force knows it. And you can't sneak toward a carrier battle group by flying close to the water, in the radar 'grass,' because patrols constantly fly around the battle group looking down with radars. A Russian bomber—even if it were on a suicide mission—would never get closer than fifty miles from a carrier, too far to put it out of action with even a ten-megaton hydrogen bomb."

"What about missiles?"

"Nope. Don't forget, nuclear warheads back then were big and heavy. The Russians didn't have a fast missile capable of carrying in a nuke, not something agile enough to avoid American radar and fighter defenses."

"I'm beginning to see the Russian nightmare. That's why aircraft carriers got all the funding they wanted back then."

"Exactly. The word went to all the design bureaus and all the designers. Whoever could come up with a surefire way to erase a carrier would be a hero." A still photo of a young, fresh-faced Russian man appeared on the display. "In 1956, a young and ambitious naval architect named Anatoly Petrov of the Malakhit Design Bureau rose to the challenge and proposed a solution so radical that at any other time he would have been shouted down or labeled a crackpot. But the Russian military was in a desperate panic, and Petrov's revolutionary Proposal Lira was given a hearing."

The screen showed a blueprint of a submarine seen from the side, the vessel's shape appearing much like the submarine photograph that had begun the presentation. Cyrillic letters crowded the blueprint, their translations flashing on the display like subtitles, the main title reading, *Golden Fish Starboard Elevation.*

"Petrov's proposal was to build an interceptor nuclear-powered submarine. Bear in mind that the nuclear submarine was less than two years old at the time, and the Russians hadn't even built one yet." Footage of the submarine *Nautilus* being launched rolled for a moment before the screen returned to the Golden Fish drawing. "Petrov suggested that this interceptor submarine would essentially be a manned nuclear-powered minisub—almost a human-guided torpedo. The sub's engines would be running at all times, with a miniature nuclear reactor—using an ultra-high-power density core—operated by a 'pen crew' at constant alert."

An animation film rolled, showing a Lira submarine at a pier, then a small group of men running out of a barracks building toward the sub, hustling across the gangway and hurrying down the hatch. The submarine headed away from the pier, an animated wake boiling up behind the vessel.

"Sort of the way bombers were treated back then," Kaminsky said.

"Right. Petrov's Lira submarine would never shut down, never sleep, just sit there at the pier, ready to go. When the word came in that an American aircraft carrier was inbound, the seagoing crew would 'scramble' to the pier from their pierside barracks, take over from the pen crew, and take Petrov's Golden Fish submarine to sea. The sub would be tiny, only fifteen hundred tons, a sixth of the size of the vessels on the drawing boards at the time."

The display switched to another blueprint. This one showed a conventional nuclear submarine of the late 1950s, labeled *November Class,* at the top. The profile of the November extended the width of the display. Underneath it a minisub, half the November's diameter and a third of its length, was labeled *Lira Class,* and was small enough to be carried on the November's hull.

"Lira would be capable of speeds approaching sixty knots, which would be required for it to get far enough at sea to torpedo and sink the aircraft carrier before the carrier reached Moscow strike range. A sixty-knot submarine in an era when twenty knots submerged was the best that technology could do. Like I said, at any other time Petrov's proposal would find its way to the dustbin, but these were crazy times."

The display changed to show an animation of a Lira class, seen three-dimensionally from the side. Near the center the reactor could be seen, glowing orange.

"Anyway, this kind of speed in a submarine would require a minimal wetted surface area of the hull and incredible power from the engines. Petrov envisioned an extremely powerful but small reactor that would be liquid-metal cooled to be able to achieve the power density in such a small package. But liquid metal freezes at room temperature, so the reactor could never be shut down, but that fit perfectly with the constant alert status of the interceptor mission. Every aspect of the design would cut weight to achieve minimum volume of the ship." The display's animation of the Lira added internal compartment bulkheads. "There would only be three compartments, with only the forward spaces manned to avoid shielding space and weight. This would require automation in an unprecedented degree, with the crew minimized to fifteen to seventeen men, all of them officers. The aft two compartments would be for the reactor and engines. The forward compartment would mostly be the torpedo room with a tiny command post. The crew would have a small berthing area with a tight galley and a one-hole toilet. The 'hotel' space for that many men would be less than the average American kitchen."

Kaminsky shook his head in wonder. "Let me get this straight. In the age of the *Nautilus,* Petrov proposes a mini-sub a sixth that size that goes three times as fast, with a crew a tenth of the size, a sub that's almost completely automatic and run by an all-officer crew that lives squeezed into a broom closet."

"That's about the size of it. The Russians were having some luck with automation in their space program, flying huge unmanned spacecraft into orbit. But a nuclear submarine is far different from a spaceship. Believe it or not, the vacuum of space is a far gentler environment than the ocean. And nuclear power plants—especially Russian-built ones—just don't lend themselves to automated supervision. Even today, fifty years later, this proposal to an American engineering board would be rejected. Our most modern submarines today rely heavily on manual control and supervision. But in a 1950s Russia anxious about aircraft carriers, it was given a serious hearing."

"Fine," Kaminsky said. "But cut to the chase, Tina—our man Petrov pulled it off, and five decades later, that's the submarine in the Terminal now, right?"

"Nope," Rancourt said, smiling slightly. "Stay with me, here, Vic. The news of Petrov's crazy proposal reached the Soviet Central Committee, and Petrov became a heroic savior in the eyes of the Party Secretary. He was given immediate funding and unprecedented authority to build this ship. Project Lira was born and given the project number 705."

The screen showed a huge bullpen drafting room, filled with designers laboring over drawing tables, with clusters of men wearing dark suits and dark ties leaning over the tables. In the background a banner of Cyrillic letters said something the screen didn't translate, but the number 705 could be made out. The screen view changed to show a black-and-white view of an oblong pool, with a steel structure in the ceiling. A small submerged submarine model was hooked up to a vertical support, and when a technician waved, the overhead structure moved the submarine model through the water of the tank, the next scene showing the model approaching the other end of the pool, with a gaggle of engineers with clipboards frowning at display readouts on a large instrument panel.

"Things were looking good for a few weeks until Petrov hit the first wall. And that was the fact that the concept couldn't work. The tiny submarine of his sketches was too small for the power plant required to propel it at the fifty-five-plus-knot speed required of an aircraft carrier intercept, even with a revolutionary liquid metal–cooled reactor. Petrov had to make the boat bigger, which made it heavier. Things went downhill fast.

"The next problems resulted from the proposed speed of the ship—Russian boats had been plagued with control surface hydraulic difficulties. This is called a 'jam dive,' where the controls jam or don't respond. By 1959 the early Russian nuclear submarines had suffered numerous jam dives at half their top speeds, and at Project 705's incredibly high speed of sixty knots, even a small control surface problem could plunge the ship much deeper than her crush depth. The deeper you go in the ocean, the more weight of the water on top of you, and the higher the pressure on your hull. You go too deep, your hull ruptures like an egg under a car tire."

An animation appeared, showing a nuclear sub cruising five shiplengths beneath the surface. The rear horizontal stabilizer suddenly went downward, and the animated ship plunged downward, heading almost straight down, then approached a red horizontal line labeled, *Crush depth.* When the ship dived below the red line, it broke apart, the animation showing scattered debris sinking to the ocean bottom.

"With the speed rating of the Lira class, the ship would need to have the capability of going much deeper than other ships of the day. The thickness of the steel that would be required to tolerate the deep depth rating would make the Lira so heavy that she would lose speed. So the reactor would have to be bigger, making the submarine bigger. You see the contradiction—you can't go fast unless your sub is small and light, but that speed requires more weight and a larger size for the reactor plant and steel hull, and the boat becomes big, which adds more skin area, which adds friction, which slows down the sub. Petrov was fighting nature's boundaries."

"The designers could have just blown off the jam-dive thing," Kaminsky commented. "That would at least save weight in the hull. So what if it became more dangerous— it was never supposed to be a pleasure cruise. The motherland was threatened."

"You're thinking like an American. Think like a Russian—you're dealing with a bureaucracy that treats failure harshly. If you're an American designer and your submarine sinks and kills the crew, you may have to testify before the Armed Services Committee, and at worst you would have to say good-bye to your Pentagon contracts, but otherwise life would go on. If you're a Russian designer and your submarine sinks, you're taken to the gulag with or without a trial. And the Russian admirals would be in the neighboring cell block. The Navy brass could make it impossible for the designers to deliver a ship if they didn't agree to the concept. From memos complaining about inadequate design to outright sabotage, the Soviet Navy had the power to keep a bad submarine design in the drydock indefinitely. The designers knew they could never get the Soviet Navy to accept the design unless they solved the speed-to-depth-rating problem. It was already an uphill battle to get the Navy to accept the idea of having a pen crew run a constantly operating reactor and a crew of almost twenty officers living on top of each other in a minisub."

The screen image shifted to a black-and-white view of a man in a space suit welding in a metallurgy lab, the man surrounded by a halo of sparks.

"The project seemed doomed, but a lone researcher named Litski in the Malakhit Design Bureau was working on titanium for hull material. As he would say at the engineer's tea area, titanium would do for submarines what aluminum had done for aircraft. Titanium was light and incredibly strong. Petrov had always dismissed Litski as a nutcase. After all, titanium was in short supply, there were no titanium mills, and the metal was difficult to weld. For years Petrov and the rest of the designers had stopped listening, but one morning they were bemoaning the depth rating and weight conundrum, and Litski spoke up and suggested titanium. He had even done some calculations showing what would happen to the hull's depth rating and weight with titanium in place of steel. Petrov couldn't believe it—Litski had just saved Petrov's career by showing that the project could succeed with titanium."

Kaminsky thought about his previous assignments and what he knew about titanium. "But Petrov was right. Titanium is a total bitch to weld. There aren't many folks in the world who can do it."

Rancourt nodded. "Titanium was the answer, but it only existed in the lab. No one could make production titanium plates. So as early as 1957, the writing was on the wall. The entire Lira project should have been scrapped. But Petrov still proceeded on, with as much funding as he requisitioned. Perhaps that was because the design bureau couldn't admit failure to the Central Committee, or perhaps in spite of 705's flaws, the idea of a sixty-knot submarine able to intercept American aircraft carriers—with the bonus that it could outrun Western torpedoes—remained attractive.

"In any case, Petrov had to create an entire titanium industry. It took until 1960 to get approval to proceed to the construction phase, and by then the projected submarine's cost increased by twenty thousand percent, and the planned production schedule grew by five hundred percent. The project was an obvious waste. The minute someone introduced accountability to the program, the Lira project would be doomed.

"Perhaps it was the invention of the intercontinental ballistic missile that brought that accountability. With ICBMs raising their ugly heads, things got a lot scarier for the Russians than a few aircraft carriers with small fighter-bombers. But since the ICBM was on both shores, in an ICBM war, the Russians could begin to compete head-to-head with the U.S. The whole idea of aircraft carrier interception became passé. You can almost guess the rest."

The screen showed several ICBM launches and an animation of the globe from above the North Atlantic, with the tracks of ICBMs traveling from the United States toward the Soviet Union, and retaliatory ICBM tracks emanating from Russia toward the North American landmass.

"A 1963 project review meeting went predictably badly for Petrov. He was fired, arrested, and taken at gunpoint to the gulag, not to be released until the mid-1970s." The screen image showed a classified film of a Siberian prison camp. "With Petrov's reputation dashed, the Soviets had a second chance to let Project 705 die. But for a second time the project survived. We're guessing that by putting it in the hands of Petrov's apprentices, the Russians felt the project would wither quietly with no further impact to the careers of the decision makers. They didn't count on the relentlessness of Petrov's understudies. A young, ambitious, and innovative ship designer named Mikhail Rusanov and his equally motivated assistant, Vladimir Romin, took over Project 705.

"When Rusanov inherited the program, it became obvious that the tremendous power—forty-seven thousand shaft horsepower—that would be required to approach sixty knots would not come from as light and small a reactor as Petrov's second design. We suspect that the project's survival in its bastardized form was because Rusanov made a deal with the Navy. He would make the sub much bigger and more operable, more habitable, in exchange for the Navy's keeping the project alive. Rusanov would allow the design to be changed, only retaining the idea of building a submarine that could go sixty knots. So the ship increased in size again, to twenty-eight hundred tons. The number of compartments grew from three to six, and crew size doubled from a lesser extent of automation than Petrov had hoped, but a degree of automation the Soviet Navy could accept."

The screen flashed a blueprint, showing the small submarine from the previous blueprint on top, a submarine twice its size below. The upper sub was labeled, *Lira Model 1.0— Original Petrov Proposal*. The lower sub was labeled, *Lira Model 3.0—Rusanov Revision*.

"The reactor systems, in addition to becoming heavier

and larger, could not be economically repaired, not even in a shipyard environment, which forced the reactor physics engineers to design the core for seventy years of operation without refueling, but such a design made the ship that much more difficult to manufacture.

"After the Cuban Missile Crisis, the aircraft-carrier threat was no longer feared in the Kremlin. By 1964 the new Russian fear—even more frightening to them than American ICBMs—was the George Washington–class nuclear submarines with their underwater-launched Polaris nuclear ballistic missiles." The screen showed an empty expanse of ocean. Suddenly an explosion of white foam erupted, and from it a nuclear missile appeared, hanging in midair for a moment before its engine ignited and it roared off vertically out of view. "A final Project Lira delay happened at the next design review, which showed the ship needed to increase in size yet *again* to thirty-eight hundred tons. And still the project lived on, perhaps because canceling it meant officially admitting bureaucratic failure. A failure not just for the Malakhit Design Bureau, but for the Navy's admirals."

The screen changed to show the sealed drydock building, with a grainy black-and-white film of the Lira being constructed, reminding Kaminsky of the new Lira submarine in the Terminal. A banner draped over the submarine's hull read, *K-377*.

"In 1965 Rusanov's new Model 4.0 of Project 705 was ready for production. The Project 705 Lira Model Four–class prototype's initial titanium hull section was laid in Sudomekh Shipyard in Leningrad in 1972, twelve years behind schedule."

The image changed to show a Rusanov version of a Lira at sea, gracefully moving through the water. After the presentation, Kaminsky stared at the moving picture, thinking about how many men had sweated and bled to make the Russian submarine a reality. He almost felt sorry for them.

"*K-377* sailed in 1972 and reached an unprecedented submerged speed of fifty-five-point-eight knots during her sea trials, a record exceeded only by follow-up Lira submarines, and never approached by any other sub class. Petrov set out to build a sixty-knot submarine, and he did it."

"So at the end of the day, the Lira was a success," Kaminsky said. "But you still haven't said anything about this beast turning the tide of the Cold War."

"No," Rancourt said. "It was a miserable failure."

Kaminsky stared at her, wondering if he had heard right.

12

The pillow was hot on the skin of his shaved head as Peter Vornado lay awake. He stared at the dark, silent room, wishing he were upstairs in the bed with Rachel. Ever since he had moved to the first floor, baby Erin had slept in the king-size bed with her mother. Beside the pillow was an intercom he could use to call Rachel, but she hadn't slept well in weeks, and he decided he could handle the rising nausea alone. He reached for the basket by the side of the railed bed and threw up. When he finished, he covered the basket, lowered it to the floor, and slowly lay back on the pillow, the dizziness spinning the room a few times before receding.

He shut his eyes and tried to sleep, but after another hour he rolled to his back and stared at the ceiling. It had been five weeks since the day the Sloan-Kettering doctor had given him sixty days to live. Two days later Vornado had undergone surgery to debulk the malignant brain tumor. There had been some pain, and a dull headache as he recovered, but the terrifying headaches from before surgery had stopped for a week, then returned with even more vigor, as if his tumor were angry that Vornado had dared to attack it.

He tried not to think about the end but it was difficult not to. He had convened with Rachel and the family attorney, getting the final estate planning finished and putting the medical power of attorney in force, so that when he eventually lost brain function Rachel could direct his withdrawal from life support. Once that was done, the nagging worry was that Rachel would be alone to raise Erin, Peter, and Marla. But even that he had come to accept. What was tougher was that when he looked into Erin's blue eyes and listened to her toddler's happy high-pitched voice, he felt guilty knowing that in another month he'd leave her. He had insisted to himself that he couldn't die. He had too many obligations to die. Too many lives depended on his. And it wasn't that he was afraid of dying. He had faced death twice, and both times he had fought it, half in terror and half in disbelief. But it was one thing to be killed in the place he had expected to die, to succumb as a warrior, another to be a victim in a hospital gown and die before his fortieth birthday. But there appeared to be no choice.

The second day after surgery, as he sat up in bed under his bandages, feeling the best he had felt in a month, Dr. Peppinger came in and spoke about a radical experimental vaccination therapy program at Duke University Comprehensive Cancer Center. The program took only a few patients nationwide, but Peppinger had gotten Vornado in. The doctor warned Rachel that this was not so much a last hope as a research program that might lend valuable data to a science in its infancy, and Vornado's results might be able to help those diagnosed in the future. Even so, there were patients who did well in the program. The Duke program had patients still living five years after receiving the glioblastoma diagnosis. Even if Vornado's chances remained zero, he could at least be doing battle with the tumor instead of just waiting for it to take him. Peppinger was insistent that they understand that this illness was still fatal. The Duke program and the vaccination might give him only a few more months. But that was all that Rachel had needed to hear.

Rachel was an energetic and successful sales executive for the eastern region of a management consulting firm. She had hated every science course she had ever suffered through, but in a few weeks had done a vast amount of research into vaccination therapy for end-stage brain cancer. She began to worry him. She had seized on the new-found knowledge as if she truly believed he would survive. For the first time since his diagnosis, there was hope in her eyes. Vornado couldn't bear to break her heart by reminding her of Peppinger's warning. She had enjoyed the trip in the car service's Town Car to Duke, despite Vornado's vomiting.

Dr. Friedman, the doctor running the program, wasted

no time. The treatment began with preprocedure MRIs and PET scans. They took a half liter of Vornado's blood and processed the white cells, altering them on a molecular level—not as the cancer cure, but to allow his body to survive the otherwise lethal effects of the vaccination. After the processing, the vaccination chemicals were added to the white cells and plasma, and the mix was injected into his groin. They waited for two days, then gave him postprocedure brain scans. He had gone back home to Virginia Beach for the chemotherapy and radiation treatments.

The drugs that allowed chemo patients pain relief and eased fatigue couldn't be used in the vaccination program, so Vornado spent hours vomiting, too weak to move. The radiation had caused most of Vornado's thick blonde hair to fall out in clumps, leaving him with patches of uneven fuzz. Rachel had agreed to shave his head, which had made Erin giggle in delight, and had left him with what he thought was a naked, vulnerable look. Rachel insisted it made him look tough in a Mr. Clean way, but he knew she was only trying to make him feel better. The chemotherapy was more torturous, but he submitted stoically. It was the nausea he hated more than the fatigue. Food made him sick, even the smell of cooking. There were times he thought he had vomited and dry-heaved more than any living human. In the past month he had lost over twenty pounds, leaving him looking bony and weak. But even with all that, he was still here, still able to talk with the kids and play with Erin. But at the back of his mind was the constant thought that his minutes were running out.

Soon he was too weak to manage the stairs, even with Rachel's help, so she had cleared out his ground-floor study and brought in a railed hospital bed. Vornado spent his days lying in the bed, little Erin sitting on the mattress beside him. Peter Junior and Marla spent their summer vacation days at soccer and tennis camp, but kept him company in the evenings. At least they could come close to comprehension of what was happening to him, unlike Erin. At first the little girl had wanted to play with him, distressed that he was bedridden. She insisted on staying in the room with him, watching television or listening as Rachel read him books. No longer did he have the concentration for his beloved legal thrillers, so she filled the shelf with Mark Twain. In the midst of a passage, when he would lean over the bed to throw up, Erin would pat his back with her little hand while Rachel held his forehead.

After three vaccinations, the Duke program shifted to an observation phase, and the chemotherapy and radiation course came to an end. After the first vaccination there had been no headaches and no discomfort. Rachel had begun to think they were out of danger, but Vornado had doubts. The headaches returned before the posttreatment trip to Duke. On the way there, Vornado had crashed, a violent seizure shaking him on the car seat. They had rushed to the nearest hospital, and he had been admitted, dehydrated, disoriented, and weak. It took hours to stabilize him. When he arrived at Duke, he was wheeled in the front door in a wheelchair and placed in a hospital bed. When the MRI and PET scan results came in, Dr. Friedman didn't need to say a word. His face said it all—the vaccination program had failed and the malignancy was back. The MRI had been clean, but the more definitive PET scan had shown a mass in the brain.

"Peter, we only have one more decision left to make," the doctor had said quietly. "Normally, at this point, we would recommend hospice care. You can go home with some strong medication for the pain, a patient-administered morphine cocktail. Your last days can be relatively pain-free. You can avoid further hospitalization, and spend some time with your wife and kids."

"You said there was a decision," Vornado said with an effort.

"You can elect to take one final but fatal risk. We'd set you up for an ultrahigh dose of chemotherapy. I'm not talking about what you had before. This would come as a single dose injected directly into the base of the brain. It will be so poisonous that there's an extreme risk of mortality. With your present condition, I'd say your chances of surviving the ultrahigh chemo are minimal. And we'd have to cut out any other medications during the ultrahigh, so you'd suffer significant pain from the dose. In addition, chemicals strong enough to kill the cancer have the potential to cause measurable levels of brain tissue damage. Odds are that the cognitive functions wouldn't be affected, but motor function, vision, hearing, and balance could be at risk."

"That's the risk. What's the possible benefit?" Rachel asked.

"Well, that chemotherapy this strong will kill the cancer in one shot. The cancer cells in the new growth are much weaker than those in the original tumor. We have a short window for an ultrahigh dose to eliminate every cancer cell. Permanently."

Vornado looked at the doctor and took a deep breath. "Doc, what would you do if you were sitting here?"

The doctor looked earnestly and somberly into Vornado's eyes. "Son, we've only tried the ultrahigh dose regimen in eight similar cases. Five patients were dead within seventy-two hours. Two slipped into comas and were gone within two weeks. The eighth recovered and is in complete remission, but may never walk again. So you see the odds we're dealing with here. What would I do? I'd go home, accept hospice care, take the painkillers, and play with the baby. Have one last party with my friends. Say my good-byes. But it's not for me to say. Talk it over with your wife. Better yet, go home and sleep on it, then call me. You can have the ultrahigh dose in Virginia Beach if you go that way instead of making the trip here."

It was hard for Rachel to say good-bye to Friedman, and to her last hope. She cried as she hugged him, thanking him, then walked beside Vornado's wheelchair to the parking lot. They rode home in silence. Rachel put Vornado in the hospital bed in his former office and sat on the leather chair in the corner.

"What do you think, Peter?" she asked.

All his life Vornado had accepted risk and even the possibility of death, but it had always been with the goal of serving his country. At sea, his death would have accomplished something. What he stood to lose now was a few more weeks with the kids. As precious as they were to him, the prospect of lying on his back for a month, high on morphine and waiting helplessly and miserably for the end, would spoil his remaining time with them. He could justify taking an all-or-nothing gamble that would yield a quick answer—either he would beat this thing or he could end the struggle. And odds of one in eight—even if survival meant living in a wheelchair—were generous compared to the alternative of being a victim and waiting helplessly for death.

"I say we go for it," Vornado said. "We're only talking about losing a few weeks if it goes wrong."

"Aren't you afraid of the pain?"

Nothing could be worse than the last five weeks, he thought. He shook his head.

"I've got to tell you," Rachel said, her eyes filling with tears, "I don't want you to do it. I have a terrible feeling about this."

"Okay," Vornado said. "We'll turn it down." Perhaps it was just as well, he thought. Maybe a month of fading away would be more healing to his family than watching him go in hours.

Rachel was silent for some time, her eyes wandering around his study, looking at the framed photos of his submarines, his officer's sword leaning against the wall in the corner, the Naval Academy diploma in a position of honor on the wall beside his submarine qualification letter and the framed Bronze Star certificate of valor for classified action in the Barents Sea last year. Something seemed to come over her, and she swallowed hard.

"Would you think I'm crazy if I said I changed my mind?" she asked.

He smiled and laughed, grimacing at the pain. "No, honey," he said tenderly. "But what's making you reconsider?"

"It's you. This room, it is filled with what you've been in your life. You're just not one to lie back and not fight. It's why I fell in love with you in the first place."

Vornado nodded, then frowned. "We probably won't win this thing, baby."

"I suppose. But I think it would be easier later knowing we tried everything."

"You're braver than I am," he said.

She fought for control, clamping her eyes shut, the tears leaking out. When she regained her voice, it was scratchy and dry. "Do you want a few days to rest first?"

"No," he said. "Let's go. Make the call."

Rachel had left a message for Friedman, spent another

hour in the study, then gone up to bed. He had lain awake since, thinking of the past six weeks, and wondering what his life would have been like right now if the cancer hadn't come. The room began to lighten with the approach of dawn, and Vornado had the thought that this might be the last morning he ever experienced. With a supreme effort he dropped the bedrail and climbed out. He walked slowly, carefully, to the east window of the kitchen and sat in a chair and watched as the sun rose over the backyard trees.

He heard the baby cry and Rachel's footsteps coming into the kitchen.

"Hi, Da-da," Erin said gleefully, grinning and holding out her arms. Rachel handed the baby over, and Vornado rested her on his lap.

He kissed Erin and tried to wink bravely at Rachel, but couldn't make it convincing.

"You still want to do this?" she asked.

"I do," he said.

The older children came in for breakfast, listening somberly as their mother told them about the treatment. They both asked if they could stay home from school, and Vornado had nodded at Rachel.

He sat in the chemotherapy chair at the hospital five miles away. He shut his eyes while waiting for the needle, thinking about prisoners undergoing lethal injections. The needle hurt, and the injection burned on its way in. Immediately he felt dizzy and nauseous, and he began to wonder if he had made the wrong decision. The drive home was torture, the five miles featuring half a dozen episodes of dry heaves. Rachel had trouble getting him into the bed, and when she did, he lay there helplessly. He didn't have the strength to thrash in the bed, or even to lift his head to vomit. The pain and nausea were worse than anything he'd imagined. It came in waves, each one more violent than the one before. During one of the terrible moments, Vornado realized a certainty—he had gambled and he had lost. It was over. He wouldn't last the night.

His only living family was his sister, Diana, who worked in Japan. She had made the trip out a month before, and he knew he wouldn't live long enough for her to cross the Pacific. He did not want to face the final sunset by himself.

He asked Rachel to bring his friends and associates over to the house, especially his old Academy roommate, best friend, and torpedo-exercise opponent, B. K. Dillinger. Rachel made the calls, her face showing that she knew he had given up. She came back with bad news. Dillinger was back at sea, on his normal command, the USS *Tucson,* and bringing him here would require heroics. Vornado nodded in understanding, beginning to realize he would never see B.K. again. For some reason he thought about Plebe Summer and Whitehead, and he smiled.

As the afternoon shadows grew long his friends filled the house. George Willey, Vornado's former executive officer, brought over the entire officer cadre and senior chiefs from the *Hampton.* Commodore Smokin' Joe Kraft and his staff came by, as did other senior officers Vornado had worked for. Kraft told him that he had ordered *Tucson* to surface so that a helicopter could evacuate B. K. Dillinger and fly him in. He had grasped Vornado's hand, then left.

Rachel had tried to be cheerful, but every one of the visitors stared at his wasted-away frame and his shaved skull, paying their last respects in advance. He struggled against tears as each person left, until the house was empty and it was fully dark. He fought the pain for another two hours, waiting for Dillinger to come. During the wait Vornado realized how weak he had grown from the visiting, a heavy crushing exhaustion making him want to sleep, but he fought the feeling, knowing that if he closed his eyes he would not reopen them. He forced himself to hang on until Dillinger could come. There was something he wanted to tell his old friend. But the hours of waiting were taking their toll. The kids and Rachel stayed beside his bed and waited with him.

A dizziness had returned, and when the front door creaked open, Vornado wasn't sure if it were real or if he had imagined it. But then the study door opened and the athletic form of Commander Burke Dillinger entered the room, wearing a wrinkled summer-weight khaki uniform. B.K. smiled courageously, hugged Rachel and greeted the children, then banged his fists on Vornado's. Rachel shepherded the children from the room and shut the study door behind her. Vornado looked up at his friend's face, hoping to keep his voice steady, but when it came out it was a hoarse croak.

"B.K., it's over. Time to close up shop." Vornado gathered the last of his strength to get out the final words. "Will you help me? Will you look after Rachel and the kids?"

Dillinger nodded and pulled Vornado into a hug, no longer able to hold back the tears. Dillinger tried to say something, but his voice failed him. Vornado dropped his head to the pillow, his own eyes becoming wet. After a few minutes B.K. stood back while Rachel brought the baby and put her on the bed. Peter Junior held his right hand, Marla his left, and little Erin rubbed his arm and said in her soprano voice, "S'okay, Daddy, s'okay." He felt her small body snuggling into his side, smelling the baby shampoo in her silky blonde hair.

He tried to form the words *I love you* to say to the baby, but he couldn't make his voice work, not even in a whisper. He mouthed the words to her, hoping Rachel would read his lips and tell the baby what he had tried to say. He squeezed Peter's hand and smiled at Marla, then at Rachel. He kissed Erin's forehead, but then he didn't have the strength to keep his head lifted above the pillow. A wave of dizziness came, the room blurring and slowly rolling back and forth, as if he were back at sea.

He had the thought that these might be his last conscious moments. He had to fight, he thought; he had to stay awake.

Just let go, an inner voice said in his mind.

He tried to ignore it, instead focusing on the faces of his son, his daughters, his wife, and his friend for as long as he could, and felt their hands squeezing his. He tried to squeeze back but soon there was no more energy in his arms. He tried to mouth more words, but his lips were chapped and dry and would not respond. When he took the next breath, it was with an effort, the one after that even harder, as if all his muscles were failing him one after another.

He felt heavy, as if he were sinking into the mattress. Every time he blinked it became more difficult to reopen his eyes. He tried to gather his strength, to stay awake one more moment, but he couldn't keep his eyes open any

longer. He felt his lids fall slowly on his wet eyes, and felt
the exhaustion overcome the pain. The feeling lasted only
a few heartbeats.

And then there was nothing.

He flew effortlessly over the waves of the sea, his body and
spirit weightless and free, the feeling of speed intoxicating.
The brightness of the noon sun dimmed slowly as clouds
rolled across the sky, and after a time twilight came, then
the blackness of the night as stars appeared over the waves.

He knew he had to do one last thing, so he turned until
he could see the sand of the beach. Brightly lit hotels flew
under him as he moved inland. The landscape flashed by
until he could see the house far below. With an effort, he
descended to the front lawn. Once stopped, he missed the
sensation of speed, but there was something important
here. He looked around him, realizing the house seemed
naked without Peter Junior's bike and baseball bat and
glove in the front yard. The driveway also seemed strange
with only Rachel's car in the driveway. He could hear a
sound coming from inside the house. At first he wasn't sure
what it was, but then recognized the sound of Erin crying.
He looked up at the window of the master bedroom, but
it was dark. Still the child sobbed bitterly. There was another sound, the sound of Rachel's voice trying in vain to
comfort the baby. He waited for a long time until the crying
stopped, then passed through the front door.

He visited his study first, as had been his habit, except
this time he had no car keys or wallet to drop into the
silver bowl on the bookshelf. The hospital bed was gone,
his office returned to the way it had been before, except
much tidier than he had kept it. He moved into the kitchen,
which was starkly clean, the usual clutter a dim memory.
He would have thought someone else lived in the house
but for Erin's crying and the contents of his study. In the
kitchen sink, a single coffee cup soaked. He stared at it
stupidly for a time, dimly aware that it meant something.

He turned and drifted slowly up the stairs. Peter Junior's
room was messier than usual. His son lay under the covers,
his eyes open as he stared at the ceiling, twin tear streaks
running down his temples and into his hair. He tried to call
out to the boy, but no sound came. He touched his son's

tousled hair, but Peter Junior didn't react. After a last glance he left the room. Farther down the hall he encountered the shut and locked door of Marla's room. He passed through it and looked at the room, which was oddly as tidy as a magazine photograph except for the black dress draped across her desk chair and black low-heeled shoes on the floor nearby. For a moment he watched his daughter sleep. He reached out to her face, but it was as if he weren't there. She turned under her comforter, a frown on her sleeping face, and her body knocked something to the floor. He looked down at it, a silver-framed official Navy photograph of an officer, the blonde man's unsmiling, tough face glaring at the camera from beneath a brimmed white officer's cap, the starched service dress white uniform colored only by the triple row of medals beneath his gold submarine dolphin pin. He tried to pick up the photo and put it on the desk, but it was too heavy. He reached out again to Marla's tangled hair, then turned back to the door. He passed through it and moved down the hall to the master bedroom.

The door was open a crack. He moved to the end of the bed where Rachel slept with Erin, his side of the bed empty, the covers undisturbed on that side. He moved closer and listened to the baby's steady slow breathing. He gently brushed a blonde lock from Erin's small face, then stared tenderly at Rachel. Even in sleep she seemed drawn and exhausted, and yet she was still as beautiful as the day he had met her. For the next few minutes he watched them as he thought about their romance, which now seemed to have been so short. He chided himself for thinking about their time together as if it were something in the past.

Something pulled him toward the master bathroom. He wandered slowly in. The moonlight illuminated the room. He looked down to see that there was only one toothbrush in the cup at the sink. He stared at it for a long time, his thoughts accelerating, until finally the lone toothbrush made him realize the truth.

The truth that he was dead and would never return.

Peter Vornado wept.

PART 3:

▼

New Orders

13

There was a growing brightness that became a glaring white light directly in front of him. He swam slowly upward toward it, the light growing even brighter. A strange feeling came over him. It was something he hadn't felt in what seemed like half a lifetime. In the dawning awareness of the moment he realized that the feeling was optimism and contentment, and the sentiment confused him.

The brightness of the light forced him to turn his attention outward. He concentrated on looking directly at it, but it was too bright. It took a long time to realize that the light was not supernatural, but a phenomenon of the earth. Slowly his senses focused on the world around him, until he was able to see his surroundings. The brightness was sunlight. Sunlight streaming into a small room from a window.

He felt his senses extending farther outward. He could feel a body, his body, but it was strange. There was something missing. Like someone waking after an amputation, he felt a momentary panic as he tried to understand what it was that he had lost. Slowly he realized that what was gone was the sensation of pain. For several moments he luxuriated in the lightness of the wonderful painless feeling. But soon he realized he had been wrong—there was pain. He could feel his lower back, and it ached. There was another ache, this one in the fingers of his right hand. He blinked several times.

Disoriented, he sat slowly up and peered at the room. His office had always been a dark cave, its windows curtained and shuttered, with a northern exposure. It would have required searchlights to be this bright. He realized the ache in his back was from leaning on a bathtub while lying on the cold hard tile floor of the upstairs master bathroom. Why, he wondered, would Rachel and B. K. Dillinger drag him up here? The thought that he might have climbed out of the railed bed downstairs and walked up here by himself without collapsing seemed impossible. Stranger still was the reason his hand ached—from how hard he'd been clutching something in his sleep. He opened his fist and stared dumbly down at his toothbrush. He tried to remember something just out of reach, something about this object that had been important, but couldn't. He shrugged and decided to think about it later.

He moved his arm up and witnessed a miracle as he was able to put the toothbrush on the counter without feeling bone-deep pain. He put his hand on his stomach. It didn't hurt. He slowly put his hands on his head. There was no headache. He turned his head slowly, waiting for the dizziness, and prepared to lift the toilet lid to vomit. But he wasn't sick. He tried to call out to Rachel, and when he did, his dry voice trembled, but at least he still had a voice. But when Rachel didn't arrive, he decided to try to get to his feet. The counter of the sink seemed a mile above him, but he reached for it and pulled, and amazingly his body came upright. He stood there before the sink, stupefied, waiting for dizziness to drop him back to the tile, but after five minutes the only sensation he felt was hunger. He glanced at his reflection in the mirror and beheld a bald stranger with a gaunt, starved face marked by black circles under each eye, hollow cheeks, and chapped lips, but there was something new, a glow to the tone of his complexion, the gray pallor of the last weeks gone. He slowly walked out into the hallway. As he walked, he realized he was limping out of habit rather than from need. He stood straighter, his body responding. He was able to walk down the stairs without Rachel holding him up. He smiled as he emerged in the downstairs foyer. He turned and opened the door of his darkened study.

Inside on the railed bed, Erin lay snoring in a deep sleep. Rachel sat on a chair by the bed, her head resting on the mattress. He shook her shoulder, but couldn't wake her. He wished he could hoist her body up on the bed, but knew he didn't have the strength. He pulled the comforter off the bed and draped it over her shoulders, then shut the door quietly behind him.

He walked into the den, where he heard snoring from the couch. When he came around the corner he found B. K. Dillinger in a deep sleep, covered by the afghan, fully clothed in jeans and a U.S. Submarine Force T-shirt, which was odd, since he'd arrived in uniform. Vornado shook Dillinger's shoulder, but he too couldn't be roused.

The insistent hunger nagged even stronger. Vornado left the den and walked slowly to the kitchen. At first he moved about the kitchen, making coffee, then toast; then shrugged and cooked bacon and scrambled eggs, whistling to himself. He set the table, pulled the highchair to the table, and just as he filled the serving bowl with breakfast Rachel walked slowly into the room carrying the yawning baby. His wife was gaunt and emaciated, her eyes frozen open in disbelief. Vornado smiled at her and gestured to the table he'd set.

"Oh, my God," she stammered. "You were in a coma for five days. I thought it was over. I tried to stay awake by your bed, and for four nights I did. I was certain that the moment I fell asleep I'd lose you. Then I finally pass out, and when I wake up, *you're gone*! I freaked out so bad I had chest pains." She collapsed in a chair, her head in her hands, and cried hard enough to shake the table. He sat beside her, his arm around her, and she hugged him.

"Are you okay?" she asked, a trembling hope in her voice.

He nodded, considering telling her where he'd spent the night. "No nausea. No fatigue. No headaches."

"Eat your breakfast while I call for the car," she said. "We're going to Duke."

The trip to Duke that afternoon seemed easy. Dr. Friedman's eyes showed a muted optimism at first. After the new round of scans, his face began to show amazement. They were asked to stay overnight so that the inventor of the vaccination program could fly in from Sweden to review the results. A hushed conference took place between the doctors, lasting hours. The vaccination designer insisted on a biopsy of the previously cancerous area, and Vornado submitted to the procedure, hoping it would be his last. On the morning of the third day at Duke, Vornado and his wife waited for the doctor in his office while he reviewed the biopsy results. After what seemed hours, the doctor entered his office. Vornado stood up. For the first time since Vornado had met him, his eyes were wrinkled in amusement.

"Well, Peter, the path report shows only normal cellular growth. It's remarkable. What you've experienced is nothing short of a medical miracle. We think the vaccination course may have been helped by the final ultrahigh chemotherapy," he said. "We're thinking of inserting that in some form into the baseline therapy. But in any case, you've beaten the cancer."

"So," Vornado asked, "am I cured?"

"For all practical purposes. We'll keep a close eye on you. There will be follow-up checkups and scans at three-month intervals until we can be sure, and then . . . well, let's see how the next year goes. Meanwhile, congratulations." The doctor broke into a sudden grin and hugged Vornado.

On the trip back to Virginia Beach, Rachel cried tears of happiness while Peter Vornado tried to get used to the idea of continuing to live. He had gotten so used to the fact that he was going to die that living on seemed impossible. The only thing that helped with the disorientation was talking to Erin, who loved the attention of her suddenly healthy father and babbled away from her car seat.

Vornado stared out the Town Car's window, lost in thought. There remained the matter of his former career. He tried unsuccessfully to imagine what would happen to his job. He decided he would report to work. He was certain they would process him out with paperwork and exit interviews. What else could they do? He was medically unfit—or at least medically fragile, which amounted to the same thing. He could no longer be relied upon to perform the missions of the past. His life was back, but his working life was still over. After the last year, he was no longer one of those men who defined their identity by their work, even though the work he had done had made other men envious. Already he missed it.

Vornado rested his head against the window and shut his eyes, knowing that he probably would not be able to nap.

As the car crossed the Virginia border, he had a thought that allowed him to fall asleep—that he had managed to let go of his life, and it had come back to him. Now it was time to let go of his career and see what came in its place. He began to snore softly.

This time, in the dream, there were two cars in the driveway, a sink full of dishes, a bed rumpled on both sides, children sleeping peacefully in messy rooms, and two toothbrushes at the sink. Vornado stood in the bathroom staring at the toothbrushes for a long time, trying to understand what they symbolized, but finally understanding that there was a simple truth in front of him: He was alive.

Peter Vornado smiled.

He had planned to begin the first day of his new life with his old routine. His eyes opened at four in the morning without help from an alarm clock. He sat up in bed and looked at the room, feeling grateful that it was the king-size bed of his bedroom and not the hospital bed of the office. The movers had come for the hospital bed Saturday and had cheerfully rearranged the heavy furniture.

Vornado shut his eyes for a few seconds, just to feel the sensation of being normal. When he opened them the world was still as it was. He turned to see Rachel in the dim light of the room. She was in a deep sleep, her arm draped over Erin's body, the two-year-old's middle fingers in her mouth as she slept curled up next to her mother. Vornado reached over and caressed his wife's hair, remembering how the night before they had made love for the first time in six months, how they had started gently and then become almost violent. He rubbed his shoulder, where Rachel's teeth had broken his skin. He smiled again, wishing his return to his life could include returning to his submarine command, but that would be impossible, even with the clout of Smokin' Joe Kraft.

Vornado stood and walked to the bathroom, and when he was through showering he walked to the closet. He reached for the working khaki uniform, but decided against it. If he were to be processed out today, it would be more appropriate to wear a service dress uniform. He pulled out the service dress khakis from the dry-cleaning bag and rigged it by feel in the dark room, snapping on the shoulderboards of rank, each with a gold star and three stripes running perpendicular to the line of his shoulders. He found the solid-gold pin on the shelf and pinned it above the left breast pocket, feeling the scaly fish of the emblem facing toward the center formed by a diesel boat conning tower—submariner's dolphins. Below the dolphin pin he pinned on the three rows of service ribbons. On the top row was the Bronze Star, a Meritorious Unit Citation and a Presidential Unit Citation—all from exploits that seemed impossibly far in the past. Vornado realized there would be no more of these coming. He debated about the third device, a gold pin with an anchor set in a small circle the size of a coin, his capital ship command pin. By now Smokin' Joe had to have named a new commanding officer as captain of the *Hampton*. Vornado shrugged and pinned it on anyway, realizing that wearing it made him no more an impostor than the rest of the uniform.

For a half second he entertained the thought of skipping the uniform altogether and wearing a civilian business suit, but dismissed it. Until the words were written on the official papers discharging him from the naval service, he was still Commander Peter Vornado, United States Navy. The last device was a black phenolic name tag reading, CDR. P. VOR-NADO, USS *HAMPTON*, COMMANDING OFFICER. This was also no longer true, but he pinned it to the uniform jacket nonetheless. He buttoned the khaki shirt, pulled on and tied his black tie, then grimaced as he pulled on the pants. They were so big on him that he would look like the "after" photograph in a weight-loss ad. At least the service dress khaki jacket would cover the pleats at his waist. He shrugged into the jacket and found his combination cap and tried it on, but it was a size too big. Even his head had lost weight. He tucked the cap under his arm and tip-toed down the stairs and into the study.

The room felt different after he had nearly died here. Perhaps he should rearrange the furniture and paint it, he thought. The old leather briefcase he had used was empty and slightly dusty. It would feel strange to come in without it, but then he realized he wouldn't need it anyway. He found the keys to the old Corvette he'd bought from Dil-linger during his friend's divorce. He left the house and inhaled the air of the early morning, smelling the salty sea air from the beach breeze. He yawned and stretched, smiling as he walked to the black sports car. As he unlocked it he remembered how he had tried to give it back when he was dying, but Dillinger wouldn't take it, saying it reminded him too much of his former life. Vornado was certain it wouldn't start, but it coughed to life and purred in the driveway.

The 4:30 A.M. drive to the base slipped by so fast he barely noticed. He drove the car to the senior officer parking lot, but not to his old space—another man would have taken that over. Vornado killed the engine and walked toward the security entrance to the piers. The unsmiling guard frowned at the mismatch between Vornado's photo and physical appearance, and asked him to key in his password, finally waving him in.

The big sign at pier three was still there, a shark pushing an eight ball, the lettering below reading, SUBMARINE SQUADRON EIGHT. Vornado walked past it to the inner security shack, greeting another guard. He had meant to walk straight to the gangway to the tender ship *Centurion,* but a strange force seemed to push him and pull him at the same time farther down the pier to the berth of the submarine *Hampton,* his former command. He bit his lip, thinking how sad the two words *former command* sounded when placed together. Listen to his self-pity, he thought with contempt, forcing himself to remember his brush with death and to feel gratitude for every breath remaining. It was then that he arrived at berth seven, resting place of the USS *Hampton,* SSN-767. She was long and sleek and slender and black from her bullet nose forward to her tapered stern. The water of the slip lapped darkly at her bulbous bow, shimmering in the stark light of the pier floodlights. He could see the seams of the anechoic rubbery sonar coating at the twelve missile doors of the vertical launch system, a reminder of the power of this ship, able to reach out from far at sea to the most remote inland bunker with a cruise missile warhead. Already enemies in another hemisphere had suffered the sting of these weapons. But they wouldn't in the future, not under his orders.

Vornado sniffed as he reached into his uniform tunic and unclasped the capital ship command pin and pulled it off. He weighed it in his hands for a moment, then looked at it in the harsh light of the floodlamps. It was over, he thought. Time to consign the pin to the sea. He tossed the insignia pin into the water of the slip, watched the ripples from it, and imagined it sinking to the bottom of the slip beneath the bow of the *Hampton*. He stared at the water where it had vanished, then heard approaching footsteps behind him.

"Captain?" an incredulous young voice called. "Captain Vornado? Sir?"

Vornado turned to see the crackerjack-clad topside security sailor jogging up to him, an expression of disbelief written across his face. The youth skidded to a halt, his body snapping to attention, his salute razor sharp. "Good morning, sir," he said, beginning to smile. "It really is you. Welcome back, sir."

Vornado returned the young sonarman's salute, smiling gently at him. "I just came to take one last look at the old girl, Petty Officer Simmons." The arrival of the sentry had broken the spell, he thought. "I should go. As you were." He turned on his heel, a lump arriving in his throat. Those first footsteps away from the submarine that he had commanded, from his former life, seemed the hardest he would ever walk. It was like leaving behind a dream. Never again would he make the orders to get the submarine under way or to rig her for dive. Never again would he make the order to submerge the ship. Never again would he feel the cool rubbery eyepiece of the periscope against his eye socket as the ship ascended from below the deep thermal layer to periscope depth, the silvery undersides of the waves lazily growing closer in his vision, the periscope view breaking through the foamy wash until the surface became starkly clear, the crosshairs framing that day's target. Never again would he feel the thrill of the crew moving to his commands at battlestations, the weapons moving into the tubes, the heavy and angry bark of the torpedo tubes, or the rushing roar of the vertical launch system as the ship attacked her enemies.

He was glad that he had made his good-bye in the cold predawn hour, when there was no one to witness his swollen eyes or his running nose. He walked quickly down the pier back to the gangway of the tender ship, climbing the steel stairs of the three-story-tall stair tower to the 01 deck.

Fortunately, he thought, the commodore was an early riser—Vornado could complete this miserable business of being discharged and go on to the next chapter of his life, whatever that might be.

He found himself at the squadron commander's outer office. Some twenty photographs of submarines were bolted to the bulkheads. Brenda, the chubby and well-endowed yeoman, was sitting at the desk. She jumped to her feet, rushed around the desk, and hugged him so hard he almost lost his balance. He stared at her, and she blushed a deep scarlet, muttering that she thought they had lost him. He smiled kindly at her, but realized she was right—the squadron had lost him. The door opened, and Commodore Kraft came out. Kraft was an imposing figure, drawing stares wherever he went. He was well over six feet tall, a former Academy brigade boxer, the runner-up for brigade champion. He was in his mid-forties but looked older by virtue of his tanned leathery face, the crow's-feet deep at the corners of his eyes. His face was thin, with stark cheekbones and a pronounced jawline. He had a full head of graying and slightly thinning blonde hair, oddly dark eyebrows, and clear blue eyes. His nose, broken in the championship fight he had lost by decision, had never been fixed and gave him a pugnacious look, although his usual expression was one of enlightened benevolence. He was thin now, having lost the bulky muscles of his youth, but his shoulders were still broad. He smiled at Vornado, revealing white but slightly uneven teeth, his face crinkling happily. His massive boxer's paw carefully shook Vornado's hand while his other hand pulled him into his second bear hug of the morning.

Kraft ushered Vornado into the commodore's office, asking questions about the course of the illness and his present medical status. For a half second Vornado felt a lingering hope that Kraft would grant him command of his old submarine, but the commodore's face had fallen as he pronounced the words that ended Vornado's career.

"Peter, I'm sorry. Rachel gave me the good news and I jumped on it. I made every call I could, called in every single marker, but you scared the type commander during that torpedo exercise with Dillinger." The type commander was Admiral Chesty Schwarz, the admiral in com-

mand of the Atlantic fleet's submarine force. "We thought
we were going to lose you at sea during an exercise that
the crew thought was war. Schwarz got burned by the
Chief of Naval Operations for not ending the exercise
when you were first experiencing severe headaches, and
in the flap a hundred memos flew about the health of
senior officers at sea and what needed to be done if a
captain got sick. Admiral Schwarz called me back and said
that even if he got a favorable medical recommendation,
he would be taking an extreme risk putting a former brain
cancer patient in charge of a ship capable of carrying nuclear weapons. Dammit, Peter, it's like they think you'll
drop in your boots two minutes from now, or in their
minds do something worse, like go crazy from a brain
tumor and jeopardize nuclear security. The ironic thing is
that it was your superb performance during that exercise
that got the attention of the brass in the first place, but
now that they're involved, they insist on doing the right
thing—or at least what's right in their minds. I'm afraid
we just can't bring you back. As far as the Navy's concerned, you're no longer physically qualified for unrestricted line sea duty. I'm really sorry."

"Thanks, Commodore," Vornado said, trying to smile. "I
appreciate everything you've done for me, but don't blame
Schwarz. If you didn't know me, you might have made the
same call. I should have expected this."

Vornado bit his lip, the office around him and Kraft
seeming far distant, as if they were playing on a television
screen in the background. His mind whirled, wondering
what his future held for him. He had refused to think
farther than this moment, his hopes riding on Kraft's
allowing him to go back to sea, or at least ordering him
to undergo a medical evaluation and letting the doctors
decide whether he was fit. Now that he was facing a door
shut in his face, he had to move on to the next chapter,
and there was a part of him that seemed directionless.
He'd have to talk to Rachel about all this. She'd always
had a level head and her own ambitions, and had given
him some solid advice over the years leading to his command position. The first thing she would ask was what
benefit it would be to him to stay in the Navy for the time
being, and how he felt about it. For a few seconds he

concentrated on how it would feel to command a desk at the Pentagon or ComSubLant or CinCLantFleet. Immediately he saw that doing that would frustrate him. Dammit, he cursed to himself. He was not even thirty-nine years old, and already he was sidelined. He would certainly be passed over for promotion to captain, and in the up-or-out naval service, that would eventually lead to the brass showing him the door. But what else was he qualified to do? By education he was a mechanical engineer. He was fluent in French and Russian, thanks to the influence of both sets of grandparents, who insisted on speaking their native tongues during their frequent visits, and from Vornado's electives in foreign languages. He began to wonder about working overseas, and wondered if there was anyone he knew in the private sector who would hire him. Perhaps he could do some good working for the State Department while he made plans to work in private industry, but he would be less useful to them if he were unable to travel. The idea of a foreign assignment, while perhaps exciting, didn't fit with his desire to be closer to his family after they had almost lost him. The idea occurred to him that he had the foreign-language skills, the top-level security clearances, and the requisite exposure to intelligence business, and that perhaps he should consider the Defense Intelligence Agency, the National Security Agency, or even the CIA. He almost chuckled at himself as he saw himself with a cloak and dagger, and then he realized Kraft had been speaking to him.

"I'm sorry, sir, could you repeat that?"

"I was saying that you were captain of *Hampton* for a year, Peter. In another two years you would be postcommand anyway. You're just arriving at the desk stage of your career a little early. You were my best submarine skipper, perhaps the best on the entire East Coast. You'll have my highest recommendation for commodore. There's no reason your career can't be just as good as it was before." The old man's voice had a pleading tone to it.

Vornado thought about it, but Kraft's suggestion seemed flawed. He'd only been in command for a year, and would have trouble commanding more seasoned submarine captains. He did love the submarine force. He loved the life, the people, the work. He could help these men with their

problems; he could still breathe this sea air of urgency, and
watch the submarines sortie for their missions, be there for
them when they needed help from home. But then the
thought of being ashore and watching the ships leaving the
piers without him seemed vastly depressing. As much as he
loved the force, it would kill him to watch it from the side-
lines. Some men made the transition from quarterback to
coach effortlessly, but perhaps not Vornado. It was time
for him to move on, he decided.

"I know, sir, and thank you. I don't want you to think
I'm not grateful. It's just that I'm different now. I'm not
the same man they medevaced out of the *Hampton*. I'm
not sure how much time I have, if this thing comes back
in a year or five years. Something is telling me to move on,
sir, and maybe I should listen to that."

Kraft opened his mouth to speak, then thought better of
it. After an uncomfortable moment, he asked, "Do you
have anything in mind for the future?"

Vornado shrugged. "I have a lot of thinking to do about
that, sir. I honestly don't know. But I have a last request."

"Anything in my power, Peter."

"I want my discharge to be effective by the end of the
month, Commodore. If I'm going to move on, I want to
get going."

Kraft nodded solemnly. "I'll see what I can do, Peter. If
I can't get a medical discharge processed that fast, I'll at
least get you on terminal leave. You can go about your
business that way."

Vornado stood. "Thanks, Commodore."

He gripped the older man's hand, then left the office.
Brenda came over for one last hug. He grabbed his cap
and walked out of the senior staff level to the long gangway
to the pier. When he stood on the concrete of pier three
he looked across the slip at the submarines of the squadron.
B. K. Dillinger's *Tucson* was docked far at the end, her
bow facing seaward, the way Dillinger liked it. It was
shortly after eight, which was too early to go over and visit
Dillinger. The ship would be a flurry of busy activity until
shortly before lunch. It would be better to go home and
talk to Rachel, Vornado thought. Perhaps later he could
see his old friend. A few beers at the waterfront hole-in-
the-wall biker bar would do his soul good after a day like

this. Shaking his head, Vornado walked slowly to his car. He looked around one last time before ducking into it for the drive back to the house. After a moment he sighed and wheeled the old Corvette back south.

14

Hank Lewis sat down at the south end of the thirty-foot-long polished oak conference table and plugged his computer into the network, then ran his hand through his thick hair as he did when he was nervous. Briefings for the Executive Committee tended to be limited to fifteen minutes, or perhaps a half hour if the project would capture the interest of the White House or the oversight committee. Late yesterday Lewis had learned that the ExComm, including the Director of Central Intelligence, would be attending Lewis's Project Goldfish cost-and-status meeting, and wanted a three-hour, fully detailed presentation. The thought of facing the director himself made Lewis sweat through his collar even in the near arctic blast of the room's air-conditioning.

Today Hank Lewis alone was responsible for keeping Project Goldfish from earning the disapproval of the DCI, who had had summary briefings on the operation but only now wanted to receive the project's details and participate in its major decisions. Lewis contemplated the months of work it had taken to penetrate the Terminal, the incredible effort it had taken to get close to the Terminal's security director, the day the first photographs had come in from inside the facility, and the two fatalities the project had already suffered—one from an accident during agent insertion, the other still under investigation. The thought of the director canceling the program or pruning it to bare bones made Lewis's stomach ache. Lewis's bosses were counting on him to present the program favorably to the director to avoid such a result. Yet Lewis had to avoid the trap of overselling the project, because stretching the truth to the director could cause one of his famous instant demotions or reassignments. There was no doubt this briefing was a high-stakes personal gamble. Lewis had stared at the ceiling half the night worrying about the presentation.

It would have been difficult enough were it simply a normal cost-and-status report with the director attending. This was much worse, because there was an issue, that dreaded term to every senior operations officer. An issue meant things weren't under precise control, which was what the clandestine service was paid for. Issues killed projects and they killed careers. Lewis berated himself that his career meant so much to him, but this was the center ring, the big leagues, The Show. Lewis might be a humble civil servant, but then how many of his Stanford classmates could claim that they had risen three levels below directorship of CIA covert operations and been named to manage the flagship project of the entire Anti-Proliferation Task Force? Lewis forced his mind back to the issue itself, the bolt from the blue from his contacts inside the Navy. Lewis had immediately called a meeting with his boss, the Director of the Anti-Proliferation Task Force, Phillip Cogsworth.

Cogsworth had grown up in the Cold War CIA, and was a ruthless and excitable operator, but to his subordinates was even, affable, and supportive. He bore an uncanny resemblance to Joseph Stalin, consciously or unconsciously sporting the same overgrown mustache and clipped hairstyle. After hearing Lewis's news from the Navy, Cogsworth hoisted a phone and called the Deputy Director of Operations, Kenneth "Roger" Bostonian. Lewis's pulse raced for a moment. Bostonian was a tough bastard, one of the senior managers best avoided if at all possible. Bostonian had crashed into the conference room, a thundercloud on his bone-thin face. It was said that if Bostonian, with his shaved head, sunken cheeks, and deep eye sockets, wore crossed human bones instead of his usual bloodred necktie, he would look like the Jolly Roger pirate flag, which had inevitably led to his nickname. Lewis explained the news from the Navy, and Bostonian's face eased into a predator's smile. In his nasal Indiana accent, Bostonian directed Lewis to bring the issue up at the briefing. Risky decisions were rarely made at a cost-and-status report, but Bostonian said that the DCI was insisting more and more on being in the flow of the real work. When Bostonian left, Lewis wondered if he had been set up, since Bostonian was notoriously treacherous. Several of Lewis's friends had Roger's knives in their backs, and though he'd never set his sights on Lewis, it was rare for Bostonian to reveal his motives. As Lewis waited for the meeting to begin, his mind raced as he went over what he would say about this, new doubts creeping in. There was a thin line between sudden brilliant, inspired ideas and half-baked, poorly conceived ones, and the more he thought about this, the more it resembled the latter rather than the former.

As the hour neared for the meeting, people began to drift into the room. The coffee and pastries arrived, a spread suitable to a Fortune 500 boardroom. The members of the ExComm wandered in as a group, including Deputy Director Spandrel, DDO Bostonian, and the deputy directors of Intelligence, Science and Technology, and Personnel. Lewis adjusted his tie and took a final sip of coffee as he waited. He looked up to see that every chair in the room was filled except for the one in the middle of the long edge of the table, facing the bank of windows. The air of expectation in the room was palpable. The clicking of footsteps outside the door could be heard, and Lewis stood.

Director Robert McKinley strode confidently into the room, smiled and shook some hands on the way to the front, then looked over at Lewis. It was startling to look at the director, Lewis thought, because he had no discernible physical flaws—it was like meeting a celebrity actor who looked better in person than on the big screen. His thick hair was perfectly clipped, his salt-and-pepper beard thick but cut close to his square jawline. McKinley had an athletic, well-muscled six-foot-eight frame draped with a custom-made suit. Lewis realized he was staring far up at McKinley's face, the director's unusual height making him that much more imposing. McKinley reached out with a firm, dry handshake and looked into Lewis's eyes.

"Good morning, Director," Lewis said, hoping he didn't sound nervous. "I'm Hank Lewis."

McKinley nodded his head enthusiastically. When he spoke, his voice was a smooth tenor with a folksy musical cadence. "I've heard great things about you and your work, Hank. Just bear with my ill-informed stupid questions, though."

Lewis stared up at McKinley, finding himself almost disarmed by how genuine and warm the man seemed. The director turned and greeted his ExComm members and found his seat, breaking Lewis's trance.

Lewis darkened the room lights and rolled the curtains closed as the shades lowered. He clicked into his notebook until the presentation appeared on the screen behind him, and he stood and narrated as the multimedia film rolled. It took twenty minutes to bring the room up to the point when the Russians had succeeded in manufacturing a sixty-knot submarine.

"I don't get it, Hank," Director McKinley said, smiling humbly. "The whole presentation so far shows that the Lira was a success. But in your introduction you said it was a failure, and then later you said it turned the tide of the Cold War. Which is it?"

"Let me answer your first comment about the Lira succeeding," Lewis said. "Technically, the program was a failure. By the time it came out, there was really no need to achieve such high submerged speeds. Soviet surveillance satellites were in orbit by 1972, and the Russians could track American aircraft carriers. They couldn't keep as good an eye on American ballistic missile submarines. The Lira couldn't help with that chore, because it had never been designed to be quiet, just to be fast. And the Lira of the 1970s didn't perform up to 1957 expectations. *K-377* had a massive and severe reactor accident during the 1972 maiden voyage sea trials. The reactor compartment was ruined, and removal of individual components became impossible because the liquid-metal coolant froze solid. The ship was broken up and the nonnuclear spaces abandoned. In 1973 Project 705 was denounced by the Central Committee Secretary for Defense D. F. Ustinov for its cramped spaces and inaccessibility for repair and maintenance. The second chief designer, Rusanov, was fired and hauled to Siberia to join Petrov, and Vladimir Romin took over for him, but it was much too late to save Project 705.

"The Lira-class submarines put into service after *K-377* were even worse, and immediately developed severe problems. The automated systems and instrumentation were unable to withstand the radiation of the high power-density reactors, and became unreliable. The subs were hated by their crews and by the hierarchy of the Soviet Navy. The deal between Rusanov and the Navy had landed both in hot water, and after Rusanov disappeared to the gulag the Navy withdrew all support. The admirals cut off funding for spares and maintenance and the sailors sabotaged the submarines whenever possible while their officers looked on. Even if the Navy had been enthusiastic about the Liras, by design they were unmaintainable, their coolant would freeze if unattended, their reactors could never be shut down, their sensors were custom-designed for the Lira class alone and had no common spare parts.

"It should come as no surprise that four of the seven Liras built would experience severe nuclear accidents, some of them fatal to crewmembers, all of them breaking those individual ships beyond repair. The Soviet Navy's funding for the Lira class was cut to zero. The Navy's own exercises with the Liras that did work showed that the Liras were incredibly loud. When they ran at high speed, the Lira could be heard hundreds of miles away even on Soviet sonars. The noise problems of the seven subs were never fixed in the shipyards, although it remained technically feasible."

A black-and-white film of a deserted arctic coastline rolled on the display. There were abandoned submarine hulls littering the frame, some listing over pathetically, one half-sunk in a shallow slip, one beached and rusting in the sandy wasteland.

"In 1982, Project 705 was declared a total loss. One submarine hull was refitted with a pressurized water reactor for training purposes, but the remainder were to be taken from active service. Reactor sections were pulled out of the submarines and laid up in abaondoned sites in the Kola Peninsula area, where high-level radioactive waste was stored. The Soviets, already financially bled by the Lira-class subs, did not scrap or decommission the reactor sections; nor did they dismantle the nonnuclear sections. The Lira-class submarine—one of the most innovative submarine designs in the world, born prematurely in 1957, a full fifty years ahead of its time—was officially dead, never to return. In a desolate city in the Russian north, Gremikha, the Lira graveyard has remained untouched since the 1980s."

McKinley frowned. "Okay. The Lira was a failure. I'm even more confused now. So far we have a failed submarine that changes the history of the Cold War."

"I know, sir," Lewis said apologetically. "It's a convoluted story, but the punch line is worth it if you stick with me. You see, from the Russian side of the story, Lira *was* a terrible failure. But had they known its effect on the West, the Kremlin would have declared it a tremendous success and made Petrov and Rusanov heroes of the Soviet Union."

McKinley stared at Lewis.

"Now comes the odd part," Lewis continued, "and the answer to why the sub was so historically important. The Lira class scared the hell out of the Pentagon and the White House. *K-377*'s tremendous speed struck fear into the Western defense community—not only could the new submarine outrun our torpedoes, it could dive deeper than the crush depth of our torpedoes. The new submarine—which the CIA knew relatively little about—was named Alfa by NATO and the Pentagon, a twist on the letter alpha, the first letter of the alphabet, the primary and fundamental letter. It made intelligence and defense headlines over here—a submarine completely invulnerable to attack, able to zip across an ocean and take out an aircraft carrier, and there was nothing we could do about it short of shooting a nuclear depth bomb at it, a nuke that would surely miss.

"Now put yourself in the mentality of an American admiral in 1972. The Soviet Union is supposedly mass-producing an ultrafast submarine that can streak across the oceans and clobber your attack subs and your ballistic missile subs, giving the Russians a gigantic advantage in sea-launched ballistic missiles. As I said before, the Pentagon was counting very heavily on the survival of the sea-launched missiles for deterrence, because they were really the only second-strike weapons we had—we expected the land-based Air Force bombers and silo missiles would be wiped out by a sneak attack from the Soviet ICBMs, but we believed our submarine missiles would keep the Russians from doing something so rash. Now, with the Alfa, an underwater blitzkrieg would take out our deterrent capability, sink all our submarines, and run faster than our weapons. The Soviets could win a first-strike nuclear war. In the minds of the admirals, the CIA, and the White House, the appearance of the Alfa submarine meant we'd lose the Cold War."

Lewis let the last sentence sink in while he clicked his notebook. The display rolled footage of the Los Angeles–class submarine plowing through the sea, its wake streaming violently behind it.

"After the initial blow, the admirals formulated a plan to counter the Alfa. They created the Los Angeles–class submarine—a much faster design than previous American subs, but still unable to compete in the same arena as Alfa—and the sixty-knot deep-diving Mark 48 ADCAP torpedo. The Alfa soon became known to be extremely noisy, but NATO believed this to be a cosmetic flaw, one that could be repaired. Alfa was only noisy during her maximum-speed run—she could flash clear across the Atlantic, slow down, and acoustically vanish."

McKinley pursed his lips. "None of this intelligence on the Lira's failure was available then?"

"That's correct. A lot of what you are seeing here was obtained in the eighties or nineties. In the mid-1970s, all we had were rumors. From our side of the Atlantic, the Alfa, if built in quantity, could defeat our entire Navy. The Alfa looked like the Soviets planned it as a preemptive naval strike, as part of a coordinated plan to win World War Three. The fact that it was born twenty years earlier as a plan to intercept aircraft carriers was completely unknown to us."

McKinley shook his head. "Good Lord, if nothing else, this is a story of why intelligence agencies are so important. Both sides chased their tails on this one."

Lewis nodded. "To the tune of trillions of dollars and decades wasted." Lewis clicked the next slide, which replayed the view of the abandoned Lira hulls in the Kola coastal nuclear waste areas.

"That takes us to today. The Kola sites hold enough submarine parts to reassemble six Liras from the remains. The cost of scrapping a contaminated nuclear submarine with liquid-metal coolant was so high that the Soviets just abandoned them in the Kola beaches, where they've been since the eighties. At least they were."

The display changed to an overhead satellite view of the

arctic coast. "Year-old routine satellite photographic passes of the Russian north coast—low-priority photo intelligence—were eventually analyzed and compared to older photos, and something very ominous was uncovered—the wreckage of the Liras disappeared."

"Taken by the men who built the Terminal?"

"Yes. At first this was a lower-level threat, because a drug-runner submarine is a problem for our national drug policy but not to our national defense. We could keep an eye on it for DEA and let them make the eventual bust. But then this happened."

Lewis's screen showed a helicopter view of a mountainside villa, a huge stone castle overlooking a vast valley.

"This is a 'before' shot of drug kingpin Orlando Suarto's estate." The display changed to show a blackened blast crater with the back walls half standing. "This is the 'after' shot."

"Christ! What happened?"

The display flashed up a surveillance film of a Middle Eastern man at an airport. "This is General Abdas al-Sattar, leader of Egypt's Ahel al Beit faction. Abdas had a short visit with Suarto a few days ago, and this was the result. We think he purchased the Lira being reconstructed at the Terminal from Sergei Kaznikov by eliminating Kaznikov's customer. Kaznikov could keep Suarto's deposit and pocket a greater price from al-Sattar."

"No honor among thieves."

"There is, but only to the extent that deals can be enforced at gunpoint. Most of Suarto's associates were killed in the assassination, so there is no one to get revenge on Abdas. And radical terrorists like Abdas are difficult to approach."

The display clicked to the same interior view of the Terminal that Lewis had shown Kaminsky, showing three gleaming metal cylinders being hoisted by the Terminal's bridge crane.

"That leaves us with this. We think they're fifty-three-centimeter-diameter torpedo tubes. These are capable of launching Granat cruise missiles. The RK-55 Granat, or SS-N-21 Sampson in NATO code, is a Russian Tomahawk with a two hundred–kiloton nuclear warhead and a range of three thousand kilometers, and can be launched from a

fifty-three-centimeter submerged torpedo tube. We believe
Abdas is having them installed in the new Lira to make
it able to launch them against Israel. We have separate
intelligence that proves Abdas has been successful in ob-
taining four Granats. In less than four months, Abdas will
be at sea with between two and four nuclear cruise missiles
in a submarine too quiet for us to find."

"Wait a minute," McKinley said. "I thought you said the
Lira was loud."

"Yes, sir, I did. I also told you that fixing the loudness
would be easy. The new construction has installed sound
mounts engineered in this decade. Equipment and decks
have been isolated from the hull. We have a big problem,
Director. The Lira is now as quiet as our Los Angeles submarine. And not only that—it can still outrun our torpedoes. This is our nightmare—a radical terrorist on an
invisible submarine that can't be targeted, capable of
speeds we can't match, armed with nuclear weapons."

McKinley took a deep breath. "I see the problem. What
does the Navy think of the new improved Alfa?"

Lewis bit his lip and admitted that no one at Defense
had been briefed, but he did mention the recent exercise
the Navy had conducted with a stolen 688 submarine and
the tasking of the *Hampton* to find and take down the
hijacked submarine.

McKinley's eyes widened. He asked if there was a presentation he could see on that. Lewis attacked his notebook
computer, finding the backup briefing Tina Rancourt had
put together on the exercise as a contingency for McKinley's famous curiosity. Lewis let the highly edited film clip
roll as the screen depicted footage taken from the commando's headset cameras and the film taken from the *Hampton*
during the mission. McKinley was impressed by the performance of the commando team, with a nod to Buffalo Patterson and naked admiration for the *Albany*'s insurgent
submarine commander—even directing that Bostonian
make discreet recruitment offers to both for assignments in
the agency. But McKinley seemed particularly struck by
the performance of the *Hampton* captain when the ship
encountered the torpedo bearing down on them from out
of nowhere as they neared the Cape of Good Hope. When
Commander Vornado fell unconscious, McKinley covered

his mouth with his hand, completely absorbed. When Lewis brought the lights back on, McKinley blinked as he asked about Vornado.

"Sir, that actually brings me to the issue of this project." Lewis swallowed, noticing McKinley gazing at him earnestly with an expression of encouragement. Lewis punched a button, and suddenly Peter Vornado's service portrait flashed up on the screen, his chiseled stern face glaring out at the room from under his white senior officer's cap. Lewis described Vornado's battle with fatal brain cancer and the treatment he'd undergone at Duke University, his miraculous cure, and his subsequent dismissal from unrestricted line duty with the Navy. "Commander Vornado is of particular interest to us, Director. He was one of the best submarine captains in the fleet. Actually, I'm understating this. An excerpt from Vornado's last fitness report reads, 'Commander Vornado is without doubt the most innovative submarine commanding officer the Navy has seen in a generation.' His boss, Commodore Joe Kraft, is beside himself about losing Vornado, but the Navy's medical requirements are severe and explicit, and Kraft's bosses aren't willing to take a risk keeping him at sea. I know what you may be wondering, sir. Why Vornado and not half a dozen other ex–submarine commanders who are presently available to be recruited?" Lewis clicked his notebook to the next slide, a page from Vornado's Navy personnel file.

"In addition to being a brilliant submarine tactician, Vornado is also a highly educated engineer. Top of his Annapolis class in mechanical engineering, MIT graduate degree in nuclear engineering, and most of his nuclear engineering doctorate requirements met at UVA. He would have completed his thesis after this sea tour. Vornado spent a split department head tour as a nuclear chief engineer in the shipyards—two years in new construction of a Virginia-class ship and two years overhauling a 688-class submarine. He certainly knows his way around a drydock. He went on to the staff of Commander Submarines Atlantic Fleet to rewrite the book on submarine operations and tactics. We became even more keenly interested in him based on his family background. Vornado's multilingual—fluent in Russian and French, the influence of both his grandparents from the old country. Vornado's talents, combined with his linguistic skills and his work and his ancestors' work at the shipyards, make him an outstanding potential recruit for this project."

McKinley looked at his watch, then stared intensely at Lewis, his encouraging expression gone. "So, Hank, where are you going with this?"

Lewis took a deep breath while holding McKinley's stare. "Sir, we could insert Vornado into the Terminal as a first-tier contingency. If the Kaznikovs manage to resurrect the Alfa, Vornado could aid in the extreme contingency plan to disable it and keep it from going to sea. If, God help us, the Kaznikovs manage to put the new Alfa to sea, we could get Vornado to be an adviser to her captain. If we can get him to sea on the Alfa, he could find a way to sabotage the ship and keep it from doing its dirty work."

McKinley kept Lewis's stare for a long moment. "What's the downside? Give me the three extremes."

McKinley was also notorious for demanding the "three extreme cases"—the best, most likely, and worst-case scenarios.

"Well, sir, all three extremes feature the possibility that Vornado might turn us down. He did just recover from a deadly disease, his heath is fragile, and he may not want to spend six months on the other side of the globe away from his family on a risky mission."

McKinley waved the objection away impatiently. "Give me mission downsides."

"Best case, Vornado succeeds in delaying the submarine or disabling it in the Terminal so long that Abdas withdraws his funding. Most likely case, Vornado helps keep the Alfa from being fully functional if it is able to go to sea, with the goal that the SS-N-21s will malfunction and fail to reach their target, or he performs actions that will allow the Navy to target the Alfa and if necessary, take it down."

McKinley's expression was somber as he nodded. "Okay. Worst case?"

"Obviously, sir, Vornado's not a trained operations officer, and we don't have time to run him through a year at Camp Peary. Vornado's an amateur, and his lack of training could cause him to make a mistake. He could be caught and tortured, and he could give away the entire operation before being killed, leading to the loss of all our assets in place. Even worse, Abdas al-Sattar gets the Alfa to sea, the Navy's not able to find it or sink it, and the SS-N-21s fly to Israel and detonate almost a megaton nuclear blast over Tel Aviv. Congress demands hearings, the whole thing becomes public knowledge, the president is impeached, and the CIA is defunded and dissolved—"

"Good God, Hank," Bostonian interrupted, his eyebrows climbing high on the thin skin of his forehead. "When you do a worst-case scenario, you take it all the way!"

McKinley suddenly snorted in laughter. On cue, the other senior managers began to snicker. Bostonian broke into a jack-o'-lantern grin. "And you forgot to mention, Hank, the end of Western civilization as we know it, and, oh, yeah, dogs will stop being man's best friend." McKinley laughed again, and the managers began chattering for a few moments. Lewis realized that he was flushing. He had never anticipated that the result of his remarks would be laughter.

As quickly as the room's levity came, it vanished. A curtain seemed to come down over McKinley's expression. His voice was flat when he glanced at his watch and said, "Hank, why don't you bring us back to the cost-and-status report?"

Lewis clicked into the main presentation, sure he was still blushing in embarrassment. Luckily, the room was still dark. McKinley and his lieutenants were sober and quiet as he ran though the financial details and the timeline of the operation and the probability arrow diagram of anticipated results and the five tiers of contingency plans written in the case of operation component failures. When he finished and turned on the lights, McKinley glanced up at him with a serious look and nodded, then stood and shook Lewis's hand.

"Thanks, Hank. Great presentation. Ken, we're late for the oversight committee prep."

With no indication of what McKinley thought of the Vornado issue, Lewis watched as the Executive Committee evaporated from the room, leaving behind a trail of empty coffee cups, napkins, and pastry crumbs. Lewis shook his head, thinking back to how ridiculous he had sounded in his worst-case scenario. He should have stopped at the Alfa getting to sea, but he had to paint the whole bloody picture.

Before Cogsworth left, he told Lewis to wait for him in his office.

Lewis walked slowly back to the task force's wing in the new administration building and waited for Cogsworth in one of his plush leather club chairs. The twenty minutes seemed like two hours. Finally Cogsworth entered, his face inscrutable. He held up a finger and took two urgent phone calls, called in his assistant and barked several terse orders, then closed the door and sat down opposite Lewis in one of the other club chairs.

"Well, sir? How bad is it?"

"Wasn't bad at all, Hank. McKinley likes you and he loved the presentation."

Lewis wanted to shout, but he forced himself to wait.

"McKinley had a word with Bostonian before he went into the prep meeting. Bostonian said he had insisted this be brought up at the meeting, but he still thought it was too risky. He recommended we turn down the Vornado recruitment. Sorry, Hank. We got a red light."

Lewis looked down at the carpet and ran his hands through his hair, feeling defeated. The idea had been solid, he thought, but he hadn't been able to sell it.

"But the idea's gotten some attention, Hank. Why don't we comb through the ops databases and see if there's anyone with any merchant marine or Navy experience? If we could find a trained operations officer, fluent in Russian, whom we could get to be part of the crew of that Alfa, we might be able to accomplish the same goal."

Lewis had already thought of that, an entire backup presentation done on his computer in the event McKinley asked the same question, and the answer was discouraging. The closest he had come was a Maine Merchant Marine Academy graduate who spoke accented Russian but had worked South America for twenty years, and who had never been to sea since his training days. He decided not to tell Cogsworth that, but returned to his office.

It would have been perfect, he thought. Vornado would have been the perfect asset in place.

"There are real possibilities, here, Chief," Deputy Director of Operations Roger Bostonian said from the plate-glass window overlooking the lush Virginia verdure of the CIA headquarters complex.

"Go ahead," McKinley said from his yacht-size oak desk. He reclined in the huge leather swivel chair and put his feet on the expanse of polished wood.

The main objective of Project Goldfish to date had been to delay the submarine, Bostonian thought, but if they could inject this new person into the mix, they might be able to contain Abdas al-Sattar once and for all. If they could control the situation, it held true promise. Bostonian saw all the possibilities, but the new Director of Central Intelligence, a political appointee who'd had a brilliant business career, did not. It fell to Bostonian to educate the director, to change him from a civilian to a clandestine service operator.

"Look at this two ways," Bostonian said. "First, without this Navy guy, Vornado. Let's say Lewis's project works. The Alfa is shut down from all the malfunctions that have befallen it thanks to Lewis's operators. It's possible our friend Abdas gets disgusted with the Alfa project and slinks away into the woodwork. Perhaps the next time we hear from him, he's got a bomb we don't know about. And this time it's going off at the Lincoln Memorial. Project Goldfish's success is our bitter failure."

McKinley nodded as Bostonian raised an eyebrow from the bar. Bostonian poured two fingers of the Balvenie Single Barrel scotch and handed it to the director. McKinley sipped, half shut his eyes, and nodded again. "You said two ways."

"Right. Now consider the same Project Goldfish with Commander Vornado in place. Except the mission parameters are subtly different. The idea is to get the submarine to go to sea with Abdas al-Sattar aboard. Get him inside the damned thing. With Vornado, we can have the Alfa into blue water, where Abdas is all alone in the ocean. There, away from the eyes of the other governments, Vornado allows us to take down Abdas. Abdas is gone forever, and the best part of it is we get all the credit. And a little bonus, boss—we can let certain details leak out, showing how close a call it was. 'Reworked Russian Supersub Seconds away from Firing Cruise Nukes at Israel'—it may not ever be a headline in the open media, but it sure as hell will be in the Congressional Oversight Committee hearing room. It's not for me to tell you the business, sir, but from my experience, at CIA we get a little more bang for our buck from close calls like this one than from tame operations that go completely according to plan. Go figure, but if you scare the congressmen, they'll stay up sweating all night and double your budget in the morning."

Director McKinley finished the scotch and stared up at Bostonian, who was nursing a Tennessee sour-mash whiskey.

"So Abdas goes down in this reworked Russian monstrosity. How does that happen?"

"I'd leave the details to Lewis and his crew. One of the options is that our shipyard crew could install a noisemaker that Vornado activates. Think of it as a tracking beacon. One of our attack submarines lies in wait, tracks the Alfa from the beacon, or from some other of a thousand tricks Vornado could pull, and the SSN fires torpedoes at the Alfa before it even knows it's had. Vornado would then disable any counterattack from the inside."

"So what happens to our friend Vornado?"

Bostonian stared back at McKinley and raised his shoulder in a half shrug. "He gives his all for the cause. We'll erect a star in the lobby of the old administration building. The president will console his widow at the top-secret ceremony. It will all be very touching."

McKinley dropped his feet to the floor and yawned. "It is promising. Let's go grab some dinner and talk about it some more."

Anti-Proliferation Task Force Director Cogsworth had been standing in Hank Lewis's doorway for some time before Lewis noticed him.

"Hey, Phil," Lewis said. "Burning a little midnight oil?"

"The word just came down," Cogsworth said. "McKinley and Bostonian have ordered us to recruit Vornado." Cogsworth broke into a grin and extended his dry, cracked hand. Lewis shook it, unable to control the expression of delight on his face. "Good job, Hank. There's just one thing. The director wants updates twice a week, just you and him, man-to-man. I hope you're in shape, because he wants his briefing done at his treadmill session at noon on Tuesdays and Fridays. You'll have to talk and run at the same time."

Lewis smiled. "No problem, boss."

"So what do you think? Will Vornado sign up with us for a mission this hazardous?"

Lewis stood up and smiled confidently. "If I can convince the Director of Central Intelligence, I'm sure I can sell it to Vornado."

But as he walked down the corridor to his office, Lewis was not so sure. He frowned, trying to put himself in the shoes of a man back from brain cancer, and couldn't do it. Perhaps he could succeed the same way he had with McKinley—by telling the complete truth.

15

Hank Lewis paced his office in the new administration building at CIA headquarters. He would have only one chance to recruit Peter Vornado, and he couldn't risk blowing it. The worst part of this was that Vornado would practically have to accept the assignment before Lewis could brief him on it, and there was no reason why Vornado would want to accept it without knowing what was involved. The work would mean he'd have to leave his family for no less than five or six months, perhaps more. Lewis pursed his lips—in reality, for Vornado, this might mean risking his life and the very real possibility of his never returning to the family. *Something that a cancer survivor would jump at,* he thought bitterly.

He had almost immediately regretted his overconfident words to Cogsworth about the Vornado recruitment. Fortunately, Cogsworth was an understanding boss, and in his thirty-five-year career had seen it all. Cogsworth had spent all day yesterday brainstorming with Lewis.

"Did you consider just using a financial package?" Cogsworth asked, meaning a payment so big that any sane man would think twice before turning it down. "Make him an offer he can't refuse. We certainly have the budget for it."

"Ah, Phil, Vornado's not motivated by money. It'd just make him suspicious. If I throw a six- or seven-figure number under his nose, he'd back away, maybe even think he's being approached by the wrong team."

"It's up to you, but you have one chance. Go in cheap and ask Vornado to disappear to a foreign shipyard and he's likely to turn us down cold. Don't forget, Vornado is as accountable to his wife as any married man—this is your weakness, Hank. You single guys just don't understand women."

Lewis grinned despite his melancholy. "Why don't you educate me, Professor?"

"Pay attention, my son. What do married women worry about?"

Lewis shrugged. "I don't know—shoes? Their butts being too big?"

"You idiot." Cogsworth smirked. "Security! Safety! *Money,* for God's sake. Show me a mother with kids, and I'll show you a creature who will jump at a shot at a million dollars. You put a nice offer in front of Vornado, make it big enough to open his wife's eyes, and he's in the palm of your hand. Trust me. This will work."

The phone rang. Smokin' Joe Kraft's gravelly voice blared in Vornado's ear: "Peter, it's Joe. How are you getting along?"

"Commodore," Vornado said, genuine pleasure in his voice. "I'm good. How are you, sir?" Vornado might be a civilian now, but he'd never be able to call Kraft by his first name.

"Jesus, call me Joe, will ya?"

Vornado laughed. "Sorry, Commodore. Old habit. What's up?"

"Well, unfortunately, Peter, all I have today is bad news. I've been pulling out every stop trying to get your medical disqualification for line duty reversed, but there's just no way. So I've been calling in a boatload of favors to get you to be considered for full retirement pay, and I'm hitting brick walls everywhere. I'm damned sorry, Peter. I just wish there were something I could do for you."

"Thanks, Commodore, you've been a stand-up boss start to finish. I appreciate it, I really do, but you don't have to keep fighting my battles."

"Least I can do, Peter. How's your head?"

"I'm better, sir." Vornado didn't mention the fatigue or recent weak headaches, which were probably just signs of stress. "They patched me all up. Good as new."

"How's the job hunt?"

"Not very promising so far," Vornado said, trying to keep his voice even.

"Keep at it, son. It'll break your way."

Twenty minutes after he hung up he got a call from Hank Lewis, who introduced himself as a vice president of advanced submarine projects at General Dynamics–Electric Boat.

16

Hank Lewis's limo dropped Vornado at the house shortly after midnight after a long dinner convincing Vornado to take a job supervising a troubled General Dynamics shipyard project in a remote locale. The catch was that it involved being out of touch with his family for four or five months, but would pay off with an enormous paycheck. Vornado stood on the front porch, watching as the big Lincoln drove away. He realized he was weaving slightly from all the wine they'd consumed. Lewis had asked him to reveal as little as possible to Rachel, but finally admitted that she'd have to know about the money. Vornado still had no idea why this drydock project was such a secret, and why its location remained a mystery, with Lewis continuing to insist that he'd brief Vornado on the plane.

As he turned to open the front door, the world seemed to keep spinning. In the last six months Vornado hadn't had a single drink, with the exception of half a bottle of wine to celebrate his return to health a few weeks ago. Now he went to a dinner and drank like a college kid. He rubbed his aching head as he entered the house, abandoning his plan of waking Rachel. They could talk about it in the morning. As soon as he found the bed he collapsed and fell into a deep, dreamless sleep.

He awoke to the sound of a shriek from downstairs. He opened one crusty eye and saw that it was barely after six. He got up and blinked at the room, again regretting how much he'd drunk the night before. As bad as the hangover felt, though, it was nothing like the headaches he'd suffered from the cancer. He took a deep breath and walked down the stairs. Rachel stood at the kitchen table holding the General Dynamics offer letter in one hand, the other palm pressed to her mouth. She looked up at him with wide eyes and threw her arms around him.

"I knew it, I knew it, I knew you could do it!" she sang. "This is amazing!"

"Whoa, hold on," Vornado said. "There're some problems with this job."

"You didn't turn this down, did you?" Rachel frowned as she dropped her arms to her side.

"Do I look crazy? No, I took the job; it's just that it's apparently in a remote location and involves being out of town for months at a time. It's not final until you agree to this."

"Can't you come back for weekends or a rest period every once in a while? My friend Vicky's husband works in Saudi Arabia, and every six weeks he gets a ten-day trip home."

"It's not like that, honey. All I know is there's no cell reception, no landlines, no Internet. Wherever this job is, it's nowhere near civilization, or it's so highly secret that I'd be essentially sequestered. Either way, I'd be off the grid. You'll be able to call my new boss to see if I'm okay, but otherwise I'll be completely out of touch for a few months. That's one reason the money is so good."

Rachel stared at him, a pout on her pretty face. For a moment Vornado thought she'd tell him to turn down the work, and it was then that he realized how much he wanted to do this thing, despite not knowing exactly what it was he was supposed to do. Finally Rachel sighed and hugged him again.

"Will they promise to fly you back if there's the slightest problem with your health? Or if there's an emergency with one of the kids?"

"I'm sure that won't be a problem."

"So when do you have to go?"

"We fly out tomorrow morning."

"USS *Tucson* duty officer Lieutenant Mercury-Pryce speaking, this is a nonsecure line, may I help you, sir?"

"Merc, it's Peter Vornado. Your captain there?"

"Oh, hi, Commander Vornado. Please stand by, sir." The phone clicked as the duty officer put the phone on hold.

Eventually B. K. Dillinger's smooth, self-assured voice came on the connection.

"Hey, roomie, how's the brain?"

"Good, B.K., good. You got time for a green alert?" A green alert was a tradition at Annapolis, when they'd become first classmen and had the privilege of calling their company officer with five minutes' warning that they were inviting themselves to his house to raid his refrigerator and guzzle his beer. Woe to the company officer who stocked less than a case of refrigerated beer—he'd find his wallet raided for the money to make the beer run.

"Come on over for lunch in the wardroom. Menu is calling for sliders—tempting, I know." Sliders were hamburgers so greasy they were capable of sliding down one's throat unchewed. "But the kids never got a chance to debrief you after the South Atlantic run. We can grab a beer after."

When Vornado arrived at the submarine, he was led below to Dillinger's stateroom. "There he is. What's happening, brother?" Dillinger stood and held out his fists. As he had since Annapolis, Vornado smashed his fists into Dillinger's, then gripped Dillinger's hand in the hardest grip he could manage, Dillinger's large hand crushing his. "Have a seat." Dillinger looked over at Flood. "Steve, you know Peter Vornado. Peter, Steve was my second-in-command on the *Albany* run. He's a damned fine pirate— I trained him myself."

Vornado took a seat opposite Flood at the café-style table against the bulkhead of Dillinger's stateroom. Dillinger sat back down in his high-backed command chair at his fold-down desk.

"How's your XO?" Vornado asked.

Dillinger shook his head. "Davey's still out on a medical." Dillinger's exec, Davey McKee, had broken both legs and his pelvis in a motorcycle accident before Vornado had left for the vacation interrupted by the South Atlantic run.

"Is he going to be okay?"

"Yeah, he'll be fine. But it'll take another year before he learns how to walk again. Steve stepped in for the *Albany* thing and the month after, but the chores of chief engineer are heavy enough without taking on the XO role. This is the new exec's first day. You can meet her at lunch."

"*Her?* Your executive officer's a woman? You're kidding me."

"The USS *Tucson* is Smokin' Joe Kraft's test platform. He and the Chief of Naval Personnel made a deal to staff us up way over the usual ten percent female compliment and see what happens. XO makes three women in the wardroom, with the sonar officer and Steve's main propulsion assistant."

"I didn't think any of the women were senior enough to be XO."

"This one is. Just left a navigator tour of the *Cheyenne*."

Flood stood and addressed Dillinger. "By your leave, Captain."

"Go ahead, Eng." Flood left and shut the stateroom door after him.

"Have you recovered from Stolen Arrows?" Vornado asked.

"I'm still behind in my sleep. We were thrown into an unconventional commando op with a team of SEALs we'd never met before, tasked with performing a mission that should have required a crew three times bigger than we had. That was one result of the critique you missed. We were so shorthanded at running the watches around the clock that by the time we reached the Cape of Good Hope, we were all exhausted. Meanwhile you guys were in a four-section watch rotation with six hours of sleep and four hot meals a day. Hell, if we'd had some goddamned sleep we would have won the exercise."

"Wait a minute," Vornado said, his eyes wide. "I had assumed you guys *did* win the exercise. Your torpedoes detonated all around us. We would have been at the bottom of the South Atlantic if it had been the real thing."

Dillinger shook his head. "After squadron analyzed the tapes they reached the official conclusion that you beat us by twenty seconds. Your SUBROCs nuked us before our torpedoes took you out."

"Oh, please," Vornado said, rolling his eyes. "That's a tie. I'd still have been dead."

"That's what we said," Dillinger said, smiling. "But Smokin' Joe Kraft ruled that you guys lived for a few seconds longer than we did, and your mission succeeded—you stopped the rogue sub from firing cruise nukes—and ours failed because we never made it inside the range circle of Tel Aviv."

Vornado remained unconvinced. "Who's to say in the real thing that the fleet commander would give us nuclear release permission in advance? No one had ever heard of that happening before. In a real operation the admirals would probably not give us nuclear weapon employment permission until the very last minute. If my SUBROCs hadn't flown when they did, early in the conflict, you'd have taken us out."

"You got early nuclear release? That bastard Kraft. That would never happen in real life, international crisis or not."

"I know. You'd have won in the real world."

"I thought I'd learned something from our Induction Day fight—to connect with the first punch. That was one of the reasons I put out the torpedo early. But dammit, anyone else would have shit their pants and run like a pussy. You just calmly stood your ground and planned your attack. If Kraft had sent any other squadron submarine commander I'd have kicked his ass and put four nuclear Tomahawks into Tel Aviv."

Dillinger had spoken as if he were joking, but he was right, Vornado thought.

"Kraft stacked the deck sending *you* out there," Dillinger continued. "He knew that I'd beat anyone else, but he didn't want the brass thinking the submarine hijacking would result in a win for the terrorists. With the early nuclear release and sending you to get me, Smokin' Joe Kraft cheated."

Vornado laughed. " 'Ya ain't cheatin', ya ain't tryin'.' "

The phone by Dillinger's fold-down desk buzzed. He hoisted the heavy black handset to his ear. "Captain," he said, his voice authoritative. "We're on the way." He hung up and looked over at Vornado. "Lunch is served."

Vornado followed Dillinger out of his stateroom and down the ladder to the middle level and across the passageway to the starboard side. The wardroom was the size of Vornado's dining room at the house, but seemed cramped from the large table that took up most of the room. The bulkheads were finished in the ubiquitous artificial wood-grain pattern laminate with stainless-steel trim. The overhead was a perforated metal mesh painted beige. The table was set with a starched linen tablecloth. The places were set with shiny china and gleaming silverware. Vornado felt the rush of nostalgia again, missing being in command as he remembered the thousand meals he had presided over in his wardroom. The chair at the end of the table nearest the galley was Dillinger's. Vornado took the guest seat to his right, the executive officer's customary seat. The XO would sit in the chief engineer's seat on Dillinger's left and bump Steve Flood down one seat. The junior officers all stood behind their seats, not at rigid attention, but in a respectful posture. In unison, as Dillinger entered the room, they all spoke up: "Afternoon, Captain."

"Good afternoon, officers," Dillinger said, smiling at the crowd. "You all know Commander Peter Vornado from the *Hampton,* the winner of the South Atlantic exercise."

Vornado greeted the officers, reaching out and shaking their hands. He remembered Communications Officer Matt "Merc" Mercury-Pryce, Damage Control Assistant Pat Schluss, Weapons Officer Lionel Tonelle, Navigator Rob Cummins, Electrical Officer Kurt Vauxhall, Torpedo Officer Dick O'Dea and Radiation Controls Officer Nick "Neon" Keondre. The two junior officer women were new to Vornado. Dillinger introduced one as Lieutenant Lena Vickerson, Flood's main propulsion assistant. The other was a Lieutenant Junior Grade Leslie Fortunato, the sonar officer. Vornado looked over at the empty executive officer's chair, wondering where Dillinger's new second-in-command was.

Just then the door to the wardroom opened and a tall, slim woman in starched service dress khakis entered. Vornado glanced up from the service plate of sliders, then found himself doing a double take as she took off her officer's cap, laid it on the sideboard, and shook her gleaming long brunette hair out of a ponytail. She was stunning, Vornado thought. Even the mannish-styled service dress khakis couldn't disguise her athletic shoulders, her large chest, her narrow waist, the generous curves of her hips, or her long legs. For a moment Vornado wondered if Dillinger were playing a joke on him—perhaps hiring one of the new exotic dancers at his favorite gentlemen's club to come by and pose as his second-in-command. But the moment her eyes turned to Vornado he knew she was genuine. She looked at him with unflinching directness, her brown eyes wide and elegant. Vornado found himself staring into her face, thinking that she had to have the most perfect features he'd seen since the day he first beheld Rachel. Her sleek brunette hair came down in bangs to her eyebrows. Her nose was a curving sculpture, her cheekbones were strong and slightly upturned at her eyes, and her lips were apple red and thick. Her chin and jawline were graceful curves formed by an inspired artist. Vornado stupidly realized he had stood up to greet her and had blocked her way.

"I'm sorry," he stammered, holding his hand out to her. "I'm Peter Vornado."

She smiled, revealing teeth as white and straight as a movie star's. Slight wrinkles appeared below her eyes as she smiled, the effect bewitching. Her hand came into Vornado's, and a tingle flashed up his spine as he felt the softness of her skin. He looked down at her name tag, which read, CDR. N. D'ASSAULT, XO SSN-750. He wondered if she used the French pronunciation, making it rhyme with *Renault,* or the American version, which would make it sound like it was spelled. It occurred to him that she might think he was looking at her chest inappropriately, and he quickly returned his gaze to her face.

"Peter, meet my new XO, Lieutenant Commander Natalie D'Assault." Dillinger had used the American pronunciation, Vornado noted. "XO, Commander Vornado. Unfortunately you missed the *Albany* mission, XO, but this was the guy who put us on the bottom."

"Pleased to meet you, Commander," she said, her voice a rich symphony, the cadence an East Coast accent, Philadelphia perhaps, and a bit low-pitched for a woman, but somehow it seemed to fit her. "I've heard nothing but great things about you and how *Hampton* stalked our crew in the South Atlantic. I saw the disk, Commander. You did a fantastic job."

Vornado felt himself blushing, unable to find words. He realized he was still holding her hand and blocking her way around the table. "Thanks, XO, but call me Peter," he said, using the universal Navy nickname for her position, which was the only thing anyone aboard would call her for the next three years of her life. Vornado sat in his seat and pulled it up to the table so she could walk behind Dillinger to the seat on his left.

Dillinger looked at his executive officer seriously. "You're late. Problems at squadron?"

D'Assault rolled her large eyes heavenward for a moment. "Scheduling officer can't schedule lunch, Captain, much less the operations of a squadron of submarines. The commodore's got to do something about him."

Dillinger nodded distractedly. "Anything shaking on the schedule?"

"Frankly, sir, there are drastic changes. I thought we'd discuss it after lunch."

Vornado watched Dillinger's interaction with D'Assault. He—and the wardroom's junior officers—didn't even seem to notice her beauty, but treated her as if she were just another senior officer. He was amazed, wondering if his crew on the *Hampton* would have been as professional.

"Fine, XO," Dillinger said laconically, with an expression that was just short of hostility. Vornado wondered if there was some problem between him and D'Assault.

The cooks continued to serve lunch off of silver platters, the tableware and ceremony of the meal starkly contrasting with the humble cuisine. Vornado accepted a roll from a server and assembled his slider, nodding as a server poured iced tea from a gleaming silver pitcher. The junior officers began to talk about sports, Dillinger and D'Assault commenting occasionally. Eventually the topic of the South Atlantic came up. Lieutenant Mercury-Pryce began shooting questions at Vornado about the *Hampton*'s experience of the exercise. Vornado described the op from start to finish, beginning with the helicopter in his backyard. The officers listened raptly. At one point Vornado saw D'Assault staring at him, making him lose his train of thought, but she jumped in to help him, asking an easy question.

Before he realized it, the meal was over. The junior officers excused themselves and rushed back to their division hassles, until only Vornado, D'Assault, and Dillinger remained.

Dillinger stirred his coffee and lifted the china cup for a sip, glancing over the rim at D'Assault.

"So, XO, what's going on with the schedule?"

"May I speak freely in front of your guest, Captain?"

"Sure," Dillinger said, nodding. "Vornado's got all the clearances, if not the need to know. But he's one of us. Go ahead."

D'Assault shook her head. "I couldn't get the full story, Captain. It may fall on you to talk to the commodore. All I could get out of the scheduling officer is that our next two quarters of planning are canceled. There's something brewing up north."

"Up north" meant the North Atlantic, the Norwegian Sea, the Arctic Ocean, and the Barents Sea, the operating areas of the Russian Republic, where Vornado and Dillinger had learned the craft of submarine operations when they were junior officers. But the Russians had been quiet since Vornado's last northern run, he thought.

"You're kidding," Dillinger said, as surprised as Vornado.

"Swear to God," D'Assault continued in her smooth, deep voice. "And whatever's going on, we're going to spend the next six months chasing it. We're instructed to drop all maintenance, button up the ship, take on stores and weapons, and hightail it to sea. Commodore Kraft expects *Tucson* to clear restricted waters by Monday morning."

Dillinger's coffee cup clattered onto its saucer as he stared at D'Assault. "A six-month northern run that starts *Monday*? Smokin' Joe never breathed a word of this."

"I know, Captain," D'Assault said formally. "Commodore Kraft sent down word that he wants to see you in his office on the tender at fourteen hundred."

Dillinger glanced at Vornado. "There goes our green alert, Peter," he said, standing. D'Assault and Vornado stood up also in recognition of seagoing tradition, that when the commanding officer was done at the meal table, the meal was officially over. "Come on up to my stateroom. At least we can catch up until I have to take off to see the boss. XO, meet with the department heads and get them going on the preunderway checklist. Then schedule a meeting with the wardroom at sixteen hundred. Cancel all leaves and get ship's force back aboard by tomorrow, no exceptions, and that includes anyone away for training. Plan on loading weapons Friday afternoon, the stores load-out Sat-

urday, and fast cruise Sunday from zero eight hundred to
twelve hundred. Liberty will be for all hands not standing
duty from Sunday afternoon until midnight Sunday night,
when I want all hands aboard and unpacked. Tell the eng
we start the reactor at zero two hundred Monday, and tell
the nav we shove off at zero six hundred."

"Aye-aye, sir," D'Assault said, her body rigid in ruler-
straight attention. "By your leave, sir."

"Granted," Dillinger said. Vornado glanced at him,
something nagging at him about the overly formal way he
spoke to D'Assault. He thought about how annoyed Dillinger had seemed when D'Assault had heaped compliments on Vornado's South Atlantic performance. As the
next thought dawned on Vornado, he began to smile behind Dillinger's back as the submarine commander led the
way back up the steep steps to his stateroom. Dillinger
threw himself into his command chair and cursed.

"Goddamned schedules keep changing," he complained.
"Who in God's name deploys a ship for six months with a
couple hours' notice? This is insane."

Vornado suddenly wished the orders were his. The excitement of the hours before a submarine got to sea were
electrifying, despite the grumbling of the crew, and every
member of the ship's force could feel it.

"Guess you need to break the news to your girlfriend,"
Vornado said. "How is she, anyway?"

"Oh, her." Dillinger narrowed his eyes. "We're on the
rocks. She took a network post in Washington. The distance has done its damage."

Dillinger and network broadcaster Dayna Baines had
been talking about getting married, and Vornado and Rachel both liked her. Perhaps that was one reason Dillinger
seemed distracted and irritable. If his relationship with
Dayna were teetering, a six-month deployment would only
send it over the edge. No relationship ever improved from
that kind of distance, Vornado thought.

"I'm sorry to hear that," Vornado said. "I like her."

Dillinger smirked. "Believe me, so do I. But the hell with
her. What was I thinking, getting serious with a woman
when I'm in this business? 'By the way, Dillinger, go steal
a submarine and disappear for six weeks.' 'Oh, Dillinger,

now take your regular command to sea for six months with no prior notice.' Jesus.''

"I miss it, B.K.," Vornado said quietly. "I wish it were me being ordered around like that.''

Dillinger looked up with an expression of surprise that changed to dismay. "Oh, God, I'm sorry, Peter. That was totally insensitive of me. You're right. I'm bitching like a sailor about doing my life's work.'' Dillinger rubbed his eyes. "I guess I'm just upset about Dayna. This deployment means I don't have any choice about our breaking up.''

"Can't you just explain all this to her?''

"Nope," Dillinger said flatly, shaking his head. "She's decided she's invested enough time in me. Before she left she wanted to set a date or she said she was done. She wants marriage and a baby immediately. I don't get it—what's the big goddamned hurry? Why would she insist on giving me an ultimatum? It's extortion—'Marry me or I'm gone.' ''

"Happens all the time. Rachel did it to me, and she was right. I'd have been content to leave her as a girlfriend forever. She wanted us to get on with our lives.'' Vornado thought about his daughter, and how he wouldn't want her wasting her life on a man who wouldn't commit, but he knew the thought wouldn't compute with his friend. There was a lot that Dillinger didn't understand about women, Vornado thought, but there was not much Vornado could teach him with words. Dillinger would only learn through experience.

Dillinger waved his hand in the air in frustration. "Ah, hell with it. Maybe a long deployment is just what the doctor ordered.''

Vornado nodded, his mind wandering to Lieutenant Commander D'Assault. He decided to broach the subject of Dillinger and his beautiful second-in-command. "What's the story on your XO? She's gorgeous. Yet none of your boys—or you—seem to notice.''

"There's something about her that bothers me, Peter. I don't know what it is.'' Dillinger's face was expressionless, his voice flat.

"I noticed. She seems to irritate you.''

"I know. It doesn't make sense. She's smart, accomplished, articulate, and a wizard at pushing the ship's agenda at squadron. She makes us all look good. The JOs love her, the chiefs respect her, and the enlisted cry on her shoulder. She's got organization skills like you wouldn't believe, and she's not one of those paper-pusher execs—as an approach officer in the simulator she's fearless and creative and aggressive, with a tactical mind as sharp as ours. And yet I don't feel like I can trust her like I did Davey. Davey and I could finish each other's sentences. And Flood could read my mind. You should have seen him in the South Atlantic—we were a hell of a team. But D'Assault is just so different from me. When I have one of my dark moods, she's bright and cheerful. If I want silence, she wants to chat. When I need input, she's lost in thought. And there's something about the way she looks at me. I can't describe it, but there's just something about her that makes it hard to look her in the eye. Dammit, I just want Davey back, or to have Flood promoted. D'Assault and I aren't going to work out, but if I ask Smokin' Joe to take her off the ship, I get a black mark for failure to develop a subordinate."

Vornado could see that his initial suspicions were true— whether it was because of Dillinger's problems with Dayna, or something Dillinger had detected about how D'Assault felt about him, or simply mutual chemistry, Dillinger was powerfully attracted to D'Assault, and he refused to acknowledge it. Perhaps it conflicted with his feelings for Dayna, or he thought it would damage his professionalism. Or maybe, deep inside, he thought that D'Assault would reject him, and Dillinger had never had any tolerance for feminine rejection.

"So is D'Assault seeing anyone?"

Dillinger frowned. "What, you want a date? Be careful, Petey, or Rachel will discipline you."

Dillinger was jealous, Vornado thought. "Hey, dark hair, dark eyes, pretty face, long hair, tall and slim, intelligent and outgoing—she's my type." Vornado smiled at Dillinger, but his friend wore a dark expression. He decided to risk confronting Dillinger. "Come to think of it, B.K., she's your type, too."

"No, she's not," Dillinger shot back quickly. "I like blondes and redheads."

"Since when? The girls you dated at Annapolis were all brunettes like D'Assault." Dillinger would have dated Rachel if Vornado hadn't found her first.

"Well, that's why I got tired of them. Anyway, you're out of luck. Natalie D'Assault is engaged to a war hero lieutenant colonel in the Marine Corps. Met at the Pentagon when she was a green junior grade."

"Good for her," Vornado said, glancing at his watch. "Listen, I'd better let you go. Your meeting with Smokin' Joe's coming up. And I've got to get ready for my trip."

"Trip?"

Vornado knew he wasn't supposed to talk about his new assignment, but B.K. had the highest top-secret clearances—perhaps he had heard something about the program. Vornado described his engagement, leaving out the description of the financial aspects. "You heard of any hush-hush Electric Boat drydock projects in trouble?"

"No," Dillinger said. "Nothing. But that's great for you, Peter. Good job. Rachel's okay with your disappearing so soon after the medical thing?"

"She thinks I'm depressed without a submarine under my boots. She thinks it'll occupy my mind."

"She's right about that."

Vornado shot an annoyed glance at Dillinger. He was not depressed, he thought, but decided not to respond. He stood up and Dillinger stood with him.

"Good luck on your deployment," Vornado said, shaking Dillinger's hand.

"Good luck on yours." Dillinger smiled, clapping Vornado on the shoulder. "Come on; I'll walk you to the end of the pier."

17

The limo took an early exit off the Beltway. At first Vornado thought that the driver knew a shortcut to Dulles Airport through the country roads of McLean, but the car rolled to a halt at a massive security entrance unlike any he'd ever seen. He looked up and noticed something on the concrete structure—a brass sign reading in block letters, CENTRAL INTELLIGENCE AGENCY. Something began to nag at his consciousness. The secrecy about this job, for instance. The payment of an absurd amount of money using a government check instead of one from General Dynamics. Being out of touch in the age of instant communication.

After two hours of being issued a badge and an orientation, he sat in one of the chairs in Hank Lewis's opulent window office.

"Obviously," Vornado said sarcastically, "you don't work for General Dynamics."

"No. I'm a senior project director working for the Anti-Proliferation Task Force, which reports through the Directorate of Operations, and which has the mission of keeping nuclear weapons out of the wrong hands. My boss is the task force commander, and he reports to the DDO, Deputy Director Operations, who reports to the Director of Central Intelligence."

"And the ship in the drydock. Was that a ruse as well?"

"Oh, there's a ship under construction. A nuclear submarine. It just has nothing to do with General Dynamics. Peter, this briefing is top secret, codename Goldfish. It should begin to answer most of your questions."

Lewis worked on his computer for a few moments, and the words *Project 705 / Lira / NATO Code Name: Alfa* flashed on the wall display screen. Lewis rolled the long version of the multimedia presentation. When the room lights came on, Vornado blinked as if he'd emerged from a dark theater to a sunny afternoon.

"Hank?" Vornado said after a long silence. "What in God's name am I doing here?"

"Peter, the submarine being built in the Terminal has been deliberately stalled by elements of my team. Call it sabotage. The original plan was to make Abdas al-Sattar suffer so many nagging delays and equipment failures that he would give up on this whole crackpot scheme and go back to conventional means of terrorism. But Abdas is a slippery character. If he doesn't go on the submarine, he may take the Granat warheads with him, go deep underground, and vanish. And when he does, every Super Bowl, every New Year's Eve in Times Square, every Olympics, we'll be looking over our shoulders, wondering if Abdas has something planned. Senior management has determined that the best way to neutralize Abdas is to clear up the problems with the Alfa and let him take it to sea. If Abdas is submerged, he can't leave the ship. If we know where the Alfa is, we know where Abdas is. And we can take the appropriate action."

"What does all that have to do with me?"

"You're taking the Alfa to sea," Lewis said, staring intently into Vornado's eyes. "You're the captain."

Vornado stared at the CIA officer. Something had just clicked inside him. The money didn't matter. What mattered was command at sea of a nuclear submarine. They had just offered Vornado the one thing that he woke from dreams about. But the mission Lewis had briefed was a dead end. Perhaps literally.

"This sounds like a suicide mission. You're going to have someone waiting in the Barents, right? Someone with two torpedo tube doors open and two Mark 48s on internal power with locked-in firecontrol solutions? I submerge the Alfa at the mouth of the Kola Fjord and bang, Abdas al-Sattar is gone and so are the Granat missiles. And so am I."

Lewis shook his head earnestly. "You've got it wrong, Peter. We abandoned that plan in the brainstorming stages, because it's possible we wouldn't hear the Alfa. If Abdas is aboard, and the Alfa gets away, we're worse off than before. No, we want you inside. Other elements of my team will go to sea with you. At the appropriate hour, there will be a mutiny. You and my team kill Abdas and his men; then you bring the missiles and the Alfa home."

"Why not just have your team kill him before he boards?"

"We thought of that, too. Abdas is a brilliant terrorist, and no one member of his crew is capable of taking over for him, but together his lieutenants could. We need to kill all twelve of his disciples, or they will return to execute his vision. If Abdas were a martyr to their cause, his executives would soldier on, and we are in the same pickle. The other problem is the Granat missiles. We have to take them out of circulation, and with all the private deep-sea salvage companies out there, the probability is too high that another group of pirates gets to them before we do. And we want the Alfa. It may be fifty years old, but it has technology that we've never been able to examine, and the intel we're getting from the inside says that the scientists at the Terminal have updated it to the point that it is a world-beater."

"They may have improved the Alfa," Vornado said, "but I doubt it's a 'world-beater.' It will still be louder than our 688 class. A Los Angeles–class submarine would still find it and trail it."

Lewis smiled. "The new Alfa has an acoustic advantage over the Flight Three L.A. class. Those frustrated scientists and marine engineers who used to sweat in the Russian design bureaus have a huge private budget now, Peter. At the Terminal they've taken all they've learned and applied it to the machinery of the Alfa. Four-dimensional fast Fourier transform sound mounts. Active quieting foundation connection points. Ultra-low-flow noise pumps and piping systems. Isolated decks. And this ship has a new sonar."

Vornado shrugged. The Alfa's legend was that it was so loud it could be heard half a hemisphere away, but maybe Lewis was correct. Lewis still hadn't answered Vornado's question. "I don't understand why you need me to execute this mutiny. If your agents are aboard, it doesn't matter who's driving the submarine."

Lewis nodded. "That's what I thought. There's a hole in the plan that you would fill. If the mutiny fails, we need a contingency plan so that the Alfa won't get away with Abdas in it. You're the contingency. If the mutiny fails, you operate the ship and the weapons systems so disaster doesn't strike. Disable the ship or the weapons or both. If you have to launch them, make them land harmlessly at sea."

Vornado understood. "But what are the chances of surviving taking the Alfa to sea?"

Lewis shrugged. "Naturally there are all the usual hazards of operating a nuclear submarine, particularly one on a maiden voyage. Flooding, fires, nuclear disasters, weapon explosions inside the hull. You've been there, but this is an untested boat with private Russian technology. Add to that the fact that Abdas and his crew are the most dangerous terrorists in the world, but subtract from the equation the fact that they will be trusting their lives to you, and they will imagine that you are one of them. That leaves you essentially with the same level of risk of just driving the submarine, until the moment that Abdas becomes aware you've tricked him."

"Hank, you're not giving me any confidence."

"Every risk we can envision, we can mitigate," Lewis said. "This is no different. The other crew members put aboard to protect the mission and to protect you will make sure Abdas is unable to harm you. With him and his men full of bullet holes, you'll drive the submarine and its missiles home. Mission accomplished."

"So why me?" Vornado asked. "There have to be two dozen people who can do this. The sub experts at Electric Boat, ex–submarine commanders, and your people."

"Nope. You're fluent in Russian, you've got ancestors who've worked in northern Russia, you're an expert in sub technology and a tactical genius. And you keep your cool in a tight situation, as we saw in Exercise Stolen Arrows. That's how we heard about you. I'm sorry about your medical discharge, but one door shuts and another opens." He paused, then leaned forward. "The schedule is tight, Peter. We need an answer. Will you do it?"

What the hell was he supposed to say to Lewis? That he'd allow them to ship him off to Russia to drive a derelict, albeit patched-together, titanium rustbucket that was probably destined for a nuclear accident on its maiden voyage? And if that weren't bad enough, was he expected to lock himself into the hull of this doomed submarine with the world's most wanted terrorist? On a mission that, at best, would bring him within a hairsbreadth of death?

Peter Vornado looked at the carpeting. If this had come up before the cancer, he would know his answer without deliberating. He would have immediately turned it down, out of responsibility to his wife and children, knowing he had no business putting himself in mortal danger when his family needed him. And the money—that he would never have accepted. He would have walked out on the dinner at that point, knowing it was too good to be true. And back then he would have resented someone trying to bribe him with an absurd amount of money, knowing he could make it on his own.

But that was before. He'd tried to minimize the impact of the cancer, but he knew the truth. It was a line of demarcation in his life. None of the equations that worked in that universe applied here. That two million dollars represented something vital to him, the freedom from worry about his family. Before he had almost shunned money, believing that the more of it a man had, odds were, the less honest he was. Now he could see how naïve and foolish that viewpoint had been. *Face it,* he told himself. That small fortune meant he had peace of mind. If he got sick again, he wouldn't have to worry about Rachel or the kids. They'd be provided for, thanks to Hank Lewis's CIA contract payment.

But Vornado knew that was only part of it. Since he was helicopter-evacuated from the hull of the *Hampton,* life had just seemed to be played at half volume. He had assumed everything would simply bounce back when he got used to being cured, but he realized it wasn't about the cancer. It was about command at sea, or the lack of it.

He chastised himself again—so it had been a defining experience, so he had been good at it, and he had enjoyed it. But that was no reason to sell his soul for one more week in command of a nuclear submarine. And what would this command mean? This ship would have no weapons other than the evil Granat city-killers. It would barely be seaworthy, filled with Moscow mobsters and Islamic terrorists, and a few members of Lewis's crew.

But even if he were thinking first of his family, wasn't that selfish in a way? What about his country? He had an

obligation to America, after all. He was a patriot and had
served his country, but now the nation needed him in a
way it never had before. If Lewis were on the level about
Vornado being the only one who could accomplish this,
then his refusal to do so would be morally wrong.

What about the risks, though? he asked himself. He answered himself—his service in the past had involved severe
risks—perhaps a fraction of what this mission involved, but
risks all the same. And he believed in himself. If the work
involved a nuclear submarine, he could do it better than
anyone he knew. He'd take the assignment, and God have
mercy on the soul of Abdas al-Sattar. In a few months the
improved Alfa submarine would be in an American drydock and he and the kids would be lounging in the pool at
the Shenandoah Mountain cabin. That way he could serve
both his country and his family.

Vornado looked at his shoes. "I'll do it, Hank. But I
need a concession."

Lewis clapped him on the back. "You're doing the right
thing, Peter. What can we do to make this better?"

"I need torpedoes."

"Torpedoes? Why?"

"I need to convince Abdas that my being in command
can protect him. If Abdas trusts me, he'll leave me alone
in the control room. I need to be the only one on board
who knows how to program the torpedoes and use the firecontrol system. In the extreme case, I could use them as a
self-destruct system."

Lewis thought for a moment. "Torpedoing your own
ship. That is extreme."

"You said yourself, you can't have Abdas in charge of
an escaped Alfa with these missiles aboard."

"But that makes it a suicide mission."

"No. Russian subs have escape pods. I could send out a
torpedo to turn around to target the Alfa itself, then evacuate in the escape pod with your agents. Abdas would be
dead, the Alfa and the Granats would be gone, but we
would survive."

"You know, that isn't a bad thought. Torpedoes being
your idea could prove to Abdas that you intend to carry
out this mission. Perfect—you'll propose that to Kaznikov."

Vornado stared at him, thinking he'd been outmaneuvered—that Lewis had said, "If you want it, go get it yourself."

"Let's go meet my bosses, and then we'll set you up in the on-campus hotel. For the next week you're going to speak nothing but Russian while you study up on the technology of the Alfa and some mission specifics. When that's done I'm sending you to the Farm, where we'll pack a year of training into seven days. By that time our people in the Terminal's recruiting and security staffs will solidify your cover story and finalize a way to introduce you to the Terminal staff."

"What is my cover story?"

"Let's save that for your training. I've got an entire staff who will educate you on that."

18

"On deck!" Lieutenant Junior Grade Nick Keondre had a projecting stage actor's voice when he chose to use it, and it was earsplitting when amplified by the bullhorn. "Take in all lines!"

Dillinger kept from scowling, but he would have taken in the forward lines first and allowed the bow to drift off the pier. Now Keondre was at the mercy of the linehandlers, and whoever pulled their lines in last. He waited patiently while the squadron linehandlers pulled the heavy ropes off the pier bollards and tossed them over to the ship, where *Tucson*'s deck crew would coil them up and stow them in the line lockers. The ship remained against the pier, the weak current apparently not able to move the hull. Dillinger sniffed the air, wondering if the drizzle would yield to the heavy rain soon. Dawn still hadn't broken. The drizzle filled the cones of light from the pier's sodium arc floodlights, and the light did little to penetrate the thick fog. In the distance a deep foghorn sounded across the water, from one of the large merchant vessels entering or exiting the Norfolk International Terminal farther upstream.

As the last line crossed over, Keondre turned to the flying bridge. "Shift colors!" The phonetalker had temporarily joined Dillinger atop the sail, and quickly hoisted the American flag on a ten-foot-tall stainless-steel mast. It hung limp and wet in the weather. Keondre reached down under the cockpit lip and pulled the lever of the air horn. A thunderous blast erupted over the calm water, the horn as loud as the one on the biggest aircraft carrier. No one within two miles would sleep through that, Dillinger thought. The horn wailed on for a full eight seconds as Keondre announced to the world that *Tucson* was under way on her own power. When Keondre released the horn, the comparative quiet was eerie.

The ship had drifted slightly into the slip, a sliver of dark water opening up between the hull and the pier. Keondre craned his neck over the side of the sail and observed the motion of the ship, waiting for the current and tide to move them away from the concrete. Dillinger made a mental note to commend the youngster for his patience.

Finally a quarter shiplength had opened between the hull and the pier. Keondre had been holding the coiled 7MC microphone connected to the bridgebox communication console under the windshield. He clicked the mike and spoke into it, the echo of his loud voice coming up the bridge tunnel. "Helm, Bridge, all ahead one-third."

Dayna, Dillinger thought. The night before, his estranged girlfriend, Dayna Baines, had come to the house to talk to him about something serious. After she'd been gone for months, she had let herself into the house an hour after he fell asleep.

Dillinger frowned and forced himself to concentrate on the ship. The pier slowly started moving relative to the hull. From Dillinger's perch on the flying bridge, the motion was evident when it was a few inches per second. The wake stirred up the glassy water aft. As the end of the pier drew even with the sail, Keondre watched it, then looked out into the river, what river they could see through the fog. Keondre reached into the cockpit for the air horn and sounded a two-second blast, announcing their presence in the channel.

"Helm, Bridge," Keondre ordered, "right full rudder, steady course zero one zero."

The bedroom door had opened slowly and Dayna Baines had walked hesitantly into the room. Dillinger looked at her and felt his heart race while a hundred emotions flooded in: joy to see her, fear that she had come to end it, attraction and sexual longing, and relief that this stalemate between them would finally be over, one way or the other. He still harbored hope that they would reconcile, and he searched her eyes for signs of good news.

Dillinger stared down the channel at the course ahead. There was nothing but a short expanse of mirror-smooth water in front of them, ending in the thick fog, with less than a hundred yards of visibility. His binoculars were useless in this.

"Slow it down when you reach the channel course," Dillinger ordered.

"Aye, Captain."

Dillinger had met Dayna Baines when she had walked aboard the USS *Miami* to do a submarine feature for the local news in Norfolk. He would never forget the first time he'd set eyes on her. He was immediately enchanted by her tall, slim body, her copper-colored hair, her pale angelic complexion, her juicy red lips, and her haunted blue eyes. Whenever she spoke to him, he lost his train of thought; he stammered and generally looked like a fool.

Slowly the ship made its way to the first turn point, then turned east toward the channel leading out of Port Norfolk. Dillinger checked his watch impatiently. It would take forever to get to the VaCapes at this speed. It was then the rain started, the drops as large as quarters. Within a minute the rainfall became a deluge, the blast of water hitting them as if from a firehose. Dillinger gathered his hood around his face, cursing the weather. The fog was unaffected by the rain.

The three-hour trip from D.C. had left her hair rumpled, and there were dark circles of fatigue under her eyes, but if anything it made her seem even more beautiful. No matter what happened between them, he would always love her, he thought.

As they plowed eastward, the wind began to blow. Almost immediately it picked up, blowing the rain in a slant from the west. As the sudden gale blew, the low clouds flew past the ship from the stern to the bow and out into the channel. The flag aft of Dillinger began to flap in the wind, the snapping loud behind him. Dillinger could feel the driving rain begin to soak through his foul-weather gear and into his cotton uniform. He shivered in the wind, but smiled as the wind finally blew away the fog, the expanse of the channel suddenly visible in front of them.

"Throttle up to standard, JOOD," he ordered.

"Standard, aye, Captain. Helm, Bridge, all ahead standard."

"I called from the car when I left," she had said. "But there was no answer." Her voice trembled as she spoke.

Dayna Baines's voice had always stirred his heart. She had hated her own voice since he'd known her, labeling it scratchy and hoarse, but he had always loved the sultry music she made when she spoke. Her south-of-Atlanta drawl and the way she caressed certain consonants had always excited him, even in the most bitter fight.

Their slow speed had allowed the deck crew to complete stowing the lines in the line lockers. They had rotated the deck cleats into the hull, and with the exception of the midhull forward escape trunk upper hatch, the deck was completely, smoothly cylindrical and rigged for sea. Soon the deck crew vanished down the hatch and shut it behind them, clearing the ship to speed up.

A slight bow wave had climbed their bullet nose, the water separating and flowing smoothly over the cylinder of the hull, the noise of it rising to compete with the roar of the wind. The Interstate 64 bridge-tunnel became visible in front of them, and Keondre adjusted their course under the recommendation of the navigator. Soon it washed behind them in their wake. Keondre turned the ship to line up with Thimble Shoal Channel.

"Kick it up to full," Dillinger shouted down to Keondre. The speed limit in the channel was fifteen knots, and full speed at 50 percent reactor power would exceed it by two knots, but that was the Coast Guard's problem. Dillinger wanted to catch up after their slow initial transit.

"Full, aye, sir. Helm, Bridge, all ahead full."

She was taller than most women, another fact she hated about herself, feeling at twenty-nine as if she were still an awkward teenager. She described herself as bony, from her small feet to her long legs past her narrow hips to a tiny waist. She'd been cursed, she felt, with a large chest, complaining that her breasts were too big and made her feel awkward. Dayna's long, elegant neck seemed graceful to him, but she always hid it with high-collared blouses or jackets, scarves, and long hair. Her face was a perfect sculpture, with each feature exquisitely shaped as if a celestial artist had planned each line and curve and surface. She didn't need makeup to be stunning, but he had never seen her without it.

The bow wave began to climb higher on the hull until it washed down the cylinder of the hull at the sail, then rose in a high standing wave to cover the top of the hull aft, then fell again by the time it reached the rudder. The noise of it became louder than the wind, which was mercifully coming from behind them. Dillinger could see the gap in the Chesapeake Bay Bridge Tunnel far ahead of them, distant by fifteen thousand yards, and an inbound lumbering tanker.

"Bridge, Contact Coordinator," Schluss's voice announced. "Inbound merchant ahead of us in the channel bears zero nine seven, range fourteen thousand yards, speed eight knots, angle on the bow port five. Closest point of approach is one hundred yards on the port beam."

"Contact, Bridge, aye."

The tanker was sharing the channel and would pass on their port side. "Give him a call," Dillinger ordered Keondre.

Two days after the *Miami* media run, Dayna had called the ship and asked for him, and that Atlanta drawl had made his pulse flutter. On impulse he asked her out to dinner, not believing his own brashness, but she surprised him by immediately accepting. It was only after he put the phone down that he became aware that she had known exactly what he would do. His hand shook as he reached for the doorknob of his stateroom as the obvious realization came to him that Dayna Baines was romantically interested in him. During dinner, she had confessed that she was smitten with him from the moment of their introduction and could think of nothing else. From the moment of their first date they had been a couple, with no thought of asking the other for exclusivity, their mutual commitment seeming natural and assumed. Three weeks later, she moved in with him. For the first time in his adult life, he was truly happy.

Keondre hoisted the microphone of his bridge-to-bridge VHF radio. "Inbound tanker at Thimble Shoal tunnel, this is outbound U.S. Navy submarine, over." The ship would never identify itself by name, only that it was a Navy warship, for reasons of security. It wouldn't do to have a spy ship receiving their radar signal correlate it to the name of their ship. It was a holdover from the Cold War, but was ingrained in the Standard Operating Procedures.

The radio on Dillinger's shoulder beeped; then a drawl-ing Southern voice crackled, "Roger, submarine cap'n, this is the *CalTex Zephyr* inbound, go ahead, over."

"*CalTex Zephyr* captain, this is outbound Navy submarine," Keondre said into his mike. "Propose port-to-port passage, over."

"Roger, submarine cap'n, concur with two-whistle passage. Y'all have a nice day in this terrible weather, out."

"Roger, *CalTex Zephyr,* thank you and good day to you, sir." Keondre clipped the VHF mike back on his jacket.

Within a few months, Dillinger had gone on to command the *Tucson* and Dayna had left her local station for the first string, the Satellite News Network Norfolk affiliate, for a coanchor slot. As combative as the relationship was, she and Dillinger settled into a quirky compatibility. Things might have progressed naturally to marriage if not for the progression of their careers. Dillinger had been spending crazy hours on the ship with a frenzied operational tempo. Dayna hated his excessively long trips and the last-minute way some of them started. They could have survived that, but then she got the offer from SNN's headquarters office in Washington to join them as a daytime anchor. For her this was the big time, the center ring, her equivalent to Dillinger's command at sea, the top of the pyramid. Dayna said she was thinking of accepting it not so much to advance her career, but because she was certain that she had only two or three years left before the news business would dump her for a younger and certainly prettier anchorwoman. She could use the gigantic salary to put away for the day when she couldn't get a job as a local weathergirl.

The visibility had finally eased enough to see through the binoculars, so Dillinger scanned the channel ahead as well. Other than the tanker, there was no one out there, just the driving rain and the gusting wind. The water of the bay was turning to short, choppy whitecaps running east. If the wind kept up, the waves would continue to grow. Dillinger shook the water off his hood, annoyed at the rain. This had to be the most miserable weather he'd ever suffered leaving port. He wondered if it was bad luck, or if the ancient mariners thought it akin to rain on a wedding day, labeling it good fortune.

With resignation Dillinger had watched Dayna reach a

decision to take the D.C. job. The interruption of their relationship would kill it, he had argued. She said it would only be for a few years, and even if it lasted longer, he would likely be stationed in Washington soon. That was not the point, he'd said. It was that he knew neither one of them would be able to sustain a long-distance relationship. She had scoffed, stating that Washington was a mere three hours away, that she had patiently waited for him when he was away, and that he was being immature. He'd maintained that seeing each other in D.C. on weekends had not been the answer—Dayna worked both weekend days and was only off Tuesday and part of Wednesday. He tried to explain reality to her, that on her days off she would be too tired from the early-morning and late-evening grind of the news business to focus on their time together, and half the weekdays he was on a short run to sea or working extreme overtime trying to get the ship ready for a run.

As they neared the bridge-tunnel, the tanker passed them by on the port side. When their crew dipped their flag on the aft deck of the superstructure, Dillinger reached behind him and lowered the flag to half-mast, then snapped it back up, the gesture one of goodwill to a fellow seafarer. The south tunnel passed under them as they continued down the channel toward Fort Story. The navigator announced the distance to the next turn point and the new course. Eventually the point came by the starboard beam and faded aft. Cummins announced the turn point, and Keondre ordered the ship to turn southward. As Fort Story went by, Dillinger could see Cape Henry Lighthouse. The periscopes rotated as the navigator's crew took visual fixes on the light and the landmarks of Virginia Beach. Dillinger scanned the beach with his binoculars, but the sand was deserted in the heavy weather. The wind blew from the starboard side and the waves traveled out to sea. *Tucson* traveled southward for some time until they reached the buoy marking the traffic separation scheme.

In the middle of the weeks-long debate, Dillinger was called to a ComSubLant conference room and told his private life was on hold, that he didn't even need to pack a bag, and that a staff truck waited to take him to the secret special warfare training center. He'd gulped but accepted the orders, while worrying that his sudden absence without explanation made it look as if he had departed in anger. Just as he'd feared, by the time he returned, Dayna had moved out.

"Bridge, Navigator, mark the turn to course zero nine zero."

The ship had just moved out of restricted waters. They were officially in the Atlantic now, although the water was too shallow to submerge until they reached the continental shelf hours east. Keondre turned the ship, steadied on the eastern course, then looked up at Dillinger.

"Cap'n, recommend flank speed."

"Very well, JOOD, increase speed to flank."

"Flank, aye," Keondre said. "Maneuvering, Bridge, shift main coolant pumps to fast speed."

"Bridge, Maneuvering, shift main coolant pumps to fast speed, Bridge, Maneuvering, aye. Bridge, Maneuvering, main coolant pumps are running in fast speed."

"Very well, Maneuvering. Helm, Bridge, all ahead flank."

The deck began to tremble beneath Dillinger's boots as the ship's reactor plant came up to 100 percent power, all 35,000 shaft horsepower forcing them forward into the choppy gray waves. He loved that feeling, the deck's shaking making it feel as though the ship were driving toward an urgent rendezvous, a mission of destiny. Of course, this time that was what he'd been told. In a few hours he'd have the tasking mission message aboard and could plan for whatever this run entailed. He turned to look aft. The shore of Virginia Beach was fading slowly into the distance, obscured by the rain and the low clouds, until it was gone, and there was nothing but the bow wave, the sea, and the wind.

Dillinger had turned on the television the first Friday night after the *Albany* run and tortured himself by turning on Satellite Network News. He watched *The Dayna Baines Report* while downing three double bourbons. He fell asleep on the couch and his head pounded all through that weekend, and perversely he blamed Dayna for it. An odd thought occurred to him, that perhaps she might be sitting by her phone, tearfully waiting for him to call. He sat at his basement rolltop desk and reached for the phone to call her, but before he could touch it, it rang. It was Rachel

Vornado calling to tell him that Peter had only a few weeks to live.

Suddenly two dolphins leaped out of the sea at the bow, their curving backs and dorsal fins visible for just a fraction of an instant before they vanished. They appeared a second time, then a third. That was definitely good luck, he thought. He extended his lanyard and sat down on top of the sail, his boots dangling inside the bridge cockpit. Now that they were clear of restricted waters, he could relax slightly.

Dillinger had spent the latter half of the summer with Peter and Rachel, their need for him helping him forget his own troubles. When Vornado overcame the brain cancer, it forced Dillinger to readdress his own emptiness, and he realized he had to call Dayna.

"Good work, Mr. Keondre. Stay alert. You may want to prompt the contact coordinator to see if he's being diligent in looking ahead."

"Aye, sir."

The waves grew as they drove out further seaward, no longer the choppy whitecaps of the bay, but now rising to three feet. The sea state was climbing, he thought. By the time they reached the dive point, this could be a serious storm. But then the ship would be steady as a building. Six hundred feet beneath a hurricane, there would be no sign of the troubled waters above.

Each time Dillinger had reached for the phone, he had stopped, thinking that she would be busy or asleep at that moment. As his courage continued to fail him, he began to draw comfort from the uncertainty, because at least there remained the possibility that she still cared about him. If he called her, she could easily shatter that illusion in a single sentence, and he wasn't sure he was ready for that. Better to let time go by and wait for her to call him. Her sudden arrival at the house the night before was completely unexpected. A part of him hoped that she would announce she had left the SNN D.C. job to return home to him, even if it meant she had been fired.

The ship trembled with the power of the flank bell. The swells began to grow in size, beginning to rock the hull far to the port side, the ship staying rolled to port for an agonizingly long time, then slowly rolling back to starboard and freezing there, then rolling back. Inside the hull, the sickening motion of the unseaworthy and barely stable submarine hull would have half the crew vomiting into plastic bags, asking over and over again the time to the dive point. But up on the flying bridge, the motion was deeply satisfying. Dillinger pushed back the raingear hood, the hurricane-force wind blowing his hair back on his scalp. He leaned against the flying bridge rails, feeling the tremendous power of the main engines, wishing he could keep from thinking about last night, but it was impossible. As much as he tried to stay in the moment, the sea and the sky seemed to vanish. He was back in his kitchen staring at Dayna Baines.

"You said you wanted to talk to me," he had prompted her as they both sat at the kitchen table.

"Burke, I don't think this relationship can survive the distance."

His heart sank as he heard her mouth the words. The end seemed suddenly and terribly real. An anger blew into his soul, mercifully cauterizing the gaping wound she'd just opened.

"You came here to dump me?" His voice was incredulous and accusatory, with a slight tremble in it.

Her eyes became swollen and red almost immediately as they flooded with tears. "You didn't answer my calls. I had to get closure even if it meant coming in person." For a long moment, she said nothing. "I've been seeing my boss, Evan English."

Dillinger stared at her in astonishment. A hundred emotions flashed through him, erupting through the curtain of numbness he'd felt since she left. It was one thing to think intellectually about her finding someone new, and another to hear her voice form the words that she was with a new man. The news knocked the wind out of him. He sat there with his mouth open and his eyes wide. He'd been betrayed, a voice said in his mind. Finally he heard himself say, in a small voice, "What did you say?"

"I'm involved with Evan."

Dillinger blinked several times. "Isn't he married?" he heard himself asking.

She dropped her eyes to the table. "He's leaving his wife. Someday."

He forced himself to take a deep breath, but he could hear his blood rushing in his ears.

"Fine, Dayna. Have a nice life. I'll have a moving company come over and pack your stuff. Leave me a shipping address, and I'll take care of it. Have a safe trip back."

Tears began to spill down her cheeks.

"You don't have to be so cold," she sobbed, her accent more pronounced. "And I never said I'm in love with him. I still love you, Burke."

He laughed harshly. "You picked a strange way of showing it."

"I mean it." She paused, trying to compose herself. "If you had just committed to me, this wouldn't have happened." She began sobbing, her shoulders shaking.

"So this is *my* fault?" he said. The words, when he heard himself say them, made him even angrier. "You're putting this on me? That you up and left for D.C., that you're screwing a married guy? And I suppose I'm also to blame that you came back down here to throw it all in my face? God, when you think about it, I'm an awful person."

Dayna swallowed hard. "Dammit, Burke, you always do this; you never see what you add to the situation. You always take yourself out of the equation. It's always someone else, because you're perfect. Evan doesn't treat me like this." The tears had streaked off her mascara. When she had wiped her face it had stained the skin under her eyes.

"So go back to him!" Dillinger shouted. "Why the hell are you even here?"

Her eyes flashed in fury but her voice was quiet and cold. "Because I wanted you to say, 'Dayna, please leave him and be with me, marry me, have children with me, share my life with me.' But you have never understood."

"Listen, Dayna, if this is what you want, run with it. If you had decided that a life with me was what you wanted, everything you mentioned—the marriage, the children, spending our lives together—it would all have come. We would have worked it all out. But you come into this house and auction yourself off like you're a goddamned painting. I'm not going to bid on you. You need to make a choice. You choose to be with that intellectual Brit with the gap in his teeth, then go back to D.C. and build your house together and get his messy divorce together and plan your princess wedding together and make goddamned gap-toothed babies together."

Her expression registered horror and shock, as if he'd struck her. She turned and put her face against the wall, then rushed out of the room.

He heard her footsteps on the wood floor of the foyer, then the door creaking open. It shut gently behind her. After a long moment he heard her footsteps on the porch, her car door opening and slamming shut, the engine starting. He walked into the foyer, her scent in his nostrils, realizing that in his impulsive anger he'd just made a terrible mistake. He looked out the window at her car's taillights fading into the distance. He put his forehead against the cool glass and thought about every word they'd said to each other, regretting what he'd said, but with no idea of what he could do to take back his harsh words.

It was over.

Dillinger sighed. If he were lucky, this run would become challenging and would take his mind off Dayna. He announced he was going below. He'd haunt the control room for a while—the XO's domain when they were on the surface—then withdraw to his stateroom. As he lowered himself down the ladder of the bridge access tunnel he could feel the slight roll of the ship as it began to labor in the waves. The deck's tremble was more noticeable inside the ship, he thought. He emerged into the control room, realizing he was soaked to the bone and leaving a gallon of water on the deck. He waved at D'Assault as he made his way to his stateroom, pulling off the raingear outside the door. He brought it inside and hung it in the stainless-steel-paneled bathroom he shared with D'Assault, then stripped off his soaked khakis. He showered and changed into his at-sea submarine coveralls, a one-piece black cotton uniform with the ship's patch embroidered on the right shoulder and the American flag on the left, with gold-embroidered dolphins over the left pocket and the silver oak leaves of his rank embroidered on his collar. He felt human again, he thought.

He stepped into the control room and spent the rest of the morning watch observing the crew and D'Assault. The more he watched her, the more he liked what he saw. Of

course, he'd yet to see her in a crisis after sixty hours without sleep—that would be the real window into Natalie
D'Assault, he thought. For just a second he compared her
to Dayna, but then stopped himself. No one would ever
compare to her.

Good-bye, Dayna, he thought.

"Thirty seconds to the dive point!"

"Aye," Lieutenant Kurt Vauxhall acknowledged the navigation technician, his voice muffled by the periscope optics module.

Dillinger squinted at the ship control panel, then took
one last glance at the chart.

"Conn, Radio," the overhead speaker squawked.

"Go ahead, Radio," Vauxhall called.

"Conn, Radio, immediate priority message from squadron marked 'personal for CO' received in the buffer."

"Radio, Conn, aye."

D'Assault glanced over. "Probably our tasking message,"
she said.

"Just in time," Dillinger replied.

"Mark the dive point!" Petty Officer Swales announced.

"Diving Officer, submerge the ship to one five zero feet
and trim the ship," Vauxhall ordered.

The diving officer, Senior Chief Mechanic's Mate Fred
Davies, who was the chief of the boat—the senior nonnuclear enlisted man aboard—pointed to the ship control
panel. "Helm, all ahead two-thirds." He controlled the
speed when ordered to dive and trim the ship. The helmsman reached down and rotated the knob of the engine
order telegraph to position his pointer at the two-thirds
position. The unit's bell rang and the pointer from the engineroom spun over to two-thirds.

Immediately the shaking of the deckplates from the flank
run stopped, and the waves seemed to begin dominating
the ship. The deck rolled far to port, then sickeningly back
to starboard. Dillinger's stomach jumped. Thank God
they'd be under this mess in a few minutes.

"Chief of the Watch, open the forward-group vents and
sound the diving alarm."

The chief of the watch reached up to the ballast control

panel's upper section and snapped up three toggle switches. Three lights on the panel, all green bars, extinguished, and three red circles appeared in their place.

"Forward vents open," the chief of the watch said as he reached up higher on the console to the diving alarm. He picked up the 1MC microphone and announced, "Dive, dive!" He rotated the diving alarm switch to the right, and an old fashioned *Ooooooooh-gaaaaah* sounded over the speakers. Then he repeated himself: "Dive, dive!"

"Bowplanes to fifteen degrees dive," the diving officer ordered the helmsman. "Sternplanes, ten-degree down bubble."

The deck slowly began to incline forward as the forward ballast tanks gave up their volume of air and water flooded in the bottom. On the video monitor, a gusher of water vapor erupted from the foredeck from the already submerged main ballast tank vents.

"Venting forward," Vauxhall called.

"Chief of the Watch, open the after-group main ballast tank vents."

The chief acknowledged and reached up to snap three more toggle switches. Again three green bar lights went out and three red circles illuminated.

The deck inclined downward further. Dillinger grabbed onto a handhold to keep his feet. D'Assault braced herself on an attack center console.

Vauxhall had rotated the periscope to look aft. On the aft deck, the waves were rising so that the cylinder of the hull was only visible between waves. Another geyser of water was blasting out the aft ballast tank vents.

"Venting aft."

"Forty-five feet," the diving officer called, reading the keel depth from the digital depth gauge on the ship control panel. "Fifty feet. Fifty-five feet. Sail's under."

On the video monitor the hull had long vanished and the waves had grown much closer to the view.

"Sixty feet. Sixty-five. Seventy feet."

The waves grew much closer to the viewscreen until one splashed up over the display in an explosion of foam.

"Scope's awash," Vauxhall said.

The view cleared, the waves marching closer until another wave roared over the scope. This time the view didn't clear. The undersides of the fierce waves appeared at the top of the video monitor, seeming even angrier from below.

"Scope's under. Lowering number two scope."

"Nine zero feet. One hundred feet. Bowplanes to five degrees dive. Sternplanes, three-degree down bubble."

Dillinger waited as the deck began to come level again.

"Sternplanes to zero bubble. Bowplanes, zero angle. One five zero feet, sir." The diving officer concentrated on the ship control panel. "All ahead one-third."

For the next twenty minutes the diving officer pumped variable ballast and transferred water from several tanks until the ship was exactly neutrally buoyant. The ship rolled slightly in the waves at this depth, but it was nothing like the motion on the surface.

"Officer of the Deck," he finally announced in triumph. "Ship has a good one-third trim."

"Very well, Dive, make your depth five four six feet. Helm, all ahead full." Vauxhall picked up the 7MC microphone, the intercom to Maneuvering. "Maneuvering, Conn, shift main coolant pumps to slow speed."

"Conn, Maneuvering, shift main coolant pumps to slow speed, Conn, Maneuvering, aye. Main coolant pumps are running in slow speed."

"Maneuvering, Conn, aye," Vauxhall said, then hung up the microphone. "Captain, proceeding deep in accordance with the op order."

"Very well, JOOD," Dillinger said. He looked at D'Assault. "Let's read the message in my stateroom."

As he stepped into his stateroom, Vauxhall announced to the room, "Captain's left control."

"What do you make of it?" Dillinger asked D'Assault. Her face was inscrutable as she read the tasking message, the new operation order.

"It doesn't make sense, Captain. We have a full weapons load. Why would we need to report to AUTEC to get another one?"

Dillinger took the message back and reread it. Its first paragraph gave them the answer to the question of whom they'd be reporting to: Task Group 2.01, an element of the National Security Council, which reported directly to the President. That alone was strange enough. Certain top-secret spy missions were known to report to the NSC, but it had become unusual. Odds were that detached duty to the NSC meant that the real mission operator was the CIA, but that wasn't spoken aloud.

The second paragraph tasked them with their first mission element, to report to the Atlantic Undersea Test and Evaluation Center, or AUTEC, at Andros Island in the Bahamas, run by RCA under contract to the Pentagon. Unlike the other islands in the Bahamas, Andros resembled the surface of the moon, and the small town that operated the sonar arrays in TOTO was populated either by the defense contractor's personnel or the Navy. TOTO stood for Tongue of the Ocean, a deep bathtub of seawater surrounded by extremely shallow shoals, making it ideal for submarine testing without being spied on by external elements. The "bathtub" was fully instrumented with three-dimensional sonar arrays, so the defense contractor could show the exact replay of a battle to the submarine crew there for tactical training. The bathtub was also used as a ship sound–silencing monitoring array. A ship would be ordered to drive through the bathtub at a certain speed, with certain pumps running, and the hydrophones would measure the submarine's sound signature. If the ship had a rattle or a rubbing pump seal, the sonar array would point it out. Better to have the contractor point out a sound deficiency than have an opponent take advantage of it. As expected, the orders required them to run the gauntlet of the sonar array for a ship's emitted sound survey, then tie up to the tender ship *Gladiator* for a quick turnaround to fix any sound shorts or rotating equipment problems.

It was the third paragraph that rang false. The tender was to give them a weapons loadout. They had been loaded up with a full compartment of Mark 48 ADCAP Mod 6 torpedoes—the real ones this time, not some disguised exercise shots. There was barely room to breathe in the torpedo room. Even the torpedo tubes were loaded. And the vertical launch tubes were all stuffed with Block IV Tactical Tomahawk cruise missiles, for use as either antiship weapons or land-attack units. There was nothing more to load the ship with, Dillinger thought.

And the most annoying part of the message was that it mentioned nothing at all about where they were eventually going or what they'd be doing. Once again, he was in the dark.

"Fucking tasking message," he heard D'Assault say softly.

He spun back around and stared at her. One of Dillinger's quirks was that he loved it when a woman cursed. It had taken him almost all of his time with Dayna to get her to curse, and when she had, it was only during sex. Hearing D'Assault swear reminded him of the scene that had just played in his mind, but it also seemed odd—D'Assault had been nothing but formal and correct since she'd been aboard. He didn't think he'd ever heard her speak in less than a complete sentence, her enunciation perfect, her speech completely polished. And yet here she was tossing the F-word around in his stateroom. She looked up and saw him staring at her.

"Sorry, sir. I'll try not to curse on board."

"I think that would be a mistake, XO," he said. Had he really almost called her by her first name? "Some situations demand swearing. On a submarine, a lot of situations require it. And if the men think you're incapable of the occasional curse word, everything they say will be obscene. They'll try to shock you. If you belt out a string of curses, believe it or not, they'll respect that."

She smiled, those white teeth lighting up her face. "You're right, sir."

"I know I'm fucking right." He smiled, then grew serious again. "Better get the navigator in the loop. Let's set a course for AUTEC. And plan to brief the officers right after evening meal."

PART 4:

▼

Resurrection

19

Peter Vornado was as exhausted as he could remember being since chemotherapy. The cramped elevator of the Hotel Arktika had a strange smell to it—rotten fish or old garbage. Finally it creaked to a halt at the twelfth floor. He followed the signs to the wing of the Y-shaped hotel that extended out toward the Kola Gulf. The room had a musty smell to it, but nothing as foul as the elevator.

He threw his bags on the floor, pulled back the bed's covers, shrugged off his clothes, and fell into the bed and shut his eyes. As tired as he was from the trip, he couldn't sleep, not immediately. He forced himself to keep his eyes shut, hoping that sleep would come. He would need to get up early for the conference downstairs, and he debated setting the alarm clock. He decided to trust his internal clock instead and turned on his side. The room was cold, but he preferred that for sleeping. Still, sleep didn't come.

He was probably too wound up about tomorrow's interviews, he thought. And the trip behind him. It began with a hop from D.C. to Miami, then an overnight stay. He'd caught a flight from Miami to Frankfurt, then a flight from there to Warsaw, where he'd spent the night. He'd awakened as if from a nightmare in the small hotel near the airport, then caught a flight to Moscow, and finally took a train from Moscow to Murmansk. He'd asked why he couldn't just fly direct from D.C. to Moscow and take a commuter plane to Murmansk. The answer was baffling—the reason was that this way was cheaper. They'd given him a few thousand dollars in cash and directed him to buy the tickets himself, and to leave all his credit cards behind. He'd left with luggage packed by the agency and a wallet with a driver's license and the cash. The license was consistent with his cover story, such as it was. It identified him as Peter Vornado, but was more recent than his real license, and listed an inexpensive apartment as his address.

He still wasn't happy with what the CIA had considered an adequate cover story. Their idea of a fake identity was just him with a nasty divorce in his recent past, with a child-support order hitting him at a time when he was drummed out of the Navy. The story maintained that he had apparently left, either to avoid paying his hated ex-wife alimony and the steep child support, or on a quest to make enough money to fulfill his new obligations. He had answered one of the Terminal recruiter's ads in a technical journal—which worked, since certain elements of the Terminal's recruiting staff worked for the agency. Once the recruiters had obtained contact information, they had requested to talk to him in Murmansk, and if he passed the interview, they would compensate him for his travel expenses. That, he was told, was why he needed to fly cheaply, because a pauper wouldn't be flying business class on a direct flight.

While Vornado was not satisfied with the cover story or the agency's precautions, at some point he had to leave his fears behind and concentrate on the task at hand—passing this interview with the people who ran the Terminal.

Finally he was ready. He waited outside the third-floor conference room until exactly eight, when he knocked. The door was opened by a pretty but prim young woman wearing wire-rimmed glasses and a midlength skirt, her fine blonde hair pulled back into a businesslike bun. She smiled at him, flashing perfect white teeth. She was tall and slender and young, perhaps only in her early twenties.

"Come on in." She shut the door behind him. "I'm Svetlana, head of recruiting. I work for Sergei Kaznikov." She shook his hand. Her accent was distinctly southern Moscow. "Don't be fooled—I'm a nuclear and electrical engineer by education. I'm the manager in charge of hiring the engineers for this project." She smiled again. "But enough about me. It's good to meet you finally, Mr. Vornado." She was holding his hand longer than was necessary, but finally released it. "Or should I call you Commander?" She blushed, or so he imagined. "Please make yourself at home." She led him into a conference room. The table was oblong, with a chair at one end, and four chairs gathered at the opposite end.

As she interviewed him, he realized that something wasn't right. She seemed interested in him, but a different kind of interest than as a hiring manager. It suddenly occurred to him that he no longer wore a wedding ring, and even the tan line from the ring was now gone. And the file on him stated that he was divorced.

"Let me tell you about today's interviews," she said. She started with Leonov Kaznikov and his commercial vision to revamp a discarded Russian submarine for sale to a "special buyer," then went on to say that Sergei Kaznikov was the person responsible for executing the idea, the more technical of the two brothers. The third man was Vasily Ilyivich, the Terminal's chief of security, and the fourth was Anton Nessov, who was the contract captain. She seated Vornado at the end of the table, where the single swivel chair was located, and pulled one of the other chairs down near his end. As she spoke she removed her glasses and looked into his eyes. She was certainly pretty, in an attractive librarian fashion, and for a moment he wondered whether it would be useful or foolish to get close to this woman. Hank Lewis's training team at Camp Peary had gone over and over this: *You're divorced, so don't act like you're still married. In a situation when a normal single man your age would sleep with a woman, you'd best consider doing it and the consequences of not doing it. Consider very carefully the particular woman and her potential contribution to the mission. If a woman comes on to you, turning her down could create a dangerous enemy, yet if she is the wife of someone powerful, having sex with her could create an even more formidable enemy.* While Vornado had been attentive, this all seemed academic, a course designed for someone else. Why would he have any kind of romantic temptation or encounter up here, in the godforsaken Kola Peninsula, on the most hazardous mission he'd ever been assigned? And yet, ten minutes into the operation, here was Svetlana, invading his personal space, her enticing perfume in his nostrils, her eyes locked on his and staring at him as if she wanted much more than his conversation.

Bile flowed into his stomach. Peter Vornado had barely

glanced at another woman since meeting Rachel. Perhaps he was imagining something that wasn't there, he thought. That had to be it. But just as he had almost convinced himself that Svetlana was all business, she put her hand on his knee as she explained about Leonov's starting the company that was building this submarine. KKS, he had called it, for the two Kaznikovs and the investment of a third person whose name began with S but who had been bought out. Uncomfortable with her hand on his knee, Vornado stood suddenly and stretched.

"Please forgive me. I can't sit anymore. It was a long trip," he said. She smiled at him, her easy blush returning. She really was extremely pretty, he thought, though far too young for him. Her blonde hair would look stunning if she were to wear it down around her shoulders. Her brown eyes and slightly dark skin contrasted nicely with the light yellow of her hair. *Probably a bottle blonde,* Rachel would pout, he thought. But with the coloring of a brunette and expertly dyed blonde hair, she looked enticing.

Was she Leonov's or Sergei's girlfriend, he wondered, or a paramour of one of the other two men? If not, turning her down could prove disastrous. Perhaps he could string her along, give her a few signals, until he could find out about her boss. He wondered if this could be Lewis's contact, but discarded the idea. She had said nothing to indicate either any inside connection or disloyalty to the Kaznikovs.

Odds were she was who she said she was. She continued with her briefing. "One of your interviews is with Vasily Ilyivich, who is in charge of security. He'll ask some of the hard questions."

"Like what?" Vornado sat back down at the end chair.

"Like why you left America. Why, if you're such a patriot, a submarine captain and all, you would turn your back on an entire lifetime of service to the USA and come here."

"That's easy," he said. "I was dismissed from the Navy with a medical discharge, even though I'm as healthy as a twenty-year-old." Her eyes widened at that. "Nothing could get the Navy medical board to listen. All I've ever done is work on or operate submarines, and suddenly I had nothing. My wonderful wife," he said, injecting as much venom into his voice as possible, "thought I was already dead, and when I regained my health, all she did was complain about how she had felt relief that she would no longer be married to me. That she realized she would be living in a world without me in it, and she could look ahead to that world, and that any sadness she felt was for the children. The day I left my final checkup was the day she served me with papers. The Virginia family court system finished the job. They levied alimony on me as if I'd done my wife wrong, and ignored the fact that I was unemployed. The judge even looked at me and said, 'With a résumé like this, you should be making a quarter mil a year.' He set child-support payments far higher than I could have paid, with the alimony, had I still been in the Navy. With my military pay and the child support and alimony, I would have had less than six hundred dollars a month to live on. A tumble-down apartment would take all that. Oh, and all the debt? The credit card bills? The mortgage? The car payments? All mine, even though my wife got the house, the kids, one of the cars, and the furniture." Svetlana stared at him in incredulity. He'd been told not to lay it on too thick, but he'd gotten carried away with his own story.

He sighed and stared at the carpeting. "I decided to see if the judge were right. If my résumé were truly worth two-fifty a year, anywhere on the planet. I found your ad in *Naval Architect's Digest* about the time that Rachel, my ex-wife, sold the house and packed the children off for California. I decided, with them a continent away, it wouldn't matter at all if I worked on the other side of the globe. At least then I could make some kind of living, hopefully something far in excess of what I owed her, and if I could mail her the child support, I'd get to see my children again."

He reached into his pocket and withdrew pictures of a two-year-old girl, an eight-year-old boy, and a thirteen-year-old girl. None of them were his, but they looked enough like him that the photos supported his story. "This is the real reason I'm here. I need to make enough money to get the children back. If money is what will buy me back the right to see my kids, then that's what I want."

He let out his breath. "I'm sorry, Svetlana. I'm here for an interview and instead of being professional I end up telling you all my troubles. Please forgive me."

"No, no," she said quietly, her hand on his shoulder, standing too close to him again. "It's okay. I'm sorry."

For a moment they were both silent.

Vornado decided to take a chance. "You mentioned that this ship is a commercial venture. That it's not associated with the Russian Navy, but is for a special buyer."

Svetlana nodded.

"What's a civilian going to do with a Lira submarine?"

She smiled. "This sub is fast. I'm guessing it's going to be used for rapid, secret undersea transport."

"Smuggling?"

"Why ask?" she said, cocking her head. "Is this a moral problem for you?"

"No. I just need to know how much money to ask for. The farther this project is from the straight and narrow, the more I can make." He smiled shyly and looked down at the carpeting. "For the next few years, I'm all about the money."

She gave him a long look of understanding. Finally she glanced at her watch. "I'd better see what's holding them up," she said.

"So," Sergei said to Vasily Ilyivich, head of security for KKS, "do you believe him?"

Ilyivich squinted at the television monitor for some time, then grudgingly nodded. "I've heard of situations like this," he said. "The Americans so punish their men for ending up divorced. But it's hard to imagine this happening just because Vornado got sick. If there is a hole in his story, it is probably that his wife caught him doing it with her best friend. A woman scorned, you know."

"Anton?" Sergei prodded the contract captain for the Improved Lira, former Russian Republic Navy Captain First Rank Anton Nessov. Nessov was short and chubby, with thinning white hair and a white beard that extended in a pencil-thin line down his full cheeks to a more generous fullness at his chin and mustache. He wore square-lensed wire-rimmed glasses, the kind of lenses that magnified his puffy, piggish eyes. He wore a perpetually jolly yet arrogant expression, which, in combination with the beard, made him seem both elfin and professorial. He wore a herringbone jacket, a tieless white shirt opened one too many buttons to show two thick gold chains, khaki pants, and a pair of odd suede crepe-soled shoes that elevated the toes higher than the heels. Nessov pulled a pipe out of his jacket pocket and stoked up a flame with a lighter, then blew out a cloud of overly sweet cherry-smelling smoke.

"Well, I just don't know," he said in a too-loud voice that made him sound as if he'd suffered some hearing loss. "If he were such a great sub commander, why would his navy toss him out like that? Odds are, they used it as an excuse, and the real reason is more embarrassing. Maybe he touched bottom or snagged a trawler's fishing net or sheared off a periscope on a supertanker hull. And Vasily's theory of him cheating on his wife makes sense."

Ilyivich nodded. "Perhaps it is both. Perhaps he was putting the sausage to his boss's wife, earning him a discharge from his military and a divorce."

Nessov sputtered a laugh, smoke erupting from his mouth. "That's good, Vasily. It has the elegance of simplicity while fitting all the known facts."

"We should check out his story in detail," Ilyivich said, stroking his chin.

"Let's go talk to him," Sergei said. "And just so both of you know, I don't care if he raped the admiral's daughter. This man could help us a great deal."

The interview had gone the way he'd expected, with one twist—the elder Kaznikov hadn't shown up, and no excuses were made about his absence, though Vornado wondered if he had been called to account to Abdas al-Sattar for the technical failures and schedule problems. The younger Kaznikov seemed at first to be a typical technocrat—focused, extremely intelligent, soft-spoken but forceful when it came to the field of his expertise, and not particularly interested in matters unrelated to that field. Sergei was a small man, thin and bespectacled, with a shaved head. He dressed in chinos, a starched white shirt, and a sport jacket. Vornado estimated him to be slightly older than himself, in his early forties.

The discussion began with Sergei carefully presenting the

project, a commercial venture conducted under the highest secrecy available outside the military to provide a third party with a refurbished, fast, quiet submarine independent of the surface. A nuclear boat, to be used, of course, for purposes known only to the buyer. He asked Vornado if he had any problems working for such a venture, and for the second time Vornado explained that he was merely a mercenary. Sergei stated that he had a full technical staff on board already, but that the submarine was plagued by mechanical, electrical, and electronic problems, that he needed someone with a new perspective, and that Vornado looked—on paper—like the answer to their problems.

Once his short presentation ended, he began cross-examining Vornado, asking mostly technical questions, probing Vornado's knowledge of nuclear engineering, at one point even arguing with Vornado over a fine point about thermal neutron flux. But the fact that they could argue about esoteric nuclear physics seemed to please Kaznikov immensely. Anton Nessov was not so easy to please. The former navy sea captain sat there smoking his pipe, asking Vornado about his experiences, seeming to probe him as if he'd done something wrong. It was difficult not to get defensive when the questions ran to, "What's the closest you've been to a nuclear fuel meltdown? And be honest." Eventually Kaznikov reined him in, insisting that the topic of conversation remain shipyard repairs. That subject seemed to last for several hours, and as the hour neared noon, food was brought in.

After lunch two newcomers arrived. The first was a tall, broad-shouldered man wearing a brown suit so wrinkled it could have spent the last ten years in a heap on the floor. He towered over the room, forcing even Vornado to look up at him. He had animated features beneath a full head of short dark hair, eyebrows that made semicircles over his wide brown eyes, a hawkish nose, and lips curled into a genuine smile. He had a brown Russian cigarette clamped in his teeth, and when he puffed it he removed it with his thumb and index finger, and he smoked it down to the bitter end. He entered the room confidently, as if he owned it. Sergei Kaznikov walked up to him, smiled warmly, and shook his hand.

"Mr. Vornado, allow me to present Superintendent Academician Yuri Belkov, the project manager and chief ship systems engineer. Yuri, this is Peter Vornado, the American submarine engineer I told you about."

Vornado stood and greeted Belkov while Kaznikov shook the second man's hand. "This is Andrei Rusanov. Andrei, perhaps you can best explain your role to Mr. Vornado."

Rusanov stood almost a head shorter than Vornado, seeming comically short next to Belkov. He was heavy and barrel-chested with a large paunch, yet still hard-looking, with bulging arm muscles and the worn hands of someone who had spent years wielding massive tools. He reminded Vornado of some of the shipyard craft personnel he'd worked with in the past, whose beer guts would only be mistaken for weakness by fools. Rusanov had blonde hair cut in a severe, short flattop. While he was jowly, his face still seemed tough and dangerous. When he spoke, his voice was resonant as a foghorn.

"It was all my idea," he said. Vornado noticed that his accent was distinctly local. "I should give the credit to my grandfather for the first Lira, but the concept of bringing the Lira back as an improved version for civilian purposes was my proposal to Leonov. Sergei here was instrumental in bringing this to fruition."

"Sit down, gentlemen," Sergei said. "Mr. Vornado, these talented engineers have a few questions for you. This won't take long, I promise."

The questions continued for hours, but as Vornado described his past exploits, parrying all their technical questions, they became comfortable. The interview's next phase began at the dinner club owned by KKS, where the wine and vodka flowed. Sergei offered Vornado the job of executive ship superintendent. The negotiation for salary lasted an hour. After protracted and almost violent arguing, Vornado had extracted almost a million dollars from Sergei, half for fixing the Lira, half as a bonus if he could get it to sea in a month. At first Sergei had doubted Vornado or anyone else could do it, but Vornado convinced him it was possible.

After another hour of drinking later, Sergei had his driver take Vornado back to his hotel. Vornado entered the small suite, realizing it smelled different—Svetlana's perfume, and the sweet smell of candle wax, and the odor of extinguished candles. He had to be completely inebriated to be hallucinating with his nose, he laughed to himself. He stepped to the end of the bed and removed his clothes, dumping them in a heap, and climbed into bed in his boxer shorts. He put his head on the pillow and shut his eyes, the room slowly rotating around him from the vodka. He took a deep breath and relaxed.

The warm hand on his chest made him sit up in fear and shock. He turned on the bedside lamp and saw Svetlana's head on the pillow. Her hair was down and draped across the pillowcase, some of it covering her beautiful face. Slowly her sleepy eyes fluttered open.

"I thought you would be out all night," she said quietly, her self-possessed manner still present even as she woke up.

"What are you doing here? How did you get in?"

"Questions, questions, Peter. The first answer should be obvious. For the second, I told the desk I needed to drop off papers, and since I made your reservation, they didn't hesitate."

Before she completed the last syllable her arm encircled his neck and she pulled him into an embrace and a deep, welcoming kiss. At first he wondered if he were so drunk as to disappoint her, but then felt himself reacting to her kiss. Immediately he was flooded with guilt that he was being disloyal to Rachel for even thinking of being with Svetlana. And then there were the mission ramifications.

The voices of his recent trainers again whispered in his ears: *Sometimes the situation will make the decision. And do not think of any encounter in Russia as cheating on your wife. You must always live inside your cover story—you are a different person from the moment you leave headquarters. And the person you are becoming is not married.*

He had the fleeting thought that the interview might still be in progress, if Svetlana were to report to her boss about anything he said about the day. He pulled back from Svetlana. He tried not to think about Rachel as Svetlana's fingers reached under his waistband and curved around him. That part of him surged lustfully into her soft hand. He suddenly realized that he must seem an inexperienced idiot after only being with one woman his entire adult life. He literally wasn't sure what to do next.

He leaned over and turned off the lamp. Then he reached out to her and felt her breast come into his hands, and her lips were on his again, her soft tongue entering his mouth and circling his, then sucking his tongue into her mouth. The softness of her mouth encircled him, just as her soft, warm hand did below. Without stopping her kiss or her caress, she rose on one knee and moved her other leg slowly up his, then rose up to straddle him. Her fingers moved on him as she guided him into her.

Her warm wetness made him moan softly as she forced him deeper inside her. She began to move over him, withdrawing from him almost completely, then quickly diving down so that he stabbed into her. She was completely in control. The motion was intoxicating, and the more she moved, the more excited he became. He heard his blood rushing loudly in his ears and his breath coming faster. Finally he burst into a climax deep inside her and she collapsed lightly onto his chest, careful to keep him inside her.

"That was great for me," he muttered to her, "but you didn't finish."

"Yes, I did," she whispered in his ear contentedly, her tongue licking upward from his lobe to the opening. "I just come quietly. Men hate me for it."

"It's difficult to imagine anyone hating you for this," he said, but he knew that in the dark he was blushing, thinking he'd just cheated on Rachel.

No, he hadn't, he insisted to himself. He was no more disloyal to her than he was to his country. It was just that regaining his life was forcing him to go through this trial, and it was all temporary.

In the misty moonlight coming through the open curtains, he saw her watching him. He smiled at her and kissed her cheek. She rolled off him, her smooth, shapely leg thrown over his wet midsection, her arm around his chest.

"May I ask you a difficult question?" he whispered in her ear. She made a moaning sound deep in her throat. "Why did you do this?" The question seemed to wake her up. Her eyelids fluttered open and she looked over into his eyes.

"I wanted you. Sergei's been thinking of nothing else for the last two months but replacing Nessov, but there was no one who could do the work. He also needed an engineer to help Yuri and Andrei with all the shipyard problems. Then we heard about you for the second problem, and amazingly you fulfill the first. When he saw your résumé he was so excited he couldn't sleep for a week, and all he talked about was you."

"I wish you'd told me that before I negotiated my pay." He smiled.

"Don't interrupt," she said, her finger on his lips. "Anyway, I decided I wanted to get to you before anyone else could."

"There are other women working in the Terminal?"

"Not many. A few in engineering and design. You wouldn't want the two hull mechanics. But the engineers are pretty. And there are bars at the waterfront where girls would line up for you."

"I'm sure no one in this entire place is anything like you."

She smiled.

"What now?" he asked, and immediately regretted it. He pressed on as she lifted an eyebrow. "Is this a onetime thing?"

"Is that what you want?"

"No," he heard himself say emphatically without thinking, another load of guilt flooding his heart.

"I'm sure you'll move on to the other women in a week or two," she said, teasing him, but he detected something serious.

"Why would you think that?"

"That's what Nessov said. That you were kicked out of your navy for womanizing."

Vornado nodded wisely. "He would think that. What is the expression? 'Husbands only look behind the bedroom door if they've stood there themselves.' "

She laughed. Her hand had slipped south to touch him under her thigh, and he could feel himself rising to meet her. It occurred to him that if he could maintain an alliance with her, he would be spared having to play the part of a cad with the other women here.

"So is it true?"

"What?"

"Are you a heartbreaker, a womanizer?"

"No," Vornado said lightly. "I'm not like that."

"I'll make sure you have no reason to dump me," she said, her hand succeeding in bringing him back to life.

He rolled her over and made love to her again, this time slowly and tenderly, and this time she came hard enough to clench spasmodically around him. The expression on her face was enough to bring him to a thunderous climax. He pulled her next to him, both of them sweating and exhausted.

The thought occurred to him that he might have been correct about this being a second part of his interview, and that if he fell asleep first, she might try something—sodium pentothal or some other truth-inducing drug. Then he wouldn't survive the next day. But her eyes shut behind her long lashes, and soon her breathing became slow and deep.

Quietly he got up from the bed and went to the bathroom. On impulse, he decided to look in Svetlana's purse for her identification. As he rummaged in her things, the thought came to him that she might be one of Hank Lewis's agents, but if that were the case, he might never know it. He'd been directed to contact a barmaid, not the secretary of Kaznikov. He found her ID, which showed her to be twenty-one years old, but that wasn't what shocked Vornado. What sent the shock of adrenaline through his system was her name: Svetlana A. Belkov.

What had he done? he wondered. The senior ship superintendent was Yuri Belkov, and he was the man in charge of the entire project, reporting only to the Kaznikovs. Svetlana could be the Lira ship superintendent's wife, for God's sake. Or perhaps worse, his daughter. Vornado could have blown this entire mission. So much for the situation determining his response.

It was after three before he fell asleep, to more dreams of Midshipman Whitehead's torture. When he woke, Svetlana was gone. He rose to get ready to report to Sergei's office. If all went well, he would be working at the Terminal within the hour. When he left the hotel, his hand trembled as he reached for the elevator button.

He'd tell Sergei it was a hangover, but as Vornado's heart pounded in his chest, he realized that he'd never been this anxious before.

20

Dillinger glanced back at the ship as the topside watch announced his departure. The ship was tied up inside the high-bay weapons loading facility building at the RCA compound at Andros Island, Bahamas. The weapons building was mostly used to load, reload, or offload submarine test torpedoes—exercise weapons with the warheads removed and instrumentation packages inserted in their stead. A sub called to fire ordnance here would have a dozen of her warshots removed and replaced with exercise shots. After her launching of the exercise weapons in the Tongue of the Ocean test range, she would return here to reclaim the warshots.

Why they were here was as much a mystery as this whole mission. For three days they had driven through the deep Tongue of the Ocean bathtub, going back and forth through the test range's sonar arrays running various requested configurations of equipment, allowing the passive sonar arrays to record their sound signature and analyze their noise emissions. The day after that, they had hovered at eight hundred feet rigged for ultraquiet while the range's active sonar hydrophones of the bathtub beeped from various angles and elevations while embarked electronics technicians calibrated and tweaked the BQQ-5E sonar suite. This afternoon he and his XO would receive the results of the sonar tests, then meet with the National Security Council representative.

The first meeting lasted an hour longer than it should have, Dillinger fumed. The technicians handed over the sound emission study, recommending certain pump and equipment configurations for the quietest conditions. The Q-5 was pronounced to be healthy and the sonar gang on board *Tucson* declared fit for duty. The second meeting would be held in an SCIF, a special compartmented information facility, in the basement of the two-story brick Com-SubLant AUTEC building. In the SCIF, Dillinger paced and ran his hand through his hair while he waited for the late NSC rep.

Finally the door opened and a man in a suit walked in. He was slightly shorter than Dillinger, and about twenty years older, with an air of authority to his body language. He had a thick head of long gray hair and an overgrown mustache. His eyes were small and dark, peeking out from under bushy gray eyebrows. Dillinger had the impression the man looked familiar, and then it came to him that he resembled Stalin. He looked at Dillinger with a serious expression and reached out to shake hands, then turned and smiled charmingly at D'Assault.

"I'm Phil Cogsworth," he said. His identification card, hanging from a lanyard around his neck, showed his picture, the words AUTEC VISITOR, and below that, DEPARTMENT OF DEFENSE. "I work for the Undersecretary of Defense. I'm coordinating Task Group 2.01, so technically once you're back at sea, you'll report to me."

Dillinger glanced at D'Assault, then back at Cogsworth. "If you're the boss, maybe you can tell us what this crazy rush to sea was all about."

Cogsworth shrugged. "Right now I can only give you a small piece of the puzzle. Please, have a seat."

Cogsworth sat at the head of the table, with Dillinger sitting next to him and D'Assault next to Dillinger. Cogsworth opened his briefcase and put it on the chair next to him. Dillinger couldn't help thinking he did that to prevent either of them from seeing its contents.

"We've had you docked in the weapons facility to remove two of your tactical Tomahawks and replace them with two RUR-5 Delta SUBROCs. Do you know what a SUBROC is?"

D'Assault looked uncertain, but Dillinger nodded. "It's a Tomahawk with the land-attack or ship-attack warhead removed and a depth charge installed. But the depth charge warhead is a hydrogen bomb."

"A W-44 warhead with a ten-kiloton warhead. Very small for a nuclear weapon, which is intentional. Large enough to kill an opposition submarine, small enough to allow your own survival in the event you are called on to use it."

Dillinger snorted derisively. "Sorry, Mr. Cogsworth, but nukes are useless."

Cogsworth raised his eyebrows. "Why is that, Commander Dillinger?" His voice had turned cold.

"Because of the excessive command and control required. I can launch a torpedo on my own authority if I'm ordered into a fight, but not a nuke. Only the president or a commander-in-chief general officer can give me nuclear release authority. And it takes a damned half hour to receive and decode the emergency action message ordering me to go nuclear. Try going to periscope depth and getting your messages in the heat of battle. It can't be done. And the president won't be issuing the nuclear release orders in advance."

Cogsworth glanced over at D'Assault for a long moment. Dillinger could feel his annoyance, realizing he was becoming protective of D'Assault. He was beginning to think of her as a younger sister.

"Excuse me, Commander, but weren't you a participant in Exercise Stolen Arrows?"

Dillinger nodded slowly.

"Good. Then I take it you withdraw your objection."

Dillinger stared at Cogsworth. The man had practically just promised that Dillinger would have an early nuclear release order, as Vornado had against the *Albany*. But a release against whom? Who was the goddamned enemy? When Dillinger spoke, an anger began to build in his voice. "Mr. Cogsworth, what the hell is our mission? What is it that's serious enough to scramble us to sea, give us a proctological sonar examination, then load us up with antisubmarine nukes and send us back out with no operation order? Does this make sense to you?"

"It does, sir. And I assure you, five hundred nautical miles from here, it will make sense to you, too. I can't tell you anything else here. There are too many mouths and twice as many ears. Once you're at sea, people can't talk."

"They'll be talking about the SUBROCs. It's not every day the crew loads on nukes."

"They don't know. They're labeled as Tactical Tomahawks. There's no nuclear safety inspector present. To anyone observing, the missiles we're loading into your vertical launch tubes numbers one and two are conventional." Cogsworth reached into his briefcase and withdrew a plastic envelope bound tightly with clear plastic tape. Beneath the tape, the envelope was stamped SECRET. "This is the tech manual on the SUBROCs. To your firecontrol system these will look just like Tomahawks, and if you can target a submarine for a Mark 48 shot, you can hit him with a SUBROC. Don't open the envelope until you get your operation order, though."

Dillinger nodded. "Is there anything else?"

Cosgworth pulled out a sheet of paper. "Inventory on the SUBROCs. You need to sign as taking custody."

Dillinger glanced at the paper and signed at the bottom.

Cogsworth put the form in his briefcase and shut it, then stood. Dillinger and D'Assault stood as well. After the obligatory handshakes, Dillinger and D'Assault left and walked down the corridor.

"What was all that about the nuclear release and the exercise?" D'Assault whispered.

"Quiet," Dillinger commanded as the elevator door opened. "We'll talk about it when we're submerged."

It took the remainder of the afternoon to offload vertical launch tubes one and two and replace them with the new weapons. The crew seemed curious, but only to the extent that they wanted to know why two perfectly good cruise missiles were being replaced with identical new ones. When Dillinger was asked by Lionel Tonelle, his weapons officer, he shrugged. "They're doing a quality-control check of what the fleet is carrying around. If they find bugs in a weapon we've had on board for a couple of months, they'll flap and flail until they find out why."

By sunset the RCA compound was fading astern and the ship passed the six-hundred-fathom curve. Dillinger took one last deep breath of Atlantic sea air and lowered himself down the hatch. Thirty minutes later the hull creaked as the *Tucson* descended to her cruising depth and sped up. Their subnote clearance message allowing them to depart AUTEC had merely told them to head northeast and proceed at a speed of fifteen knots. All Dillinger could do was wait for further instructions.

He wasn't good at waiting, he realized as he drummed his fingers on his stateroom's desktop.

The tall, coverall-clad form of Ship Superintendent Yuri Belkov arrived and rescued Vornado from the hours-long security indoctrination that would allow him to work at the Terminal. When he saw Belkov, Vornado felt suddenly guilty, remembering the evening before with Svetlana, but Belkov was either ignorant of their rendezvous or a good actor.

Belkov was ebullient that Vornado was joining the team. He took Vornado up a flight of stairs to the main level of the Terminal. For a long time Vornado simply stared in awe at the facility and the graceful form of the submarine nestled inside levels of scaffolding and equipment. Belkov was content to watch Vornado's expression of admiration.

"Oh, my God," Vornado finally breathed. "It's beautiful."

Belkov laughed. "The shipbuilding room or the Lira?"

"Both. Yuri, I think I've died and gone to heaven. Who built this? It's an engineering triumph."

"I did. Rusanov had the original idea. Leonov had the commercial contacts and the ability to obtain the hull hulks from Gremikha."

"What's that?"

"A submarine decommissioning facility four hundred kilometers northeast of here. The Russian Navy's been scrapping the older nuclear submarines, but there's been a long delay for the Liras because no one from the government has come up with a practical way to scrap a liquid metal–cooled reactor. They built a process and completed it, but it won't work and would be unsafe, so it was abandoned. The Liras would be beached in the wastelands there for decades. It was a huge problem, and it was about to erupt into a scandal. Just as the experts were scratching their heads, Leonov made them an attractive offer. He proposed to the government a revolutionary, cheap way to decommission the liquid-metal reactors. As far as the outside world knows, the reactors are broken up and the radioactive material is put into lead-lined casks and returned to Gremikha for long-term storage in a secure facility, and the ship's steel and titanium is scrapped, with the Kaznikovs keeping the money. Except the radioactive material storage casks aren't filled with waste liquid-metal coolant, just more lead to make them appear heavy and some radioactive waste to make them register on a radiation monitor. And instead of scrapping the metal from the Liras, we're rebuilding them. Rusanov got a waterside warehouse near Gremikha, so he only had to have the hulls towed a few cliks. The towing of submarines is routine there, so another one being pulled in the middle of the night is not noticed. I built a facility inside the warehouse there that breaks up the hull sections into modules that can be unobtrusively shipped by barge to the Terminal."

Vornado stared at Belkov, idly comparing the facial features of the energetic shipyard engineer to Svetlana's. The nose was different, but he could see Svetlana's eyes and facial bone structure in the older man. "So your government thinks you're scrapping the Liras here. What about the nuclear fuel—isn't that controlled material that could go into a bomb? Isn't that rigidly inspected?"

"Ah." Belkov waved his hands. "Leonov buys that on the black market for some of his other businesses. For him, bomb-grade uranium and plutonium are a commodity. Expensive, yes, but available. He simply returns some unprocessed nuclear fuel to the same authorities he bought it from in the first place. The inventories all match, the inspectors are happy, the people Kaznikov bribed are happy, and he doesn't lose money because he makes it up from our customer."

Vornado had never felt that he could be much of a businessman. A Byzantine operation like this would never have occurred to him, and even after having it explained in the simplest terms, he still had trouble comprehending all the deception that was required to make such a plan work.

"What about the danger of doing this here, near a city?"

"To the government, we're doing the radioactive operation up at the Gremikha warehouse, and this is only where we scrap the hulls with their steel and titanium. The beauty of the operation is that if we don't get a buyer for the second and third submarine, we will actually scrap them, in total fulfillment of Leonov's contractual obligations."

Vornado nodded. It all tied together. He wondered how much of this Lewis and his team knew.

"So how do you get this beast out of Murmansk if this is so secret? It would be a disaster if it sailed north up the fjord when it's supposed to be scrap."

Belkov smirked, a conspiratorial expression passing across his face. "Wait and see," he said. He frowned and looked up. "Now, what you see here is the hull and reactor module of the old *K-493*. We chose that one to do first, since its mechanicals were in good shape and its reactor compartment was the easiest to repair. Some of the other ships had nuclear accidents, so for the second and third submarines we will have to mix and match parts. If we sell a fourth Lira, we'd have to build most of its reactor compartment from scratch, which would add a year to the schedule, but still is feasible. If we kept doing that, we could sell units five, six, and seven."

"Does it have a name?"

"Not really. The customer has the honor of naming the vessel, and he doesn't care. We simply call it Lira Unit One, or Unit One for short."

"Who is the customer?"

Belkov shrugged. "I have no idea. Not my job. But I imagine him as someone who just cares about the financial aspects, his eyes only on the ledger."

Vornado nodded. "You said you had problems that you needed help with."

"You ready to get dirty?"

Vornado smiled.

Belkov took Vornado on a long tour of the exterior of the submarine. Aft, it was missing the final module, the sternplanes and rudder section. The ship ended abruptly, resembling a fish with its tail sliced cleanly off. At each point in their walk, Belkov reeled off the technical problems. A write-up of them would take up a very long manual, Vornado thought.

Belkov walked Vornado to the middle of the hull and upstairs to the top of the deck. Vornado gaped at the long, smooth curving sail. It was so faired into the hull at its bottom that there was nowhere to walk on the hull to get from the afterdeck to the forward deck.

"How do you go from back here to the foredeck?"

"Through a tunnel in the fin. Follow me." Belkov walked onto the spongy foam-covered hull. The foam was lighter than that on the *Hampton,* and gave under his boots. Belkov walked to the rear sloping end of the sail—no, the fin, Vornado corrected himself. There on each tilted aft side was a hatch four and a half feet tall and two feet wide. Belkov opened the starboard one and disappeared into the fin. Vornado followed him and found himself in a dimly illuminated cramped tunnel running forward. He had to duck to walk behind Belkov as the tunnel made a gentle curve around what must be the periscopes and masts taking up the center of the fin. Eventually they emerged into a wider spot in the tunnel. A single hatch led to the forward deck. Vornado crouched down and looked through the opening toward the bow. Inside the fin, behind the forward door, was a hatch ring that came to Vornado's shin. It was the upper part of a cylindrical tunnel that led vertically down into the pressure hull. But instead of going down, Belkov opened a hatch that led out of the fin to the foredeck.

There was a gangway to the scaffolding platforms that surrounded the ship at all elevations. Belkov left the hull, walked onto a platform, then ran up two flights of a stair tower. Vornado followed him, one eye on the ship below him. Belkov hurried aft along the top of the fin. Vornado could see the openings for the masts, which were being worked on by crews of technicians. One-third of the way back along the long fin was an odd thing—a three-windowed windshield, but the windows were horizontal and faired into the top surface of the fin.

"On the surface, this is the topside command post. The older navy men called this the bridge." Belkov hit a hydraulic control button on the scaffolding column and the entire windowed assembly rotated slowly vertical. When it stopped, Vornado could see that it formed a place out of the wind for the officers conning the ship. He liked it—it was a much more elegant solution to the problem of wind on the bridge than the American design, which had "clamshells," or fiberglass doors that rotated downward into the cockpit, requiring them to erect a separate Plexiglas windshield. Here, with one hydraulic button, the ship built a weatherproof enclosure around the men on the bridge. Vornado followed Belkov down a short ladder to stand on the bridge. It was odd, Vornado thought, because it was much wider than American bridges, but had its cylindrical tunnel leading vertically downward in the center of the cockpit, and the hatchway was so tall that it was flush with the top of the fin.

"Why's this hatch so tall? Why not at the deck level?"

"Because it's dual function, Peter." Belkov climbed up to the top of the hatchway and threw his leg into the vertical tunnel, then disappeared down inside. Vornado waited, then climbed up. He glanced down, but the interior was dark. Vornado lowered himself further down the tunnel. It was about two feet wide, but only six feet tall, which was strange, since Vornado guessed they were twenty feet above the deckplates of the upper deck. He lowered himself and emerged into a tight compartment, barely seven feet tall, with a hatch at the bottom. The space was cylindrical, perhaps ten feet in diameter. The circular walls had empty brackets and racks, and on one side at the top was a small control panel.

"What is this?" Vornado asked. "There's more to this than a bridge access tunnel."

"It's an emergency escape vehicle. It can separate from the hull. This is the only place we could put it, in the fin. It's one thing that makes the fin so wide. If there's an emergency, the entire twelve-man crew can get into here and leave the submarine. Escape vehicle disconnection circuits are on the control panel there."

"Does it work?"

"Controls are disconnected. The customer saw no value in expending the amount of funds it would take to make it work. Let's go below." Belkov spun the control ring of the hatch at Vornado's knees, pulled the hatch open, and disappeared down the vertical tunnel. A faint light drifted into the combination escape pod and bridge access trunk from below. Vornado followed, lowering himself down the second six-foot-long tunnel.

As his head emerged into the ship's interior, the smell he'd sensed before became stronger. The interior was lit by several strings of temporary lights, some of them strung through a hatch behind him. They were maintenance lamps connected together by their reinforced power cord. He found himself in a cramped vertical accessway, a closet, with his boots on grating. If he stepped aside, he would barely have room to move the grating up and lock it into position so he could lower himself down the opening in the deck to a ladder to the next deck down. Behind him, leading forward, was the open hatch to the next compartment. Vornado turned to face aft and fully opened the door of the closet he was in. As soon as he did he froze, his eyes wide in astonishment.

Yuri Belkov stood in the center of the most advanced control room Peter Vornado had ever seen in his life. He could barely breathe until he was fully inside the oblong room. He stood surrounded by a long, horseshoe-shaped wraparound panel. The deck was about fifteen feet wide from the edge of one panel on the port side to the panel on the opposite side. The panels consisted of sloping sections at a seated man's lap, then a vertical section, then a back-sloping high section. There were seven high-backed leather command chairs at the panels. The centerline of the room had four vertical poles, the penetrations for the masts. One of them had to be the periscope, Vornado thought.

"Welcome to the Lira's automated command post," Belkov said.

The room was quiet, with a dim hum of electronics. Vornado glanced at one of the panels. It resembled photographs he had seen of the control panel of a modern jetliner, the kind with the "glass cockpit," with flat panel displays taking the place of gauges and dials. Each sector of the panel except the lower sloping part was a flat panel display. The lap portion of the consoles was a dizzying assortment of keyboards, trackballs, fixed function keys, toggle switches, cup holders, pencil cups, and clipboard hangers. While Belkov watched in amusement, Vornado began his walk around the horseshoe, starting on the forward port side. The first part of the wraparound panel was a section facing forward, immediately to port of the closet entranceway. The panels there displayed the bowplanes, the sternplanes, the ship's angle, the rudder, and the status of all the ship's fixed and variable ballast tanks.

"Ship control center," Vornado said. Belkov just nodded.

The next panel, forming the corner of the horseshoe, had displays showing the ballast volume vent valves, another display of the tank levels, and several variable ballast pumps. There was a panel showing the hydraulic system, and another showing the snorkel system and the diesel engine and control layout.

"Ballast control center." Again Yuri nodded.

Farther aft there was a panel devoted to displaying the status and controls for about a thousand automatic valves. Aft of that Vornado correctly identified the steam plant control center, the reactor plant temperature-monitoring panel, and the reactor control center. He returned to the head of the horseshoe at the entrance and began again. The forward starboard corner had all black screens.

"Firecontrol center," Yuri offered.

Vornado continued to the aft section. He found the radio control center, the electronic surveillance measures control panel, then a double section of the panel aft devoted to sonar. The aft starboard corner was formed by the navigation equipment, with a huge horizontal flat panel display showing the chart. In the center was Murmansk, and a small yellow blip flashed on the riverbank.

"That's our position," Yuri said.

Vornado walked aft through an opening between the reactor plant control center and the navigation panel, and found himself in an electronic equipment space, with vertical cabinets stacked from the deck to the overhead. Yuri pointed out the areas: navigation electronics and ship control systems on the starboard side, then the four-hundred-hertz rectifiers and the whining gyroscopes and inertial navigation binnacle in the center, the reactor control electronic cabinets to port of the centerline, and the far aft port side taken up by the firecontrol and sonar equipment cabinets. All in all, it was quite compact, perhaps a third the amount of cabinet space taken up by all the similar controls for a 688-class submarine, even bearing in mind that the Lira was fully automated on all levels, and so automated in the engineering spaces that they were unoccupied at sea.

Vornado returned to the center of the control room and spun around and around. "I want to take this ship to sea so bad I can taste it," he muttered. Yuri grinned.

"I had it all set up to show you. Let's head to the middle level so I can let the workers back in here." Belkov walked forward to the access closet and clicked an intercom button on a small communications panel. "We're done in the command post." He stepped to the narrow side area and lifted the grating and latched it in place, then vanished down the ladder to the middle level. Vornado followed him. For the next four hours, the two men crawled through the submarine, exploring every level and every room. Vornado examined each piece of equipment, asking questions and making mental notes.

Finally, after climbing out of the reactor compartment hull-cut into the radioactive access trailer, Vornado sighed. "I need a shower."

"And I need a drink," Belkov said. "Let's clean up and go to the KKS company dinner club."

After a long evening of keeping Yuri Belkov company, Vornado was too drunk to do much more than wave at Svetlana and stagger to the bed. Sometime during the night, he rose to get water for his alcohol-parched mouth. When he returned to bed, he found he couldn't sleep. It was as if the vodka and wine had evaporated, and all he could think about was the Lira submarine. He kept seeing its interior as he was walked through the spaces, the knowledge given him by Yuri spinning in his mind and melding with the older information learned during his career. He realized he was too excited to sleep. There was only one other thing like this experience, he thought, and that was the obsession that came from being in love.

He looked over at Svetlana, whose sleepy eyes had opened. She stared at him raptly, as enamored with him as he was with the Lira.

"Hi," he said.

"Hi," she replied, her eyes brightening. She got up on one elbow and reached her hand to his boxer shorts' waistband. He grabbed her wrist.

"Not tonight. I'm much too tired."

She pouted, but nodded.

"May I ask you a question? What's your relationship to Yuri Belkov?"

She smiled. "He's my father. You didn't know that? Didn't I tell you that was the reason I began to become interested in you? Dad talked about you day and night."

Vornado sighed. "No, actually you didn't mention it."

She nodded, a slight smile on her face. "If I had, you wouldn't have touched me. Like tonight."

Vornado frowned. "Get some sleep. Tomorrow's going to be a long day." He didn't tell her he'd be returning midday to check out of the hotel. At the KKS dinner club, Vornado had insisted to Belkov that he be given a private office inside the Terminal, and that it be equipped with a cot, a refrigerator, and a bathroom. For the next few weeks he would be working twenty-hour days, as he had as the chief engineer of the *Augusta,* when he had caused a shipyard uproar by moving a cot into his barge office and working around the clock for two years to return the ship to seaworthiness, taking only catnaps and a few hours of sleep at a time. He'd also insisted on having a notebook computer loaded with all the Lira's plans, specifications, drawings, shipyard logs, work orders, discrepancy reports, and quality-assurance documents. Yuri promised it would all be ready by the start of the dayshift.

21

In the middle of the night, the phone buzzed. "Captain," Dillinger said into the phone.

"Officer of the deck, sir," Matt Mercury-Pryce's voice said in his ear. "Zero five fifty, Cap'n. We have one of the alphanumeric call sign letters aboard via ELF. Request to slow and come shallow in preparation for coming to periscope depth."

Extremely low frequency radio waves, the only kind able to penetrate a thousand feet beneath the surface, were received by one of the radio antennae in the sail. It was only capable of transmitting one letter every twenty minutes, the data rate of the radio waves that low, and it took tremendous transmitting power and hundreds of acres of transmitting towers, but that was sufficient to transmit a call sign that would alert a deeply submerged submarine to rise to periscope depth to collect a UHF burst transmission from the military communication satellite.

"Very well," Dillinger said. "Come shallow and prepare to come to PD. If the XO's asleep, wake her up."

This was it, Dillinger thought as he stepped into the bathroom and tossed off his T-shirt and boxers. They'd come to periscope depth and get their radio broadcast and one of the messages would be their operation order. He intended to take a one-minute shower. Ever since Plebe Summer, he had been able to step under the water, wash his hair, lather up, rinse off, and towel-dry inside of three minutes. He shut off the water, opened the shower cubicle door, stepped out, and reached for the towel when he looked up to see Lieutenant Commander D'Assault standing less than two feet from him.

She smiled at him. "Sorry, Skipper." Her glance flashed down to his midsection and back up to his face, and her cheeks became suddenly red. He became aware that she was standing too close to him, but it was probably just that the room was so small.

"Natalie," he said as he found the towel, glad that his voice sounded deep. "I think if one of us is naked we should be on a first-name basis."

"Okay, Burke," she said quietly, still standing in front of him, seemingly undeterred by his nakedness. He could see her chest rise and fall as she breathed. "Or do you prefer B.K.?"

He looked at her, amazed that he was considering her question instead of ordering her to leave.

"Everyone else calls me B.K. But it's okay with me if you want to call me Burke," he said finally, the words coming from somewhere else.

"Burke it is," she whispered. Her hand reached out to him and she touched his chest with her index finger. She stepped suddenly away from him and opened the door to leave. She tossed him one last glance and a smile. Then she threw him the towel. He looked down and realized he'd never actually taken the towel off the hook, but still stood there naked, the towel now hanging in his hand. He shook his head, telling himself that he was still asleep and none of what he thought had happened really happened. But he kept thinking of the way her eyes had widened as she looked at him. He could still see the light brown irises of her eyes, which had dilated fully open even in the harsh light of the bathroom.

She likes me, he thought, a sudden ray of happiness penetrating the darkness of his mood since Dayna had left. *Shut up and go back to work,* he commanded himself, but he knew he was grinning to himself as he toweled off.

He dressed in a fresh uniform, slipped into his at-sea black sneakers, and emerged into the control room. Natalie—*dammit, the XO,* he corrected himself—stood at the chart table.

"Where are we?" he asked her, realizing too late that the question could be taken more than one way. Her eyes rose slowly to his, and he was aware of the tiny flecks of gold in them, and her luxuriously long, dark lashes.

"We're here, Captain." She pointed to the chart, one

long fingernail tapping on the display. It was the same finger she had used to touch his chest.

What's wrong with me? a voice inside him yelled. He awoke from a dream of Dayna, was seen naked by his second-in-command, and suddenly his hormones were erupting? He had to get control of himself.

"Captain?" Mercury-Pryce interrupted. "Both letters of our ELF call sign are on board. Ship is at one five zero feet, course north, speed six. We've conducted a full baffle clear with no close contacts, one distant contact, merchant bearing two seven eight, beyond closest point of approach and opening, range in excess of ten thousand yards. Request permission to come to periscope depth to receive our broadcast, sir."

Dillinger took a quick glance at the room. So much knowledge could be gained from one half-second glance at the control room. "Off'sa'deck, proceed to periscope depth."

Dillinger watched as Merc conducted the dangerous evolution of bringing the vessel shallow enough that her periscope with its radio antennae could penetrate the waves. As soon as he'd brought the ship up and the periscope cleared the waves, he raised the BRA-34 radio antenna and received the ship's broadcast messages, which transmitted every seven minutes. Once the radiomen confirmed they had the messages, Merc took the ship back deep.

Dillinger and D'Assault opened the door to the radio room to read the message. When Dillinger finished, he lifted his eyes to D'Assault.

"Lying bastard," he said.

"Who?" she asked.

"Smokin' Joe Kraft. He told me we weren't going on a northern run. This op order puts us right north of Murmansk in the Barents. Can't get much more north than that."

D'Assault looked at the message board in Dillinger's hands, getting close enough to him to touch her shoulder to his arm. He felt an electrical tingle flash up his arm from her touch, but was determined not to betray the feeling to D'Assault. She nodded, then looked over at him.

"It just says to go north of the Kola Peninsula. It doesn't say what we're doing there."

Dillinger nodded. He was becoming used to just-in-time information.

"OOD, get the navigator to the control room." The nav would need to lay in a new course to the position on the op order. "Take her deep and return to course zero four zero at standard."

"Aye, sir," Mercury-Pryce acknowledged. "Dive, make your depth five four six feet. Helm, all ahead two-thirds, right five degrees rudder, steady course zero four zero. Sonar, Conn, going deep. Lowering number two scope."

As *Tucson* tilted downward and accelerated to the northeast, Dillinger reread the operation order, wondering what in God's name they were going to be doing in the arctic waters north of the Russian Republic, armed with two antisubmarine nuclear weapons.

Peter Vornado sank into sleep five minutes after sitting down at Svetlana's dinner table. She tried to wake him, with no success. She put the food away and walked him slowly to the bed, then laid him down and pulled off his clothes. For a long time she watched him as he lay naked on the bed. When he was asleep, he looked like a little boy. Sometimes he would suck on his lower lip, and she would watch it pulsating, wondering if he were thinking about her breasts, or perhaps his ex-wife's or mother's. She lay down beside him and stroked his hair, smiling to herself about today's developments.

Two weeks ago Peter had convened with Yuri, her father, and Rusanov to lay out his plan. He had assembled fifteen integrated teams of workers per shift—organized mostly by major systems such as reactor plant mechanical and electronics, electric plant, main steam plant, drive train mechanical, masts and antennae, periscope optics, emergency diesel, atmospheric controls—with each discipline represented, including hull mechanics, electricians, nuclear and nonnuclear electronics technicians, pipe fitters, pipe and hull welders, machinery mechanics, and internal communications technicians. With Svetlana insisting she wanted to use her engineering knowledge, he had put her to work on the dayshift, managing the dayshift teams under his general supervision. The second shift belonged to her father, and Rusanov ran the graveyard shift.

Peter was tireless, usually at the Terminal for the last four hours of Rusanov's shift, then helping and advising her through her shift, then staying at least five hours into Yuri's shift. When Peter was present, the entire Terminal staff was whipped into an absolute frenzy, inspired by his fingers-in-the-lube-oil leadership. There were times when she watched him and thought that he had missed his calling, that he should have been a battlefield general, and then she would remind herself that he had been a military hero until his health betrayed him. There was no telling where he would have ended up had he been allowed to remain in his American navy.

Svetlana had traded her business suits and pumps for shipyard coveralls and work boots. Her hair hadn't been out of a ponytail for the last two weeks. At the end of each day, she was covered in grime and stinking of sweat and dirt, but she was happier than she could ever remember. Peter gave her new insights every time she hit a snag. He also supported her by giving her a lead foreman who ran herd over her entire fifteen-man operation, a shaved-headed, broad-shouldered hull mechanic named Viktor Danalov, whom she herself had recruited early in the Terminal's operation. She knew that Peter wanted her shift to go smoothly when he wasn't there, and she knew he lacked the fullest confidence in her, because she was young, inexperienced, and, of course, a girl. But she didn't care. Taking the position meant hour after hour with Peter, at a time when he didn't wave her away as being a distraction. She had successfully placed herself at the center of his problems, and hence at the center of his world.

That night, while Peter was at her apartment after working till after one in the morning, the phone rang. It was her father, Yuri, calling to tell her that there had been a terrible automobile accident. Anton Nessov's limo had been smashed in half by a heavy truck between the Terminal's dinner club and his apartment, and there was barely enough left of his body to bury. The funeral would be in the evening of the next day. She had been shocked and dismayed. She knew Peter didn't care for Nessov, but she

had been the one who recruited the crusty ex–Russian
Navy submarine captain. Had he suffered? she asked. Odds
were that it happened too fast for him to realize much,
Yuri answered, and if he had followed his usual routine,
he would have been fairly intoxicated by the time he left
the dinner club. Just before Yuri hung up, he asked her to
relay the news to Vornado. She blushed when she looked
at his naked body in the bed as her father acknowledged
her relationship with the brash American submarine
engineer.

It had been a busy two weeks for all of them. The
teams that Peter had formed had made great progress. At
the end of each shift, Peter debriefed the team foremen,
relentlessly going over the list of equipment problems,
whittling the list ever smaller. He was never satisfied
when the gear didn't cooperate, many times making the
off-going foreman stay well into the next shift while he
and Peter dived into the piping and instrumentation dia-
grams and control schematics. Sometimes Peter and the
foreman would spend three or four hours in the submarine's bilges, tearing apart a trim pump or crawling
through a ballast volume trying to troubleshoot a sticking
vent valve.

Peter's reputation was becoming legend inside the Terminal. Sergei Kaznikov watched him from an upper-level
mezzanine, nodding in satisfaction. Svetlana knew he was
coming to a decision to offer Nessov's position to Peter,
and there had been another crisis brewing, this one over
the staffing of the submarine once it would go to sea.
Nessov had wanted his old cronies from the Russian Navy
hired, but Svetlana had yet to be impressed by any of
them. They were all lazy drunkards, and she knew that
Peter wouldn't accept any of them. Before she had joined
Peter on shift, she had discreetly tried to recruit other,
more professional ex-Navy men from the Russian submarine force, and had found them equally lacking. She had
upshifted the search to an international inquiry, but the
applicants were either nonnuclear submarine sailors or
discontented British or French expatriates with the same
problems as the Russians. Peter had listened to her dissat-
isfaction with the situation, and had calmed her down by

telling her not to worry about it, and to stop wasting time with the search.

"When the submarine goes to sea, we'll take members of the Terminal construction crews. It will be easier to train an expert at the ship's systems and construction in the field of operations than it will to take an operator and school him in this ship's complexities. The operators will be under my supervision, and I'm the best submarine operator here, and I know how to train men." There had been no arrogance in his statement, merely simple honesty.

A small hope dawned in her mind that perhaps she could impress Peter enough that he would appoint her as one of his operators. How thrilling it would be to see him at sea, in his element. She would work on that, she decided. There was not much time. Barely two weeks after Nessov's funeral, Peter had eliminated all the major problems that kept the ship from making progress. Kaznikov's gloomy but realistic forecast of eleven months to prepare the ship for its at-sea mission had shrunk to a mere three weeks, all thanks to Peter's inspired leadership and detailed knowledge of submarines and their construction. Kaznikov had the happy duty of notifying the client that his product was back on schedule.

The client was now becoming the problem. As soon as Kaznikov hinted that the ship might be coming along better than his last forecast, the customer representatives had swarmed all over the Terminal, all of them Egyptian advance men wearing robes and turbans. Svetlana had watched them walking through the shipbuilding room. One of them had registered shock and revulsion that she was a woman wearing coveralls and boots and holding a drawing. She found it difficult to be professional around them, client or not. They were pigs, even if they were paying for all of this.

The client representatives started to make arrangements to load their things on board the ship, even before Peter set the date for the vessel to become waterborne. When he heard about it, he was furious. The ship, to hear Peter speak, was his, and no one did anything to it without his permission. The client reps proposed an odd arrangement—instead of trucking their belongings to the Terminal and flying in separately, they insisted on bringing their things, and the personnel making the sea voyage together in a caravan of four huge buses. They wanted to park the buses inside the Terminal a week before sailing so that they could offload them of the secret cargo they would be carrying, and to use them for accommodations until the moment the vessel sailed. Just before departure they would load their baggage on board, and finally the small client group who would be sailing would board the ship under a veil of secrecy, so that no one from the Terminal would know who they were. They would leave their luxurious buses inside the Terminal until they completed their maiden voyage, when they would have them claimed and driven to the vessel's destination port.

Peter had objected. He didn't want distractions inside the Terminal. He wouldn't allow the buses in until the ship was waterborne and cleared of all system problems, loaded with lube oil, diesel oil for the emergency generator, hydraulic oil, potable water, steam system makeup water, reactor plant makeup liquid-metal coolant, reactor shield tank water, refrigerants, steam generator chemicals, atmospheric control chemicals, and liquid oxygen. Only then, he said, would he allow the clients to come aboard and load their illicit cargo, whatever it was. Kaznikov agreed with him, but said that it would be difficult to convince the client. Peter's jaw had clenched, the way it did when he was enraged, and he'd said to let him talk to the client. Sergei had shaken his head and said he'd get his older brother involved. Leonov Kaznikov could make progress with the Egyptians where Sergei would come away empty-handed. Reluctantly Peter agreed.

When Peter woke up before dayshift this morning, she thought, he would begin the most significant day since he arrived, the day the ship was lowered into the water and brought to final readiness. Had he not been hired as the ship's at-sea commander, his duties would have been completed by the next day, after the ship's chemicals and fluids were loaded and its reactor and steam plant started up and its main and emergency systems tested. Since he was going to be the vessel's captain, today would mark the day he would begin to shift gears. It was so exciting, she thought as she stroked his hair.

She decided to wake him up the way she'd wanted to since she'd met him. He slept while she pulled the waistband of his boxers down, but he was awake soon after.

22

The insomnia was getting worse. It usually happened during the tensest times of a mission, when trailing a hostile target or when submerged in a shallow inner harbor of a foreign nation eavesdropping with an antenna raised to record radio transmissions and private phone conversations. But they were still two days from being on-station and the sleeplessness was on him full force.

Whenever it happened to him, Burke Dillinger did what his own captains had done when he was a junior officer—he leaned over the navigation chart, shot a hundred questions at the officer of the deck, wandered aft and harassed the engineering crew, and then, after all else was exhausted, he sank into his chair in the wardroom and socialized with the officers. It was shortly after 2300 when Dillinger went to the wardroom. The room was deserted except for the duty cook, who set the table for midnight rations, the meal served from 2330 to 0030. Dillinger lifted his elbows so the cook could spread out the linen tablecloth.

"What's for midrats?" Dillinger asked.

"Beanie-weenies over rice with crackers, peanut butter and jelly with white bread, iced tea, bug juice, coffee, and milk, sir," the cook replied. Typical belly-busting midnight-rations fare, good for one thing—keeping the midnight watchstanders awake by any means possible, including indigestion.

Dillinger nodded. If he had any intention of sleeping, the fare tonight should best be avoided. He found the remote control to the television, opened the cabinet housing the plasma display, and turned it on. He scrolled through the menu to find the latest news download from the communications satellite. A burst communication could download a five-minute news update, filmed in a networklike studio.

Occasionally, if the Navy broadcasters considered the network news acceptable, they would just send that. Dillinger clicked the play key and the news segment began, starting with a date-time stamp, since the news was always delayed by a day or so by the time the crew could watch it.

The logo of the Satellite News Network flashed on the screen, then dissolved to show the face of Dayna Baines above a banner reading, BREAKING NEWS—TAIWAN/CHINA TENSIONS ESCALATE WITH TAIPEI'S THREATENED ATTACK ON BEIJING.

"Good evening from SNN World Headquarters," she announced in her heartbreaking Atlanta accent.

"Oh, shit," Dillinger said.

"Is that any way to greet your executive officer?" Natalie D'Assault smiled at him from over his right shoulder. He hit the pause button on the remote and looked up at her with a smile.

She wore black coveralls with the emblem of the USS *Cheyenne* rather than her usual blue set with the *Tucson*'s logo. It was common practice in the submarine force to wear coveralls with the badges of the *Ustafish,* a slang generic term for one's former submarine. But rarely did the senior officers engage in the practice unless the laundry service were behind. Her hair was pulled pack into a partial ponytail, the gleaming raven-black hair in back falling straight to her shoulders, the hair on the side of her face pulled back and clipped behind her head, with her bangs still falling on her forehead. If she were wearing makeup, he couldn't tell. Her naturally long eyelashes framed her dark eyes, and her lips seemed fuller and redder than usual. He could detect just a trace of the scent of her perfume. He thought about the incident in the shower that had happened over two weeks ago, just as they got the op order, and how since then he had taken longer showers, but there had been no other encounters in the bathroom.

She had been standing command duty officer watch since they began the transit north, coming on at 2330 and relieving him of the burden of hour-to-hour command, allowing him to sleep until 0600. She took her sleep during the evening watch, the traditional time when the ship relaxed slightly, when the crew's mess rolled the nightly movie, as did the wardroom, and the smell of theater-style popcorn

wafted throughout the ship. During the morning and afternoon watches, she concentrated on her paperwork, the
ship's schedule demanding even though they were on a long
mission. She also spent considerable time managing the
personnel aspects of the crew, working with her main ally,
the chief of the boat. The COB was the senior nonnuclear
enlisted man aboard, who helped her deal with the hours
of work a crew of 130 required. There were promotions,
fitness reports, disciplinary actions, qualification boards,
and interviews to be conducted. The XO was traditionally
the busiest human being aboard, and D'Assault was no exception. She seemed to relish the work, her attitude always
making her seem fresh and ready for more, which contrasted starkly with how Dillinger had been as an XO. By
watching her, he saw how well the XO job could be done.
He remembered his own dark moods and the way he used
to snap at the COB and the crewmembers, and the ruthless
way he'd ordered the junior officers around. D'Assault handled it all with so much more aplomb, using psychology
when Dillinger had relied primarily on brute force. He began
to wonder anew if his ascendancy to commanding officer were
the result of Dayna Baines's broadcast segment on him,
when he remembered the paused broadcast.

"Hello, XO. I was just talking to my old girlfriend. How
are you? How's the crew?"

D'Assault glanced at the screen as she gracefully sat in
the chair immediately to his right. The chair was the executive officer's customary chair, and had she been a man she
would have plopped down in the same chair, but there was
something about the fact that the room was deserted and
she was sitting so close to him that made his pulse race in
his ears.

"Your girlfriend? Oh, I see. You men—always falling in
love with the weathergirl on television," she said to him, a
tease in her voice.

"No, I mean it," he said. "She was a local Norfolk news-
caster and did a segment on the *Miami* when I was XO.
After the piece aired, she asked me out." He gave her his
most dashing smile, or at least what he guessed passed for
dashing. "I mean, let's face it—how could she possibly
resist?"

D'Assault looked at him seriously, one eyebrow lifted

just slightly, a quick glance at the screen; then her eyes returned to Dillinger's. "Oh, exactly, Skipper," she said quietly. "Who could blame her? I know how she feels."

He stared back at her, stunned, then looked away at the instrumentation cluster on the outboard bulkhead, pretending to monitor the ship's course, speed, and depth, even though the needles hadn't budged in twenty hours. "Not that it matters," he said, trying not to allow the heaviness into his voice, but not sure he had succeeded. "She took the SNN job in D.C. a few months ago and then took up with her new boss. We broke up on the eve of departure."

D'Assault was silent for a moment. "If it's any consolation, Skipper, I recently went through the same thing," she said, her expression compassionate. "Charlie and I ended our engagement just before I reported aboard. He found someone new." She shook her head, but there wasn't a trace of sadness on her face. "These things are always painful, even if they eventually put you in a better place."

Dillinger looked at her dumbly, realizing his mouth was open. He'd had no idea. She had just never acted single. He glanced at her left ring finger. She'd always worn her Academy ring there, he thought, as she was tonight. It had never occurred to him that she might have broken her engagement. He'd just assumed she wasn't the type to wear an engagement ring.

"Anyway, sir, you asked about the crew. Things aren't good."

Dillinger snapped back into the moment. "What do you mean?"

The cook entered and set a coffee cup in front of Dillinger and poured it full of the steaming brew. D'Assault accepted a cup, then waited for the cook to leave.

"Well, sir, the op order hinted that the Task Group 2.01 commander might monitor all outgoing and incoming private communications. They've done far more than that. No one has received an incoming e-mail message since we got the op order. I've sent out my share of e-mails, all of them official except one to my mother, and all of them have bounced."

Dillinger frowned hard at her. "You should have told me this immediately. I would have bitched in a message to

2.01." He should have known all this without having to be
told, he thought, but he had had no reason to send any e-
mails. To whom would he send a note? His old girlfriend,
Dayna? Fat chance. His old pal Peter Vornado? He was
laboring in some godforsaken shipyard someplace with no
cell phones and no Internet uplink. He could have sent a
message to Rachel Vornado, but she was probably as in
the dark about Peter as Dillinger was. In a way it was
depressing just how isolated he was becoming. He glared
at D'Assault, trying to concentrate on what she was saying.

"I know, sir, and that's why I didn't tell you. We don't
need to be complaining to the mission commander because
Suzie back home can't send a flowery love note to Petty
Officer Smith."

"Yes, we do," Dillinger said, anger rising in his stomach.
"What about emergencies? What about Lieutenant
Schluss's expectant wife? What about Chief Keating's kid,
who has leukemia? If the fleet cuts off our e-mail, we lose
the loyalty of the crew."

She put her hand on top of his, just for a moment, as if
she were a mother trying to calm a hysterical teenager.
"All those urgent private communications are coming over
in the submarine broadcast in the form of family-grams,
sir." Family-grams were how the fleet had handled personal
communications in the old days before fleet e-mail, coding
personal messages into the official submarine message
queue, delivered by the radiomen directly to the crewmember addressed. D'Assault removed her hand and put it
in her lap, and just then Lieutenant Pat Schluss, the damage
control assistant reporting to Engineer Steve Flood,
walked in.

Dillinger nodded, his anger evaporating. "Hey, Pat," he
said, deciding to test Natalie's statement. "Any word on
Mama?"

Schluss smiled. "Got a family-gram last periscope depth,
Cap'n. She had her last ultrasound and everything's fine.
They said it's a boy. Actually, the nurse's exact words were,
'Oh, that is *definitely* a boy.' Apparently he takes after his
old man, physically, I mean—"

Dillinger held up his palm. "We get it, Patty. That's
enough. You've got mixed company on board."

"The XO, sir? Skipper, XO's one of the guys. No disrespect intended, ma'am. I mean, it's a compliment."

D'Assault smiled at the young officer. "I know Patty, and thank you."

Dillinger stared at both of them. He decided to let the issue pass until he was alone with D'Assault. "Well, now, DCA," he said, addressing Schluss by his job title, "can we offer you some beanie-weenies?"

Schluss nodded, moving farther into the room. He turned to see what was on the video display and smiled when he saw Dayna Baines. As he turned his back to retrieve his napkin from the sideboard drawer he made a comment over his shoulder: "Your girlfriend's looking mighty fine tonight, Skip."

Dillinger looked directly at D'Assault, a slight smile on his face. "Believe me, I know," he said, hoping she knew he wasn't talking about Dayna. She looked back at him, her gaze as naked and smoldering as his, her eyes wide, until finally she blinked and looked down at her plate.

Just then Navigator Rob Cummins came into the room. "Evening, Captain, XO," he said in his surprisingly high-pitched voice. Genetics had played pranks this time, Dillinger thought, that Cummins could be so intimidatingly huge, yet have such a soft voice. He got his napkin and sat down next to D'Assault. The cook returned and took orders, and within a minute had served the officers.

Cummins glanced up at the video screen. "Anything yet?"

They'd been scanning the news reports to see if there were anything in the open media about northern Russia, which might help give this odd mission some context.

"Nothing," D'Assault said.

Something was different, Dillinger thought. He glanced over at the instrumentation cluster on the outboard bulkhead, which displayed speed, compass bearing, and depth. The speed indicator had fallen below their usual fifteen knots to eleven and was continuing to fall.

Seeing his attention on the speed indicator, Rob Cummins spoke up. "Skipper, at this point on the chart the PIM slows to five knots."

They were near the top of the world now, well into the

Barents Sea, north of the Arctic Circle, heading east in the
waters north of Sweden on the way to the Sweden–Finland
border, and from there directly into Russian waters north
of the Kola Peninsula.

Dillinger nodded at the navigator as the phone from the
control room buzzed. "Right on cue," he said as he pulled
the phone handset up from under the table. For just an
instant his hand brushed D'Assault's knee, and as the
sparks flashed up his arm he wondered if he were blushing,
just before he wondered what her leg was doing so close
to the under-table phone. His eyes caught hers, and he
thought he saw the corners of her eyes crinkling in a secret
smile. "Captain," he said.

"Captain, Officer of the Deck, sir," Lieutenant Mercury-
Pryce's voice said crisply over the circuit. "We're at point
Kilo on the secret chart. The op order calls for a reduction
of speed to five knots in accordance with PIM. Accordingly,
sir, I've slowed to all ahead one-third, turns for five knots."

"Very well, OOD. Where are we with respect to PIM?"
Dillinger asked. PIM was the op order's point of intended
motion, a place on the chart where the task group commander wanted them at any given time, which up to now
had traveled at fifteen knots, which was relatively fast to
report to hostile waters. Fast enough to make speed over
ground, but slow enough not to broadcast own-ship's noise,
and slow enough that their sonar search wasn't impeded by
their own machinery noise. But it was still too fast when
close to a paranoid former adversary.

"Two miles ahead, sir. Op order prefers us to be within
ten miles but allows us to be twenty miles from point of
intended motion."

"Very well. Anything else?"

"Yes, sir. Request permission to rig ship for ultraquiet
red."

Dillinger glanced at the bulkhead chronometer. Rigging
ship for ultraquiet meant shutting down the galley, and he
wanted the off-going watch section to get one last hot meal.
The "red" codeword was Dillinger's invention on the
Miami, when he ordered switching all overhead lights in
the forward compartment from white to red to remind the
crew that the ship was on its tiptoes.

"Off'sa'deck, rig ship for ultraquiet red with the exception of the galley. At zero one hundred, bring the ship to the full rig.''

"Aye, sir, rig for ultraquiet red except the galley until zero one. Sir, request to shift main coolant pumps.''

The rig for ultraquiet required they reconfigure the ship's pumps so that they would run the quietest combinations, as dictated by the sound surveillance report from AUTEC.

"What've you got now?"

"One, two, four, and five in reduced freq. We need to run three, four, five, and six."

"Very well, inform the engineer and shift reactor recirc pumps."

"Aye-aye, sir. That's all."

Dillinger hung up the phone. As he put the phone under the table he felt D'Assault's soft finger stroke his hand. For just a moment he let his hand freeze there, feeling the warmth of her finger and the cool sharpness of her long fingernail on the back of his hand. He realized that his eyelids were going half-shut as he concentrated on her touch. He caught himself, and opened his eyes wide. Her finger left his hand and he put the handset back in its cradle, but before he brought his hand back he touched her knee, this time giving her a deliberate squeeze, while he turned his head to watch the ship's speed display. When he pulled his hand back he realized he was breathing much faster than normal.

Control yourself, he thought. He was acting like a teenager. He blinked as he folded his napkin. He felt D'Assault's knee touch his under the table. With his best stony face he stood, knowing he had to take this out of the wardroom, and wanting to talk to D'Assault.

"I'll be at the chart, XO. I'd like to see you in my stateroom in five minutes," he said in his best businesslike voice.

"Aye-aye, sir," she said, her voice slightly hoarse.

As he left the room, the overhead fluorescent lamps clicked out, the darkness startling. After a half second, red lights clicked on, then off, then back on, flickering for just a moment before stabilizing. The passageway was illuminated in a haunted-house blood red. The bass noise of the air handlers suddenly changed, the fans downshifting. The submarine was whisper quiet. Dillinger quietly hurried up the stairs to the control room.

"Captain's in control," Mercury-Pryce announced.

Dillinger waved to him as he examined the chart. They were close now. In a matter of hours they would be in Russian waters, hovering at the last chart point mentioned in the operation order, Point November, north of the Kola Fjord—the river leading northward from Murmansk. The only thing that would bring them here was a new Russian submarine, Dillinger thought. This was one of the places a Russian new-construction submarine would emerge from the building ways on sea trials. This was the old game, lying in wait for a new-construction Russian nuke so they could get a broad-spectrum close-range sound recording of the new ship's tonals and transient noises, so that in the future they would be able to search for submarines of that class with the same sound signature. But what did that have to do with loading two antisubmarine hydrogen bombs on board?

Their operation order required them to minimize periscope and radio-mast exposure once north of the Arctic Circle. If Dillinger were satisfied with the accuracy of his navigation gear this far north, he was ordered to avoid the surface altogether, and only return to periscope depth if called from the deep by an ELF call sign or when they reached their destination, Point November. Once there, they were ordered to come to periscope depth for an op order update and an intelligence briefing, unless the task group commander came up with the news earlier. Dillinger would be relieved when the op order addendum came out. He wanted to get the answers to the questions everyone had been asking, and to come clean with the crew about the SUBROCs. Satisfied that he had the picture, he stood erect.

Mercury-Pryce asked if he could give Dillinger a post-watch report now that he'd been relieved by Steve Flood, who was taking over the OOD watch for the midnight watch. Dillinger listened attentively, then dismissed Mercury-Pryce and nodded a greeting to Flood. The engineer stood on the periscope stand wearing red goggles despite the red light of the room to ensure that his eyes were night-vision adapted in case the ship needed to come suddenly to periscope depth, and the green readouts of the attack center could interfere with his retinal shift to night vision.

Dillinger walked forward to his stateroom and retracted his bunk to form the café-style booth. On impulse he leaned over and locked both doors, the one to the control room and the other to the passageway. He sat in his high-backed leather command chair and waited for D'Assault, wondering what he had called her in to say. Were his intentions to tell her they needed to stop this thing before it started? Or to negotiate a relationship, with all that meant? Oh, God, he thought. He hadn't asked for this. He didn't need this. It was just happening. It was happening despite the fact that he'd been picked for command because of his self-discipline in addition to his nautical skills. And here he was acting like a teenager with his executive officer.

A part of him blamed the shore command. What did they expect, knowingly putting two young single officers in a situation that demanded they work hand in hand, far at sea, for months at a time? He wasn't a machine, he fumed. He had blood flowing through his veins like any other man, and Natalie D'Assault was a gorgeous flesh-and-blood woman in the prime of her sexuality. Biology didn't freeze in its tracks because of the damned Navy Regulations book. The thought came to him: Why couldn't Smokin' Joe Kraft have sent him someone ugly? And then he laughed out loud at how ridiculous that seemed.

Just as he was laughing, the door to the head that connected his cabin with the XO's cracked open. "Captain?"

"Come in, Natalie," he said, his voice warm. Perhaps he would just see what cues he picked up from her. If she had a cooler head than he did, she might tell him to stop this foolishness. If she did, he was prepared to agree with her, despite how much he wanted her. But when he looked up at her, desire flooded him, filling his lungs with a gasp and making his pulse flutter. He bit the inside of his lip to try to get ahold of himself. "Sit down."

"Listen, Skipper, before you say anything, please let me apologize for—"

He saw her expression, her face seeming closer in the red-lit cabin. She registered pained regret, and he saw that she was going through the same torture he was. He decided he wouldn't allow her to suffer because of him.

"Natalie," he interrupted, "don't you dare apologize. You did nothing wrong. If there is any blame, it is reserved entirely for me. I have to confess, I'm losing control. If we met in other circumstances, our relationship would be completely different. We would be free to . . . well, you know . . ." His voice trailed off as he ran out of words to describe how he felt about her.

She seemed glum for a moment, her lips forming a delicious pout, but at the word *relationship* something on her face changed.

"Burke, what are you really saying?" There was that word on her lips again, he thought. When he heard her voice say his name, something inside him completely melted.

Dillinger sighed. "Please help me through this, Natalie." He looked away, the ship's glowing red speed indicator by the head of his bunk reading five knots, the compass showing course east, the digital depth-indicator readout showing keel depth of three hundred feet in the shallow Barents. "I've got feelings for you that have nothing to do with how a captain feels toward his exec. When you're near me, I'm just a lonely man looking at and thinking about a beautiful woman. A woman he cares about deeply in a hundred ways, not one of those ways appropriate for a commander to feel for his second-in-command. I'm so sorry, Natalie. I know it's unprofessional. I didn't intend this; it's not who I am as an officer. I just . . ." He held out his hands with his palms up in a gesture of helplessness and looked into her eyes.

She looked back at him, her eyes completely liquid, as if she were on the verge of tears. Her lips parted just slightly. He saw her tongue quickly moisten her lips, and then she half stood. Her hands touched his shoulders as she bent over to come closer to him, and as he looked up at her, her lips suddenly met his. All he could feel was the wet warmth of them, and her hands touching him, and without volition his arms reached out for her and he pulled her closer, kissing her like he'd never kissed a woman in his life. He could feel her eyelashes flutter against his cheeks, and he opened his eyes and saw her staring at him lovingly while she kissed him. Her tongue circled his gently yet urgently, the skin at the corners of her eyes crinkling in happiness. As he cupped her breast in his hand, the phone's buzzer sounded loudly. He jumped, and as suddenly as she had come into his arms, she sat back down on the café bench. When she separated from him, he felt as if half of him had been abruptly torn away, leaving him bleeding and alone.

He licked his lips, breathing as if he'd just sprinted forty yards. He could still taste her, and he longed to kiss her again. He took a deep breath, trying to control his breathing, and picked up the handset.

"Captain."

"Cap'n, Off'sa'deck, sir," Steve Flood said. If Flood had any idea what was going on, he didn't betray it. "We've got the first letter of our ELF callsign aboard. Recommend coming shallow in preparation to coming to periscope depth."

Dillinger shook his head. He was getting used to getting his mission information in tiny doses, each preceded by an ELF order to come shallow. "Very well, OOD. Report all contacts."

"No sonar contacts, Captain. We're alone up here."

"Take her shallow and clear baffles; then take her up to PD."

"Shallow, baffle clear, PD, aye, sir."

"I'll be in radio." Dillinger hung up and looked seriously at D'Assault. "Keep your door locked when we're together," he whispered. "Turn up the phone so you don't miss a call. And for God's sake, don't give us away in public." They both stood and he pulled her close, then kissed her again, this one as electric as the first, but lasting only a second. He pulled away and looked into her eyes. Her gaze shifted from his left eye to his right as she tried to look into his soul.

"I'm so glad, Burke," she whispered. "I've spent the whole run falling for you."

He put his finger on her lips to quiet her, then turned to his sink in the corner. There was lipstick on his lips, and his hair was disheveled. He brushed his hair and washed off Natalie's lip gloss, and when he stood up to towel off, she was gone, back through the head door. He shook his head and took another deep breath, trying to bring himself back to the moment.

He walked to the upper level and keyed in the combination lock at the radio room door, then came in. The deck

tilted from port to starboard as Flood brought them up to
periscope depth. The surface would have to have a high
sea state to rock them like this at periscope depth, Dillinger
thought. There must be a storm blowing topside.

After a wait of a few minutes, every second of it spent
thinking about Natalie, the radio chief handed him the two
messages. He scanned them both quickly, not sure which
one was the more astonishing—the emergency action message granting them full nuclear weapon release permission
as of right then, or the operation order update message
directing them to sail into the deep channel of the mouth
of the Kola Fjord to await the sortie of an outbound Russian nuclear submarine.

The answer was the second, he decided. The submarine
leaving the Kola Fjord was a rebuilt Improved Alfa nuclear
submarine, one with all the terrifying speed and depth capability of the old Alfa, but with revolutionary new sound
quieting—one that they were directed to trail in complete
stealth until it reached open water. The final paragraph
ordered them to shoot to kill the Alfa, provided there was
no one around them in the seas who could testify to the
explosions of their torpedoes and nuclear SUBROC
missiles.

Natalie came into the room behind him, and he was
aware of every molecule of her. He passed the messages to
her, and watched the planes of her face harden into a scowl,
then form an expression of shock and awe.

"Oh, my God," she said, rereading both messages.

"Exactly," Dillinger said. "I don't care that it's the midwatch, XO," he ordered, once again her captain. "Get the
officers together in the wardroom for an op brief. And get
out everything we have in the secret safe about the Alfa.
And XO . . . it's time to tell our officers about the SUB-
ROCs. I've got a feeling we may be using them."

Dillinger reread the message. He wondered if, between
all that had happened with Natalie and these crazy orders,
he were really asleep and simply having freakish midrats-
induced dreams.

23

The countdown to lowering the ship into the water was in its final hour. Vornado sat at his desk in his dark office, his thoughts turning to what would happen after they got to sea. Hank Lewis's mission plan stated that once the Lira was in deep waters, Lewis's agents aboard would mount a mutiny and take over the ship. Danalov was obviously one of Lewis's assets in place. Vornado knew because there was no mistaking that face. It was the same man who had saved Vornado's career so many years ago during Plebe Summer, after he and Dillinger had executed the recon raid against Midshipman Whitehead. Midshipman First Class Victor Kaminsky had eventually become CIA officer Viktor Danalov. No amount of years could remove Kaminsky's voice from Vornado's memory. Not even plastic surgery—if he had had any—could take away Vornado's memory of Kaminsky's eyes, the same eyes that had drilled into his while he had pointed the stereo remote control at the huge speakers and asked Vornado if he had hurt Whitehead. The same eyes that had looked back at Vornado from the fifth-compartment lower level as Danalov worked on a sticking hull seawater valve.

As he had been trained during his whirlwind session at Camp Peary, Vornado registered no recognition of Kaminsky when he saw him. Apparently real spies ran into each other all the time, but no one ever broke his cover story, not even with a nod or a wink. Vornado knew the recognition was completely one-sided. He could name every one of the firsties who had trained him during his plebe year at the Academy, yet had forgotten every name and face of the plebes he had trained when he himself was a firstie. And that was why Victor Kaminsky—now Viktor Danalov—showed no recognition of Vornado whatsoever. Perhaps since they knew Vornado would know Danalov, Lewis had not identified Danalov early. There had been no conversations since he had worked here with a CIA contact, so how did Lewis know Vornado would pick the right at-sea crew?

The only other explanation was that Svetlana was working for Lewis. He had considered that possibility two dozen times, and each time it didn't feel right. She was who she claimed to be. He was certain of it.

If Vornado's guesses were correct, Danalov would be the man who would help get this mission accomplished. Under Lewis's premission instructions, Vornado had made several demands when the Kaznikovs offered him the job of being the Lira's captain. The first was torpedoes. That had caused an argument that lasted half the night, but Vornado had threatened to walk.

Finally they had grudgingly agreed to find five UGST torpedoes, which were the Russian equivalent to the Mark 48. And once again, the Russian technology wasn't in answer to the comparable American iron, but an independent development. The only disadvantage the UGST had over the Mark 48 was that its chase speed was ten knots slower. In every other category, it was superior. Unlike the Mark 48, which took half a village to program, shoot, and steer, the UGST was a true "fire and forget" weapon, with a development the Russians called the "Planshet algorithm," the Holy Grail of torpedo design, a reality-modeling fuzzy-logic targeting program that prevented the torpedo from becoming confused by enemy countermeasures and that could distinguish the target from the firing ship and from friendly units in the area based on the battlespace environmental picture as of firing time. An operator would tell the UGST firecontrol program if the target was a surface ship or a submarine, the approximate location of the target, and any knowledge of friendly forces, and then set it loose. Its computer would do the rest, although it could be given postlaunch instructions like the Mark 48.

His next demand was that the escape vehicle be made fully functional, in order to make the clients feel safer. The Kaznikovs had agreed. Vornado had then demanded that he be allowed to take five of the Terminal's staff as his crew. At this the Kaznikovs had balked, but Vornado had eventually prevailed. His list included the talented Maslov brothers, Viktor Danalov, Svetlana Belkov, Yuri Belkov, and Andrei Rusanov, who would be Vornado's second-in-command.

When that was settled, Vornado made his final demand. "I'll need personal sidearms," he had said. "I require a Smith & Wesson stainless-steel forty-five-caliber pistol, model 4566TSW. I'll need six of them, with one belt holster. I'll also need six Walther P99 model nine millimeter pistols with the fifteen round magazines with one shoulder holster, and two Walther PPK 7.65-millimeter pistols with the seven-round magazine with an ankle holster. I want five boxes of ammunition in each caliber and four spare clips for each weapon. I want the three holsters and one of each weapon delivered in a package to me with two clips of each caliber. The other firearms, clips, and ammunition need to be locked in the captain's stateroom safe. If the safe's not big enough, install a bigger safe. Immediately."

"What's all that for?" Sergei had asked in astonishment.

"Client control," Vornado said with a straight face. Both Kaznikovs burst into laughter. Leonov slapped Vornado's shoulder.

"Believe me, we understand," Leonov said, still chuckling. "We'd like to use some of that kind of client control ourselves."

"I mean it," Vornado said, his jaw clenched. "If I am in command of the Lira, I am an absolute dictator. Your client can control the mission, but I command the submarine, and anyone who doesn't understand that will see an example of what I mean. It should only take one bullet. Anyway, I will need to test each firearm in a shooting range. It wouldn't do for me to load pistols that don't work."

"You're serious."

"Listen, I'm taking your best talent to sea with some of the most dangerous terrorists in the world. I won't risk having your people roughed up by cowards. The Egyptians must not think of us as their bus drivers. We'll attempt to earn their respect, but if they begrudge it, we'll obtain it from the barrel of a gun." Vornado made the speech as nonchalantly as he could, but he had been rehearsing it in his mind for weeks, as he had the torpedo request.

Sergei shrugged. "Why not? You'll use them responsibly, I'm sure." He scribbled on his pad and looked up. "That's all?"

Vornado thought for a long minute. He shook his head. "No. I'll need a handshake agreement that I will be awarded the building work for Unit Two in the event it sells. My salary requirement is two million base pay with a bonus of an additional two million if I beat the schedule, which we'll agree now will be a target duration of half of the Unit One timetable."

Sergei scribbled busily. "Would you consider a second at-sea mission?" Leonov asked.

Vornado hesitated. "Depends. It will cost you. And I may require more than five paltry torpedoes."

Both men smiled and agreed. After that, they spent the next two hours drinking to future success, with Sergei occasionally making cell phone calls to arrange what Vornado had demanded.

With Vornado's sidearms, they would quarantine the terrorists. Lewis had left the tactics up to Vornado, but Vornado and Lewis's final plan was to mutiny with weapons that Danalov would obtain and lock the terrorists up in a confined space, and if that weren't possible, to kill them outright, then drive the ship back to Norfolk. The U.S. Navy would then have an unmatched prize, and Abdas al-Sattar and his lieutenants would either be caged and turned over to the FBI or lying in the frozen stores compartment, ready to be examined before burial.

Vornado entertained the thought that Lewis might have ordered a U.S. sub to trail the Lira and preemptively shoot at it, therefore killing Abdas and his men before they could do any damage, with complete assurances that they had scored a lethal kill. It would, of course, sacrifice Vornado and Danalov. Vornado had no idea whether the CIA was accustomed to killing their own operatives if the target were as high-value as Abdas, but he could see the decision going that way. It had a logic to it. Vornado's family was provided for, and Danalov was a professional. The only thing that made him disbelieve that scenario was the Lira submarine itself. The CIA recognized the Lira's value as a supersub. Certainly they would order it captured alive. Which was what he would be watching for. If he could lock up Abdas and fend off a hostile intruder sub, he could drive the Lira back home. And then this damned ugly mission would be over.

The thought occurred to him that then Svetlana Belkov would be walking the same Virginia Beach streets as Rachel. If she were Lewis's agent, she would forget about Vornado and return to her duties, and his worries would be over, because her assurances that she loved him would prove to be merely her duty as his contact. In the more likely event that she wasn't Lewis's girl, she would return to Russia and to her previous life. What if she wanted to stay near him? he wondered. That would be a disaster. They didn't mention anything about this at Camp Peary. What did the professionals do when a cover-story romance became sticky, for God's sake? He put his worries aside as the driver arrived at Svetlana's building.

Fortunately she was already asleep. He climbed into bed next to her as quietly as he could. She made a sound in her throat and snuggled her naked body up to him under the covers, aware of him even in her sleep. He tried to fall asleep, but his mind turned to thoughts of the sea mission. He wondered how he would get along with terrorist Abdas al-Sattar, whom he would meet in two days, after the ship was waterborne with all systems started up.

Finally he fell asleep, and as he had every time he slept for the last three weeks, in his dreams he struggled to survive the hazing of Midshipman Whitehead, the only thing good about the nightmare his memories of Midshipman Dillinger.

Peter Vornado accepted the steaming hot cup of coffee from Svetlana. He had just returned from a subbasement stockroom that he'd used for a firing range to test the firearms Sergei had brought. One of the Smith & Wesson .45 pistols was holstered at his hip. Inside his coveralls, nestled in a shoulder holster, was one of the Walther P99s, and in a special ankle holster he wore one of the tiny Walther

PPKs. Vornado liked the heavy feel of the weapons. He couldn't imagine going to sea with the Egyptians without them.

They stood on the railed mezzanine overlooking the Lira. It finally looked like a submarine, he thought. The Terminal's scaffolding, man lifts, and scissor lifts had been removed from the hull. The thousands of feet of power cords and gas hoses had been cleaned up. The ship was finally ready to be lowered into the water. It would descend vertically into a flooded pit below the floor level of the Terminal, just like the construction table at Electric Boat, but this mechanism was inside the building. Beside him on a small console were the controls to the massive hydraulic system that would turn the huge screw columns connected to the table. As soon as he got the word from Rusanov that the ship was ready, Vornado would energize the hydraulics to the columns, and the Lira would begin its descent to become waterborne.

With nothing to do until Rusanov emerged from the hull, he smiled at Svetlana and noticed that, for the first time in weeks, her hair wasn't pulled back in a bun or a ponytail, but flowing in shining waves to her shoulders. She was so young, he thought, barely eight years older than his daughter Marla. With that thought a stabbing feeling of guilt flashed through him, because whenever he thought of Marla, he thought about how she reminded him of Rachel, and thinking of Rachel while looking at Svetlana was enough to sear his heart. Quickly he turned back to the submarine below them.

Rusanov arrived along the mezzanine, huffing from his haste. "Ship's ready to get wet," he said. He stared at Vornado's gun. "Well, I see you're not a man to trifle with."

Vornado nodded and opened the control cabinet. He rotated the control switch from the REMOTE to the LOCAL position, then rotated the power selector from AUTO to DOWN. A groaning metallic screech sounded through the cavernous Terminal building, and a vibration shuddered through the floor, shaking Vornado's teeth.

"Down she goes," Svetlana said.

Vornado watched as, inch by inch, the ship was lowered into the water. It would take two hours for the vessel to

sink to the point of her final draft marking. Until then, the
ballast volume valves were opened so that she wouldn't
become unstable and roll over. Vornado stood there for
the next two hours until the ship was fully waterborne. The
entire time he thought about how he would take the ship
over from Abdas al-Sattar.

"Here's a list of people I want brought into the lower conference room." It was five in the morning by Vornado's
watch. It was Sunday, he thought, having to calculate the
day of the week. Since he'd been working on the Lira,
there had been no weekends, which made every day a Monday. "Bring them in at nine."

"But it's Sunday. It's A Crew's day off."

"Find them. Those people are going to sea on the Lira
when we shove off Tuesday night." Rusanov dropped his
jaw and stared at Vornado in incredulity. "Including you,
Andrei. You're my second-in-command. Pack a bag."

Rusanov finally found his voice. "Um, sir, I'd be afraid.
I don't like the idea of being on a ship and going underwater—I just can't do it."

"Andrei," Vornado said, "after an hour you'll be used
to it. No arguments. I need a crew, and you know the
vessel's every nut and bolt. You'll be so busy keeping it
in working condition, you'll barely notice it's at sea. Your
grandfather would be proud of you."

Rusanov looked cautiously at Vornado, as if measuring
him. "You'll keep me safe?" He sounded like a child talking to his mother, Vornado thought, a sudden empathy filling him for the younger engineer.

"I'll keep you safe, Andrei," Vornado said quietly, his
hand on Rusanov's shoulder. "I promise."

Rusanov nodded, a look of anxiety coloring his features.
"I'll do it, sir."

Vornado walked toward the stern of the ship—toward
the river—when he heard the rumbling of the bridge crane,
which was odd, since nothing heavy remained to be lifted
for the submarine. The escape pod crew wouldn't need the
crane, and other than the torpedoes it had been over a
week since the heavy crane had rolled through the building.
Vornado walked to the edge of the manufacturing floor,
near the handrails guarding the narrow slip of water that

the Lira floated in, where he saw the huge blue bus being lifted by the crane.

The clients must have brought the buses in by barge, he thought. What an odd way to get buses to Murmansk, but anything in the river under a barge tarp went unmolested, while trucks and cars and buses could be searched by border guards and local and provincial police. The client obviously didn't want questions asked. The crane set the bus down at the end of the floor, near the bow of the Lira, then slowly returned to the barge offloading room. As Vornado watched, three more buses were offloaded, the others placed behind the first, extending in a line down the length of the slip beside the submarine. It didn't matter, since the floor wasn't going to be used anyway, now that the ship's construction was complete. Still, it had to be the strangest way he'd ever seen a bus arrive.

Men in robes and turbans walked from the barge offloading room toward the buses. The clients, he thought. Most of them were older, with heavy beards and tinted glasses, but there were a few younger men. There was not a woman among them. One of the younger ones barked orders at some of the Terminal crew, shouting at them to retrieve their luggage and supplies from the bus to load onto the Lira. Even though Sergei and Leonov had told him about the client, Vornado could feel a resentment that he would share his submarine with these men, who in their arrogance were ordering around skilled technicians as if they were slaves. He glared at them, revulsion rising in his throat. He doubted that the cultural awakening he'd felt with the Russians would happen with the Egyptians. From a hundred feet away he didn't like them, yet couldn't have verbalized why. Perhaps it was simply because these men intended to slaughter millions of innocent people because of a centuries-old quarrel. Children, Vornado thought. They would willingly kill toddlers like Erin if it served their purposes, and that was what made them different from him. He himself would kill in a battle without a second thought, as he had been trained all his career to do. But he would never knowingly push a button that would launch a weapon that would kill an innocent child. War or no war, he wouldn't shoot at hospital ships or cruise ships or launch missiles at civilian populations. He felt his hand rise to his throat, missing the Saint Christopher's medal that Rachel had once given him, yet another of his possessions that he had not been allowed to bring with him.

He decided to go aboard the sub to see what the clients were doing. He boarded the narrow catwalk to the foredeck and ducked into the forward sail hatch and then into the vertical access tunnel. He emerged into the brightly lit torpedo room, where Rusanov and his men were working on the torpedo interface panel. The torpedoes were all loaded onto the racks and secured by rubber-coated wire-cable clamps. When Rusanov saw him, he came hurrying over. He wanted to say something, a look of worry on his face, but Vornado spoke first.

"Andrei, I want all five torpedoes to be tube-loaded, not rack-stowed."

Rusanov didn't hear him. His breathing was coming in gasps. "I have to tell you something, sir. I found out from the clients—they went back to the command post. They want to load something in the tubes." He stepped close, glancing around them, his voice a murmur. "They were painted over, but I used to work in a weapons depot and I know what they are, sir. They're RK-55s. Granat missiles. Four of them, Captain. They're cruise missiles. The ones they want to load have nuclear warheads. These men . . ." His voice trailed off to a whisper. "They want to hurt someone bad. I don't like that, sir. I don't want to be any part of it. Sergei would *never* have built this ship if he knew what these men intended to do with it. This was supposed to be a *smuggling* ship, hauling harmless marijuana or illegal immigrants. Not nuclear weapons. My grandfather is rolling in his grave. He would never have wanted this. This ship was built to defend the Motherland against invading American aircraft carriers and nuclear submarines, not toss hydrogen bombs at innocent women and children." Rusanov struggled for breath. "I won't go with you, Captain Vornado. I won't do it." He shook his jowly face, his eyes round and haunted as he realized what he'd been working on for the last year.

Here it was, Vornado thought. There was no way he could breathe the words that the client would never fulfill their mission, but if the rest of the prospective crew knew that the ship was going on a mission of destruction with nuclear weapons, they too would refuse to go on the trip, and knowing how treacherous the Ahel al Beit terrorists were, anyone who turned down the mission would likely not survive the next day, not with knowledge of what the mission involved. And yet, if they believed that he would stop the terrorists, that rumor would reach the ears of the clients, and he would not be captain for long. He had thought about what his response would be to Svetlana when she eventually found out what the mission entailed, but he hadn't expected Rusanov to be the one to ask. Rusanov was the tough, muscular, silent type, but already he had revealed his vulnerability to Vornado. People would always surprise him, he thought. He had to find a way to make Rusanov understand while ensuring he wouldn't tell anyone else the truth that these missiles would never fly.

"You're correct about *one* thing, Andrei," Vornado said quietly, his eyes drilling into Rusanov's. "Submarine operation is a hazardous business. The only thing more dangerous is rocketing into space or flying high-performance fighter jets. And if we're not vigilant, accidents could happen." Vornado touched the butt of his .45, snug in its holster. "It's our job to make sure we manage our voyage so that there are no accidents. *No accidents,* Andrei. The only thing that happens when we're at sea is what *we* intend to happen." He stared into Rusanov's eyes without blinking. Rusanov finally nodded as if hypnotized.

"Sir," he whispered, "are you saying you'll prevent the clients from firing their missiles?"

Vornado frowned. He clenched his teeth and spoke, his voice low and menacing. "Listen carefully to what I'm going to tell you. I'm the captain of this ship. The captain's job is to fulfill the mission to the fullest extent of the client's desires. If I hear any of my crew saying anything to the contrary, they will be left behind." He lifted an eyebrow at Rusanov, as if to enclose the statement in quotation marks.

Rusanov frowned in confusion for several seconds, but a dawning comprehension came to him, and a smile slowly spread over his heavy features. He nodded. "I understand, Captain. I withdraw my objection."

Vornado narrowed his eyes, his expression serious. "Good man." He clapped Rusanov on the shoulder.

"Should I load the client's weapons now?"

Vornado nodded. "Bring them aboard. Tube-load one of them and rack-store the others."

"They won't like that. They said to put them all in the tubes."

"I wasn't aware the client was in command of this submarine."

Rusanov smiled. "Don't worry, sir. Nothing happens unless you order it to happen."

"That's right, Andrei. Don't forget it. Did you pass the word to the people on the list?"

"Yes, Captain. They'll be here."

"Carry on, Andrei." Vornado stepped to starboard and ducked through the bulkhead hatch to the second compartment, through the motor generator room and to the hatch to the third compartment upper level. The hatch was crowded with hoses and power cords and lifting tugger cables for the work on the escape pod. The noise of air-impact wrenches was loud in the confined space, the workers above shouting over the racket. Vornado ducked through the mess and pulled open the partition door that separated the vertical accessway to the bridge above and the middle level below. It was a tight squeeze, but he got by the door and shut it again. After he latched it shut, the room became instantly quiet.

The interior of the command post had started to become almost like a cathedral to Peter Vornado. Since the vessel became waterborne, the Exaquantum Yokogawa plant information management-distributed control system had been running constantly, its screens configured the way Vornado had insisted, with ship control, navigation monitoring, and propulsion plant control on the port side, and battlecontrol, firecontrol, sonar, radio, electronic countermeasures, and navigation display to starboard. The lighting was deliberately dim, with only the glow of the panels illuminating the room, to allow better display from the screens. The forward center of the room was penetrated by the smooth stainless-steel pole of the periscope. Vornado had ordered it surrounded with stainless handrails in a circle four feet in diameter, so that people walking into the room wouldn't smack into the scope or the pole, and so that someone doing a periscope observation

could make rapid circles without banging into someone.
The room was normally whisper quiet, with a slight high-
pitched whine from the electronics cabinets aft of the display consoles.

Gathered just aft of the periscope were a dozen Ahel al
Beit Egyptians, all of them clad in their white flowing robes
with capes and turbans. Vornado could smell them almost
before he could see them, either from whatever different
food they ate, or from their hygiene habits. They were all
at least a head shorter than Vornado except for two, one
of whom was tall and gaunt, with a bloodred cape, the
other wide and muscular. They all had belts around the
waists of their inner robes, the tallest of them wearing a
red one studded with jewels, and they all had knives in
ornate scabbards. The tall, thin one's jeweled belt had both
a knife and a long scimitar sword, which looked heavy
enough to cut down a small tree in one stroke. Vornado
focused on him, since he was apparently in charge. He was
about Vornado's height and age, but there was something
distinctly disturbing about him. He gave Vornado the same
disquieting feeling one gets on a visit to a mental institu-
tion. He seemed to be calm, but also gave the impression
that at any moment he could erupt into violent fury. Yet
in an odd way he reminded Vornado of old Easter movies
that all seemed to feature the actors portraying Jesus Christ
as a dreamy, blue-eyed, dark-skinned, heroic yet supernatural character. It was his eyes, Vornado thought, since they
didn't seem to focus on the room, but in the far distance,
as if he saw something no one else could see. His blue eyes
were odd, since all of them but him had coal-black or
brown eyes. He had a slightly hooked nose between stark
cheekbones, chiseled facial structure, and a pointed chin.
He wore a peculiar goatee. Under his jawline, the beard
was shaped like arrowheads pointing up to his ears, giving
him a sinister look. The mustache was trimmed and thin,
but extended farther than his lips. The effect, in combination with his long flowing hair, made him seem like a ro-
manticized painting of a pirate.

The man seemed to be a natural leader. The others de-
ferred to him. He spoke in a quiet but projecting tenor
voice with a melodic cadence. When he stopped speaking,
three of his subordinates jumped in, their obnoxious voices

clamoring for the leader's attention, the sound of them disturbing, profane, and blasphemous in the usual silence of the room. Then two of them bent over the keyboards of the consoles, pressing the keys and fixed function buttons.

The presence of the Egyptians here, in the command post, with their noise, and their taking liberties with Vornado's equipment, suddenly caused bile to fill his stomach. He had figured there would be some kind of a confrontation between him and the terrorists, but he wasn't prepared for it to happen before he was introduced to them.

"Hey, get your hands off my machinery," he spit in a commanding tone. In the room, with its curving smooth overhead and tiled computer deck, his words sounded harsh and loud, a gunshot booming inside a church. He barely realized he had spoken in English for the first time in a month. "Get out of the command post. No one enters here without my permission. You could endanger the ship or yourselves. Your staterooms are on the middle level. I suggest you go to them or leave the ship."

"What?" the larger of the tall men said in amazement, his accent almost British with Middle Eastern overtones. This was the one who had pressed the navigation-control fixed-function key. He was broad shouldered and beefy, unlike the others. Vornado wondered how he had gotten down the hatch. He had a thick neck and a huge face with coarse features above a tangled goatee. "What does a servant infidel dare to say to me?"

He walked up menacingly and stood close enough for Vornado to smell his sour breath, his hand moving beneath his white cape to withdraw his knife. Vornado refused to move, a part of his mind wondering if this would be his end. In slow motion he saw the knife, its flat black blade twelve inches long. Vornado felt its cold steel on the soft flesh in the front of his neck. The sharp point broke his skin. He felt the track of a drop of blood as it ran down his throat. He stared at the man's eyes, his own open and intimidating. The large Egyptian obviously had his attention focused on the knife and Vornado's throat. He never saw Vornado's right hand go to his holster or heard the snap of the cover. Vornado brought the heavy .45 pistol up in a swift but smooth arc and poked it in the man's left eye. The man staggered back a half step, blinking in frightened

surprise. This close, Vornado thought, the barrel of the gun
had to look bigger than a cannon.

The problem was that the .45, while loaded with a full
clip, was uncocked. Vornado hadn't even considered pulling
back the slide, disengaging the safety and holstering the
weapon so that it would be ready in a second. When he
thought of the pistol, he had believed that it was mostly
for effect, to enter the consciousness of the clients purely
for intimidation. It had never occurred to him that he might
have to shoot the weapon in anger in a split second. Vornado had even judged it irresponsible and unsafe to holster
a cocked semiautomatic pistol. As he tried to stare down
the huge Egyptian, the man lunged at Vornado with the
knife, the blade coming up from below and stabbing up
toward his heart with tremendous speed. Reflexively, Vornado pushed the .45 as hard as he could into the man's
chest in an attempt to push him away, but it was like pushing on a stone building, and the force of the shove only
served to tip Vornado backward. As he fell to the deck he
saw the barrel of the gun rising between him and the big
Egyptian. Instinctively he pulled hard on the trigger, but
uncocked, the gun did nothing. Vornado hit the deck, landing on his seat, his head continuing to fall until he hit the
back of one of the control seats, which slid in its fore-and-
aft track to dump Vornado on his back. Incredibly, the
Egyptian calmly and deliberately switched his grip on the
knife so that he could stab downward with it instead of up,
and as Vornado watched in disbelief, he raised the knife
over his head and began to lunge at Vornado.

Finally Vornado regained his presence of mind, the moments of the assault up to now hypnotizing him in shock.
His left hand shot to his right side, grabbed the barrel of
the .45, and pulled the slide back, the weapon cocking, the
sudden click loud in the silent room. He let go of the barrel
and brought the weapon up to fire at his assailant. But the
huge Egyptian didn't seem to care. While still holding the
knife with his left hand, his right reached under his robe
and produced the biggest handgun Vornado had ever seen.
He'd seen it in pictures and heard people talk about it, but
here it was close-up, a black MAC-10 automatic assault
pistol. Deliberately he brought it straight out to aim at
Vornado.

"Good-bye, infidel." He aimed directly at Vornado's eyes.

Vornado could barely believe it—less than five minutes after meeting the client, he'd either kill one of them or he'd be shot. He tensed his finger on the trigger, wondering if he would live long enough to empty the clip into the man before the MAC-10's rapid-fire bullets cut Vornado's body in half.

A sound louder than a gunshot rang out in the room then, a human voice—Abdas's voice—saying something in Arabic. As if he were a toy turned off, the huge attacker stopped in his tracks.

"Holster your weapon, Arsalaan," Abdas shouted at the big man in English. He looked over at Vornado. "You. Holster your firearm and rise to your feet."

Vornado followed the second order but not the first. While keeping the barrel of the pistol pointed at the client group, Vornado carefully regained his feet, staring at the Egyptians. So far they were frozen in disbelief. Depending on how he conducted himself, he might live though this after all. He aimed the gun carefully at the leader with both hands, police style, deliberately sighting down the barrel with one eye shut, hoping that his hand wouldn't shake and give away how terrified he was.

The Egyptians' faces stared at his gleaming stainless-steel weapon. The leader was the only one who looked calm. Arsalaan, the huge one who had come after Vornado with the knife, glared at him, but sheathed his knife and put the MAC-10 away.

"Who are you?" the leader asked, as coolly and with as little interest as if they were in a civilized conference room, completely ignoring Vornado's pistol.

"Peter Vornado," he said guardedly. "Who are you?"

The man inclined his head, as if royalty addressing a commoner. "I? I am Abdas al-Sattar. You may address me as Holy One." He paused. "Am I correct in assuming you are chief of security at this facility?" His eyes were cold. Vornado kept the gun aimed at his face.

"I'm the captain of this ship." He heard his voice, and said a short prayer of thanksgiving that it was even, deep, and threatening. "While I'm pleased to meet the owner, I don't appreciate being attacked with a lethal weapon on the decks of my own vessel. I must restate to you that this room is off-limits to you and your men.''

Vornado waited with his heart in his throat and his gun aimed at the chief terrorist. Abdas al-Sattar's eyes bored into his, staring down the gun barrel, and by the expression on his face, he acted as if the gun weren't loaded. When he spoke, his voice was quiet and authoritative, but without hostility.

"While I am dismayed at your attempted use of force against one of the owners of this ship, I am glad to see that our captain is a fearless warrior." He nodded, liking the sound of his own words. "That will benefit us far at sea. Leonov was correct about you."

Very slowly his expression changed, his frown easing, his face relaxing back into that freakishly calm look. "Arsalaan is impulsive," he said, as if his large bodyguard were not in the room. "I have told him many times that Allah will strike him down for his anger." His voice was melodious and cultured, his words sounding as if he had rehearsed them a hundred times.

Vornado took a deep breath. Apparently the confrontation was over. From now on, he promised himself, the .45 would remain cocked in the holster. Vornado engaged the safety and holstered the cocked weapon.

"These are my principal lieutenants." Abdas introduced them by name, gesturing toward each, but Vornado didn't acknowledge them, his eyes locked on Abdas. He couldn't afford to lose the gains he'd made by accident, and if he bowed or nodded or greeted them, they would disrespect him. Abdas finally pointed to Vornado's attacker. "And this is my half brother and security chief, Arsalaan."

Vornado looked at al-Sattar's brother. He needed to avoid angering Abdas unnecessarily, but he needed to enforce his rules about the command post. "I regret that this almost became violent, sir," he said. "However, he—and all of you—needs to understand that this room is critical for the operation of the ship. This is a dangerous business. Misoperation of any of the ship's controls could kill us even here at the Terminal's slip."

Abdas held up his palm. "I like you, Captain Vornado." He struggled with Vornado's name. "I am glad to be under the command of someone so . . . decisive, should I say? But I really must insist that we be able to observe what you are doing here in your operations center."

Vornado nodded. "Fine, but only one at a time, and you will only converse with the watch officer present if he agrees to talk to you. I can't have you or your men distracting my crew. You're welcome to look at the displays, but no one touches a single button, display screen, toggle switch, fixed-function key, or trackball, unless invited to by the deck officer on watch. Are we agreed?" He forced himself to say the next words, controlling his expression to be deferential but tough. "Holy One?"

Abdas al-Sattar smiled and gave a half bow. "That will be satisfactory. Let's go, gentlemen. I will be occupying the stateroom directly underneath this room, on this side," he said, pointing to the port corner. That was the captain's stateroom.

"No, you won't," Vornado said, his voice controlled but commanding. "That's the captain's stateroom. It's the closest one to the command post on purpose, because in an emergency I need to be here within two seconds. You want to delay my trip, it could cost you your life."

As if in punctuation of Vornado's words, someone up in the escape vehicle slammed the lower hatch hard. It reverberated throughout the room, the titanium hull of the ship making it a giant metal drum. The men standing by Abdas all ducked in terror, including Arsalaan, then frowned as they realized they were in no danger. Abdas was in charge for a reason, Vornado thought. He hadn't jumped a millimeter.

"The other staterooms are too small," Abdas said with a stern expression. "I will require a room identical to yours."

An idea came to Vornado that would disarm this standoff and allow Abdas to save face. "If you will grant me one day, Holy One, I will have two of the present staterooms converted to one exactly like mine, except slightly larger. A bigger table, I believe, for your men." During that day he would finish the escape pod and the interface panel for the UGST torpedoes, he thought, and Abdas wouldn't stop his vital work, since his own stateroom construction would be holding up departure.

Abdas smiled. "That would be acceptable, Captain Vornado, but do not install the table. We will use the increased floor space to pray. It is time we prepare to go to prayer."

He stood and left through the forward hatch. Vornado sank into a control seat, sighing and realizing that his coveralls were soaked with sweat. Above him, the intercom beeped.

"Captain Vornado?" Rusanov's voice clicked from a hidden speaker.

Vornado clicked a toggle switch on the panel in front of him.

"Go ahead, Andrei."

"Sir, the crew is gathered in the lower conference room."

"Very good. I'm on the way."

As he opened the partition to the vertical accessway, a crew of Egyptians came in through the second compartment hatch. When they saw him they retreated quickly back to the second compartment, their eyes averted. Good, he thought. He wanted them to fear him. And so far, other than Abdas himself, the Ahel al Beit terrorists were no more than common thugs, and cowards at that. It made sense, he thought, seeing how their mission to destroy Tel Aviv was an act of cowardice. Abdas's brother Arsalaan was a bully, but at least he'd had the heart to stand face-to-face with his enemy. Not even Abdas could say that, which was probably why he had backed down so quickly.

Vornado realized how tired he was when he felt dizzy climbing out the vertical access tunnel. The world seemed to float around him. How long had he been awake? he quizzed himself. Sixty hours? Seventy? He had to get some sleep soon, he thought, or he would collapse.

Vornado had crawled onto his office cot, completely exhausted after being awake for days on end. When the knock came at the door, he didn't even open his eyes, expecting it to be Svetlana or Andrei reporting the status of the Lira. But instead it was Danalov.

Danalov walked close to Vornado's cot, so close he could whisper in Vornado's ear. When he did, Vornado sat up, startled. He had said, "Head of white."

Head of white, Vornado thought. *Whitehead.* It *was* Vic Kaminsky, the firstie who had saved Vornado's career so

many years ago. He narrowed his eyes and looked at Danalov in the dimly lit office.

"What's the plan?" Vornado asked.

"Mutiny on the high seas," Danalov said. "You're loyal
to Abdas al-Sattar, but from the middle level the rest of
the crew comes at the Ahel al Beit with guns. When they're
all gone, we take the ship to the Atlantic. You can guess
the rest."

"Guns?" Vornado murmured back.

"Only yours," he said quietly. "You got more than we
needed by yourself. Once we're at sea, you'll need to give
me your safe combination so I can distribute them without
the Egyptians finding out."

"It's risky," Vornado murmured. "A bullet though an
electronics cabinet could kill us all. And if one of the Egyptians survives, he could make a lot of trouble for us. Odds
are, we won't all survive a mutiny."

"You got a better plan?"

Vornado held Danalov's glance. *The torpedoes,* he
wanted to say, but he didn't feel that the thoughts he was
thinking about them made sense. It was just a contingency
plan, he thought. The torpedoes were for show, to make
Abdas al-Sattar trust him. Still, there was a way he could
use them so that would avoid the mutiny plan. A mutiny
was unpredictable, and would be bloody and ill-fated, if
Vornado's instincts were to be trusted. But it didn't make
sense to talk about it. Not here and not now.

"No. We'll go with the mutiny."

Danalov left and Vornado shut his eyes. After a few
minutes another knock came at the door. Vornado shouted
for the person to come in, and sat up in bed again. It was
Yuri. Vornado had meant to check with him to ask about
the escape pod work, and the UGST interface cabinet, but
Yuri's face was a thundercloud.

"I can't go with you, Peter, and neither can Svetlana."

"Why not?"

Yuri was furious. "I was never happy with her working
here. She's a child, Captain Vornado. I can't have her at
sea on a submarine. On a mission so dangerous that . . .
well, you know what I mean."

Vornado would be shorthanded without her, but if he
felt anything at all, it was relief.

"Of course I understand," he said.

Yuri seemed embarrassed by his outburst, apparently expecting Vornado to argue. There was a moment of awkwardness before he turned and left. A few moments later Svetlana opened the door and shut it behind her. She walked up, her eyes red from tears.

"You heard?" she asked.

He nodded. "Yuri told me." He looked at her, noticing that she had dressed today the way she used to, in a business suit. She leaned close. "I'm coming anyway. Father can't stop me. I'll bring the things I'm packing to your office. Please make sure you bring them aboard." She turned, her shining golden hair spinning off her shoulders, and left the office, her heels clicking on the tiled floor.

Vornado shut his eyes in exhaustion.

He slept for nearly thirty hours.

24

The USS *Tucson* had been bottomed two miles north of the mouth of the Kola Fjord for nearly a week. During that time the ship was rigged for ultraquiet red with no exceptions. Dillinger had ordered the towed sonar array streamed before the bottoming, which presented extreme risks of losing it from a snag on the rocky bottom, but Dillinger didn't care. Lieutenant Commander D'Assault had questioned him on it, worried that they needed to be free to vertically rise to periscope depth to see who was leaving from the bay, but Dillinger had refused, insisting that when the Alfa exited the Kola Fjord, it would be loud enough to detect with the broadband sonar sphere of the BQQ-5, and with the towed array streamed, they would be able to catalog its narrowband frequency signature, which would come in handy later if it managed to get away.

It was a tactic that Dillinger had invented while staring at the walls of his stateroom, trying to distract himself from his feelings for Natalie. Since they had locked the stateroom doors and kissed, absolutely nothing had happened. There were a hundred perfectly rational explanations for it. For one, they were on a mission, and since sleep was the enemy of command at sea, D'Assault took over his duties on the midnight watch. That meant her day began at eleven at night, when she took her wake-up call and showered, went to midrats and socialized with the junior officers going on and coming off watch, then barricaded herself in her stateroom while doing her paperwork, stopping to visit the control room every hour or so. Officers of the deck, in her opinion, were like first graders—old enough and independent enough that they didn't need to be directed every minute, but inexperienced enough to require frequent adult supervision. Dillinger believed differently, that they were submarine-qualified officers, and as such, were essentially in command of the submarine during their watch, and he refused to qualify them for OOD duty unless they knew the one supreme rule—when to call the captain. He ruthlessly enforced their boundaries, insisting they know what things required his permission, which required notification after the fact, and which they could perform without disturbing him.

With Natalie working the midnight shift, she was tired and irritable by the end of the afternoon, and she insisted on working during the dayshift and afternoon shift, despite the fact that they were rigged for ultraquiet, which truncated much of what she could do. She couldn't run propulsion plant or forward casualty drills, and training was secured, as were daily meetings with the junior officers. The ship existed for one thing right then, and that was to capture the outbound Alfa and get it in trail, follow it to deep waters in the North Atlantic, and sink it. And yet she still buried herself in the meaningless administrative work of the submarine. Whenever he knocked on her door, she had her headphones on and was concentrating so deeply on her computer screen that he had to tap her on the shoulder to get her attention, and when he did, he felt like he was interrupting. She disappeared to sleep shortly before evening meal was served and wouldn't appear until midrats. She never knocked on the door leading from the head they shared to his stateroom. When she wanted to talk to him about what happened on the midnight watch, she did it in the wardroom, where he went to get coffee after his morning shower.

While a part of him was relieved that she wasn't demanding anything of him, he felt like he was going crazy. Had he been dreaming the night she'd kissed him in his stateroom? Her finger stroking his hand under the wardroom table had been real. Her knee next to his had been real. And that kiss was definitely real. But since then she'd been missing in action. It could only be one of two things—either she regretted making her move on him, and had changed her mind about a romance, or she was just trying to remain professional. He had decided to bide his time, but over the last week he'd felt like punching the bulkhead.

In any case, this new nonrelationship with Natalie had given him plenty of time to plan his tactics for capturing the Alfa. He had driven the ship slowly due east with the towed array streamed while descending to a depth where there were barely twenty fathoms beneath the keel. Dillinger ordered the ship to slow to a halt and hover at that depth, knowing that the slightly negatively buoyant towed array would slow in a line across the bay and sink down onto the rocks and sand. After hovering for a good twenty minutes, making sure the array was on the bottom, Dillinger ordered the outboard lowered. The outboard was a small thruster mounted in the lower level of the aft compartment, which could allow them to maneuver off a pier when there were no tugs, the way he had maneuvered the *Albany* during Exercise Stolen Arrows.

With the thruster lowered, Dillinger ordered it rotated to face the stern and started it, so that it began to pull the ship backward. He had originally intended to use the screw and back down, but D'Assault had convinced him that doing that could cut the towed array cable, which met the hull too close to the screw blades. Once the ship had crawled backward a few hundred feet or so, Dillinger judged that there was enough slack cable that they wouldn't part it when the time came to leave the bottom, and the coiled cable on the bay floor would allow them to vertically rise to periscope depth if they had to without moving the linear array.

Dillinger had ordered a negative depth rate inserted into the hovering system so that they would plunge slowly vertically downward. The ship came to rest on the bottom at a slight list to port and a slight incline, at a keel depth of only 120 feet. The deep channel in the center of the fjord widened and deepened at the river's mouth, the Barents Sea's rocky bottom sloping gently twenty miles farther north to a hundred fathoms, but Dillinger wanted them closer. This was deep enough that no ordinary freighter ships would hit their sail or an extended periscope, but just barely. If a fully loaded supertanker happened by when the periscope was raised, it would be bad news, but he doubted any ships that big made the trip south to Murmansk. The traffic seemed to be predominantly local barges, either pushed by old rusting tugs or pulled from short towlines.

There were small freighters, medium-size container vessels, and frequent midsize tankers, but nothing with a draft deeper than thirty feet. Sonar had cataloged all the ships coming in and out, and the sonar supervisor, salty Senior Chief Harlan Keating, was so bored that he had taken to seeing if he could recognize the tugs by their frequency signatures.

After four days on the bottom, with nothing but ordinary shipping traffic overhead, and no ELF calls to periscope depth, Dillinger felt himself start to unravel. He had never been patient or good at waiting, and the elusive Alfa hunt and Natalie's aloofness were conspiring to drive him over the edge. Finally, during a slow afternoon watch, he stared at his notebook computer, lying closed on his fold-down desk. It was connected by the LAN cable to the ship's intranet, so that the officers, chiefs, and leading petty officers could e-mail each other and the shore facilities. E-mail had become one of the blessings and curses of the fleet, because it could become too easy to just send an e-mail rather than walk to the engineroom to talk to the electrical chief. There was too much of a temptation to stare at the screen rather than manage one's division, but so far no one on the *Tucson* had abused the system. Until now. Dillinger booted up the computer and stared at the e-mails in his queue. They were all routine, most of them addressing maintenance or personnel issues. He sorted the list by name, finding several dozen unread messages from D'Assault. He decided to open them. For the most part, when she sent or forwarded a message, the subject line was detailed and descriptive. *Sr. chief leave request, Jan 10–24*, or *Navy commendation medal for Lt. Vauxhall.* He looked at each one briefly, finally reaching the one message that had no subject line.

Hi. I thought maybe we could talk using the system. Too many eyes and ears prowling the decks. If this gets out, we could lose the loyalty of the crew. You're too good a captain for me to let that happen to you. But you're also too good a man for me to not tell you how much I care about you. Please write back. Miss you. Natalie.

It was four days old, for God's sake. The one after that was from this morning.

I'm sorry. I guess I misinterpreted what happened. I'll give you the apology that I should have the night in question: I'm sorry I stepped out of line and was unprofessional. If you can forgive me, I'll try to be the best executive officer to you that I can. And don't worry about your side. Being on the rebound can distort your feelings. I understand completely. Again, sorry. I messed up, but I'll improve. LCDR N. D'Assault.

Dillinger stared at the second message, then toggled back to the first. *Dammit,* he thought. Why hadn't she just told him to check his e-mail? Then he remembered: She'd mentioned the e-mail system at least six times in the last three days, and he'd waved her off, thinking that the administrative duties could wait, and if they couldn't, D'Assault would approach him in person.

He hit the reply button to the first message, deciding to ignore the second. He stared at the blue screen for a long time, but there was something about it that didn't feel right. Finally he shut the system down and pulled out his stationery, with the ship's emblem on the upper right, the Department of the Navy seal on the upper left, and the ship's mailing address in between, and bold letters spelling CDR. BURKE K. DILLINGER, USN, COMMANDING OFFICER. The paper was a heavy parchment that always felt best with an expensive pen. He withdrew the Montblanc pen that Dayna had given him, which he had put in his desk but never used. Ironic that the pen she'd given him would find its first use writing a love letter to another woman. He put his pen on the paper, wondering if the block he'd had with the e-mail screen would affect him on paper, but was thankful it didn't. As soon as he touched the pen to the paper, the words spilled onto the page:

Dear Natalie, I didn't open my e-mail until now. Don't send anything more on the system. The eyes and ears see and hear all that as well. If we get caught, we may as well be caught when we're face-to-face. I can't take being distant from you like we've been the last few days. I need you. I want you. Come to my stateroom at 0200 tonight so I can tell you how I feel about you. And if you're

*willing, I'd like to show you as well. I'll know you're
coming tonight if you go to bed early in the afternoon
watch. But I'll understand if your answer is no. Maybe
you've changed your mind, dearest Natalie, but I know I
haven't. Burke.*

He reread it four times and almost wadded it up into a
ball, but then bit his lip and tried to remember what the
father of the American Navy, John Paul Jones, had said:
He who will not risk, cannot win. The quote reminded him
of the time he had memorized it, so long ago during Plebe
Summer, when being able to spit it out along with a hundred other trivia items had been mandatory. That thought
reminded him of Whitehead, and thinking of Whitehead
made him think of Peter Vornado. He wondered where on
earth Peter might be. He couldn't wait to have a beer with
him and tell him about this crazy mission, and ask his advice about Natalie. For the first time in his life he realized
that he couldn't wait to introduce a girlfriend to Peter and
Rachel. They had said they liked Dayna, but she was too
strange, and it had been an embarrassment to Dillinger. By
comparison, Natalie D'Assault was so balanced, so direct,
so professional, so mature, so competent, and—he realized
it suddenly—so in love with him. Never in a thousand years
would Natalie date a married man to try to leverage him
into a more serious relationship the way Dayna had. As
the thought came to him he decided to go ahead with sending the letter. He put it in an envelope, sealed it, and wrote
Natalie on the outside. He shook his head, removed the
letter from the envelope, ripped up the envelope, and re-
sealed the letter in a fresh one, and on this one he wrote,
Personal and confidential for XO. That would keep the eyes
and ears guessing, whereas the first would feed the rumor
mill. He slipped the note under her door.

It wasn't two minutes later that a knock sounded on the
door to the head.

"Captain?" she said, her voice tentative.

"Come on in, XO," he said.

She poked her head in. Her hair fell to her shoulders, its
highlights shining in the red-lit room. She smiled at him,
an easy, all-knowing smile of fulfillment. She was still his,

he thought, his heart flooding with an unfamiliar emotion. So this was what joy felt like.

"Hi," she said, her voice low and hoarse.

He had no idea how he could wait twelve hours to hold her, but he had to. Steve Flood had the watch out in control, and Flood tended to call frequently during the day to give Dillinger updates.

"Hi," he said. His tone of voice and his expression made that one simple word say everything he wanted to say to her. Her eyes shone as she looked back at him. But when she spoke, her voice was all business.

"Anyway, Captain, I just thought I'd let you know I'm missing some sleep. I'm going to turn in a few hours early this watch, so I won't be at evening meal. But I'll be awake to relieve you at eleven."

He looked into her eyes and realized she was the one he'd been waiting for his entire adult life. He had to finish this goddamned mission and get back to Norfolk, he thought. It would feel so good to have her in his house. There would be no ballistic coffee cups, he knew, but there would be passion all the same, and something more, something he'd never had with a woman—security and comfort and contentment.

"Fine. Sleep well, XO," he said crisply. No one listening would ever know what was on his mind. He winked at her, and she winked back and disappeared into the head.

Dillinger felt his heart pounding. It was like being in love for the first time, he thought, or an illicit affair. Which it was, if Navy Regulations had anything to say about the matter. Like a hot dog tasting better at a ballpark, love was always more intense when it was forbidden. He wondered what Natalie would be like if she were his wife. Would she stay in the Navy? Or if she quit, what would she do? Did she want children? And what would children she bore him look like? A million questions, he thought, and he'd have to wait for the answers. Perhaps that was something he could wait for.

Dillinger stood and walked out into the control room to get an update on the Alfa. Flood looked up and nodded. "Captain's in control," he announced to the room.

Just barely, Dillinger thought, smiling at Flood. "What's

shakin' topside?'' he asked, his old swagger back. Nothing like having his romantic doubts eliminated to make him feel like a submarine captain again.

"We had a fairly big tanker lumber by overhead. Did you hear the screw?''

Dillinger shook his head. He must have been too involved in his correspondence and conversation with the XO.

"Outbound?''

"No, inbound. Chief Keating said it was the deepest draft we've had yet, but still only in the upper end of the medium-size bracket.''

Dillinger grinned. "Is he still getting narrowband signatures of merchant shipping out of boredom?''

Flood smirked. "Down to the names of the captains. I think if we don't put a torpedo in something soon, the senior chief's going to go a bit batty.'' Flood glanced at the closed curtain to sonar. "I hope he didn't hear that.'' The conn open mike was piped into sonar, so that Flood wouldn't have to pick up a microphone to talk to the sonar supervisor.

"Conn, Sonar, didn't hear anything,'' the overhead speaker buzzed with Keating's Tennessee accent.

Dillinger snickered. "Carry on, OOD. I'm going to make a tour.''

Flood nodded.

"Captain's left control,'' Flood announced.

Dillinger walked forward as he checked his watch, counting the minutes until the hour of 0200 arrived.

Peter Vornado sat up on the cot, his head spinning. The dizziness had to be from sleeping for so long, he thought. He could tell he'd slept for a long time, maybe days on end. When he went for a long time without sleep, at some point he would collapse. As a midshipman, he habitually slept for more than three days straight after final exams. Other than the cancer, nothing hurt as much as the bone-deep pain he felt when he woke from a long sleep like this. It eased slightly as he sat a few moments. He stood and turned on his light. He reached into the closet for fresh coveralls and a towel. The water flow in the closet-sized bathroom's shower was stinging and hot. He got out and changed into fresh coveralls. He noticed something different about the room. By the door a heavy fur parka and cap hung on a coatrack. At the foot of it was a packed bag with an envelope on it. He looked inside the bag. It contained five sets of new coveralls, underclothes, and black sneakers, all in his size. Inside the envelope was a note in loopy feminine handwriting.

Dearest, when you wake up, I'll be gone. I've changed my mind about going to sea. Not because of you, but because my father has begged me with tears in his eyes. To honor him, I've agreed. I'm going on a long visit to see my mother in Moscow. She and my father have been separated for years, and it will be good for me to get to know her for a few months. I want you to know how much you have meant to me these last weeks. I can honestly say that I love you more than I will ever love anyone. It breaks my heart to know you are far at sea, without me, but I am glad, because I know in my heart I will see you again. Until that day, my love, please take my love with you. I love you. Svetlana.

Vornado looked up at the wall, the strangest emotion filling him, one of loss and heartbreak. He never thought he would feel this way about Svetlana, but now he doubted he would ever see her again. True, he had no business being with her—he was in love with Rachel, and Svetlana was far too young for him—but despite all that, they had shared something incredible and precious and special. He felt his eyes grow moist as he stood there, feeling like a fool, yet feeling sorry for himself. *I'm not ready for us to be over,* he thought, surprised to find himself thinking that. *And I never even got to say good-bye to you,* he thought, the misery something heavy and cold in his chest. He sniffed, trying to control himself, telling himself it was for the best.

She'd said she would be with him at sea no matter what her father said, but obviously she had changed her mind while he slept for so long. Dammit, he cursed, why couldn't he have awakened after a few hours? Then all this wouldn't have gotten out of his control.

The packed bag made him think that the ship must be ready to be pulled out of the slip. He checked his watch, but it had stopped. Annoyed, he threw the old Timex in the garbage. He put his toiletries in the bag and looked around the room, making sure he wasn't leaving anything, and he'd almost forgotten. After fishing for the key to the desk drawer, he opened it and withdrew the stainless-steel .45, its belt, holster, and two clips of ammunition. He cocked the weapon, put the safety on, and holstered it. Also inside the drawer was the notebook computer Yuri Belkov had given him, which he would need at sea. The thought occurred to him that if anything happened to him or the Lira, this computer's records would allow the U.S. Navy to build one from scratch. If he kept a log on it at sea, if the ship survived and he didn't, they would also be able to profit from the work he'd done before dying. He was being stupidly morbid, he thought, and it had to be because Svetlana was gone. After putting the heavy notebook computer in its protective sleeve and tucking it into the duffel bag, he walked out to the mezzanine carrying the parka, hat, and bag. He stopped dead in his tracks after two steps.

The Lira was gone.

So was the slip of water in the center of the shipbuilding floor. The table had been raised the way it had when the ship was under construction, but the vessel had disappeared. When his heart started beating again, he ran to the stairs and took them two at a time, nearly knocking over Andrei Rusanov at the bottom. The burly Russian wore a fur parka and cap, and both were powdered with snow.

"Oh, Captain," he said, with an oddly pleased look on his fleshy face. "You just saved me the trip. Svetlana tried to wake you up, but nothing worked."

Vornado blushed as the image of how she'd last awakened him came to mind.

"Where's the damned ship, Andrei?"

"Come with me," Rusanov said, smiling.

"Dammit, Andrei, you've moved it without my permission," Vornado said, a smoking anger filling him. His hands trembled. "How many goddamned times do I have to tell you people who is the captain of this fucking submarine?" He made it a point to avoid cursing, but when he was furious he let it all out, which seemed to work for him, because then his crew knew exactly how he felt.

"Sir, you gave us permission. In fact, you directed us to do this."

"I did?" *Oh, no,* Vornado thought. When he was missing sleep for several weeks, he would reach a point where he would be unable to be awakened, and he would talk in his sleep—often quite lucidly—in an attempt to say whatever he had to so that he could go back to sleep. On the *Hampton,* the officers had standing orders, when they suspected he was sleeptalking, to give him an oral quiz. Day of the week. Ship's position. Last time of periscope depth. At some point he would just stop talking and fall back asleep, and they would have to stand him up to wake him. Obviously he hadn't told the Russians this, and when they tried to wake him he'd told them to move the ship out to the river.

"Yes, Captain, you did."

"Oh," Vornado said, instantly contrite. "I'm sorry, Andrei."

"Perfectly all right, sir." He smiled. "Leave your bag here and put on your coat and hat. You'll need it."

Vornado put on the hot parka and hat, feeling as though he'd just donned a bear suit. There were gloves in the pockets, so he pulled those on as well. Rusanov led him to the ladder to the roof, which Vornado had never climbed. It was dusty and rusted, but he followed Rusanov up the creaking ladder to a hatch in the Terminal's roof. He wondered if Security Chief Ilyivich would disapprove, but forgot the thought completely when he climbed up to the roof.

In the arctic November it was dark most of the day, but in the glow of the city lights, through the falling snow, Vornado could see the fjord below. There, below them, was a large rust-bucket freighter ship. It was probably forty- or forty-five-thousand tons, tied up pointing north, downriver, with its starboard side made fast to where the barge unloading facility hung out over the black water. It looked as if it had seen better days, and had to date back fifty years, judging by the rust on the deck and the gunwales. He could see lights coming from the superstructure, and a dim lamp lit a gangway that was placed between the barge offload facility to the freighter.

"What in God's name is that?" Vornado asked.

Rusanov could barely contain his mirth. "That, sir, is the motor vessel *Kirovsky*. Our ride."

"I don't get it, Andrei. What the hell is going on?"

"Looks like a normal freighter, right? You wouldn't give it a second look, right?"

"Yes, yes," Vornado said impatiently.

"The Lira's inside."

"Say that again."

"Inside. It's not really a freighter at all, and underneath all that rust is a fairly new seaworthy vessel with its bottom cut out for a length of ninety meters. Which is quite convenient, since the Lira is eighty-one-point-four meters long." He paused and watched the expressions change on Vornado's face.

For a full two minutes Vornado simply stood there with his mouth open. Finally he found his voice. "But how?"

"Winches. Extremely powerful winches. Three under the superstructure and three in the bow, reeling in cables made fast to the Lira by circular clamps of steel. It took about ten hours to lower the Lira to be submerged and winch it over to the *Kirovsky*, then slowly readmit compressed air into the ballast tanks to allow the Lira to rise up into the *Kirovsky*'s hold. It took another four hours to tighten the cables and secure the Lira in place, then an hour to install the temporary gangway from the bridge hatch to the interior of the *Kirovsky*. And the last few hours we spent supporting the divers who went down to bolt in the stiffening struts under the Lira hull that connect the port and starboard side of the freighter, to keep it seaworthy despite this gaping hole in its keel."

"Who . . ." Vornado stammered. "Who was in charge? Who submerged the Lira?"

"I did, sir." Rusanov beamed at him like a child who had just ridden his bicycle around the block for the first time.

What could he say? he thought. "Good job, Andrei. Excellent work. I'm awed." But then he grabbed the big Russian by his shoulders and glared into his eyes. "You ever pull a stunt like this again, you're dismissed. I expect you to wake me up when you need my attention, and I don't care if it takes a nuclear bomb to do it. Do I make myself clear?"

Rusanov had a new confidence after moving the Lira. He simply smiled, nodded, and said, "Yes, Captain, I understand."

Vornado blew his breath out through his lips, fog forming around him from the cold. In the falling snow, the world was incredibly quiet. "Show me the inside," he said.

"After you, sir."

Vornado lowered himself back down the ladder to the inside of the Terminal, then followed Andrei through the door of the barge unloading facility to the gangway to the *Kirovsky*. Up close, it looked even worse than it had from above. In addition to the rust and disrepair, it smelled fishy and stale. Rusanov led him through a hatch to the interior of the superstructure and down to the lower decks. There was a paint locker on the forward bulkhead. Rusanov moved a paint can and the entire shelf of paint moved on a hinge, a hidden door behind the shelf. This would normally be the bulkhead separating the ship from the oil hold. Rusanov unlatched the door. There was a space about two feet wide, the lining for the tank. On the other side was nothing but rusted metal. Rusanov pushed on it, and it opened on a hidden seam.

Vornado gasped. Bright white lights illuminated the interior of the ship, the metal freshly painted, the bulkheads looking like they'd come out of the new construction shipyard the week before. Vornado stood on a railed platform overlooking a narrow slip of water, and below him was the cylinder of the Lira's hull. Forward he could see the fin, a wooden platform erected over the bridge. The ship was a tight fit inside the hold, the flanks of the submarine almost rubbing against the sides of the freighter. A number of rubber fenders were installed port and starboard between the freighter and the submarine, and the decks of the sub were interrupted by two dozen ten-meter-diameter clamps with four cables turnbuckled to each clamp running to steel bullnoses welded to the freighter's structural frames. It was ingenious.

"Amazing," he breathed. "How long did it take to make this?"

"A lot less time than the Lira," Rusanov said.

"Why didn't you tell me?"

"Security, Captain. The fewer people who know, the less chance word can get out."

"When do we leave?" Vornado asked.

"Ten minutes, sir. Yuri Belkov and the Kaznikovs wanted to say good-bye to you first. The clients are all aboard, and the freighter's engine is idling."

"The Lira is on internal power?"

"We started the reactor, energized the turbine generators, and separated from shore power before we moved the ship."

"Andrei," Vornado said in exasperation, "what else have you done without my permission?"

"Let's see. I loaded lube oil, makeup liquid-metal coolant, deionized water, battery dielectric, alcohol, diesel fuel, hydraulic oil, liquid oxygen, hydrogen to cool the turbine generators, compressed air—"

"That's enough, Andrei. I can't hear any more of this. It will drive me mad. Trust me, I will never sleep again, not while you have the keys to my submarine." He paused. "Did you say alcohol? What equipment is that for?"

Rusanov grinned.

"Never mind," Vornado said. He was so used to the U.S. Navy's prohibition on drinking at sea that it never occurred to him that Rusanov would think nothing of loading a few cases of vodka into the frozen stores locker.

They left the freighter and walked back across the gangway into the barge unloading facility. Andrei led him into the door to the empty shipbuilding room, where both Kaznikovs and Yuri Belkov waited for him with smiles on their faces.

Yuri spoke first. "You remember the day you interviewed with us?" he asked.

"I will never forget." Vornado smiled.

"Remember how you told us you pawned the watch you loved, the Rolex Submariner?"

Vornado began to suspect something. Belkov produced a green box.

"For your brilliance as a submarine engineer, and for what we know will be a luck-filled voyage," Leonov said. "Go on, open it."

Vornado opened the box. Inside was a gold Rolex Submariner watch with an azure face, almost like the one he'd worn since Rachel bought it for him when he was appointed to command the *Hampton,* except that watch had been stainless steel and gold, and this watch was solid gold. For the second time in an hour, Vornado felt his eyes grow wet.

"I don't know what to say," he stammered. "I'm overcome. Thank you. Thank you so much."

"Don't forget to read the inscription, Peter," Leonov said.

On the back of the watch the tiny inscription was in Russian, its Cyrillic lettering spelling, FOR THE BEST SUBMARINER OF BOTH EAST AND WEST. HAPPY VOYAGES, PETER, FROM ALL YOUR FRIENDS. Vornado felt his eyes misting up, despite the fact that he was here on false pretenses as part of a CIA operation. These were real people with real feelings and real problems, and he had suffered through the bad times with all of them. He felt a tear leak from his eye and fall down his cheek. He wiped it away before anyone could see it, and hugged Leonov, then Sergei, Yuri, and finally Rusanov.

"Put it on," Yuri laughed.

Vornado strapped on the bracelet, loose, the way he liked it. The watch felt heavy and big. He shook his wrist, positioning the ocean-blue dial. He felt an odd feeling, like the beginning of his old, familiar reality returning to him once more.

The three men clapped him on the shoulder and wished him good luck on the mission, and said they waited for the moment when he would return. Vornado bade them farewell. As he turned to wave good-bye to them for the last time, the shipbuilding room seemed odd and forlorn without a ship to occupy the table. The bright lights of the facility remained lit, but the only thing on the floor were the Egyptians' buses, their windows dark, still lined up nose-to-tail, waiting to be reclaimed after the mission.

He hated good-byes, Vornado thought, as he walked slowly to the barge offloading room and over the gangplank to the *Kirovsky*. It was a heavy, choked feeling that invaded his chest and throat as he stepped onto the gangway. As he reached the end of it, he tapped his Naval Academy ring twice on the metal of the handrail, an ancient gesture of farewell.

I miss you already, Svetlana, the unbidden thought came to him. He would have to control himself better than this, he thought. As he boarded the freighter, the bridge crane of the Terminal pulled up the gangway, and a few of his shipbuilding crew tossed over the heavy mooring lines. The *Kirovsky* was under way. The vessel sounded a blast of its horn, the sound lonesome on the calm water of the river. The water at the stern of the ship rippled, and slowly the ship moved forward, so slowly and evenly that it seemed that it was stationary and it was the land that was moving.

He made his way through the superstructure of the freighter until he reached the bridge. On the afterdeck, looking over the fantail, he found Rusanov standing at the handrails and smoking. He accepted a Russian cigarette and watched the lights of Murmansk fade slowly astern of them. Eventually the river made a gentle bend, and Murmansk was gone. Vornado sighed and walked down into the superstructure and back to the secret hold of the ship, to the gangway, and then to the escape pod. He lowered himself into the vertical access trunk until he was inside the escape pod.

He noticed something different immediately. It wasn't the fresh paint or the functional control panels or the life-saving equipment loaded onto the bulkheads of the escape vehicle; it was the smell. No longer did the ship have the smell of the shipyard. This smell could only be one thing— a nuclear submarine. He took in the aroma, identifying lube oil, ozone, cooking oils, cigarette smoke, diesel exhaust fumes from the testing of the emergency generator, cleaning fluids, the sharp taste of pure oxygen, and the tang of atmospheric-control amines. It was a good smell. Vornado looked at the Rolex watch face. He was a submariner again, he thought.

He continued down the ladder to the uncluttered accessway and stepped into the command post. The humming whine of the machinery was intoxicating. Dmitri Maslov, the electrical and electronics engineer, stood the watch, sitting in the control seat at the after port corner of the room, the propulsion plant controls. Dmitri was the taller, thinner, and older of the two Maslov brothers, his red hair and freckles making him seem younger than his forty years, the impression vanishing when he opened his mouth, his baritone serious voice commanding and confident. As he always had when Vornado entered a room, Maslov stood and brought himself to military attention, the mannerism strange, since Maslov had always been an academician.

"Good evening, Captain," he said.

"Hello, Dmitri. Please, relax."

"Yes, Captain."

"How's the reactor and steam plant?" Vornado asked.

"Liquid-metal pumps running in slow speed, reactor power is fifteen percent, both turbine generators supplying AC loads. The main engine's been on the turning gear. I think it's time to take it off the turning gear and warm it up. We can spin the shaft every minute or so to keep it warm."

"How far are we from being able to separate from the *Kirovsky*?"

Maslov walked to the after starboard corner, where the horizontal navigation display was shown. "We'll reach the mouth of the bay here. Let me calculate."

"Wait a minute. Are the ship's clocks set to Greenwich Mean Time?"

"No, Moscow time."

Vornado shook his head.

"GMT it is, Captain," Maslov said, resetting two brass chronometers bolted to the upper consoles on the port and starboard sides. He sat at a control seat, brought up the Yokogawa-distributed control system's configuration screens, and changed the time zone. Satisfied that the computer had received the command, and that it had not caused a problem in the navigation module, Dmitri returned to the navigation display.

"Where was I? We'll pass north through the mouth of the Kola Fjord a little after two in the morning GMT. We're going about twelve knots, and we'll turn west here. The water's shallow, only a couple hundred meters, but it's deep enough that we can separate here, about fifty nautical miles northeast of the Russia–Finland border."

"Good," Vornado said, tapping the .45 in its holster. "Where are the clients?"

"They wanted to be where the action was, up on the bridge of the freighter." He smiled. "I think you scared them too much for them to trespass here again."

"They'll be back. Give them a few hours submerged in their little sea cabins and they'll be knocking on the command post door." He turned to leave. "You have permission to take the main engine off the turning gear and warm it up, but I want Rusanov in here before you start."

"Yes, sir," Dmitri said.

Vornado ducked into the door to the vertical accessway, pulled up the grating, and continued down to the third compartment, middle level to his stateroom. He shut the door behind him and took off his heavy coat and hat and hung them in a closet cubbyhole. His coveralls were neatly hanging in the closet. Someone had unpacked for him. His notebook computer was bolted in a special docking station on his corner desk. He sniffed the air. He could smell Svetlana's perfume. Hallucinations weren't unusual at sea, particularly auditory and olfactory ones. After fifty days submerged, men heard their wives' voices and smelled their mothers' cooking, but he was fully rested and hadn't been at sea for more than a half hour. Maybe it was just that he was thinking about her.

He opened the door to his private bathroom and there was Svetlana, leaning against the stainless-steel wall, dressed in blue coveralls that emphasized her slim figure, her fine blonde hair falling down to her shoulders, her smile angelic even in the bright fluorescent lights of the head. The emotion that flooded him was one of relief and joy. But then he frowned—the clients would not appreciate a woman on board the submarine.

Before he could complete the thought she unzipped his coveralls and pulled them off him, then pulled him into an embrace. He kissed her deeply, an irrational exhilaration filling him. His body responded to her, and in spite of everything going on, all he could think about was having her.

"I missed you," he said. He kissed her again, her mouth drawing him in.

"I hoped you would," she whispered. "Come on, let's try out your new bed."

There was nothing to do for the next few hours until the freighter was alone in the Barents Sea. He decided to make love to her one last time, then insist that she remain on board the *Kirovsky* and return to Murmansk.

As it turned out, once wasn't enough for him.

25

The midwatch in the sonar room of the USS *Tucson* was far from routine. The ship lay on the rocky bottom of the mouth of the bay at a slight incline, which Senior Chief Sonarman Harlan Keating considered perfect. The bottom characteristics and the funnel shape of the opening of the mouth of the Kola Bay meant excellent sound reception. They could even make detects far upstream and around bends of the river because of the rocky geography.

Keating was thirty-seven years old and had been a sonarman almost nineteen years. He was tall and thin, with dark hair and rugged features. His Tennessee accent was so thick as to make him nearly unintelligible in normal conversation, but oddly, when he got excited, he annunciated as clearly as a network broadcaster. He had selected the midwatch for his watchsection, because it always seemed that whenever he had been on a northern run to catch a Russian, the bastards always tiptoed out of town in the middle of the night, unlike the U.S. Submarine Force, which could be counted on to begin all their secret missions precisely at eight o'clock on Monday mornings, just as this one had begun, even though it was an emergency operation. He checked the digital chronometer on the bulkhead, which read zero one forty-seven. He decided to call for his second half-pot of coffee early. Fortunately it was doughnut night, and the cooks would be delightedly making preparations for the morning's treat. If he were lucky, Keating could claim a chocolate with sprinkles before the rest of the crew grabbed them.

It had been a long run for Keating, and while he was glad to be doing his life's work, this operation couldn't have come at a worse time. His six-year-old daughter had been diagnosed with leukemia three weeks before they left. He had planned to put in for hardship leave, but his wife, Diane, had pulled him aside after they'd gotten Becky to bed the week the op had been announced. "Harlan," she had said quietly, "Becky already knows about this deployment from Fred Davies's daughter. If you stay home, you're going to frighten her. She's a smart kid and she picks up on anything unusual. She's used to you disappearing to take your sonar set out in the ocean. If you stay here, lurking around all day, it'll damage her. She'll think she's dying, and it could make her sicker. Just go to sea. I'll take care of her, and you'll be back in a month."

Diane was a successful child psychologist with a busy practice, and yet for their entire marriage he had teased her that he knew more about children than she did, coming from a family of seven kids, but this time he knew she was right. When he said good-night to Becky late Sunday, Diane flashed a warning look at him, reinforcing her demand that he not say anything to Becky that would indicate how sick she was, and for God's sake not to cry. He had read Becky four of her favorite books, then smiled at her and kissed her forehead, and she wished him good luck on his trip beneath the seas. Having a father who was a big shot on a nuclear submarine had captured her imagination, and many were the Saturdays he had brought her aboard the *Tucson*. Captain Dillinger was good about having children aboard, and had even asked the two of them to have lunch in the wardroom with him the Saturday before departure.

Keating had put on a brave face for little Becky, but as soon as he shut her bedroom door he had shouldered Diane aside to hurry to the garage workbench, the one place in the house that was totally his, and he had sat on his stool and cried his eyes out, his shoulders heaving with the strength of his sobs. He didn't want Diane to see him, because he knew it wouldn't be good for her to see him so weak, but he felt her hand on his shuddering shoulder and looked up at her through the tears.

"She's going to be okay, Harlan," Diane said, but her eyes were red and swollen.

"Jesus, Diane," he'd said, his voice trembling. "Why would God do this to a child? Why Becky? Why not me? *Why the fuck not me?*"

For once Diane had no words, and the two of them had just hugged there in the dirty garage, soaking each other's clothes with their tears. Eight hours later, Keating stood in this room on the upper level of *Tucson*'s forward compartment quietly reviewing the preunderway sonar checklist and praying that Becky would be spared.

The coffee arrived steaming hot, the aroma of it filling the sonar room. As Keating took a sip, he looked around him. The sonar room was an oblong space, and calling it a room flattered it. It was smaller than the bathroom in his father's Memphis house, all of five feet wide from the edge of the starboard line of consoles to the bulkhead on the port side, and fifteen feet long from the curtained door that led aft to the control room to the room's forward bulkhead. The row of consoles had three sonar stations, each station having two large displays—one in the vertical and one on the upper section that gently sloped toward the operator. There were three operator's high-backed swivel chairs, each bolted to the deck, and behind them a high stool where the sonar supervisor of the watch could see all six displays.

Each watch's sonar supervisor configured the panels to his taste, but Keating liked his operator to set up the two panels on the left, the forward console, as the broadband displays. These showed the data received on the spherical array in the nosecone, the noise raw and unprocessed, just displayed showing the bearing of the noise and its sound pressure level, or intensity. The sound volume was shown by the brightness of a trace, and the direction was shown on the horizontal axis. Keating had lined up south, 180 degrees, as the center of the screen since the threat vector—the direction from which the Russian target would approach—was to the south. Bearings 181 to 359 extended to the right of screen center, and 001 to 179 were to the left. A bright trace on the screen at bearing 180 would indicate a possible approaching ship or submarine.

The screen then scrolled downward over time. A noise from due south at 180 degrees would make a bright trace, and if it were a steady noise, the trace would continue vertically downward with all the rest of the data, while the readings from all bearings would also scroll slowly downward, which was why the readout was called a "waterfall display," since the data fell downscreen with time.

The spherical array was a "broadband" receiver because it heard all frequencies, making it much like the human ear. A trace on the screen was either loud or soft, but no other information about it could be gained from the display. It could be the high-value submarine target or just a school of fish, such as shrimp clicking away at each other. The sonar operator, through his headset, could direct the system to pipe into the earphones the noise that the particular hydrophones heard at that angle, which made the sonar sphere one gigantic directional microphone. A good operator could tell a lot about a sound through the headset. A surface ship's screw made a rhythmic noise as it cavitated through the water. It made a *whoosh-whoosh-whoosh* noise, in time to the rpms of the screw. With a quieter screw, as with a submerged submarine that didn't cavitate the seawater to make water vaporize into bubbles on the low-pressure side of the screw blades, the noise might be the flow noise of the seawater pumps or the sub's huge reactor recirculation pumps.

With quieter submarines, the broadband system wasn't enough for distant detection. Narrowband sonar had been invented to fill the requirement to find quiet submarines farther out. It searched for frequencies—bell tones, or tonals, as they were detected from the towed array, the 250-foot-long hydrophone towed on a mile-long cable. The array was currently expertly placed on the bay floor by Captain Dillinger, the long linear sonar hydrophone lying at a right angle to the direction of the river. The towed array picked up all noise that hit it, as the sphere did, but it was processed differently, the electrical pulses from the array's segmented long hydrophones passed along the tow cable to the BQQ-5's powerful narrowband processor computer, which was an extremely sophisticated frequency filter. The last thirty years of refinement had mostly added computational power to allow more rapid sifting of the haystack of ocean noise in search of the needle of a submarine. Raw noise was filtered by frequency, so that noises of a particular steady tone could be detected. These tonals could be displayed in a narrow graph, and the graph could immediately allow the operator to discriminate between natural broadband noise—waves and wind and rain and shrimp clicking and lava boiling seawater to steam—and narrowband noise, such as from a ship's turbine generator or main seawater pump or reactor recirculation pump. A natural frequency tone from the ocean would make a sloppy hump on the graph, but something man-made made a distinct spike.

The trouble with the damned thing was that there was so much noise in the ocean at so many frequencies that the BQQ-5's computers could choke on it, and couldn't keep up with the incoming data fast enough to show a meaningful result. This was nothing like the movies, Keating thought, where a submarine lurking in the sea knew everything about the ocean around it, and target submarines were blips on a radar screen. Here, at the bottom of the Kola Bay, they lived in uncertainty, with graphs of mathematical probability determining whether there might be an enemy submarine out there.

The way the Q-5 had dealt with the flood of data was to slice it up and focus on small parts of the whole. The towed array had the ability to "form a beam," to discard all incoming data except that coming from a narrow sector—a cone—of the ocean. If the sonar operator knew the threat vector, he could concentrate on that one beam. In the middle of the ocean, the operator didn't have the luxury of knowing in advance which beam would get lucky, so they made up a sonar search plan that looked at one beam for fifteen minutes, then threw the data away and checked the next beam for fifteen minues. The second way the Q-5 handled the information was by focusing on a very few select frequencies. Intelligence gained from recording target submarines revealed that each type of sub made its own individual signature of frequencies, including American subs. The sonar intelligence specialists knew what four or five frequencies were made by Russian Akula subs, Sierra subs, and of course, the Alfa subs. They also knew what tonals were emitted by the American Seawolf class and the Los Angeles class. This information only could be found out if the target were recorded up close, so the recording sub had to get close to the new sub as it left port on its maiden voyage.

Unfortunately, to find a target submarine, one had to know *exactly* what to look for. But if the operator knew what possible targets he was seeking, the rest fell into place.

The Q-5 would be configured to check for four or five frequency ranges of four or five expected tonals, and the operator merely watched the developing graphs for spikes and discarded the data and began processing all over again, every fifteen minutes. In the situation of the *Tucson,* it became even easier, because there were only four towed array beams that had any meaning with the way the array was laid across the bottom of the bay. They knew they were seeking an Alfa, and no matter what the shipyard had done to it, if it were an Alfa, it would have a signature of a very narrow range of frequencies.

On the two center screens there were four graphs, each one seeking the principal Alfa frequencies. The graphs had frequency on the horizontal axis and sound intensity vertically. The two right screens displayed the secondary frequency "buckets" that were also reported from the Alfa. The trouble was, no one had seen much activity from the Alfa since the late eighties. It had always been a troubled boat, Keating thought, all raw horsepower and no subtlety, an automated submarine driven by an all-officer crew.

There had been the usual rebellious jokes in the crew's mess, that if the Alfa were manned only by officers with no enlisted men, that the *Tucson* had nothing to worry about. The teasing between officers and enlisted men had been a submarine force tradition since the first diesel boats, a result of cramming the crew into such a small space and sharing such danger. It tended to break down the formality between officers and enlisted. It wasn't that they were on a first-name basis with each other, but in the sub force they understood each other and had tremendous mutual respect, though if anything that made the banter that much more intense. Of all the enlisted men aboard, the sonarmen were the most important, Keating would maintain in the mess, because without them the ship was nothing but a deaf, dumb, and blind tube of steel underwater, helpless against enemies. The beefy nuclear technicians who ran the propulsion plant back aft, the "nukes," scoffed at Keating, insisting that the "sonar girls" just watched their televisions every watch, took three showers a day, and stank of French perfume. Let them drag their knuckles from the engine room every watch, he thought. The real work of the submarine happened right here.

"Anything?" Keating and his watch partner, Sonarman Third Class Antonio "Pup" Morales, shared the three consoles and the computers in the room during the watch. Morales was a pimply-faced, studious youth, bone thin, with black hair he parted in the center above his wire-rimmed glasses. He was green, but with a good head on his shoulders. At the end of this run he would earn his silver submarine dolphins, and then could advance up the ladder. Until then he shared the watch with the most senior sonarman, taking advantage of Keating's experience and, truth be told, being punished for being the most junior in the division. Morales could have gone to a good college had he chosen to but, like Keating himself, had been too impatient to get some adventure in his life. While some might not define sitting in this green-and-red-lit room for hours, staring at slowly moving screens an adventure, Keating knew that it was, and young Morales shared that view. The nukes from back aft had chosen to adopt the young petty officer, and had insisted on taking him with them to the usual biker bars, teaching him how to drink like a sailor and defend himself against the civilian Harley riders, but at sea they left him alone.

Young Morales divided his time between the broadband displays and the narrowband, with Keating directing the dumping of data and reinitialization of the frequency buckets, and Morales listening to broadband noises and alerting Keating to anything unusual.

Keating checked the chronometer again. The watch was crawling, he thought, but if they didn't get the Alfa tonight, maybe he would poke his head out tomorrow. Keating yawned, zeroed all the frequency buckets, and watched the sound flow into them.

The aft stateroom door to the control room was locked, as was the second door to the passageway. The overhead red lights of the room were clicked to the dim setting, which turned off half of the light fixtures. It was almost two in the morning. The stateroom was cold even with the air handlers turned low, because of the arctic cold of the northern water, so Burke Dillinger wore his old wool West Point bathrobe, a prized possession from his academy days when Navy beat Army's heavily favored football team and the

Navy midshipmen won their trophy robes. He sat on the bed, staring into space, wondering if Natalie would join him, and wondering if what he was about to do was as irresponsible, ill-advised, and crazy as he thought it was.

He could almost hear what they would say at a court-martial or admiral's mast, the administrative proceeding to determine fault and punishment of an officer in command. Even saying something to Natalie that hinted he had feelings for her could result in his removal from command and ruin his career. Even if they were ashore in Norfolk, on a Saturday night, in the privacy of his house, he wasn't allowed to treat her any way except as his junior officer. They could be friends, of course, even drink and joke together till the bars closed down. He could put his arm around her to keep her from stumbling drunkenly into a ditch, but the moment he put his arm around her as a man embraces a woman, he could be court-martialed. And to think of touching her at sea was absurd, the most taboo thing the Navy could imagine. The scandal that could erupt with an affair between the commanding officer and the executive officer on a nuclear submarine at sea would make headlines. And it was worse than that. He wasn't about to touch Natalie on a milk run in the VaCapes Op Area; he was about to touch her here, in the Barents Sea, within the sacrosanct twelve-nautical-mile limit of another nation's sovereignty. The orders to penetrate Russia's twelve-mile limit had come from the president himself, since no one else had the authority to order it, and the message had been deleted from the buffer and shredded as soon as he, the XO, and the navigator read it. No, he decided, there would be no administrative proceeding, no cozy admiral's mast; this would be a fully staffed courtroom case, a formal United States Navy court-martial.

So here they were, on a covert spy mission, inside the twelve-mile limit on purpose, bottomed out in a Russian harbor, with their sonar gear straining for an enemy submarine, rigged for ultraquiet, with orders to shoot the submarine to kill, on a voyage so top secret and so vital that he would probably get called to the Pentagon—no, the White House itself—to tell the tale, and yet here he was, sitting on his bed at two in the morning, perhaps the watch when

the target submarine would emerge, waiting for his XO to
come into his stateroom so he could commit a crime that
had only to do with his human frailty.

For the first time in months he thought about his father,
Kinnaird "Kin" Dillinger, who had seemed ten feet tall
until the moment he revealed that he had lived a false life.
Dillinger thought back to the way he'd seen his father, before the revelation, and smiled at his childlike hero worship
of Kin Dillinger. What would the old man say about this
situation? Would he disapprove and tell his son to distance
himself from this woman, and to straighten out and be a
professional? Or would he tell him that a woman like Natalie came by but once in a lifetime, and to go ahead and let
himself love her? Or would he advise him to do both—to
push her away now and be with her later? Dillinger thought
he knew the answer: that it would be to do the thing that
was healthiest for him, while honoring and respecting the
things in his life he loved, such as his career, his submarine,
his crew, and Natalie. But how could he find the balance?
he heard his own voice as a child ask. The answer seemed
to come from outside of him—that he would know. He
knew how to run this submarine, he knew how to lead the
crew, and when the time came, he would know how to
love Natalie Whitworth D'Assault, lieutenant commander,
United States Navy.

The creak of the door to their shared bathroom made
him return to the present, and he turned his head as the
door came fully open. Natalie stood there in the dim red
light. She was five feet away from him, wearing a long white
T-shirt that extended halfway down her bare thighs, but he
could see her body draped under the cotton fabric, which
fell across her full breasts and revealed her curving hips.
Her hair fell down to her shoulders, the red lights of the
single lit fixture giving it gleaming highlights. He stood to
look at her, her shining, liquid eyes seeking his. Her perfume was in his nostrils, a faint but beautiful scent, something he had sensed before but could no longer remember.
She stepped closer, looking up at him.

He knew he should tell her that this couldn't be, that
they must save their careers, that what they were doing
here in the Barents was much too important for them to
distract themselves with a romance that had no business

existing. A romance that was forbidden, prohibited, for all the right and logical reasons. She came an inch closer to him, her lips, made redder by the light of the red lamps, parting slightly. In his heightened awareness, he could see the slight gloss on her lower lip from where her tongue had been for just an instant. Her lips opened just slightly more, as if she were about to say something to him. She was closer now. He could see the part in her hair, and how each individual hair swept up from her shoulders to her head, and the strangest thought came to him—that he loved every hair on her head.

Tell her this is wrong.

He reached out to her, his hands touching her soft shoulders. He pulled her close to whisper in her ear.

Tell her this won't happen. That you can't do this. That your duty to the country and the Navy and the crew and the mission means you can't, no matter how much you want to.

She stood close to him, his hands on her shoulders, her arms helplessly at her sides, her face inclined to look up at his face.

Tell her this is over.

Her eyes began to shut, her lids closing on her beautiful brown irises with their dilated pupils, her long eyelashes meeting her cheeks. There was a small constellation of freckles on her cheeks and the bridge of her nose. He barely believed it when he felt her lips on his. Had she moved up to him? No, he thought, it was he who had come down to meet her.

You can't do this. Stop it now. Explain it later.

Dillinger could feel the soft, wet warmth of her mouth caressing his. He felt every molecule of her lips on his, the incredible softness of her tongue as it teased him, drawing him into her mouth. He felt his heart pounding, the blood rushing in his ears, and he felt her arms encircle his back, the cool skin of her forearm on his neck pulling him down to her. In response he held her tighter, the passion rising in him in a surge of desire, and he kissed her harder. She moaned, just slightly, and the sound brought him back to reality—no one could know about this.

This tempts fate. Tell her you can't do this, not now, not here.

He moved her to his bed and laid her down on the mat-

tress, the T-shirt rising to reveal simple white cotton panties, with the shape of promise beneath. He joined her, his
arm encircling her, her arms around him again, their
mouths meeting. Her hand reached out to his and pulled
his touch under her shirt to her breast. He shut his eyes,
the flesh of her breast warm and soft, her nipple hard. He
kissed her hard then, squeezing her breast harder.

Her hot breath was in his ear, and then her tongue slowly
circled the center. She moved beneath him, and he realized
she had pulled her panties off, then moved one of her knees
to the wall. She reached up and pulled on his robe, and he
sat up and removed it and tossed it to the deck. He was
naked underneath, and he felt her touch on him, her fingers
cold, the sensation sending a roar of rippling tingles up his
spine. This time it was he who moaned, but she kissed him
then to keep the sound down, and it was then he knew she
was as worried as he was.

She pulled on him, bringing him closer to her, her encircling fingers urging him into her. He was surprised that she
was ready for him. Dayna had always needed more coaxing,
but Natalie was soaking, the soft, downy fur there wet. He
thrust into her, seeing her eyes shut again, and the world
seemed to whirl around him, dissolving into a swarm of
flying incandescent sparks that surrounded the two of them,
the rest of the world vanishing into a dim red darkness. He
moved into her, slowly at first, but then unable to control
himself as her breathing became heavy in his ears. He
thrust harder and faster into her, feeling the wind at his
back, the hurricane force of it moving him closer to the
center of Natalie, and he whispered her name in her ear,
her eyes opening. For just a tenth of a second he saw what
he considered the most beautiful sight in the world—the
happiness on her face.

"Oh, dear Natalie," he murmured. "Oh, God."

"Burke," she whispered, her hand rising to run her fingers through his hair. "I love you." Her lips found his, her
teeth biting his lower lip.

The sound of her voice saying those words played over
and over again in his mind. How many women had said
that to him, he wondered, and when they did, how many
times had it spoiled the moment? He knew that never had
another woman's declaration of love done to him what

those words did when Natalie said them in her gorgeous silky voice. And then it happened. He hadn't meant to think it, much less say it; and even if he thought it, he knew he would be able to control himself. But he had been wrong.

"I love you, Natalie," he said.

She kissed him then, her fingers running down his back to his hips, and she pulled him in deeper, urging him to a faster rhythm, her breathing coming faster and harder. He shut his eyes and felt the closeness of her body, the places it was soft, the places it was hard, the smoothness of her skin, the tightness and warmth and wetness of the inside of her. She moved faster under him. He opened his eyes and saw her frown in concentration, her hips moving faster, her motion becoming more sudden, until she suddenly froze beneath him, her mouth opening slightly, her lips shining in the red light, and she exhaled in a long *oooohhhhhh,* then seemed to relax slightly beneath him. Her eyes opened and she smiled at him.

He wasn't sure what it was that brought him over the edge. Maybe it was the happy, satiated expression on her face, or the way she had told him she loved him, or the sound she had made when she came, but in a sudden tidal surge, he felt himself swept into an ecstasy so intense it was almost painful. For long seconds his sense of self vanished and there was only the two of them. Suddenly he felt cold and he shivered. He felt her arms around him and he opened his eyes and saw her shining eyes looking up at him.

He'd never seen such love in the eyes of a woman, and to see it from her made him want to make love to her again. He saw that he was in uncharted seas, because never before had he felt any impulse after having sex with a woman except to sleep or to withdraw, to return to his friends or his basketball game or his gardening or his house projects, including every encounter with Dayna. But he looked at Natalie and realized that nothing would ever compare to the feeling of being in her arms, and he knew that he had meant it when he had told her he loved her. He never wanted to leave this moment or this place, nestled in her arms with her smooth, bare, warm legs locked around him. He kissed her and looked into her eyes, sighing in fulfillment.

"I meant it," he whispered in her ear.

"What?" she asked, smiling at him, her fingernails stroking the skin of his back.

"When I said I love you."

Her expression became serious, a frown of consternation appearing. It was amazing how each emotion on her face made her beautiful in a different way. "Do you really?" she asked. There was a childlike vulnerability in her voice, and it made him love her even more.

He nodded. "I do. Did you mean what you said?"

She put her face between his chest and his neck for a moment, kissed his throat, then rose, her eyes seeking his again.

"I've loved you since the first moment I saw you," she whispered.

Petty Officer Morales saw the glowing mark on the short-time waterfall before Senior Chief Keating, which was a professional triumph. Keating nodded as the youngster pointed it out. A fairly distinct broadband trace emerged from the south. Probably an outbound merchant, Keating thought. He put on his headphones and trained the bearing of the noise to the south. He'd been right. It was a loud surface ship. Three-bladed screw, going slowly, about thirty rpm. This one sounded familiar. Keating nodded to himself. It was the deeper-draft freighter he'd caught going into port a week ago, the one he'd christened "the Buff," which stood for "Big Ugly Fat Fucker." He clicked his boom microphone.

"Conn, Sonar, new sonar contact, designated Sierra Eight, held on broadband on the sphere, bearing one seven nine, merchant ship, making three zero rpm on one three-bladed screw. He's far upriver and probably coming outbound. Believe it to be the Buff."

"Sonar, Conn, aye," Lieutenant Mercury-Pryce's voice came over the headset, piped from the conn open mike. Mercury-Pryce always tried to sound bored and calm, even in the tensest situations, as if in imitation of his fighter pilot brethren.

Keating poured another cup of coffee and sat down in the left console seat to watch the broadband display. The trace moved right, then left as the Buff followed the curves of the river. The sound traces on the broadband displays were getting brighter. The Buff was getting closer.

But what was this? he thought, frowning at the center display. The 254-hertz frequency bucket started jumping. There was a definite growing spike at 253.8 hertz. Keating hit the keyboard, dumping the old data and starting fresh, the towed array beam that looked downriver now empty of information, the unit starting over to "integrate" the new, fresh data. Keating glanced at the broadband display to see where the 254 was coming from, but other than the Buff, there was nothing. The 254 searching bucket was tied to the beam that looked directly south, but by virtue of how beams were formed, they could also get a frequency detect on the tonal from due north—which was in the submarine's baffles. Keating switched to the middle seat and watched as the 254-hertz tonal began to grow again on the frequency display. It was a definite spike. Keating glanced down at the lower buckets, his mouth dropping open. There was a double spike growing in the 308-hertz frequency bucket, one at 307.5, the other at 308.7 hertz. This happened when there were two "spinners," rotating machinery side by side, running at slightly different speeds from being loaded differently, like the port and starboard turbine generators when one unit's speed regulator was a bit out of tune, or there were two pumps and one had more of the work of pumping the fluid from an irregularity in the piping system.

Keating jumped back to his stool so he could see the entire picture. There was no doubt—he had Sierra Eight, the Buff, coming downriver, now at 45 rpm, and from the same bearing he had a 245-hertz tonal and a 308-hertz doublet.

Both of the tonals were classic signs of the Alfa. And the Buff hadn't made any tonals like this when it had roared by the first time, when it had been inbound.

"Conn, Sonar," he said, trying to sound calm, but knowing that his accent had just flattened out. "New sonar contact, Sierra Nine, narrowband contact, on the central beam of the towed array, bearing either one eight zero or zero zero zero, with a two-forty-five and a three-oh-eight doublet. Sierra Nine is classified as a submarine. Believe Sierra Nine belongs to the Alfa class."

Mercury-Pryce's voice was no longer calm, his words rushed. "Sonar, Conn, aye. Designate Sierra Nine as Master One. Any sign of broadband from Master One?"

"Conn, Sonar, no."

"Supervisor to control."

Keating hung up his headset, opened the curtain to the control room, and looked up at Mercury-Pryce, who stood on the periscope stand, a long cold cigar clamped in the young lieutenant's teeth.

"Yes, sir?"

"Is it possible the Alfa is shadowing the Buff, maybe submerged under him to sneak out of port?"

"Water's pretty shallow in the deep channel, OOD," Keating said. "But the Alfa could be following the Buff out, with the intention of submerging under him to avoid our detecting him."

"You're sure this is the bad guy?"

Keating nodded. He would bet ten years of his life on it.

Mercury-Pryce tossed the cigar into the butt can. "I'll call the XO. Thanks, Chief." Keating hurried back to sonar in time to hear Mercury-Pryce order over his shoulder, "Chief of the Watch, man silent battlestations."

For a long time he held her. Her breathing descended to the rhythm of sleep, her lovely hair spread out on his pillow, her arm around him. He watched her sleep, her eyes shut, her eyelashes on her beautiful cheeks, her chest rising and falling. He kissed her forehead, feeling it still slightly damp from the sweat of their coupling. Maybe, Dillinger thought, he could hold her for another hour before anyone wanted her.

As if answer to the thought the buzzer from the control room phone buzzed back in her stateroom. There was no way Dillinger could wake her in time for her to get the call without sounding groggy or winded from the sprint to her sea cabin, so he grabbed the heavy phone. They were on the same circuit—only the buzzer location was different.

"Captain," he said, his official voice deep and normal-sounding, thank God.

Natalie's eyes flew open in panic and she launched herself out of his bed, grabbed her panties, and shut the bathroom door quietly behind her.

"Sorry, sir, but I thought I'd buzzed the XO. Sir, we have—"

"XO," Natalie's voice said suddenly on the phone. He could still feel her, as if she were still hugging him. He wondered when he could be with her again, but the thought evaporated in Mercury-Pryce's next words.

"Captain, XO, we have the Alfa."

26

Andrei Rusanov stood on the aft superstructure observation platform overlooking the *Kirovsky*'s fantail. The white foamy wake boiled up astern of them, leading south to the Kola Fjord. He looked at the craggy hills of the Kola Peninsula as they moved past the flanks of the ship and faded southward, until the last of them moved by. The ship had moved out of the river and made its way into the Kola Bay and on into the Barents Sea.

He glanced at his watch. It was five minutes before two in the morning, just slightly ahead of schedule. He decided to watch the coastline until it faded over the horizon, then go belowdecks. It wouldn't hurt to get a few hours of sleep before they separated from the *Kirovsky*.

He slapped his gloves together, feeling the late-November cold, and idly thinking about whether a drink would warm him up, when he saw one of the clients emerge onto the railed deck. He nodded at the man, but the Egyptian looked at him as if he were an offensive eight-legged insect. The man turned his back. Curious, Rusanov craned his neck to see what the man was doing. He held a phone, one bigger than a normal cell phone, with a fat antenna coming out the top. A satellite phone. Rusanov could hear the machine beeping as the Egyptian pushed the phone buttons, then listened. Rusanov thought it odd that the man never spoke into the phone, but just pushed the phone buttons. He must be checking on his damned Swiss account, Rusanov thought. Eventually the Egyptian hung up. He turned and glared at Rusanov and went back into the superstructure.

The Egyptian hurried through the passageway and up the steep ship's ladder to the bridge, where Abdas al-Sattar sat in the captain's seat, his subordinates circled around him. Abdas looked up.

"Holy One, it is done."

Abdas smiled.

The timing was perfect. Not too soon after their departure, or else the emergency authorities would see them and ask questions, perhaps even delaying their exit from the mouth of the Kola Fjord. Not too much later than their entrance into the Barents, though, or else the principles of KKS and the key employees of the Terminal would live to tell the tale of this submarine, and that would be unacceptable. A surviving employee could blow this secret and vital mission.

Far over the horizon to the southeast, in the ten seconds after the satellite call, the four computers hidden under the floorboards of the four buses in the Terminal received the command detonate signal, and four sets of blasting caps sparked into incandescence. Aboard the four buses, a combined total of forty thousand pounds of Semtex RDX/PETN moldable plastic explosive exploded. In the first milliseconds of the blasts, the buses ceased to exist, a high-energy fireball taking their place in the space on the shipbuilding floor of the Terminal building. As time passed, the fireballs grew and reinforced each other until they reached out to the walls and the ceiling of the building.

In the next hundred milliseconds the structure of the Terminal building became unrecognizable. Every steel wall column melted or became fist-sized chunks of shrapnel, and every ceiling girder vaporized. The outer brick walls of the formerly decrepit building became crumbling bullets, accelerating to near sonic velocity, ten thousand cannonballs aimed at all points of the azimuth. The wood of the roof disintegrated into shards and splinters flying skyward, though there were some chunks as large as billboards that flew upward, engulfed in fierce flames. The explosion ripped downward into the ship construction table, the heavy metal slamming down into the water cavern under the building.

In the second hundred milliseconds the Terminal ceased to exist, its steel and brick and glass structure now a million missiles flying skyward and outward. Had that been the only result of the Semtex detonation, it would have kept the sky lit in roaring fires for the next twenty hours, but the explosion caused a white-hot, flaming half-ton piece of steel to fly into the side of a relatively small ten-thousand-gallon kerosene tank at the neighboring Murmansk Oil Company. The explosion of the kerosene set off fires at all the nearby tanks in the forty-acre tank farm, one of them a 500,000-gallon tank of unleaded gasoline. The gasoline tank explosion was the equivalent of almost ten thousand tons of dynamite. The shock wave from the blast reached out to pound the city, knocking over the twenty surrounding buildings, which caused natural-gas fires throughout the waterfront district.

Two miles away to the south, every north-facing window of the Arktika Hotel shattered and blew hundreds of thousands of shards of glass inward as the gasoline tank erupted in its tremendous detonation. A mushroom cloud nearly a hundred meters in diameter rose up over the dockside buildings, the cloud a rolling orange conflagration rising over the city, the November dimness becoming as bright as noon at the equator for a full minute, until the orange fireball turned to black smoke. The thirty-block area of the waterfront was reduced to flaming ruins.

It would take more than two weeks for the Murmansk Fire Protection Directorate to put out the flames. They would never find the bodies of Yuri Belkov or the Kaznikov brothers, who had been drinking champagne to celebrate the success of Lira Unit One in the Terminal's lower conference room.

Dillinger had jumped into his coveralls and sneakers and rushed to the control room. A second after he arrived, Natalie walked in, looking calm in her coveralls, her hair pulled back into a professional-looking ponytail. As he pulled on his cordless boom microphone he caught her eye. There was absolutely nothing in her glance other than the acknowledgment of an executive officer toward her captain. What an incredible woman, he thought, who could show this level of discipline and strength. His heart swelled with love for her for just a fraction of a second. Maybe she saw it in his eyes, because she smiled just slightly before scowling at the officer of the deck.

"What've you got, OOD?" she asked crisply. It was supposed to be Dillinger's line, he thought, the part of him that swirled with emotion for Natalie suddenly shoved back into its compartment, and his mind returned to its uncluttered state of fierce clarity that he had always privately called his battle-stations zone.

Mercury-Pryce looked up, one eyebrow lifted. "We've got Sierra Eight, broadband merchant outbound from the bay. He passed overhead about two minutes ago. We've also got Master One, definite Alfa-class with a two-fifty-four and a three-oh-eight doublet."

"Status of battlestations?" Around him, the control room—normally cramped—had become as crowded as a skyscraper's elevator at one minute to nine in the morning. The attack center seats were occupied by three officers. The weapons officer manned the weapon control console while wearing a special headset with a dual circuit to the torpedo room and to the control room. The dual navigation tables were more crowded than a winning craps table in Vegas, with the navigator at the center of the action, plotting the "solution" to the target on the starboard plotting table, then spinning to update the navigation picture on the port table. A table had been folded down in the aft corner for the time-bearing plot and the time-frequency plot. The watchstanders would perform dual methods to get the target—one using the ship's battlecontrol system, the other using raw bearing data and inputs from the ship's inertial navigation system. In a calm, single-target environment, the manual plots could come up with an acceptable solution, and they were a hedge against a loss of the firecontrol computer, but it tripled the number of people in the room. Even in the arctic temperatures around them, the room had grown hot. D'Assault had already rolled up her sleeves and taken her coverall zipper down a few inches. Dillinger turned to hear Mercury-Pryce's report on the manning of battlestations.

"Fully manned except my relief, Mr. Flood, who's being relieved aft."

"Very well," Dillinger said, crossing his arms as he stood in front of the starboard side attack center consoles. "Sonar, Captain, bearing to Master One?"

"Sir, ambiguity holds him either northwest or southeast."

"Coordinator," Dillinger said to Natalie. During a battlestations approach, the XO became the firecontrol coordinator, or simply "coordinator." "Let's get the array off the bottom and get some speed on." Dillinger turned to the periscope stand, where Lieutenant Commander Steve Flood, the most senior and experienced conning officer, was relieving Lieutenant Mercury-Pryce, who stepped down and took the control seat in front of the second position of the firecontrol console, becoming the "pos two" operator. "Off'sa'deck, vertical rise to depth one hundred."

"Vertical rise to one hundred, OOD aye," Flood acknowledged. "Chief of the Watch, engage the hovering system and insert positive zero point five feet per second depth rate to one hundred feet. Diving Officer, maintain one hundred feet."

Dillinger watched the digital depth gauge as the ship rose slowly off the bottom. He glanced at D'Assault, whose lips had narrowed as she concentrated on the sonar repeater display. She looked up and frowned.

"Something's wrong," she said.

"What?"

"No broadband on the Alfa. He's got to be within two thousand yards, but all we have is Sierra Eight, the Buff."

"We may never have broadband on him," Dillinger said, looking away. "He's much quieter now. We'll have to track him with his tonals on narrowband."

"Sonar, Coordinator," D'Assault said into her boom mike. "Report signal-to-noise on Master One's tonals."

"Coordinator, Sonar, both are around positive eight decibels."

Dillinger raised an eyebrow. That was loud. "Sonar, Captain, what's your guess on range?"

"Captain, Sonar, close."

"But no broadband?"

At first there was no answer, but then Senior Chief Keating spoke quietly. "It's possible Master One's hiding behind Sierra Eight, or submerged under him, or even towed by him."

"Any evidence of a screw with more than three blades?"

"Conn, Sonar, no."

"What the hell's going on?" he asked, looking at Flood. Flood, as OOD, worked for him on the battlestations firecontrol party as an assistant approach officer, while the XO was sort of his peer, making independent judgments about the target's motion. Dillinger could override the XO, but it was rarely done.

Flood glared at the attack center consoles and the dual sonar repeater screens, unconsciously imitating Dillinger's crossed arms and stiff posture. "I think he's being towed astern of the Buff. This close, we'd hear his screw. No screw, no broadband, but he's moving and his bearing is tracking with Sierra Eight's."

Dillinger shook his head. "Is there a chance he's on the bottom, listening? That would explain the absence of a screw noise."

D'Assault turned and shook her head. "No, Captain, he's moving. He's moved from the athwartships beam all the way over to the three three five slash two zero five beam. I think he's moving with Sierra Eight, the freighter." She glanced at Dillinger, a tough expression on her face. "Russians have been known to pull tricks like this, sir."

"Sonar, Conn," Dillinger said, his tone showing irritation. "Up to now we've assumed Sierra Eight is the freighter that came in. Is it possible that Sierra Eight *is* the Alfa? Noisy, with a three-bladed screw?"

"Captain, Sonar, wait."

"OOD, depth one hundred feet, sir," the diving officer announced. Chief of the Boat Fred Davies, the former auxiliaryman chief who had been promoted to COB this year, was the best diving officer aboard, and it was said he could maintain depth control in a category-three hurricane.

"Bring her ahead slowly, OOD. Two knots."

"Helm, all ahead one-third," Flood ordered. "Maneuvering, Conn, make turns for two knots. Helm, steer course east. Dive, maintain depth one hundred feet. Helm, mark speed one knot."

"Conn, Sonar, we've got loud transients on the towed array. Unit is dragging. Loss of Master One."

Dillinger waited in the tense, quiet, red-lit room for the speed log to show the ship moving. The drag of the towed array on the bottom would tend to slow them down, but the screw easily had the power to cut the tow cable, even at bare steerageway.

"Sonar, Conn," Dillinger barked. "Supervisor to control." What the hell was going on with the answer to his question? he wanted to know. While the towed array was dragging on the bottom, they'd lost the Alfa, so Dillinger could talk to Keating face-to-face. The door to sonar opened and Keating came into the room, his face drawn and lined. What heart the man had, Dillinger thought, going on this deployment while his little girl was sick back in Norfolk. But personal problems aside, Dillinger needed his sonar supervisor on his game, especially now.

"Skipper," Keating said, "Sierra Eight is definitely the same big freighter that came in a few days ago. That screw is big, sir, maybe fifteen feet in diameter. There's a pattern of transients—creaks and moans—that only comes from surface ships. And we saw this freighter before. I was the one who named it the Buff. And he didn't have any of these tonals before. I was on watch, and I was looking for these particular tonals. There's no way the detect at the bearing of the Buff is a submarine. Master One's close to it, maybe even on the same bearing, but it's not the same ship."

"One knot, sir."

"Sonar, Conn," Flood called, "putting on turns for two knots. Advise status of towed array."

The voice of Sonarman First Class David Orleans, Keating's second-in-command, came over the circuit. "Conn, Sonar, we have . . . we have loud transients from the south-southeast. Sounds like an explosion."

"Request to return to sonar," Keating said.

Dillinger nodded and waved Keating back to sonar while staring at the sonar display. A loud blooming trace had erupted to the south.

"Plot it on the chart," Dillinger ordered Rob Cummins. "Bearing one six nine." Cummins whirled the bearing ruler to the bearing of the noise, laid it on the table, and drew a pencil line from the illuminated light on the chart that shone up from the navigation table's inner workings.

Cummins looked up. "It lines up with Murmansk, Captain. Maybe a gas-main explosion."

"Sonar, Captain, is the explosion coming from the water? Any bubbles, shock waves, hull breakups?"

"Captain, Sonar, no. We're getting it from the air. Something on land."

"Attention in the firecontrol party, we think something may have blown up on the Kola Peninsula, but let's not allow it to distract us. Forget the explosion and keep focused on the Alfa. Carry on. Sonar, Captain, you got the towed array back?"

Dillinger bit the inside of his lip, knowing that with the elusive Alfa held only on the towed array, it would be the end of the mission if it got hung up on a rock on the bottom and the ship's speed cut off the array.

"Conn, Sonar, loud background from the towed array is diminishing. Believe the array is mostly off the bottom."

"Sonar, Conn, aye," Flood said, his eyes on the towed array display on the dual sonar screens. The graphs had gone crazy with the intensity of the sound from dragging the unit on the bottom.

"Conn, Sonar," Keating's voice crackled on the phone circuit, "Unit's off the bottom."

"OOD, eight knots," Dillinger ordered.

"Helm, all ahead two-thirds," Flood said.

Dillinger checked the overhead chronometer. It had been only twenty minutes ago that he was in a different world. He looked over at the sonar repeater panels. By going east, they had gotten the towed array to come off the bottom, but Sierra Eight was going northwest out of the bay.

"Bring her around to the northwest and speed up to twelve knots." That was the speed the Buff had been going before they lost the Alfa, Master One.

"Helm, all ahead standard, left ten degrees rudder, steady course three three zero. Maneuvering, Conn, make turns for twelve knots. Sonar, Conn, maneuvering to the northwest." Flood walked back to the chart. Dillinger followed him. They watched and calculated as the ship slowly turned to follow the big freighter.

"Attention in the firecontrol party. If we follow the freighter, we should be able to reacquire Master One," Dillinger said. He could sense Natalie looking at him, but he kept his eyes on the sonar panel.

There on the 308-hertz graph the spikes began to grow vertically upward out of the noise of the ocean. Dillinger smiled. They'd done it, he thought. They'd taken the risk of laying the towed array on the ocean floor, which wasn't recommended, and by doing so they'd caught the Alfa when it sneaked out of town towed by the freighter. Now they'd successfully gotten the vital array off the bottom with no damage. All they had to do was establish the exact location of the Alfa, follow it out to deep water in the Norwegian Sea, then torpedo the son of a bitch to hell. Then he could hightail it back to Norfolk, brief the brass, and ask Natalie out for their first date. Dillinger smiled and looked over at the XO. Her face was as emotionless as if they had nothing personal between them. She half nodded to acknowledge him and turned back to the attack center.

"Conn, Sonar, reacquisition of Master One, bearing three one five, roughly coincides with the bearing to Sierra Eight at three two zero."

"Gotcha," Dillinger said.

"Sonar, Conn, aye," Flood acknowledged.

"Captain, request you and the OOD on the conn," D'Assault said.

Dillinger nodded. It wasn't unusual to have an offline conversation between the three heavies in the room—Flood as officer of the deck, D'Assault as coordinator, and Dillinger as approach officer—during battlestations, particularly when there was so much uncertainty in fighting a submarine. Yet that uncertainty couldn't be acknowledged to the crew, or they would lose their confidence in the senior officer. So whenever tactics during doubtful times or disputed decisions needed to be discussed, the "three wise men" would gather between the periscopes, away from the other watchstanders, and debate the issue, their hands covering their boom microphones. In the tight confines of the ship, there was no real way to get away from the ears of the watchstanders, and with their leadership sometimes divided, every ear in the control room was tuned to their conversation, but it gave them the illusion of confidentiality, which was often more important.

"Captain," D'Assault began. "It's my responsibility to advise you that we could shoot him now and make sure he doesn't get away again. It would fulfill our mission."

"While disobeying the order to avoid being detected while taking down the Alfa," Flood interrupted. "We're supposed to do this away from prying eyes. The freighter would live to tell the tale."

"Or we could miss and hit the freighter," Dillinger added.

"I know, Captain. I'm just pointing this out. We're close with no broadband on the Alfa. If he gets away from us, we could regret not putting a bullet in his forehead now."

"Understood," Dillinger said. D'Assault was being needlessly pessimistic, he thought. He turned to Flood. "OOD?"

"Captain, I'd wait. I think we're missing broadband because the Alfa hasn't started his main engines and reduction gear and screw. Once he opens the throttles, we'll have him. We should let him get a few miles over the horizon from the freighter, then shoot him."

"Torpedoes?"

"Well, yes, of course."

D'Assault picked up Dillinger's meaning. "We *could* punch him with the nukes. Much shorter time of flight, a definite kill, and we have full permission."

Dillinger shook his head. "No. The mushroom clouds would be seen far over the horizon by the freighter and anyone else on the Kola Peninsula. Plus we'd have a sonar blue-out over that entire sector of the ocean. On the off-chance that we miss, we'd never be able to confirm a kill, and it would hide a furious Alfa. He'd come out of a blue cloud with vengeance in his heart. He'd be looking east, with clear sonar reception in that direction, toward us, and he could surprise us with a Russian torpedo. If we have a reasonable shot with torpedoes, we'll use them."

"Agreed, sir," D'Assault said. "Captain, the missiles can be powered up for hours, but they take ten minutes to spin up. In the heat of battle, waiting ten minutes may not be a survivable option. Maybe you should warm one of them now, just so you can fire it if you get in a hurry."

"That's another gyro spinning close to the hull, Captain," Flood said. "It could put out some detectable noise. But I'd risk it."

Dillinger thought about it for a second, then nodded. "Weps, make the SUBROC in vertical launch tube one ready in all respects with the exception of opening the outer door."

After Tonelle acknowledged, D'Assault spoke up. "Let's

do some target motion analysis on Sierra Eight. We've got
the bearing to the Alfa, but not his range, and I want to
know his exact course. If we lose him, we can input a guess
that he'll keep going on that vector."

If they could understand the distance from the *Tucson*,
knowing the ship's position, they could chart the position,
course, and speed of the Alfa on the chart. That way, if
they lost him, they could look for him down the course that
he'd been going.

"OOD, take her southwest."

The *Tucson* turned to the southwest while her sonar
arrays and the BQQ-5 processors sliced and diced the data
from the freighter and the Alfa.

Peter Vornado turned off the shower water and dressed
quickly in his coveralls, debating whether to spend a few
minutes topside on the observation platform of the *Kirovsky*. When he emerged from the small bathroom, Svetlana sat up in the bed, her hair mussed from the last hour
they'd spent together.

Vornado smiled at her. "If I'd done my job, you'd be
asleep now," he teased her.

"You'll have to work harder," she said, a smile gracing
the lovely curves of her face. Vornado stood looking at her
for a long time, wondering for the thousandth time how he
would ever say good-bye to her when this ended. A fugitive
thought stole into his mind: that they might not survive the
next week.

Vornado's smile vanished. "Listen, you can't show your
face, not with the Egyptians and their attitudes toward
women. First, they'd want you in a black gown with your
face covered; second, they'd want you restricted to the
kitchen; and third, they wouldn't want you on the ship at
all. Bad luck."

"I can't hide in here, and I came because you need me,
not just here, but in the command post."

"You'll have to dress like a man, then. You can take
some of my coveralls and bulk yourself up with a pair of
sweatpants underneath. I'll have to cut your hair." It would
be a damned shame to cut her shining blonde locks, he
thought, but better he cut her hair than the Egyptians use
one of their knives on her. "And do something about your

face. Can you use some makeup that will make it look like you have a five-o'clock shadow?"

She fished in her bag for a pair of scissors, and ten minutes later she had a blonde crew cut. She frowned at it in the mirror.

"It needs to be darker," she said. "Go on. I'll join you in a while."

"Lock the door behind me."

Vornado left his stateroom and climbed the ladder to the upper level. He walked into the command post. Dmitri Maslov still had the watch. Vornado bent over the navigation console and checked their position. It was almost time to stop the freighter and send the divers down to unbolt the stiffening girders and separate the submarine from the freighter.

Maslov crossed the room to switch seats, a blinking annunciator on the sonar panel.

"Something's wrong," he said.

"What is it?" Vornado looked over his shoulder.

"A loud roaring sound from the southeast. The history module shows it started some time ago."

"How long ago?"

Maslov shook his head. "Dammit, Captain, it didn't get really loud till two minutes ago, but there was a spike from that direction here, at time zero one fifty-five hours, and the sound was three decibels over background." Maslov tapped the display. "Damned thing should have annunciated. I was involved in reactor plant temperature trends."

"It's okay, Dmitri. Can you listen to it?"

"Here."

Maslov handed Vornado the headset. The sound was like a howling wind, broken by a crackling explosion.

"What is that?"

"It's not coming from the ocean, at least I don't think it is. There's trouble back on the peninsula."

"Stay alert," Vornado ordered. "We should be monitoring the narrowband processor in case we're being followed by a submarine from the West."

"Yes, Captain, but not much chance of that."

"Watch it anyway. I'm going topside to get the crew and the clients from the *Kirovsky*," Vornado said. He started up the hatch to the escape vehicle, but men were already lowering themselves down the upper ladder. As he watched, the Egyptians came down one by one, continuing downward to their staterooms on the middle level. Finally Abdas al-Sattar climbed down and nodded at Vornado, then continued to the middle level. The Russians came down next, the last man down Andrei Rusanov, who pulled down the lower hatch and spun the dogging ring.

"Is the bridge rigged for dive?"

"Excuse me?"

Apparently the English phrase didn't translate well into Russian.

"The bridge. Did you bring down the cockpit windshield and latch it in place, and make sure there's nothing up there to rattle?"

"Yes, sir," Rusanov said. "We're going to be stopping any minute so the divers can unbolt the stiffener struts."

Vornado took a deep breath, then turned to check the navigation chart. When he turned, he saw a thin man leaning on the periscope pole. He had closely cropped black hair and stood half a head shorter than Vornado. His skin was slightly dark at his mustache and chin and cheeks, but otherwise he had feminine features.

"Sorry," Vornado murmured, "but you don't fool me."

"You're not the one I'm trying to fool," Svetlana said in a deep voice, the same one she used when making fun of the stupid things men said to her.

"You're right," Vornado said. The way the Ahel al Beit terrorists disregarded the Russians, she would barely be given a second glance.

Rusanov stood beside Vornado, a frown on his face. "Who are you?" he asked.

"Hi, Andrei," Svetlana said, still using her male voice.

He looked closely at her. "Svetlana?" he whispered.

"No," she said, as if insulted. "My name is Ivan. Ivan Mironov."

"Sure it is," Rusanov said. "Captain?"

"It's fine, Andrei. The Ahel al Beit don't take kindly to women aboard. Put Ivan here in the watch rotation. He's standing watch like the rest of us."

"We've stopped, Captain," Maslov interrupted. "*Kirovksy* will be dropping us any moment."

"How will we know it's time to separate?"

Rusanov spoke up. "We open the ballast volume vents. When the *Kirovsky* lets go of us, with the vents open we fill up with ballast water and sink away from her. It's shallow enough to bottom-out here. Once *Kirovsky* is clear, we'll pump out the variable ballast, balance the ship, and we'll be on our way."

Vornado nodded calmly, but inside he began to have misgivings about the ship. It was untested and had sailed with a green crew, and was performing tactics foreign to Vornado. He'd be glad when this damned run was over, even if it meant he had to face the Svetlana problem.

PART 5:

▼

No Regrets

27

"Conn, Sonar, a thousand transients coming from Master One," Senior Chief Keating's voice announced on the fire-control circuit.

Dillinger glanced at Steve Flood, who had donned his red goggles, just in case they had to come to periscope depth in the darkness. The Alfa had stopped, as had the Buff, Sierra Eight, the massive freighter. For the last fifteen minutes, the oddest and loudest noises had been coming from the freighter, the noises classified as transients, because rather than the constant noise of a screw or a turbine generator, they were ephemeral. Transients included dropped wrenches on the deckplates, a slammed hatch, falling pots and pans, the roar of a steam generator blowdown, or even music played too loud on a stereo system that was acoustically shorted to the hull.

"What do you think the problem is?" D'Assault asked Keating.

"Conn, Sonar, it's possible they're having trouble disconnecting the towing rig. If that's what's going on."

"Sonar, Conn, aye." D'Assault glanced at Dillinger. "At least we have him, sir." She covered her microphone with her hand and stepped close to him, her eyes rising up to look in his, except now she was all business. "We could shoot him now, Captain."

He shook his head. "The freighter is right here. He'd witness the explosion. Op order forbids it. Or worse, we could hit the goddamned freighter. That's not something I want to explain to Smokin' Joe Kraft."

She nodded and stepped away. He turned back to the sonar screen, one eye on the dot-stacking display on the BSY-1 firecontrol system. If the dots stacked vertically, it meant the assumed solution—the contact's course, speed,

and range—was matching the data coming in from reality.
When the line of data diverged to one side or the other, it
meant the guess wasn't predicting reality. The officers on
the attack center consoles would then dial in more realistic
assumptions of range, course, or speed to bring the dots
back in line. If the target were moving steadily, and if they
maneuvered in three-minute "legs" or segments of time on
a course, with the legs far enough from the target's course,
the computer could determine a unique solution for the
target, meaning only one combination of course, speed, and
range would create a vertical line. Speed clues came from
sonar—the turn count from the screw would reveal a slow-
moving target or one that was hauling ass, and those clues
could be used when dialing in an assumed speed. Range
could also be guessed at rationally. A far-distant target
might only be held on narrowband bottom-bounce, so
they'd dial in the range to be tens of miles away. A close
broadband contact, perhaps one seen on the periscope,
would make the attack center officers dial in closer ranges.

The trick came when the target was maneuvering or
knew they were out there. Then both the computer solutions and the manual plots fell apart.

"Captain, recommend we come up to PD and take a
look for ourselves," D'Assault said. "If he's having trouble
disconnecting the tow rig, maybe we can get a look at him.
At the very least, we can get a periscope photo we can use
as a trophy to prove we had the guy."

"Best idea I've heard all night except for one," he said,
wondering if D'Assault read his meaning. "Sonar, Captain,
we're going to vertical rise to periscope depth."

Things were tense in the command post when Abdas al-
Sattar entered in his white flowing robe and his bloodred
cape, his scimitar sword bouncing against his thigh. If he
felt uncomfortable being without his lieutenants, he didn't
show it.

"Captain Vornado, I should like to speak with you."

"Not now, Holy One," Vornado said without looking at
the Egyptian. "We're busy."

A loud thundering boom sounded from above them as
the ship detached from the *Kirovsky*. The depth readout
at the ship control station showed them sinking rapidly,

since Andrei had fully flooded the variable ballast tanks. The deck inclined downward. They were heavy by the bow. Rusanov sat at the ship control station, the corner consoles at the port forward corner of the room, frantically manipulating the displays to avoid crashing to the bottom nose-first.

Abdas grabbed a handrail of the periscope stand. Vornado had never seen him move so quickly. He always had acted with deliberate, calm grace, but he must be feeling the same anxiety Vornado was.

"Dammit, Andrei, pump forward variable to sea, max rate!"

"Pumping, sir. Depth fifty meters."

Slowly the incline came off the ship. "Don't go too far, Andrei. Secure pumping."

The deck was almost level but the ship was still sinking too fast.

"Pump centerline to sea, now."

Rusanov pumped and the depth rate slowed.

"What's the depth here?"

Rusanov was busy on his panel. Vornado walked to the aft starboard corner of the room and selected the sonar display to show the bottom sounder. He worked through the software to sound a single ping. On the bottom of the keel, a small hydrophone emitted a short, high-frequency beep, then listened for its echo. The time between ping and echo was measured by the computer and converted to water depth based on water temperature and how that correlated to sound velocity. The system added the depth of the keel at the time of the ping to come up with a total water depth.

"Two hundred eighty meters," Vornado announced.

"Depth two hundred meters," Rusanov announced. "We're steady, maybe rising a bit."

"You've got control?" If Rusanov had depth control, there was no need to bottom the ship. They could hover here for a moment, then move slowly ahead to get away from the *Kirovsky*. Vornado looked over at "Ivan," who leaned over the navigation display. The unit showed the chart using a horizontal flat-panel display, its software obtained commercially. The charts of water depth were updated from some Russian Navy secret charts, which had

been obtained the usual way, through the Kaznikovs' brib-
ery. It would be hard to get used to a chart that wasn't
paper, but technology moved on.

Rusanov nodded. "I've got control. Steady on depth two
hundred five meters."

Dillinger snapped the next order. "OOD, bring her up
slowly to PD."

"Aye, sir," Flood replied. "Chief of the Watch, rig control for black. Diving Officer, vertical rise to make your
depth six seven feet."

The optics module came slowly out of the periscope well.
Flood crouched down and snapped the grips into position
and put his eye on the eyepiece before the unit had risen
more than two feet out of the well. He rose with it, his
right hand making sure the scope was in low power, his
left rotating to train his view directly overhead.

"I can see the surface," he said, his voice muffled by the
periscope optics module. "Shimmering light from the
waves."

"One hundred feet, OOD."

"Very well, no shapes or shadows." Flood was rotating
the scope once every two seconds, turning it around and
around, the waves far overhead spinning around his head.
He flattened the view slowly to try to pierce the darkness
and see farther out.

The silence in the room continued. Dillinger waited, his
eyes on the attack center. Once Flood had the scope dry,
he'd take over from him. It was best not to look too anxious. That would make the crew think he was worried. He
needed to appear steely to them. In the green glow of the
attack center, he could sense D'Assault's eyes on him, and
he longed to look back at her, but he knew he couldn't
afford to, or he would lose his concentration.

"Seven zero. Chief of the Watch, flood depth control
two. Six nine. Six eight, Chief, secure flooding. Six seven
feet, sir!"

On the periscope stand, Flood rotated in three quick circles. The lights of the freighter came into his view to the
northwest, then disappeared, showing only the dark horizon
and a faint trace of the far-distant cliffs of the Russian
coastline. With nothing close, he slowed his search.

"No close contacts!" he announced. He trained the periscope to Sierra Eight, the freighter. In the clear moonlit night, the waves were gentle, whipped by an eight-knot wind, and they shimmered in the silvery moonlight. The freighter just sat there, dead in the water, its running lights on. There was no sign of anything wrong except for the fact that it was stopped.

"Let me look," Dillinger said over Flood's shoulder.

"Low power, on the horizon, bearing three five zero relative."

Dillinger took the periscope, the eyepiece warm from Flood's face. There in the crosshairs was the stopped freighter. Its superstructure was lit with several interior lights and a few lights on the ladders between external platforms. The cabin lights of the superstructure shone in the darkness. There was none of the activity he'd expected on the fantail, where he thought he'd see a crew of twenty men disconnecting a heavy tow cable. He turned the scope to do a high-power search of the horizon. Obviously the Alfa was surfaced nearby, and they couldn't see it because its running lights were off for stealth. But when he'd completed the circle, he came up with nothing.

"Sonar, Captain, I have visual on Sierra Eight but nothing on Master One. Do you still hold Master One?"

"Captain, Sonar, towed array is drooping with zero speed, so we've lost narrowband, but we now hold Master One on broadband sonar. Signal-to-noise on broadband is high. Lots of transients, and he's close, sir."

"What about deflection/elevation?" D'Assault asked.

The term *deflection/elevation* referred to the sonar sphere's ability to look up or down. If they had contact on the Alfa with broadband sonar, the sphere's hydrophones would indicate which elevation at that bearing was most active.

"Coordinator, Sonar, we have a zero D/E on the target, I say again, zero D/E."

Which meant the submarine was horizontally near them. That was impossible.

"Sonar, Conn, what the hell?" D'Assault's voice was irritated. "Supervisor to control."

"Yes, ma'am," Keating said from behind her.

"What took you so long?"

Keating's frown didn't ease. "I know this sounds nuts, Captain, XO, but the Alfa's not on the bottom and he's not surfaced. He's at our depth."

"It does sound nuts, but thanks," Dillinger said. Keating withdrew back to sonar. "Junior Officer of the Deck, take the scope," Dillinger ordered Lieutenant Nick "Neon" Keondre. "Coordinator, OOD, step up on the conn," Dillinger said, lowering his boom mike and covering it, as did the other two officers. "What do you think?" he whispered.

"I say we wait a few minutes," D'Assault said. "He's here, he's submerged, we've got strong broadband contact on him, and he's getting rid of the tow rig."

Dillinger thought for a moment, then nodded.

"Andrei, the main engine is warm?"

Vornado had a feeling he hadn't had since another lifetime. He was submerged and in command. It was a feeling of exhilaration that almost no one would ever understand. In the palate of human experience, perhaps only maneuvering a fighter jet through supersonic barrel rolls or walking in space in low earth orbit or jumping across the surface of the moon could compare to this. And yet, in hours or days or weeks this would be over, and he would return to his life as a civilian. He put the depressing thought aside and concentrated on the moment.

"Yes, Captain, clutch is engaged and the screw spins freely. Ready to answer any engine order."

"Very good. Dead slow ahead. Watch your depth and your compass heading." Vornado leaned over Rusanov's shoulder. "When we get a little motion, three knots, test your rudder."

"Yes, sir." Rusanov put his hands on the aircraft-style throttle and moved it slowly forward.

As Vornado watched, the ship's speed indicator on the display climbed slowly from zero to one knot. Vornado looked aft. Dmitri Maslov was watching the reactor plant.

"How's reactor power?"

"Rising, sir. Temperatures are normal. Reactor power fifteen percent."

"Two knots, Captain. Three knots."

"Test the rudder."

"Yes, sir." Rusanov grabbed a joystick from the panel,

the configuration of the ship control screens, rudder pedal, and stick intentionally imitating a fighter airplane's cockpit. Rusanov adjusted the joystick pad down farther, so that it was between his legs, the stick protruding just above his crotch. In other circumstances Vornado might have considered it funny, but this was dead serious. Rusanov put his feet up on the rudder pedals. "Testing rudder in the right direction." The rudder indication on the panel showed the control surface moving to the right. Vornado concentrated on the compass, which began to spin slowly from due west toward the north. "Five knots, Captain."

"Test left rudder." If the rudder jammed, the mission would be over.

Rusanov pushed on the left pedal; the indication changed to show the rudder moving back to the centerline of the ship and beyond, continuing to the left.

"Good, Andrei. Steady on course two nine zero."

When Rusanov was back on the northwestern course, Vornado ordered him to test the bowplanes, then the sternplanes. After ten tense minutes, it appeared everything worked. If any of the control surfaces disappointed them at speed, they could be dead in seconds, particularly if either the bow or sternplanes jammed in the dive position. They'd poke a hole in the sea floor and keep going.

"Andrei, the towed array—is it ready to be deployed?"

Rusanov selected a new screen for the side readout. He nodded. "Yes, sir."

The system to eject the towed array cable came from main hydraulics, the same system that drove the bowplanes. Since the bowplanes had worked, the array should be able to deploy. The sixty-meter-long cable was stowed in a tube between the outer hull and the inner pressure hull, with the cable reel contained in a free flood space above the torpedo tube door mechanisms forward of the first compartment.

"Deploy the towed array." Vornado watched it, an unbidden image flashing in his memory of little Marla, back when he was a junior officer standing duty and she was three, and he had shown her the control room and sonar. When the sonar chief mentioned the towed array, she thought he had said "toad Ray." The next time he had duty, she wanted to know if he would be talking to that toad named Ray. God, he missed his daughter, he thought, and his son, and his wife. And his life.

"The array is fully deployed, sir."

Vornado looked aft at Svetlana, who had joined them in the room. He hadn't noticed when he was busy with Rusanov. It seemed ill-advised, especially since Abdas al-Sattar was here as well. But if she were working on a panel, Abdas would have less reason to focus on her.

"Ivan?" he called. She looked up at him. "Bring up the sonar system in narrowband mode. Transfer the processors from the conformal hull array to the towed array, and initiate a multifrequency automatic search." Svetlana nodded, probably because she didn't trust her "guy voice" around Abdas, and started a sonar search using the towed array.

Once she was in the system, Vornado walked aft to check the reactor plant console, then came back to the ship control screens. He had been having an internal debate with himself, whether to put the ship through some trials, or to just move quietly toward the North Atlantic. The prudent course would be to do the minimum, to travel slowly and quietly with no risk, and to get the mutiny under way and dispose of Abdas while he was still getting used to being submerged, but Vornado's instinct told him Abdas and his men were at their maximum alertness. Better to let several watches go by, and allow them to get bored. Let the middle of the night come tomorrow. By then Vornado could meet with Danalov, hand out the weapons, and plan the event. Vornado checked the chart and the seawater depths ahead. They were in a deeper trench here that extended to Nordkapp, Sweden, and beyond, into the Norwegian Sea, with water depths going down to almost a thousand fathoms. There was no doubt—if he did a maximum speed run, he would know the ship's capabilities.

But what if he were being followed, he thought, by a Western boat in trail? It might be a good thing, Vornado thought. A trailing American submarine would be his ally, he decided. The CIA wanted Abdas and they wanted this submarine. Anyone out there would be there just to keep track of them. And if that were the case, going swiftly would make noise, and making noise would beckon the submarine tracking him.

The decision was made, Vornado thought. He'd let the horses run.

"Conn, Sonar, we've got something changing," Keating reported. "Transients are gone. We hold Master One on broadband and narrowband. Both indicate Master One is moving."

Dillinger glanced at Flood, then D'Assault. The waiting was over.

"Let's get our game on," Dillinger said. "OOD, let's get eight knots going north-northwest and get a broadband leg."

"Helm, all ahead two-thirds," Flood said.

"Conn, Sonar, Master One is accelerating."

"Sonar, you got a blade count?" D'Assault asked.

"Conn, Sonar, not yet," Keating said.

Dillinger watched the attack center plots, occasionally glancing at the geographic plot and the navigation chart. The *Tucson* was speeding up to the northwest, her towed array straightening. The data from the Alfa, Master One, continued to cascade into the BQQ-5's narrowband and now broadband sonar processors. Dillinger was supremely confident—Master One was theirs.

"Let's go, Andrei. Kick it up to fifteen knots."

"Manual or autopilot, sir?"

"Keep it in manual for now."

"Fifteen knots, sir." Vornado watched as Andrei advanced the throttle slowly forward. The deck didn't vibrate at all. Vornado watched the depth display. The ship was rock solid. He turned aft, stepping the three meters to glance at the reactor display.

"Everything healthy?"

"Perfect, sir," Maslov said. "Passing twenty-percent reactor power, and main seawater injection pumps have switched off automatically, Captain. We're on scoop injection."

Reactor power had barely budged off the idle marking, the indication showing 25 percent power. The main seawater pumps were quiet now, the ship's forward velocity ramming cooling water into the main condensers. With new unfouled condenser tubes, up here in the freezing arctic the ship should be faster than it ever would be. Maybe even faster than the old days. Maybe, Vornado thought, they could do fifty-seven or fifty-eight knots.

"Andrei, give me twenty-five knots."

"Yes, sir, twenty-five knots." He pushed the throttle slowly forward. The deck was still as calm as if they were stopped.

Vornado moved aft again. Reactor power had finally moved, the indication displaying a power level of 40 percent. At this speed, his old *Hampton* had been at 50 percent power, just at the point that the main coolant pumps would need to be upshifted to their noisy fast speed.

"Twenty-five knots, Captain."

"Good," Vornado said. "Thirty knots."

Again Rusanov throttled up, and the ship was rock steady. Vornado ordered forty knots, then forty-five. This was five knots faster than he'd ever sailed submerged.

"Fifty knots."

Rusanov accelerated, and still there was no discernible vibration. Still smooth as silk. At this speed, they'd have left the *Hampton* in the dust, gaining twelve nautical miles on her every hour. The huge thrust bearing was the difference, Vornado thought, a smile coming to his face as he leaned over the ship control console. He turned to look at the reactor plant display. It showed they still had 20 percent to go. It was time to push it and see what the Lira could do.

"Conn, Sonar, Master One is heading out of town fast. I've got fading signal-to-noise on broadband and the two tonals. Recommend increasing speed to full."

"Full?" Dillinger said on the circuit. "Goddammit, Chief, are you out of your mind?"

"Conn, Sonar, signal-to-noise on the tonals and broadband is still diminishing. Conn, Sonar, loss of broadband signal."

"OOD, full speed," Dillinger ordered, hurrying to the sonar room. He ripped open the curtain, his face a mask of fury. "What the fuck is—"

Keating interrupted, staring intensely at Dillinger. "Captain, we've lost Master One."

* * *

"Andrei, coordinate with Maslov and take it slowly up to a hundred percent reactor power. Let's see what she can do."

"Yes, sir." Rusanov enlarged the reactor power readout at his station, then advanced the throttle slowly. As the steam turbines pulled more energy from the core, the rod control system withdrew control rods to increase power level. Vornado wouldn't exceed 100 percent, but he should safely be able to climb all the way to the maximum rated thermal power of the core.

Reactor power climbed into the nineties. At 95 percent power, at fifty-nine knots, the deck gave a slight tremble. Vornado stared at the speed indicator. Either it was out of calibration, or the ship had exceeded his every expectation. As the speed indicator settled at sixty-one knots, the deck's trembling intensified. Sixty-one knots and the vibration continued, but not bad enough to spill a half-full cup of coffee. This ship was a miracle, he thought.

At this speed, just a small problem with the control surface hydraulics or a momentary inattention from Rusanov could kill them all. It wasn't worth the risk to keep this up. He'd save this incredible speed for the day the ship was chased by a torpedo, but running from an enemy submarine wasn't its destiny. The only matter at hand was figuring out how to contain Abdas and his Ahel al Beit terrorists.

"That's enough, Andrei. Engine stop. Let her coast down."

"Engine stop, sir." Andrei pulled the throttle back to the stop. The throttle's track had a stop and a side track. For him to reverse the main engine, he needed to push the throttle to the side from the stop point, then pull it aft. But reversing the shaft at this speed could stress it enough to crack it in an instant, and if the shaft parted, the ship would flood through the hole where the shaft had penetrated the pressure hull.

As Vornado watched, the ship coasted slowly to sixteen knots.

"Main seawater pumps started automatically, Captain," Maslov reported.

"Andrei, half speed ahead, turns for fifteen knots."

"Fifteen knots, sir."

"Ivan, towed array still with us after all that?"

Svetlana turned from her sonar console and nodded. Satisfied, Vornado moved back to the navigation display, where Viktor Danalov stood, checking out the system. Vornado looked into his eyes for a second, then down at the chart.

Abdas al-Sattar joined them at the navigation display.

"Captain Vornado? Is now a better time?"

"Certainly, Holy One," Vornado said. "What is it?"

Abdas glared at Danalov. "If we could speak in private."

"My stateroom?"

"No, here at the map."

"In a submarine it is called a chart."

Abdas glared coldly at Vornado. The Holy One didn't take kindly to being made to wait, nor to being corrected, but that was his problem, Vornado thought. He felt the comforting weight of the Smith & Wesson .45 at his hip, the Walther P99 in its concealed shoulder holster, and the ankle-holstered Walther PPK. One way or another, he would make sure he returned to Rachel and the children, he thought.

"Viktor, if you could excuse us. Why don't you relieve Ivan at sonar?" It wouldn't do to have Svetlana visit his stateroom, not with the Egyptians thinking she was Ivan Mironov. He needed to make sure she didn't return to his room except to take her things. She'd be bunking in with the Maslovs, he decided. "Don't you have some unpacking to do in your stateroom? Stateroom five, right?"

She nodded and stood to give the seat to Danalov, then disappeared down the forward accessway. Abdas never looked up from the chart.

"Where is the closest point we can shoot at Tel Aviv?" Abdas asked.

Vornado stroked the keyboard embedded in the aft part of the navigation table, the scale of the chart changing until it seemed that they looked down upon the earth from high above Europe. He selected Tel Aviv as screen center, then ordered a three-thousand-kilometer circle drawn around the city.

"Granat missiles have a three-thousand-kilometer range," Vornado said quietly, one eye on Maslov and Rusanov, the other on Abdas. "As you can see, we're here, outside the circle. The only way to get inside the range circle is to transit through the Strait of Gibraltar, here. Even then, we don't intercept the edge of the circle until we're north of Algiers."

Abdas seemed satisfied. "How long to get there?"

"I've ordered a fifteen-knot transit." Vornado touched the display and a calculator appeared. By touching the screen he could make calculations and unit conversions. Handy little feature, he thought, wishing it had been aboard his previous submarines, but then there was a hell of a lot he'd like to borrow from the Lira to bring home. If he had the presence of mind when the time came to take the notebook computer with him, it would have every detail of the Lira's construction and characteristics, for detailed analysis by the Navy. Hell with that, he thought. If it went according to plan, he'd bring them the entire ship. "That gets us to Algiers about ten days and two hours from now."

"You could go twice as fast, easily. Four times the speed, from what I just saw."

Vornado was about to argue with the Egyptian when Abdas raised his palm. "Wait, before you say anything. I want you to turn back."

"What? Why? I thought you wanted to get on with your program." Vornado was going to say "mission" but it seemed a misuse of the word. A mission was what the good guys went on. This was an errand of evil.

"For this, I will need to speak to you in your stateroom. But before you go, turn the ship back east, but proceed slowly."

Vornado shrugged. "Andrei, slow to ten knots and return to course east."

Rusanov acknowledged and brought the ship around. Vornado turned to Abdas. "Give me five minutes. It is disgracefully untidy. I want to be able to receive you."

"Very well."

Vornado hurried to the ladder, hoping Svetlana had known enough to evacuate. But when he arrived, everything was in its place, and her baggage was gone. He opened the door to his private bathroom and saw that the hair on the floor had been cleaned up, and none of her toiletries was visible. For a moment he felt a tinge of sadness. For the hour they'd had together here, she'd made this place part of her. God, he thought, how would he be able to go back to his old self?

And the real question was, would Rachel know?

"Dammit," Dillinger cursed. He glared at D'Assault. "You were right, XO. We should have torpedoed him when we had the chance."

"It's okay, Skipper," she said, her eyes on the sonar repeater, as if by staring hard at it she could bring the Alfa back. "How were you supposed to know the fucking thing would take off like a bolt of lightning?"

The Alfa had disappeared without a trace. The tonals they'd detected, the 246-hertz spike and the 308-hertz double bell tone, were detectable only when they were in close. They'd never even gotten a low frequency analysis of the screw to figure out how many blades the damned thing had.

There would be hell to pay now, Dillinger thought morosely. With the loss of the Alfa during a mission so serious they were ordered to torpedo it, he would probably be investigated and lose his command. If he were dismissed from submarine command, he wondered, how much would D'Assault love him then? That was a vicious thought, and he berated himself for it. She didn't deserve that. He looked over at her. She returned his glance, and there was only compassion and shared misery on her face. Seeing that made something move inside him. His mood rose from dark despair to a shallower, lighter depth. They'd fight this; they'd find the Alfa.

"Captain," D'Assault said quietly. "We could extrapolate his position from his previous course and put out a SUB-ROC. If we're close, we could kill him, even though we don't have sonar contact on him."

Dillinger shut his eyes for just a second. It was tempting, extremely tempting. But he'd never be able to confirm a kill, and they'd never gotten a good enough read on the Alfa's course to be able to get the SUBROC warhead within twenty miles. To come even that close meant they had to assume a speed. What should they put in for velocity—forty knots? Fifty? Sixty? The Alfa might be cruising at forty-five knots, or it could be hauling ass at fifty-eight.

There was too much doubt. At the end of this mission, Dillinger would have to face Smokin' Joe Kraft and account for his actions. Impulsively launching a nuke at the dust of a retreating contact was no way to ensure the best kill.

"No," he finally said. "Much as I'd like to deploy a couple of hydrogen bombs right now, we just won't be able to make sure we've hit him."

"We could go active," Flood said. "Ping out an active pulse and see what we come up with."

Dillinger waved him off. "It's been seven minutes since we lost him. At his speed, he could be fourteen thousand yards downrange."

"That's within active range, sir," D'Assault said.

Pinging active sonar would give away their position, and Dillinger wasn't willing to do that. The battle wasn't lost, he decided. He had ordered full speed to the north-northwest to try to reacquire signal on the Alfa, but as he leaned over the chart table he decided to change that. He'd maneuver the *Tucson* to make a high-speed run along the coastline on the shipping route to the North Atlantic, where the Alfa was obviously headed.

That was the first thing he could do. The second would be even more effective. His submarine could go thirty-nine knots. But one of his torpedoes could go fifty-five.

"Weapons Officer," he said to Lieutenant Commander Lionel Tonelle. "Can you program a torpedo and link it into the Q-5 active sonar like we did on the *Albany*?"

Tonelle looked at him seriously. "I can, sir, but it'll take time. Twenty minutes."

Dillinger should have had the tactic preloaded. He invented a new submerged attack in an exercise and had neglected to use it in this odd one-shot war. This time, if they got a sniff with the remote torpedo, he'd vector it in to attack the Alfa first, and second, he would employ a second lesson from Exercise Stolen Arrows—he'd program a SUBROC and hurl it over the horizon at the detect position. He, and all of them, had been guilty of underestimating the Alfa. They wouldn't commit that crime a second time.

"Wire it up, Weps," he ordered. "Mr. Schluss, take over the weapon control panel, and Mr. Vauxhall, take over for Mr. Schluss."

D'Assault raised an eyebrow. While they waited, he might as well tell her about the tactic.

Inside the captain's stateroom, Abdas waited for him. As usual, the terrorist was taking advantage, sitting in Vornado's high-backed command chair. Vornado told himself he should just let it go, but realized it would be the wrong thing. It seemed like every shared moment with Abdas turned into a confrontation, a goddamned pissing contest.

"Get out of my damned chair," Vornado growled. Abdas smiled, as if to say Vornado was being unreasonable, but he rose and sat in one of the other chairs.

"So," Vornado said, sinking into his command chair. It felt better than the chair he'd had on the *Hampton*. "Why am I going east instead of west, and what is it that's so secret you have to take me aside?"

"The freighter ship."

"The *Kirovsky*?"

"Yes. You have torpedoes on board?"

Vornado nodded, his eyes narrowed at the Egyptian.

"Good. I want you to sink it."

Vornado let a moment pass, but apparently Abdas had no intention of telling him any more. Abdas half rose from his seat as if getting ready to go.

"Wait, for God's sake." Abdas froze. "Why am I sinking the freighter?"

"For security reasons," Abdas said, as if that explained it all. "If anyone on the freighter tells the tale, we will be stopped before we can complete our holy task."

Something began to come clear to Vornado. "There was an explosion from the direction of Murmansk. Did you blow up the Terminal?"

Abdas merely looked at him without blinking. Vornado looked away, wanting to strangle the skinny bastard. He rose suddenly and left his stateroom, slamming the door of the stateroom hard, an unquenchable anger rising up in him. He crashed into the command post, his face a mask of fury.

"Yes, Captain?" Rusanov said.

Vornado said nothing, but energized the firecontrol subpanel, the displays coming to life in the forward starboard corner of the room. Within the hour, he thought, he'd know if the torpedoes worked. He couldn't believe he was about to do this, but he steeled himself. *Get used to it,* he thought. As the displays came to life, he wondered how many crimes had been committed in the name of keeping a cover story intact.

28

Vornado tried to compartmentalize his distaste for what he was about to do, but it wasn't easy. It wasn't like the *Kirovsky* were a warship dedicated to fighting in combat. It was just a helpless freighter, with a crew of twenty souls who were about to be floating in freezing water in the middle of the night. There wasn't even the possibility of asking al-Sattar if they could stop and pick up survivors—the whole reason they were torpedoing the freighter was to destroy all evidence of the Lira's existence, and a large part of that evidence was the crew.

The Ahel al Beit terrorists would surely treat their crew onboard the Lira the same way, Vornado thought. He wondered if they suspected that the Lira crew knew it, or if they cared. It did make plausible grounds for Danalov's coming mutiny. Vornado wondered if it might be a good idea to hurry up that maneuver, and take over the ship now, but Abdas's violent brother Arsalaan was wandering the first three compartments, his MAC-10 at the ready. If they enacted a mutiny, they would have to start it when Arsalaan and Abdas were asleep, or at least Arsalaan. Once Danalov got the guns out of Vornado's stateroom and distributed them, this nightmare would be close to ending.

The entire crew had reported to the room. Rusanov took the ship control station. Dmitri Maslov took his control seat at the propulsion plant controls. Mikhail Maslov stood at the navigation plot, where Abdas al-Sattar was loitering. Svetlana had taken the sonar console, and Danalov sat at the firecontrol console, which was perfect, because Danalov was the one Vornado knew had been sent by Hank Lewis. There would be no hesitation from Viktor Danalov when it came time to shoot the freighter.

"Attention, crew," Vornado said. "We've been ordered by our client to do something very painful, but we're going to do it nonetheless. In a few minutes, when we intercept the freighter *Kirovsky,* we will be torpedoing it. This is an attempt to ensure that the departure of the Lira is not spoken of by anyone. If there is anyone here who has a problem with this, speak up now."

"Conn, Sonar," Keating announced. "Reacquisition of Master One!"

"Sonar, Captain, report," Dillinger said. Lionel Tonelle was still trying to wire up the Mark 48 to the active sonar suite, and it seemed to be taking forever.

"I have Master One on narrowband, and his signal-to-noise ratio is getting stronger. I believe the Alfa's approaching us. It's possible he turned around."

Dillinger scanned the sonar repeater. The bearing to the Alfa was west-northwest.

"Coordinator," Dillinger said. "Get a leg and see if Keating's theory checks out. And reset pos one to snapshot mode."

A snapshot was a tactic stolen by the Americans from the Russians. With Russian acoustic inferiority, the Soviets had pioneered ways to launch torpedoes on the first sniff of a hostile submarine. If a captain were unable to launch a torpedo within sixty seconds of the detection of an enemy, no matter what time of day or night, he would be fired, and the second-in-command would find himself promoted on the spot. The BSY-1 attack console's snapshot mode was a comic-book overhead view of two rowboats. The one at the top was the target, the one at the bottom own-ship. The line connecting them was the line of sight, and the angles of own-ship and target to the line of sight were determined by the sonar data and guesswork, but even a rough guess of the target's motion might be good enough to kill him, and if it didn't, it sure as hell would be good enough to scare him away so a more measured ambush could be conducted.

After one tense minute, Dillinger turned and drove the ship south. The dots on the firecontrol position two console began to stack vertically. D'Assault stared at him.

"He's on the way back. How do you account for that?"

"Maybe he's going home. A short maiden voyage. Or maybe a vital piece of equipment has burned up." He smiled at her. "Maybe they forgot their keys."

"In any case, sir, we have a firing solution. Recommend firing point procedures, tube two."

"Very well. Sonar, Captain, bearing to Master One?"

"Captain, Sonar, bearing two eight five, assuming beam ambiguity resolved in favor of the northwest."

"Very well. Coordinator, snapshot tube one!"

"Snapshot, tube one, aye, sir," D'Assault said. She leaned over pos one, where Lieutenant Patrick Schluss dialed in the line-of-sight bearing to be 285 degrees true. Own-ship was automatically shown going on course 290. That left the target ship's range to be dialed in.

"Pos One, dial in a range of twenty thousand yards, course one one zero," D'Assault ordered. "We can correct if Master One's closer. The course should correlate to him returning toward Murmansk."

"Aye, Coordinator," Schluss said, making the panel read what D'Assault wanted to see. "Set."

"Stand by," Tonelle said.

"Shoot!" Dillinger commanded.

"Fire!" Tonelle snapped.

The torpedo tube firing mechanism exploded in the room, slamming Dillinger's ears hard.

"Unit one launched electrically," Tonelle said.

"Conn, Sonar, own-ship's unit, normal launch."

"Captain," D'Assault said. "Request you and the OOD on the conn."

"What is it, Coordinator?" Dillinger whispered.

"Sir, we could launch the SUBROC now. Our solution isn't great on the Mark 48, but we have him close enough to nuke."

"No," Dillinger said. "If we have a reasonable chance of killing the Alfa with a Mark 48, we will do that. But mark my words, if he runs again for any reason, I'm going to hammer him with a SUBROC. For now, he's coming back east. We've got a torpedo going right down his throat. Let's take advantage of the situation and kick his ass."

The Maslovs took the news that they would sink the *Kirovsky* the hardest. Mikhail, the younger one, stared at

Vornado with his mouth open. "Sir," he stammered, "we'll be picking up survivors?"

"No," Vornado said through clenched teeth. "I won't lie to any of you. The purpose of shooting the freighter is to kill the crew. It is regrettable, but necessary. This submarine is too secret to allow a crewman of the *Kirovsky* to talk about it at a waterfront bar."

Maslov stood there, his mouth opening and shutting like that of a beached fish.

"Oh, for God's sake, Mikhail, go below if you can't take this," his older brother, Dmitri, barked. Mikhail Maslov wandered forward and disappeared down the accessway.

"I apologize for my younger brother," Dmitri said. "He is still very young, in many ways."

Vornado turned without acknowledging. He didn't blame the younger Maslov, but he couldn't have the rest of the crew imagine that he forgave what amounted to a disobeyed order. The thing about it was, Mikhail Maslov was the only virtuous one of them aboard. With an effort of will, Vornado forced himself to focus on the task at hand, horrible as it was.

Dillinger leaned over the plot table. They'd turned and moved off to the north, quickly but quietly. They still had sonar contact with the Alfa, but still only on narrowband, which was frustrating.

"Conn, Sonar, Master One has transitioned off the athwartships beam. He's in the second aft cone."

"Sonar, Conn, aye," Flood acknowledged.

"What do you think, Coordinator?" Dillinger asked D'Assault.

"It correlates, Captain. We're heading north, so I'd expect Master One to come out of the west beam and transition to the southwest beam."

"Only if he's closer than we have on the pos two solution," Dillinger said. "Dial in something closer on pos two and see how it stacks."

"Pos Two," D'Assault ordered Mercury-Pryce, "dial in a closer range."

Merc's plot was a vertical haze of dots, each one a fixed-interval data unit, or an average of thirty seconds of sonar bearings. With broadband, Merc would have had a clean,

ruler-straight course of FIDUs, but with narrowband the
data packets were all over the damned screen. If Merc's
assumptions of the target's course, speed, and range correlated to reality, the FIDU dots would stack vertically, showing that the predicted bearing to Master One matched the
data. Mercury-Pryce reached for the range dial and rotated
it from twenty thousand yards to ten thousand. The vertical
blur of FIDUs blurred over to the side. It didn't correlate.

"Try a slower speed," D'Assault said.

Mercury-Pryce dialed the Alfa's speed from thirty-five
knots to twenty. The dot stack came back toward the centerline. At a speed of twelve knots the dot stack was
again vertical.

"We need to maneuver, Captain," D'Assault said.
"Without another leg for this solution, the Alfa could be
anywhere." Unless the ship turned and did target motion
analysis to get rid of this solution ambiguity, too many
guesses about the Alfa's speed and distance worked. If the
ship were driven south, only one speed and distance would
make the dots stack.

Steve Flood came down next to D'Assault. "If we turn
to get another leg on Master One, Skipper, we could lose
him. If he's transitioning into the narrower beams, he's getting closer. If we wait, he could go by the end beam, and
that will take the ambiguity out of the solution. At that
point we could turn east to keep up with him, and that
would give us a rough leg. Good enough to shoot on without the possibility of losing contact on him."

Dillinger considered, remembering the despair of losing
contact with the Alfa.

"Coordinator, we'll suffer having a degraded solution for
now. I want us to maintain contact on the Alfa. We turn
the towed array a hundred and eighty degrees, it'll take ten
minutes to stabilize."

"Agreed, sir, but I highly recommend a slow, large-radius
turn to the northwest. We'd stay out of the Mark 48 search
cone but close the distance to the Alfa. Chances are, his
signal-to-noise ratio will grow stronger. We may get broadband back on him if we close the distance. Once we get
him broadband, there's no escape for him."

Dillinger liked the sound of that. "Attention in the firecontrol party, we are maneuvering to the northwest to close

range on the Alfa and improve narrowband signal-to-noise ratio. Carry on. OOD, take us to the northwest. Increase speed to standard until we steady on the new course, then drop back to ten knots."

As the ship turned, Dillinger found himself in prayer. *Please don't let us lose the Alfa.* He got an immediate answer.

"Conn, Sonar, we have the Alfa on broadband, bearing two zero five."

Dillinger could have hugged Senior Chief Keating, until the sonar chief's second announcement came.

"Conn, Sonar, own-ship's unit has shut down."

The torpedo they'd launched to chase Master One had eventually run out of fuel.

Goddamned Mark 48s, Dillinger thought. Its search cone was too damned narrow. If the target weren't within a six-degree cone, it would miss. It was like sending a search team into the forest with a narrow-beam flashlight and ordering them only to search straight ahead. Unless the target's position were known, a torpedo launched on a guess would miss.

The question now was, had the Alfa been alerted to the torpedo? Had he heard it launched, or did he hear its motion as it blindly stumbled through the ocean clumsily looking for him?

It was too late to worry about it, Dillinger thought. The fortune of war had made its ruling, that the torpedo fired in the dark was a miss, but now they had something more valuable than gold—Master One, back on broadband sonar.

"Weapons Officer, cut the wire to tube one, shut the outer door, and reload tube one. Make tube two ready in all respects.

"Attention in the firecontrol party, my intention is to do a three-minute TMA leg on Master One held in broadband, then shoot tubes two and three. Carry on. OOD, turn left and take us across the line of sight to course one five zero. Hustle through the maneuver."

"Aye, sir. Sonar, Conn, turning to the left. Helm, all ahead standard, left ten degrees rudder, steady course one five zero."

It was tense while the ship turned. Dillinger wondered, would the gods punish him for not shooting a snapshot before the turn? He was one to learn from experience, and up here, in this battle, experience seemed to be telling him that shooting torpedoes without a solution to the target was like trying to net a fish with only a rough idea of where the fish was. And if he shot a torpedo down the Alfa's bearing line, the slippery bastard would take off again in one of his unbelievably fast sprints and fade from the sonar screens, and in all probability would never be seen again. There would be no more wasted shots, Dillinger decided. This time they would sneak up on the bastard, get in close, find out exactly where he was and where he was going, and put a torpedo right through the center of his heart.

29

The navigation chart showed them nearing the point where they'd submerged. If the *Kirovsky* had turned back to the east-southeast and sped up to twelve knots, its cruising speed, they would intercept it in another ten minutes. He looked at Viktor Danalov on the firecontrol console.

Danalov looked pale in the dim lights of the room. Vornado assumed he was as sick about the task ahead of them as Vornado was.

"Mr. Danalov, please power up the UGST torpedo in tube six." Back on the *Hampton,* he would have been able to command the weapon made ready in all respects and the weapons officer would take care of everything, but here, he was the only one who knew what he was doing. There was good news in that, he thought, because when Danalov executed his mutiny and put Vornado at gunpoint, Abdas would believe that his mission was over.

"I need help, Captain."

Vornado stood behind him and prepared to walk him through the gyro power-up and the testing of the connecton between the tube and the torpedo through the long coiled guidance wire. But apparently Danalov just wanted to talk to Vornado up close.

"What are you doing?" Danalov said, without moving his lips, while manipulating the panel.

"I'm shooting the freighter," Vornado said. "What are my choices?"

"Start the mutiny now."

"We can't," Vornado hissed. "The clients are full of adrenaline. I've never seen people so alert. They'd be instantly suspicious of your going below now. Now shut up; we're being watched."

"You're making a big mistake. You could use your personal weapons."

"Arsalaan has a MAC-10 automatic," Vornado whispered back. "I saw it. He pulls that out, my popguns would be overcome instantly."

"I say face the devil now."

Vornado ignored him and concentrated on the panel. He had spent the long hours waiting for the Lira's construction completion studying the UGST and its interface panel. When the torpedoes were loaded, he and Andrei Rusanov had connected each weapon with the black rubber connection plug to the torpedo tube power and signal source, then tested each unit. Against the objections of the clients, torpedo tubes one through four and six were loaded with UGSTs. Tube five was loaded with one of the four Granat RK-55 nuclear-tipped cruise missiles. The other three missiles were rack-stowed in the torpedo room to await their time, which Vornado knew would never come, not if he had anything to do with it. He'd carry out this attack against the freighter, despite Danalov's objections, but he'd die—in excruciating pain if he had to—before he would launch a nuke at a civilian city. At the moment he was the only one who knew how to launch it. Rusanov and the Maslovs could figure it out given time, which was another reason they had to get this mutiny done as soon as possible after they departed the area once the freighter was down.

The torpedo was powered up and the self-checks were satisfactory. Vornado glanced at the chart. It was time to slow down.

"Mr. Rusanov, half speed ahead, turns for twelve knots."

"Twelve knots, sir."

The ship slowed. From the aft corner of the room Dmitri Maslov spoke up. "Main seawater pumps energized in automatic, sir." The scoop injection no longer had enough forward velocity to ram cooling water through the main condensers, so the pumps came on.

"Very good, Mr. Maslov. Mr. Mironov, devote particular sonar attention to bearings zero eight zero to one zero zero, where I expect the freighter." Vornado had intentionally begun to use more formality in the command post. Somehow it didn't seem appropriate to give a torpedo launch order by using someone's first name. "Mr. Danalov, flood and vent tube six."

"Tube six is flooded, sir," Danalov said. "Flood valve shut, vent valve shut."

"Open the outer door, tube six."

"Outer door coming open."

"Captain," Svetlana said, "Sonar holds the freighter at bearing zero nine three."

If they could hear it, that was enough to program the UGST torpedo. "Send the bearing to the freighter to UGST in tube six."

"Bearing sent, sir."

"Sir," Danalov said, "outer door to tube six is open and locked."

"Good. Pay attention while I configure the weapon, Mr. Danalov." Vornado selected the torpedo program mode. "Surface ship targeting is here. We'll select that. Wake homing is active; torpedo approach will be in medium speed. We have the choice of an active ping or passive-listen sonar. We'll select passive. Detonation will be by both direct contact and magnetic proximity. Now we'll lock in the settings by selecting this. When I call out a range to the target—the distance from us—you'll enter it here. I'll give you an 'enable' range, which is the distance the weapon will travel before arming. You'll click that in here. Got it? Think you can do it again if you need to?"

Danalov nodded.

"Mr. Rusanov, line up the forward ballast transfer pump to the starboard bank torpedo tube flush tank and start the pump."

Andrei acknowledged, pressurizing the flush tank from the Russian equivalent to the trim pump. On the *Hampton*, high-pressure air would pressurize a ram piston that would pressurize the water-round-torpedo tanks to eject a torpedo, but the Russians had eliminated the machinery and fuss of the ram system by simply using a trim pump, though arguably the American system would be more reliable in battle, if heavier and more space-consuming.

"Pump started, sir, and starboard flush tank is fully pressurized."

"Mr. Danalov, select the aft tank flush valve on your panel and place it in 'firecontrol automatic.' "

"Yes, sir, aft flush valve in firecontrol auto."

"Attention, crew, I intend to take the ship to periscope depth to send a final bearing to the firecontrol system, and to witness the freighter sinking." Vornado looked aft at Abdas. "It is important that the client see that we have fulfilled his orders, so he will also observe the freighter going down." Abdas gave no indication that he had been mentioned or addressed. "Mr. Danalov, kill the command post overhead lights." The room became dim, lit only by the displays of the screens. It was better with no glare on the displays. Perhaps Vornado would keep it this way after the attack. "Mr. Rusanov, engine stop, report speed six knots. Rise to depth three zero meters."

"Engine stop, three zero meters. Speed eleven knots, Captain."

"Very good." Vornado waited as the ship coasted down. The deck inclined upward as the ship ascended.

"Speed six knots, sir."

"Very good. Dead slow ahead, turns for four knots. Rise to keel depth twenty meters."

"Dead slow ahead at four knots and rising to twenty meters."

Vornado entered the periscope railing and reached into the overhead. Rather than the control ring of American submarines, there was a simple hydraulic control lever. Vornado rotated it upward, and the periscope began to slide upward out of the well. The optics and capabilities were nothing as advanced as the Type eighteen or twenty-two, but they would suffice. The eyepiece module came out of the well, rising to chest level. Vornado snapped down the periscope grips and put his face to the cold rubber eyepiece.

"Conn, Sonar, we've got transients from Master One," Keating announced.

"Sonar, Captain, describe the transients."

"Conn, a groaning sound. Could be raising a mast or periscope."

Dillinger looked at D'Assault. She glanced at the pos two display, then back to Dillinger. "He's going to PD, Captain. Wait a minute." She leaned over the pos one display and whispered into Schluss's ear, who played with the dot stack. "Sir, can you give me a leg to the northwest again? I've got a theory."

Dillinger nodded. He ordered Flood to take the ship back to the northwest. It took two minutes for the ship to steady on the new course and another two minutes for D'Assault and Schluss to gather and sort their data. The entire time Dillinger kept his eyes on the bright trace to the south, Master One.

"Coordinator, report," Dillinger said, impatient to shoot the damned Alfa.

"Our theory is on the geo display," D'Assault said triumphantly. "Look, Captain, the Alfa's returning to Sierra Eight, the Buff freighter. Remember we were trying to figure out why the Buff was at all-stop for over an hour? And now he's barely going five knots? The Buff must be in distress, and the Alfa's coming back to render assistance."

Dillinger checked out the God's-eye view. The computer showed the Alfa returning from the west-northwest to return to Sierra Eight. His course would lead him right to the Buff. The trouble was, that presented certain ethical and operational problems. Dillinger looked at Flood, who had grasped the situation as well.

"Captain, now we're back where we started," Flood said. "If we shoot him within view of the Buff, we're in violation of our op order. And if the Alfa's at periscope depth or surfaced, we can't put in a ceiling setting. That means a Mark 48 could miss and take down the goddamned freighter. Now you've got a civilian ship sinking and a very annoyed, fully armed Alfa submarine, who knows where the torpedoes came from."

"Captain." D'Assault's tone was almost desperate. "We let the proximity to the freighter stop us last time. My strongest recommendation is we disregard this part of the op order. It is better to risk having the freighter witness the explosion that takes down the Alfa than for us to lose him, probably for good this time. If the freighter sees the Alfa die, so what? They'll assume it's another *Kursk* or another *Scorpion,* one more victim of its own weapons exploding inside the hull."

"If we shoot him here, he could be salvaged," Flood said. "The Russians would figure out we killed him."

"Not if we put five shots into him," Dillinger said. "There won't be anything left after his own weapons go off. But that's not our concern anyway, OOD. Our orders are to shoot the Alfa, because for some reason either we're sending a message to the Russians, or. this guy's an out-of-control rogue and needs to be taken down. The way I read the tea leaves, it's imperative that we kill him, and doing it in private would be nice but not required. Let the freighter see him go down."

"How do we keep from hitting the freighter?"

"We'll watch the bearing we input into firecontrol, and if the torpedoes misbehave, we'll steer them or shut them down," Dillinger said.

"And if we lose the wire like we did unit one?" Flood's wide eyes could be seen behind his red lenses.

Dillinger frowned. "Then it'll be a fucking bad day for the freighter." He could be court-martialed for saying that, but he no longer cared. He turned back to the attack center. "Attention in the firecontrol party, my intention is to target the Alfa as soon as we have a firing solution."

The ship took three minutes to speed through a final turn to the southwest and steady on course to collect sixty seconds' worth of broadband data. With two legs on the target after he went to periscope depth, they had him at range seven thousand yards, bearing 198, on course east at five knots. A junior officer at submarine officers' basic course could take him down with this data.

"Captain," D'Assault said, "we have a firing solution. Recommend shooting tube two."

There was no sound, unlike the slamming, booming roar of the American high-pressure air-induced torpedo launch. All that had happened was that a ball valve in a piping system at the aft end of the tube opened, admitting high-pressure water from the flush tank, which was pressurized from the ballast transfer pump to the rear of the torpedo, ejecting it out of the tube. The torpedo software would start the torpedo's turbine engine, and the torpedo would suck water in its ducts and pump it out the aft nozzle. On the firecontrol panel, the green light extinguished and several other displays flashed up. One of them indicated the torpedo had been launched.

"Torpedo indicates launched, Captain."

* * *

"Firing point procedures," Dillinger said, an electricity shaking every nerve in his body. In overtime, he was in sight of the goal line and about to toss the game-winning touchdown. "Tube two, Master One."

"Ship ready," Flood called.

"Weapon ready," Tonelle said.

"Solution ready," D'Assault snapped.

"Set," Mercury-Pryce said, locking his solution into the weapon control panel.

"Stand by," Tonelle said.

"Conn, Sonar," Keating interrupted. "Torpedo in the water!" The Alfa had fired a torpedo at them.

Dillinger ignored him. "Shoot!" he ordered, not caring about anything except getting the shot off. He'd deal with the torpedo from the Alfa in ten seconds, but right now he wanted the bastard dead.

"Fire!" Lionel said as he hit the function key. The resounding boom slammed Dillinger's eardrums, the sound once again deeply satisfying.

"Torpedo in the water bears one nine five!" Keating announced.

"Firing point procedures, tube three, Master One," Dillinger said, standing his ground in the face of an incoming torpedo from the south. *Damn the torpedo,* he thought.

"Set!"

"Stand by."

"Shoot!"

"Fire!"

Another loud boom sounded throughout the ship as the torpedo was launched.

"Tube three fired electrically," Tonelle reported.

"Helm, all ahead full, right full rudder, steady course north! Sonar, Captain, clearing datum to the north."

"Captain has the conn," Flood announced. The moment Dillinger gave an order to the helmsman, he had taken over from Flood.

"Conn, Sonar, own-ship's unit, normal launch. Also, Captain, you've put the torpedo in the baffles."

"Helm, steady course three four five." That would keep the Alfa's torpedo where they could hear it.

"Sir, recommend withdrawal at flank," Flood said.

Dillinger shook his head. Doing that would mean upshifting the four reactor recirculation pumps, which would triple their sound signature and invite another torpedo from the loudness of their departure. "Wait to see what the torpedo's doing. Maybe it's a snapshot, as poorly aimed as our earlier ones were."

Dillinger had an odd thought then, that even if the *Tucson* took a hit, the Alfa would be just as dead. Unlike the first units, these two Mark 48s would be dead-on.

"Ivan, take the periscope," Vornado ordered. He didn't want to see the freighter's death. It would be enough to hear the explosion. He turned away as Svetlana took the scope. He leaned over the firecontrol panel, watching the indications coming back from the torpedo. The fins had clicked open. The pump jet propulsor had spun up to full revolutions to get the weapon out of the tube, then had throttled back down to medium approach speed. The torpedo rose to a depth of five meters, searching for the disturbance in the water from the freighter's wake. The panel flashed as the torpedo sent back word that it had detected the wake. It kept on its chase, the indications coming more rapidly. Finally the torpedo, in its final phase, sped up to its full speed of forty-eight knots and aimed for the hull of the target.

Suddenly the indications went blank. The torpedo was dead.

"What the hell?" Danalov said. "No data! It malfunctioned!"

"Oh, my God," Svetlana breathed in awe from the periscope.

"No," Vornado said. "The weapon doesn't exist anymore, so it can't send back—"

The sudden explosion boomed through the command post, the ship shuddering violently. The sound roared around Vornado, the noise rising to an eardrum-piercing volume. He clapped his hands on his ears, but had to let go to find a handhold as the deck lurched. On the periscope, Svetlana winced, but he wasn't sure if her cry was from the pain in her ears or from the shock of what she saw. Vornado turned and saw an orange light illuminating the circle around her eye socket from the ball of flames coming from the freighter.

"Conn, Sonar, bearing rate to the torpedo is steady. Believe torpedo is *not* coming our way."

"Helm, all stop!" Dillinger snapped. Running from a torpedo that would miss in any case was suicide, because going full speed was so loud that the Alfa could retarget their torpedo—did their torpedoes even have wire guidance?—or the Alfa could shoot another one, this one better aimed.

At fifteen knots, Dillinger decided to turn to the west. That would bring the sonar sphere to bear on the torpedo rather than risking the torpedo's going into the baffled area where the sphere was deaf.

"Helm, left five degrees rudder, steady course west."

The ship turned, the compass spinning slowly on the ship control console. Dillinger watched the geographic plot, an odd idea coming to him.

"Coordinator, what the hell is he shooting at?"

The explosion hit them then, the force of it rocking the deckplates and reverberating through the hull. Dillinger put his palms to both ears. It was the loudest thing he'd ever heard in his life, and his ears rang in the seconds afterward. Forward, in sonar, Senior Chief Harlan Keating threw his headset to the deck and screamed in pain. The deck trembled and four books fell out of the periscope stand bookshelf. Dillinger grabbed the conn handrail, his knuckles white.

"Sonar, Captain, report status!" What in God's name was going on?

"Let me see," Abdas al-Sattar said, shouldering Svetlana aside and looking through the periscope. He began singing something in a foreign tongue, his robe moving as he danced behind the periscope.

Vornado changed his mind. He had brought death down on the innocents aboard the freighter. It was punishment for him to look, but he deserved it. It would probably be the least that he would suffer over this mission. "Holy One, please allow me to look," he said. Reluctantly Abdas moved aside, and Vornado put his face on the warm, slick

eyepiece. The sky was bright as noon as the freighter's fuel
tanks exploded, the secondary detonation rocking the ship.
Vornado could make out the forward half of the ship settling into the water, the forecastle pointing toward the
heavens as it slid backward. The water was crowded with
flotsam, much of it burning. He thought he could make out
two thrashing arms, and his stomach turned in revulsion.
He pushed the scope away. "Go ahead," he said to Abdas.

For the next two minutes he allowed the terrorist to examine his handiwork. Vornado glanced at his Rolex, the
solid gold of it heavy on his wrist, the azure face and bezel
shining in the light of the glowing display panels. It had
been a half hour since they began the approach on the
freighter. "Holy One, it is time we returned to our western
transit. We need to get out of this area, or we will be
discovered."

Abdas watched for another minute, but finally surren-
dered the periscope to Vornado, who took one last look.
The bow gave up the surface in a burst of foam and disappeared. There was nothing but the flames on the surface,
a few Dumpster loads of garbage, and four men. Vornado
clicked the high-high optic power, and the faces of the men
came into view. Three of them were panic-stricken as the
ice-cold water began to kill them; the fourth man's expression was frozen in horror, the left side of his face on fire.
Vornado shut his eyes, clicked the unit back to low power,
and lowered the periscope.

"Mr. Rusanov, left ten degrees rudder, steady course two
nine zero, descend to depth one hundred meters and accelerate to fifteen knots."

"Captain," Svetlana called in her normal voice. The
sound shocked Vornado, and he shot a warning look at
her, but Abdas al-Sattar had hurried to the forward vertical
accessway, presumably to report the news to his troops.

"What? Be careful, Ivan."

She gave him a naked look of pure fear. From where he
stood, he could see her trembling. "Torpedoes," she said.

Vornado felt the acceleration of time that came with the
sudden dose of adrenaline. He pushed her out of the sonar
console seat and flashed through the display. The annunciator was flashing, the computer detecting an incoming torpedo, then a second. The data was several minutes old, for

God's sake. They had been too busy on the periscope to imagine they were being followed.

Who the hell was shooting at them? Vornado wondered. And why?

Because, he answered himself, whatever submarine was out there, lurking in trail of them, had heard Vornado's torpedo, and assumed it was coming for *them*. This must be some kind of defensive counterfire, Vornado thought. A snapshot, most likely poorly aimed. Two snapshots, he corrected himself.

The bearing of the torpedoes was from the north. That eliminated the possibility of running north, but to try to outrun them by going south would be suicide—he'd run out of ocean before he'd put ten minutes into the run. That left either east or west, and the ship was already speeding up to fifteen knots heading east-northeast. All he could do was accelerate to maximum velocity in the direction he was already going.

"Andrei, engine ahead full! Maximum rate of acceleration!"

Vornado hurried to the ship control console as Rusanov pushed the throttle forward, the deck shaking slightly as the ship went through thirty knots. That resonance hadn't been there before, Vornado thought.

"Hurry, Andrei, get it up to ninety percent." Vornado rushed back to the propulsion control panel. Good Lord, he thought, he was the only one here who knew what he was doing, and with that thought the headache bloomed behind his eyes. "Maslov, I need to overpower the reactor. Is there a single point where you can override all reactor protection circuits and interlocks?"

"No, Captain. I'd have to dig into the software and override the power limit, core reactivity rate limit, and all the temperature limits. There must be forty things the reactor can trip on, sir. I can try to override them all, but if I miss one we'll lose the entire propulsion plant. Maybe, sir, it's safer to just keep going at sixty-one knots."

"It's not enough." If they were being chased by ADCAP Mark 48s, he thought, they'd be barreling in at fifty-eight knots, and his maximum speed only had three knots on them. If he'd been too slow to accelerate, they could be right on his rudder now. "Dammit, Maslov, override them one by one, then, and hurry. And don't fucking miss any of them!''

American ships had a "battleshort" switch that in one motion took out all the safety interlocks, so the reactor wouldn't trip out on them in the middle of a torpedo evasion. Why hadn't he thought of that during the construction? he scolded himself. The answer made him feel foolish—he'd never expected to have to run from a torpedo or fire one himself. The torpedoes he'd insisted on loading, despite his claim that they were to defend the ship, were for a contingency plan that he'd told no one about, and had nothing to do with enemy submarines.

"I think we can safely do a hundred and ten percent, sir," Maslov eventually said.

Vornado had a dark moment then. He'd already made the mistake of assuming that a trailing submarine would just follow them at a safe distance. This one must be trigger-happy, because it had responded to the UGST torpedo with a counterfire. Whoever that captain was, Vornado thought, he was in deep trouble right now. If Vornado had made a mistake like that, Smokin' Joe Kraft would have his dolphins. But the mistake was made on the Western submarine's side, and now there was the second mistake on Vornado's side to match it—his failure to design a single-switch battleshort circuit.

And now he was about to do something that might turn out to be his third mistake—overriding reactor protection circuitry, executed in a piecemeal fashion in the panic of the moment, could lead to them failing to cut out one reactor shutdown. And when Vornado ordered the reactor power above 100 percent, it would shut down. The ship would coast to a halt while two fifty-eight-knot torpedoes came soaring in to get them. After that, there would be no more mistakes. But if he could just evade these two weapons, there would be no more. The Western captain wouldn't make the same mistake twice, and though he'd fired in a moment of fear, he wouldn't shoot any more weapons.

Time to decide, Vornado thought. He returned to the sonar console and tried to divine the distance to the incoming torpedoes, but the system was overwhelmed. Without maneuvering the ship, they only knew the bearings to the two incoming weapons. But on the screen they looked powerfully loud. And with that thought, the decision was made.

"Andrei, indicate one zero nine percent reactor power," Vornado ordered. "What's your speed?"

"Sixty-one knots, sir, maybe a little less."

"Throttle up slowly."

Andrei Rusanov curled his fingers resolutely around the throttle lever and pushed it gently forward. His reactor power indication climbed from 100.0 to 101, 102, then higher. Vornado breathed easier. At 104, the deck began to tremble, and at 105 percent power, the ship began to vibrate violently. *Let it shake,* Vorando thought.

"Sixty two point five knots. On hundred and five percent reactor power."

"Keep going."

Rusanov pushed the throttle forward again, and as he did the lights went out, the consoles all went black, and a loud siren sounded from aft in the room. The deck's vibration had gone suddenly quiet.

"Reactor shutdown!" Maslov shouted in the dark room. "Dammit, Captain, I overrode that trip, but it took us out anyway."

With two fifty-eight-knot torpedoes on the way in, the Lira submarine began to coast down as her steam plant shut down in response to the reactor control rods being driven into the core automatically by the machinery that thought that something was wrong.

Three mistakes, Vornado thought. Those three mistakes would now prove enough to kill him. As he rushed back toward Maslov's station, the thought occurred to him that he would now die in this dark command post in this titanium coffin under three hundred fathoms of frigid arctic seawater, and he wondered, Was this truly better than dying in his hospital bed in his own home, surrounded by his family and friends?

And what would B. K. Dillinger do right now? Vornado thought in despair. *He'd fight,* a voice inside him shouted. *He'd fight to the death with no regrets.*

He missed B. K. Dillinger, Vornado thought, wondering if that would be his last thought on earth.

30

The USS *Tucson* slowed to eight knots, heading west. Behind them, to the southeast, the explosion lit up an entire sector of the broadband sonar screen.

"Conn, Sonar." Keating's voice came over the circuit. For the first time since Dillinger had known him, his voice was tentative. "I can barely believe the data, sir. The Alfa shot at the Buff. It's a direct hit. I have bulkheads rupturing and twisting steel. There was a secondary explosion. Probably fuel tank going off."

D'Assault was the first to speak. "Supervisor to control." When Keating stepped out of sonar, he seemed dazed.

"Senior Chief, are you certain? That just doesn't make any sense. He wasn't shooting at us?"

"No way. The bearings don't work. We're over his left shoulder. I had transients, Captain. I think he went to PD, took a look, and put a torpedo right up the freighter's ass. It was deliberate, sir."

Dillinger stared at Keating. "Senior, are you absolutely sure?"

Keating nodded.

"If I had the leisure time to go to periscope depth, Senior, I would. Let's finish off Master One first."

Keating returned to sonar. Dillinger looked at the weapon control panel.

"Weps, status of our torpedoes?"

"Still on the run to enable," Tonelle said. "Should be enabling at any minute."

D'Assault stepped closer to him. "We should shift the search from passive to active," she said. "All the noise in the water from the freighter blowing up will lower the signal-to-noise ratio from Master One."

"Good idea. Weps, shift from passive search to active, both units."

"Active search, aye, sir. Weapons will go to active search at the enable point. Three, two, one. Unit three enabled, sir. Unit four enabled. Units are indicating active."

"Sonar, Conn," D'Assault said, "do you have pinging from the units?"

"Conn, Sonar, yes."

"Any response from Master One?"

We have you now, you bastard, Dillinger thought. What kind of an asshole would torpedo a defenseless freighter, the very ship that towed him out of the river in the first place? No wonder ComSubLant and the Department of Defense Task Group wanted this guy on the bottom. He was some kind of rogue submarine bent on sinking commercial shipping in international waters. How many innocent sailors had just died? Dillinger wondered.

"Conn, Sonar, Master One is speeding up. He's going supersonic again, Captain."

"Goddammit," Flood cursed. "This guy can outrun a torpedo, Skipper. And who knows, he may be able to dive deep enough to evade a torpedo. Our units go to crush depth pretty shallow compared to what this guy can dive to, and the water is deep out here."

"Weps," Dillinger said, "any sign of a detect?" He began to think about shooting one of the SUBROCs now instead of waiting. If Flood were right, the Alfa might be able to outrun a Mark 48.

"Conn, Sonar, transients from Master One. Conn, Master One is slowing."

As the command post consoles flickered back to life from the forward batteries feeding the four-hundred-cycle inverters, a part of Peter Vornado came back to life as well. There was still something he could do, Vornado thought.

He could use residual steam for propulsion, using the temperature of the hot liquid-metal coolant to boil the steam in the steam generators. It presented a severe risk of lowering coolant temperature so fast that it would shrink as it cooled, perhaps even freezing it, and that could exert so much thermal stress on the reactor vessel that it would shatter, which was the worst nuclear accident they could suffer. After that, the nuclear fuel would melt down inside the reactor compartment and would melt through the hull, and when it hit seawater, the resulting steam explosion would rip through the third compartment aft bulkhead. It would kill them in seconds, roasting them with high-energy radioactive steam.

Of course, that was the worst-case scenario. In the more likely case, Vornado would just use the residual steam he needed and the reactor would be fine. But if he were wrong, the only thing that would change would be the manner in which he died. And right now, if he absolutely had to die, he'd just as soon die fighting.

Fight to the death with no regrets.

"Captain Vornado? Captain Vornado!" It was the voice of Abdas al-Sattar.

"Vornado!" That was the Holy One's evil brother Arsalaan, the one Vornado had almost shot in the command post.

"What's going on?" Abdas asked.

Vornado ignored them. "Andrei, configure to use residual steam, quickly."

"Yes, Captain, I'm ready," Rusanov said, his voice too loud in the quiet space.

"Engine dead slow astern, Andrei."

"Astern, sir?"

Vornado's eyes had grown accustomed to the dim light of the backup powered distributed control system console displays. He could see Andrei putting the throttle lever in the reverse track and pulling it slowly back. The rpm meter showed the screw reversing.

"Ten rpm, sir."

"Give it twenty, then thirty."

Rusanov pulled the throttle further aft. "You know you're risking thermal shocking the primary system?"

"I know it."

The sound of a torpedo sonar howled through the command post, the sound of the Mark 48 seeker sonar loud inside the hull. They were close, Vornado thought. Obviously they'd been configured to switch to an active search when they got a sniff, which meant they had detected the Lira. But an active search was perfect, because they were also designed to reject all sounds that returned the same frequency as they transmitted. It was called a Doppler filter, and it avoided the inconvenience of the torpedo attacking the stationary waves above or the sea floor below, despite the fact that they returned echoes of the torpedo's active sonar. Anything that wasn't moving didn't register. It was like being chased by a wolf that could only see moving prey, Vornado thought. That didn't mean it was preferable to stand still when a Mark 48 was coming in, but if all else failed, being stationary in the sea was better than stupidly coasting down from twenty knots to fifteen when the torpedoes went active.

"Forty rpm, Andrei. What's your speed?"

"Eight knots ahead. Making forty rpm astern, sir."

"Reactor coolant temperature is crashing," Maslov shouted from aft. A whining shriek came from the other side of the fourth compartment bulkhead as the thick metal of the reactor protested. The metal wouldn't appreciate going from 2,500 degrees to 800 inside of sixty seconds as the steam turbines robbed the coolant of its thermal energy. Any more and the liquid metal would freeze, and the reactor would never start again in the best case, and would experience a "thermal implosion rapid disassembly" in the worst case, a variety of nuclear accident that could befall only a liquid-metal-cooled reactor.

"Engine stop, Andrei!"

Rusanov pushed the throttle to the detent stop. "Engine stopped, Captain."

"What's your speed?"

"One knot. No, less. Point six knots and slowing."

Vornado took a deep breath. The torpedo sonars were getting closer. They were the only sound in the room until Abdas spoke up again.

"Captain Vornado! I must insist you tell me what you're doing," Abdas asked. "What did you do to the lights?"

There was nothing to do but wait for the incoming torpedoes, Vornado thought. In the time he had to wait for them, he might turn this situation to his advantage. He might be able to fight the ship and take care of Abdas at the same time. But first things first. He turned to Maslov.

"Dmitri, can you recover the reactor?"

"I don't know, Captain. Main coolant temperature is less

than eight hundred Celsius. The reactor vessel survived the
shock of being cooled down that fast, but it may be so
weak now that it may not handle being warmed up."

It only needed to work once, Vornado thought. "We'll
take that risk. Warm up and restart the reactor, Mr.
Maslov."

He could see Svetlana's eyes shining at him in the dimness of the space. Seeing her reminded him of being with
her in his stateroom, and that made him think of the weapons there. He pulled Danalov close to him and whispered
in his ear.

"Left eighty, right nineteen, left fifty-eight. Got it?"

Danalov was sharp, Vornado thought. Without even a
nod of his head he left for Vornado's stateroom, where the
weapons were waiting in the captain's safe.

The active sonar bleeping sounds continued to grow
closer. They'd been coming for several minutes since the
reactor shut down. The sounds grew louder, if that were
possible, but the sound power required to detect a submarine tens of miles away was immense, and up close it could
deafen a swimmer. Vornado was tempted to put his fingers
in his ears, but instead he pulled Abdas al-Sattar close.

"You hear those sounds? Those are incoming torpedoes.
We're under attack, Holy One. There was a lurking submarine waiting for us here. Waiting for you. Attempting to
kill you."

Abdas was silent for a long moment. The incoming AD-
CAPs were shrieking now, the sonars so loud it was hurting
Vornado's already sore eardrums. Vornado spoke again be-
fore Abdas could say anything.

"The escape vehicle, Holy One. If you and your entou-
rage get into the vehicle, you can separate from the ship.
You'll float to the surface. You'll escape the wrath of the
enemy submarine. We will fight on down below. If we survive, we will pick you up. If we don't, you will live on. I
assume you have satellite phones and radios? You could
summon help for yourselves?"

Abdas's face was shrouded in shadows, but Vornado
thought he saw his expression change from fear to a cunning smile, then to an expression of loss.

"What about the cruise missiles?"

The Mark 48s were close now, perhaps only a shiplength away. Vornado didn't want to have to shout over Abdas, and he wasn't truly sure his tactic would work. In training, doing this only fooled the torpedoes one time in three. He wondered if his outer steel hull and inner titanium hull could really take a direct hit from a torpedo and survive, as the design criteria of the 1950s claimed. They had only contemplated the torpedoes of fifty years ago, which were nothing like the ADCAPs screaming in now.

He held up his finger to Abdas and left him to sit at the sonar console. The sonar display was completely deafened by the incoming weapons, but at least if the 48s hit them, Vornado could die here and have this be his last stand rather than have Abdas's face be the last thing he saw. As he watched, the display changed, and the shriek of the Mark 48s suddenly became a lower-pitched hum.

They had gone by without impacting! The tactic had worked, at least for now.

"Wait a minute," D'Assault said. "Senior Chief, he's *slowing*?"

"Conn, Sonar, yes. He's putting out a lot of broadband. I think he's using his astern turbine. It's incredibly loud. He's slowing even more."

"Oh, shit," Flood said.

"What?" Dillinger asked.

"Captain, he must know about our Doppler filters. On an active search, the torpedoes are filtering out noise from echo returns from stationary objects. If Master One stops and hovers, he'll be invisible to the torpedoes."

"What if we shift them back to passive?"

Tonelle turned and shook his head. "Still too much noise from the freighter breaking up, sir."

"Any detection from the torpedoes?"

"Nothing, sir."

"Conn, Sonar, Master One has shut down. Loss of broadband and narrowband on Master One. He may have stopped, hovered, and scrammed his reactor, sir. I've got nothing at all from his bearing."

Whoever the captain of the Alfa was, he was crafty. And he'd been schooled well in American tactics. Now there was only one thing to do, Dillinger thought. This time there wouldn't be an encounter session with Flood and D'Assault. This time he would dictate the outcome.

Vornado heard Rusanov and Maslov cheering just as Danalov came back into the dark room, his pockets bulging. Vornado caught his eye and turned back to Abdas.

"What happened?" Svetlana asked.

"Torpedoes missed," Vornado said, winking at her.

"The torpedoes are gone, Captain. Can't we stay on board the ship? We can't abandon the cruise missiles."

"The torpedoes are coming back, Holy One." The sound of the torpedoes changed again. Out in the sea, the units had turned around and were coming back, their active sonars pinging again. "The Americans call that 'reattack.' If they lose the scent, they come back for a second try, then a third. Eventually their processors will correlate this return to their target, or the mother ship will reprogram them to remove the Doppler filter and they will see us, even though we are stopped. You need to evacuate until we've won this battle. Your cruise missiles will be here, Holy One. We will keep them safe. We will fight for this ship's survival. I promise you, no crew will fight harder. If this battle is survivable, we will survive it. When we do, we will surface next to the escape vehicle and bring you back aboard. If we don't appear, you can call your contacts for help. There is heat and air and food in the escape vehicle, and if the seas are calm, you can open the upper hatch for fresh air."

Abdas didn't say a word. He rushed to the accessway, dragging Arsalaan with him.

"What the hell did you do that for?" Danalov hissed.

"Watch," Vornado said.

"You fool, *they're* going to escape and *we're* going to die. It was supposed to be the other way around. The idea was to shoot them here, then take this ship home."

"You wouldn't get them all, Vic. They would hide in the middle level with their weapons. The only way to get rid of rats from a ship is to sink the ship."

"Is that what you're going to do about the enemy submarine out there? Let us sink?"

Vornado listened. Something had happened to the noise

of the torpedoes. He stepped to the sonar console and smiled. Both units had shut down. The Mark 48s had run out of gas. Vornado's tactic had paid off. This time. If he were correct, there would be no next time, because he'd give the Western submarine no cause to shoot again.

"The weapons are dead, gentlemen," Vornado said. "Mr. Maslov, status of reactor startup?"

"I've pulled control rods and I'm heating up, now, Captain. I'm twenty minutes from having propulsion power."

"What's the holdup?"

"Reactor vessel head stress, sir."

They were in a tactical situation, but he decided to allow the startup to be done slowly. In the unlikely—no, impossible—case that they were fired upon again, he would hustle the startup and risk cracking the reactor vessel, but until he had an indication they were in danger, he would sit tight here.

"Well?" Danalov asked. "What are you going to do about the enemy submarine?"

He turned to Danalov. "Nothing. Hush, here they come."

The Egyptians came galloping into the command post, the lower-ranking members of them carrying their things. What did terrorists pack for a trip like this? Vornado wondered. Codebooks? Radios, satellite phones, computers? Twinkies? Whatever it was, they were ready to load it all into the escape vehicle.

"Andrei, secure your post at ship control and assist the Ahel al Beit in getting into the escape vehicle. Show them how the upper hatch operates, and the heater and lights." He almost added "the first-aid kit," but bit his tongue. No need to have the terrorists suspect they would be in danger in the pod. "Inform me when the lower hatch is ready to be shut."

"Yes, sir."

Danalov's eyes bulged out in frustration. "Vornado, how is this going to work?"

"Trust me," he said. He looked over, and the Egyptians were almost finished climbing up into the large escape pod. He was surprised that they were going so quickly without asking any further questions. He had imagined it would take a gun battle or taking one of them hostage, but up they went all by themselves. Perhaps he had underestimated the amount of fear that two incoming torpedoes could cause to a landlubber.

Since the Egyptians were so cooperative, it was time for Vornado's contingency plan. "Ivan, man the sonar display, and be wary for any more incoming torpedoes." That was more for show for the Egyptians, since they could hear the conversation until they shut their lower hatch.

"Mr. Danalov, man the firecontrol panel. Let's prepare the weapons in tubes one and four." He worked with Danalov to repeat the sequence they'd used to prepare the UGST torpedo to shoot at the freighter. At least the dead men on the freighter were about to have their revenge.

Rusanov returned to the command post. There was a strange expression on his face. Perhaps shock, Vornado thought.

"They're all in the vehicle, Captain. We're ready to shut the lower hatch."

"Arm the release mechanism and pass control to the dead man's panel," Vornado ordered.

He walked forward to the break in the wraparound consoles to the vertical accessway portal. He opened the door and climbed two rungs of the ladder. Inside the pod, the lights were lit, the interior dim and stuffy and cold.

"Holy One," Vornado said, his voice trembling with emotion. He climbed all the way into the pod. It was a tight squeeze with all the Ahel al Beit terrorists there. There was a main level and a half-level shelf up above that could be used for sleeping. It looked like it could sleep six, with room for twice that many below if they used the area of the lower hatch. Vornado counted heads. All of them were here.

"Yes, Captain?"

"I wanted to ask if you could say a prayer for us and for our safety," Vornado said, an earnest expression on his face. "For us, and for the safety of your cruise missiles, and that we may continue our mission."

The leader's face became calm and distracted, as if he were meditating, his mind far away.

"It shall be done. Go in the peace of Allah, Captain Vornado. We look forward to your success in battle. And we will say prayers for you until you triumph."

"Farewell, my master," Vornado said, reaching up for the hatch. "Go with Allah," he said to the terrorists, then pulled the hatch down and spun the engaging ring, then lowered himself down the rungs through the lower hatch and shut it, then spun its dogging ring. He looked up at the dead man's panel and pulled the protection cover off the release toggle switch. There was an identical panel inside the pod, but he'd armed this duplicate panel, which was installed for redundancy. It was called the dead man's panel, because if it had to be used to eject the pod, the man remaining to release the escape vehicle would go down with the ship.

"Go with Allah," he said again as he held his hand over the release toggle switch. "Better yet, go *to* Allah, you motherfuckers."

He punched the switch to detonate the explosive bolts and immediately a large blast rattled the ship, shaking the deck hard enough that he had to grab the ladder to the hatch above. The sound was loud enough to pound Vornado's ears and intensify the headache that had been cooking since the first torpedoes were launched. The roaring noise lingered, a long, deep screech of metal. He looked at the panel, which showed the "vehicle released" indication.

The rule of Abdas al-Sattar on the Lira was finally over.

"Attention in the firecontrol team. Master One is proving too slippery for us to hit with a Mark 48. Either he's been briefed on our tactics or he has the intuition of a genius. In any case, he knows we're here, and he'll be firing at us any minute. I don't intend to wait for Master One to shoot us. I intend to nail his position down now. He knows we're here, so an active sonar pulse will not give us away. We will ping active at him, and when we have his range and bearing, we will be launching the SUBROC in vertical launch tube one at Master One. Carry on. Weps, status of SUBROC unit one?"

"Warmed up, just waiting for a firecontrol solution. Recommend you hover at seven zero feet."

"Very well. OOD, take the conn and hover at seven zero feet. Sonar, Captain, we're about to stop and hover to shoot a SUBROC. Prepare to go active against Master One."

"Conn, Sonar, wait one."

"Helm, all stop," Flood ordered. "Diving Officer, hover at seven zero feet."

Dillinger checked his watch impatiently, knowing it would take time to prepare to go active. It wasn't a frequently used tactic, and it was more art than science. In the worst case, all that would happen was that they'd give away their own position while still not seeing the Alfa.

"Sonar, Conn, transients from Master One."

"Anything recognizable, Sonar?" D'Assault asked.

"Whoa, *loud* transient from Master One," Keating said, his usual discipline temporarily lost. "Sounds like something exploding. Maybe an internal explosion."

"Torpedo status, Weps?" Dillinger asked.

"Reattack mode, Captain. Neither one has him."

"Conn, Sonar, this is wild, but I have loud surface noises. Sounds like something on the surface."

Vornado hurried back to the command post. Danalov glared at him accusingly.

"You've failed us, Vornado."

"I've not yet begun to fight," Vornado said, quoting John Paul Jones, another plebe rate he'd had to recite for Victor Kaminsky so many years ago. "Attention, crew. My intentions are to put a UGST torpedo into the escape vehicle."

The room abruptly erupted into a cheer. Vornado stared at the people in the room, amazed. He'd thought it was obvious. Danalov's mouth hung open before a smile came to his face.

"You dog," Danalov said, shaking his head. "You had this planned all along."

"It was just a hazy idea stuck in the back of my head. A contingency plan that we were fortunate enough to use," Vornado said. He looked up into the overhead, thinking that the Ahel al Beit were still up there, and his job wasn't over yet. "Mr. Rusanov, vertical rise to nineteen point five meters, slow ascent rate. Raising the periscope."

Vornado hit the hydraulic control lever to raise the periscope. As the eyepiece module came slowly out of the well, he put his face to it and stood erect out of his crouch as the scope rose fully out of the hull.

On the surface there was some light with the coming of dawn. It was cloudy overhead, with a choppy surface, the waves rolling by in long swells from a stiff wind, maybe twenty knots steady, with gusts to thirty knots. He turned the periscope in a slow circle, stopping when he saw the escape vehicle close in the view. It looked like a large section of the fin itself had risen to the surface. The pod was attached to the upper curve of the fin and the sloping sides. The entire upper part of the fin went with the pod, the spherical section almost completely submerged below the fin cap. The cap floated five feet tall in the waves, the windshield of the bridge half-raised. It must have been jarred loose when the vehicle broached. Vornado had worried that the vehicle would present too small a target, but it looked like it would suffice.

"Sending firecontrol bearing now," he said, hitting the bearing button.

"Firecontrol accepts the bearing," Danalov said.

"Set range at ten meters." The weapon was in surface target mode, with wake homing disabled, magnetic hull detection, and direct contact fuses both on.

"Firecontrol accepts the bearing, but the torpedoes are locked out by safety interlocks. How are you going to shoot the escape vehicle? It's right where we are."

"In the West, this is called an 'over the shoulder shot.' We shoot the torpedo out to the north. It travels a thousand meters, then turns around and comes back."

"But it will come back right to us."

"I'm inserting a floor setting. I would have liked to see the pod explode while I watch in the periscope, but I'll need to be below the floor setting so my own torpedo doesn't hit us." Vornado put the floor setting in at fifty meters. His hull would need to be deeper than that for this to work.

"Ready, Captain," Danalov said, his previous cooperative attitude back. "Safety interlocks are shunted. Torpedo accepts the firecontrol directions."

"Fire the UGST," Vornado ordered, looking over Danalov's shoulder. The noiseless torpedo launch again seemed strange. The wire guidance showed the position of the torpedo as it headed out to the north.

"Mr. Rusanov, vertically change depth to two hundred meters."

"Two hundred meters," Rusanov acknowledged. "Flooding centerline variable ballast."

"Very good. Lowering the periscope."

On the way back down, Vornado concentrated on the firecontrol display. The UGST transited north at thirty-five knots, a fairly fast clip, then executed its turn to come back to the firing position and ascended to a depth of two meters, blasting in toward them just below the waves.

The unit's active sonar came on, pinging in rapid machine-gun bursts, then pinging again at a different frequency, the tones seemingly chosen at random. Vornado watched the panel as the torpedo came flying in. If it made a mistake in its floor setting, or if they had programmed it wrong, it was a bullet headed right for them.

"Sonar, Coordinator, is it possible Master One surfaced?" D'Assault asked.

"Conn, Sonar, unclear."

"Captain, recommend check fire on the SUBROC. If he's surfaced, the depth charge will be much less effective."

"Captain, unit two has shut down," Tonelle reported.

"Dammit," D'Assault said.

"Conn, Sonar, we have a torpedo tube door coming open."

"Unit three shut down," Tonelle said.

"Fuck this," Dillinger muttered. Both his torpedoes—the ones fired with satisfactory firecontrol solutions—had missed. The damned Alfa was just too good. It was like he had some kind of divine shield. Well, Dillinger vowed, it wouldn't last much longer. "Attention in the firecontrol party. Firing point procedures, SUBROC unit one, tube one, Master One."

"Conn, Sonar, torpedo in the water."

Dillinger wasn't surprised. Nothing this slippery bastard could do now would surprise him. He had to make the command decision, Dillinger thought, the one no one could help him with. After fighting this elusive Alfa all night, and watching him elude four torpedoes, with the son of a bitch in his sights with a nuclear depth charge, should he delay the attack and run from the Alfa's torpedo, or should he stand his ground for a few more minutes and fire the SUBROC?

No wonder the Academy kept drilling into their heads the value of courage and sacrifice in battle. So many people pictured what he did as pushing a button and the enemy disappeared. If they only knew how much uncertainty there was in this business. And now he was presented with two options—running from the Russian torpedo and losing the Alfa yet again, or staying and fighting and risking eating the torpedo.

"Sonar, Captain, track the torpedo. OOD, all stop and hover at depth seven zero." If the under-ice evasion tactic could work for the Alfa, maybe it could work for Dillinger. As a bonus, that was missile firing depth for the SUBROC.

Over the next few minutes the UGST torpedo got louder and louder, until its pinging rose to a crescendo. It was so close Vornado could hear its pump-jet propulsor. The sounds were coming from up above.

"Here it comes," Svetlana said, using her normal voice. "Congratulations in advance," she said, smiling at him. He nodded at her, a serious expression on his face. He waited for the torpedo to explode. It occurred to him that if the weapon malfunctioned, it could drive right into the Lira and kill all of them in one brutal punch.

All he could hope for, in that case, was that he would be dead before he suffered. He caught Svetlana's glance then, and hoped that she would live. On this mission he had committed crimes he would never forgive himself for— killing the men of the *Kirovsky* and making a mockery of his marriage and dishonoring his wife and his children. He could accept his own death. But Svetlana didn't deserve such a fate. Before he could complete the thought the torpedo sonar grew earsplittingly loud, and he thought he heard a metal-to-metal click. Instinctively he clamped his eyes shut, wondering if his fourth mistake had been to order a torpedo detonation so close to his ship.

"Conn, Sonar, Master One's torpedo has *down* Doppler. Master One has turned his torpedo around. Conn, Sonar, Master One's torpedo shows it's returning on its original bearing, on a reciprocal course."

"Could tonight get any stranger?" Dillinger asked D'Assault, shaking his head in astonishment. "He turned his torpedo around on *himself*? What, is he committing suicide?"

"Conn, Sonar, Master One's torpedo is going active. Torpedo bearing is now the same as Master One's."

31

"Holy One, I think I hear something," Hameem Farruhk said. Hameem was the closest any of the Ahel al Beit came to Abdas's second-in-command, a tall, thin, earnest youngster completely devoted to the cause, but perhaps lacking the ruthlessness and cunning of Abdas himself. That was a commendable combination, though, because when Abdas himself was the number two to Surayj's Ahel al Beit, he had had ambition. That ambition had led to Surayj's fiery death in the horrible bombing attack at the café that Abdas had engineered. The explosion had brought Abdas more than command of the Ahel al Beit; it had brought him wisdom. Wisdom to realize that ambition in a subordinate would never be tolerated in his regime.

Shortly after he took over, Abdas had conducted a purge, although he never used a word for it. Anyone loyal to Surayj had terrible accidents, ending up just as dead as Surayj himself, or in cases where Abdas was inclined to be merciful, they ended up in secret Ahel underground prisons with their hands cut off and their tongues removed so that they would never tell the tale. Since then the fortunes of the Ahel had multiplied as his financing sources saw the heart of a warrior, and saw how serious he was about wiping the scourge of the Israeli state from the face of Allah's holy earth.

The mission with this submarine had not been Abdas's idea, but it had been brilliant nonetheless, and he had told his financial backers to watch for something spectacular, which would come—as prophecy had declared—from the seas. The Lira submarine, while impressive, had disappointed him. He would have expected that with all the work that went into it, with all the claims that it was a supersub, that it would have easily dispatched any enemy, but here it was helplessly stopped in the ocean while torpedoes attacked it, and forcing Abdas and his holy warriors to leave the vessel in this overgrown lifeboat.

Abdas sat in the center of the bottom circular bench, an arctic parka wrapped around his bony shoulders against the cold. The escape vehicle rocked slightly in the swells of the surface as Abdas waited patiently for the outcome of the battle.

"My lord, we have the radios ready in the event that Captain Vornado loses the battle," Hameem had said a few moments before.

Abdas al-Sattar had held up his palm to command silence. "No, Hameem, there will be no talk of Captain Vornado losing this skirmish. He will prevail. I can feel it from deep inside. I have watched him closely, and I believe that Captain Vornado is ready to come to Allah on his knees. He will win this, and we will be back aboard with him soon, and we will execute our holy task before Allah. The Israelis will burn in the fires of purification that we will deliver."

Of course, once the mission was completed, Captain Vornado and the Lira submarine would have to be destroyed, just as the Terminal had been, and the *Kirovsky* after that. There could be no trace of the fingerprints of the Ahel al Beit on this mission other than Abdas's own statements after the plan succeeded. The strange thing was, Abdas had developed a deep respect for young Captain Vornado, who was certainly one of the boldest sea captains in history. It would pain Abdas to kill him, but then, his spirit would go to the most merciful Allah, even though he was an infidel. Perhaps Vornado's assistance on this mission would help him in the face of the one true God, Abdas thought, smiling to himself.

The noise Hameem pointed out sounded like a rushing from directly below.

"Holy One, perhaps Captain Vornado has launched a torpedo."

The fading sound of the weapon whooshing away could clearly be heard through the thick titanium of the escape vehicle.

"Good, Hameem. That means that there will not be much time to wait. The lurking Western submarine will be crushed." Abdas closed his eyes in prayer, his eyes moving back and forth under his lids.

The sound of the torpedo faded away in the distance. Abdas waited, his eyes still shut.

"I'm cold," Arsalaan complained in his barbaric voice.

Abdas looked up at him in irritation. "Creature comforts have always been more vital to you than the cause," he said calmly. "Allah uses this event to try to teach you something."

"It would be fine with me if Allah made it warmer in here. Hameem, can you turn on the heater?"

"Holy One," Hameem asked, uncertain if he should leap to the orders of Arsalaan, who was out of favor with the master. "Would you desire me to—"

The noise of a whining shriek came from the same direction that the torpedo had left. It continued to make the noise, but it was a different sound pattern from the torpedoes that had hunted them before. That could only mean one thing—that there were *two* Western submarines out there, perhaps from two different nations, and this new model of torpedo was launched by the second submarine, and if Abdas's submarine were directly below them still, this second infidel's weapon was coming right for Captain Vornado.

"Let us pray," Abdas said. "Let us pray that the new torpedo coming for Captain Vornado malfunctions and misses its mark. Let us all pray for Captain Vornado."

The screeching sound changed, becoming a series of rapid beeping pulses, growing steadily louder and louder, from the same direction. Soon there was another noise, the same rushing sound they had heard when the Lira launched the torpedo a few minutes before. Both the pinging and rushing noises grew so loud that conversation could only be conducted by shouting.

"Allah, in your holy vision you have seen fit to spare us from this battle, and for that we thank you," Abdas prayed, his voice rising over the hellish noise of the torpedo. "We come to you now, in all humility, to ask for your blessing for—"

The explosion ripped the escape vehicle into ten thousand pieces, the biggest no larger than a toilet seat, the smallest the size of a splinter, with much of the mass vaporized in the high-energy fireball. The blast and shock wave pulverized the bodies of the men of the Ahel al Beit, leaving only scattered bodily fluids and bone fragments. The metallic debris from the explosion rained slowly down through the thousand-meter-deep Barents Sea, the larger plates from the fin cap floating slowly down like feathers falling from a tree, the smaller chunks floating downward more quickly. Among the metal detritus were the remains of a gold-plated scimitar sword, the handle melted away so that only the blade itself fell toward the ocean bottom. After a five-minute fall, the blade stabbed into a patch of sand between outcroppings of rock on the seafloor. The jewels on the blade could no longer be seen in the coalmine darkness of the bottom.

The sword was the only earthly thing remaining of Abdas al-Sattar and the Ahel al Beit.

The explosion was so close the deck lurched to starboard, tossing Vornado into the console. Svetlana landed on him, her head smashing into his back. The lights went out and the consoles lost power again. The noise was worse this time, the ringing in his ears much worse. He felt his head, which had hit the console display hard enough to crack the glass. He had a bump the size of his thumb rising on his forehead. The pain of it extended into his skull, joining the headache that had taken root behind his eyes. Up till now he had been able to ignore it, but it was starting to remind him of the *Albany* run. *I hope the tumor's not back,* he thought.

"Andrei, isn't there anything we can do about the four-hundred-cycle power?" he said in irritation, rubbing his sore forehead.

"Temporary battery inverters coming back online," he said. The console displays flashed as they came back to life.

"You okay, Svetlana?"

"I'm fine, darling," she said, rubbing her shoulder. "Oh, sorry. I relaxed a little too much when you got rid of the clients."

"Which reminds me," he said. "We need to look topside to make sure we hit it. Mr. Rusanov, vertical rise to nineteen point five meters. Raising the periscope."

From the deep looking upward he could see the debris. As the periscope cleared, he saw ten acres of foam across the water, with a hundred pieces of floating wreckage. He could see a life jacket from the escape pod, a blanket, a battle lantern, but this time there were no bodies.

"Lowering the scope. Mr. Rusanov, vertical dive to two hundred meters. Mr. Maslov, status of reactor startup."

"Sir, I'm fully warmed up and ready to start the steam plant. I'll have all turbines ready in a few minutes."

"Conn, Sonar, loss of Master One's torpedo."

A roaring distant explosion came through the hull from the southeast.

"Conn, Sonar, Master One's torpedo has exploded."

"Obviously," Dillinger said. "Sonar, do you still hold Master One?" Maybe this battle was over, and Master One had done them a favor. Still, this would take quite a bit of explaining to Smokin' Joe Kraft.

"Conn, Sonar, we've lost Master One on broadband. Too much noise from the explosion. But we hold Master One on narrowband. He's still kicking."

"Someday maybe we'll figure out what just happened," Dillinger said to D'Assault. "Sonar, are you ready to pulse active?"

"Conn, Sonar, yes."

"Sonar, Captain, ping active at Master One."

The sonar pulse was loud enough to rattle Dillinger's teeth. He could hear it echoing through the ocean. He hated that sound. It said, "Here I am; come and get me." But in this case, he was so frustrated trying to nail the Alfa that he didn't care. Between the enemy's annoying tendency to disappear at supersonic speed and evade torpedoes by stopping, he had no idea how to kill him other than nuking him. Every other tactic had failed, and his orders were clear—the Alfa had to die. So if active was what was required, so be it.

A second pulse went out into the ocean. Dillinger had hoped sonar could do it with one, but apparently they were having trouble.

"Conn, Sonar," Keating reported in a deadpan voice. "We have him. Bearing one six four, range twenty-six thousand four hundred yards. Data sent to firecontrol."

It was a little close for comfort, Dillinger thought. The spec on distance was twenty-five miles, or fifty thousand yards. Shooting the Alfa meant the nuke would blow up thirteen miles away. He could make a little of that up by running, but the time of flight of the SUBROC was a little more than ninety seconds. He couldn't run far in a minute and a half. But he was here at the decision point again. Either he risked the ship and killed the Alfa, or his mission went unfulfilled and the ship was safe. It wasn't a choice. If the ship suffered, so be it.

"Firing point procedures, vertical launch tube two, Master One," Dillinger ordered.

A faint noise sounded through the hull. It was ghostly, a piercing whistle, not unlike a whale call, but more electronic. There was only one thing that made that noise—a BQQ-5 sonar system, as installed on a Los Angeles–class submarine. Vornado hurried to the sonar console. He could see the sound of the sonar on the screen. The display was called the multifrequency sound-pressure level display, the Russian version of broadband sonar. On the sonar screen, which was white to indicate the absence of noise and black to depict a sonar contact, there was a heavy stark-black trace that correlated to the tone that came through the hull.

The wailing noise came again. There was no mistake. Vornado would never forget what that noise sounded like. There was an American submarine out there. At first he felt relief. Since it was American, he and the crew were safe. If it had been British or French or Russian, there was no telling what their governments had told them about the Alfa. And since he had sunk the freighter, a foreign submarine would have assumed him hostile and would have had cause to shoot him. He knew now that those torpedoes were defensive shots, fired in haste and in fear, in reaction to the torpedo he had fired at the freighter. They had thought that torpedo was for them, and had fired back. But now that he knew it was an American sub, this run would soon be over.

It did raise the question of what to do now. Obviously the Los Angeles class was pinging active in an attempt to communicate with them. It was a signal, and a sign that the long dance between them was over, thank God.

Vornado knew a way to hook up a microphone to their own active sonar system to make an underwater telephone of sorts, but it would take too long. Perhaps he should just ping active back at them.

"Shoot on generated solution," Dillinger ordered.

"Set."

"Stand by."

"Shoot!"

"Fire!" Tonelle took his hands off the panel and watched, a slow smile coming to his face. The sound of rushing gases could be heard from forward. "Tube gas generator ignition and missile ejection," he said triumphantly. As fast as it had come, the noise faded, and then a much louder noise roared from the bow—the sound of solid rocket fuel igniting.

"Conn, Sonar, own-ship's unit, solid rocket fuel ignition."

"Helm, all ahead flank!" Dillinger ordered. "Steady course three two zero! Dive, make your depth one thousand feet! Maneuvering, Captain, cavitate! Sonar, Captain, hauling ass to the northwest."

There was nothing to do now but run away from the Alfa and pray the SUBROC landed on target. D'Assault sought his eyes, and he could see admiration for him in her expression. She shouldered up to him. "You did good, Captain," she said quietly.

"Couldn't have done it without you, Coordinator," he said. "Sonar, Captain, keep a weather eye on Master One. If the SUBROC is a dud, we will immediately slow and fire a salvo of Mark 48s at Master One."

Vornado found the screen of the sonar module that would let him configure for an active sonar pulse. As he was about to ping back at the American submarine, Danalov stiffened next to him.

"Captain," Danalov said. "Look at this."

Vornado looked over at the multifrequency display. There was a black trace that was much stronger than the previous sonar pulse, yet this noise didn't come through the hull. Vornado plugged in a headset to listen to it. He trained the sphere's pickup hydrophone to that bearing, almost due north, and listened. He was no sonar expert, but he could swear that what he was hearing was a rocket. That was right; it was a definite missile. The bearing of the noise was changing rapidly. That meant it was either very close or very fast. The noise got quieter, and the streak turned to gray from its previous black, but it was still coming. During the boost phase, the missile's bearing changed from north to north-northwest in a few seconds, but then it steadied at about 330.

What the hell would cause a rocket motor ignition? A Tomahawk missile? What would a Tomahawk be targeting? Unless it was a SUBROC. *Dear God, there is a SUBROC on its way in!* What in God's name was the Los Angeles sub doing? Didn't they get the word? The torpedoes had been mistakes, Vornado was certain. But this . . . this could be no mistake. The American sub was trying to kill them with a nuclear weapon!

When Lieutenant Commander Lionel Tonelle punched the "fire" fixed-function key, the firing circuit sent current to the ignition mechanism for the gas generator of tube two, which was a charge of solid rocket fuel aimed downward into a reservoir of deionized water. The rocket fuel ignited and sent a large jet of flames toward the water reservoir, which erupted into steam, expanding in volume a thousandfold. Under the pressure of the expanding steam, the RUR-5 Mod Delta SUBROC missile was ejected rapidly from the tube.

The skin of the missile never got wet as it rose in a bubble of rushing steam, which formed a tunnel all the way to the surface. The missile rose from the sea, still traveling upward from the force of its ejection from the tube. Eventually it slowed as gravity pulled it earthward, but as it passed through zero g, the firing circuit inside the missile's computer shut, and the missile ignited its solid rocket booster. Flames shot out the aft end of the missile, and for a brief instant it just hung there over the boiling water with the rocket thrust building, but then it accelerated upward, slowly at first, then faster, until it flew so fast that it passed through Mach 1 on its way up. The first stage of solid rocket fuel was small, only enough to gain a thousand feet of altitude, and as quickly as it had ignited, it was exhausted. A ring of twenty-four explosive bolts detonated, and the solid rocket stage was jettisoned, tumbling astern as the weapon continued in its arc of flight.

On the way up, the winglets had snapped open, giving the weapon-control computer directional control. Under the cylindrical belly of the missile, an air duct popped open, admitting high velocity air into the missile, through the compressor blades, through the combustion chambers, and out through the turbine and the rear nozzle. At first the air did nothing but flow through the missile, windmilling the compressor and turbine assembly. The missile continued upward, eventually reaching the second point of zero g at the top of its parabola. The control surfaces rotated, taking the missile back down toward the sea in a steep dive. As the missile accelerated back to earth, the air windmilling the compressor sped up, and the compressor rotational speed came up until the air in the combustion chambers reached three atmospheres, just enough so that combustion in the chambers wouldn't backfire through the compressor.

The weapon control computer directed fuel injection, the fuel pump spinning up and delivering jet A fuel to the combustion chambers. The computer lit all six combustion chamber spark plugs, and the fire began inside the missile. As the flame fronts stabilized in the combustion chambers, the pressure rose at the entrance to the turbine, and the turbine began spinning faster and faster, and since it was connected to the compressor by the central shaft, the compressor spun faster and compressed the incoming flow more, until the jet engine was fully self-sustaining. The weapon computer throttled the jet engine up to full power and rotated the winglets, pulling the missile out of its steep dive just in time to avoid crashing into the cold water of the Barents Sea.

The missile stabilized its navigation and rotated the nozzle to turn toward the attack vector, and as it turned, its GPS system confirmed it was going the right direction and to the right position. Only then did the arming circuit of the nuclear depth bomb energize, the hydrogen bomb fully ready.

Vornado bolted from the sonar console to the propulsion plant displays. "Mr. Maslov, I need power immediately. What's your status?"

"Blowing down the steam headers now. Steam piping will be warm in ten minutes."

"No, it'll be warm in ten seconds. Open the main steam stops and spin the turbine generators, now!"

"We'll wreck them with moisture droplets, Captain! They'll throw turbine blades all over the fifth compartment!"

"You're relieved," Vornado shouted, pushing Maslov out of the chair. He looked up at the software and overrode all the permissive interlocks to start the port turbine generator. He spun it up to three thousand rpm, then engaged the power to the turbine generator breaker and started both reactor coolant pumps in slow speed. He spun the starboard turbine the same way, paralleled it into the electric plant, and upshifted both main coolant pumps to fast speed, then engaged the clutch.

"Andrei, engine ahead full speed! One hundred percent reactor power. Report reactor power level and speed, and steady on course three three zero." He stood. Maslov looked at him as if he were a defenseless puppy who had been kicked by a heartless and cruel master. "Take the plant back, Dmitri, and cheer up. Your reactor has just saved our lives."

"What the hell's happening?" Danalov asked.

"The trailing submarine just launched a rocket-mounted nuclear weapon at us."

"Fifty percent power, forty-seven knots, steady on course three three zero."

"What? A *nuke*? You're serious?"

"Seventy percent power, fifty-five knots."

Vornado ignored Danalov and sat at the sonar console.

"One hundred percent power, sixty-one knots."

"Well, what are you going to do about it?"

"What am I going to do about it? What can I do? Run away as fast as I can and hope to hell it's a dud."

Danalov's face grew threatening. "Figure something out, Vornado. Defend this ship. Find a way. Do something."

Vornado stared at Danalov. He was right. There must be something Vornado could do to fight the American submarine. But why had they attacked with such overwhelming force? It came to him that they were trying to sink the Lira because they had found out that it was under the control

of the Ahel al Beit. How were they to know that Vornado
and the crew had just rid the earth of the terrorists? The
same problem would have existed had Danalov's mutiny
plan been executed. The net result was that the attacker or
attackers out there were following rational orders.

It was all clear to him now. The Los Angeles–class sub's
captain must have thought that the mutiny plan had failed
when the Lira had attacked the freighter. They never expected him to follow such a brutal order. That was the
moment the battle had turned, he thought. They must have
believed that when the Lira attacked an innocent ship on
the high seas, that Vornado had been killed. And if Vornado were obviously dead, the CIA believed that Danalov
couldn't get the ship back to Norfolk on his own, and with
the vessel in the hands of the Ahel al Beit, without Vornado, letting it leave the Barents Sea was too dangerous.
That must have invoked the CIA's contingency plan. And
the plan, when all else failed, called for the Lira to be
torpedoed. And when the torpedoes had failed, and knowing how fast the Lira was capable of going, the Los Angeles
submarine had pulled out all the stops and launched a
SUBROC.

It all made sense, Vornado thought, because it was what
he would have ordered had he been calling the shots for
the CIA. He couldn't blame Hank Lewis or the CIA, or
the crew of the opposing sub. None of them were to blame.
It had been a terrible mistake to shoot the freighter. Danalov had been right after all. Vornado should have let Danalov start the mutiny then, he realized. But it had all
happened so fast, and he had been feeling his way through.
And now his own mistakes were conspiring to kill him.

This is the end, he thought. All his work had been for
nothing. All his plans were nothing but smoke. He, Rusanov, Danalov, Svetlana, the Maslov brothers, and the Lira
itself would soon be gone. But at the same time, the actions
of that submarine were about to result in his death, and
didn't he owe Rachel and the children the chance to have
a husband and father?

Dammit, he thought in anger. What would B. K. Dillinger have done? He answered himself immediately. Dillinger wouldn't have hesitated. He wouldn't have spent a
half second wallowing in guilt for torpedoing the freighter.

And it wouldn't matter to him that his attacker was a fellow American. He would have said, "So what?" And he'd sit down at the firecontrol console, load one of the RK-55 Granat missiles, and launch it at the attacking submarine, legitimately defending himself.

But would that work? It was a land-attack cruise missile. It couldn't detonate beneath the water. It might not have a warhead in the form of a depth charge, he thought, but it had a two-hundred-kiloton hydrogen bomb in it, a detonation that could be rigged to go off at sea level. The warhead was twenty times bigger than a SUBROC's warhead. The explosion from that would have severe results beneath the sea. The pressure wave would be able to cut a submarine to ribbons, if he got close enough to it.

But that was the conundrum. He didn't want to kill the other sub. He just wanted to scare the hell out of the other captain, perhaps frighten him off long enough for Vornado to drive the Lira out of here. That was the only goal, Vornado thought, to get out of here, into the Atlantic, and from there, *home*.

Vornado threw himself into the firecontrol seat and brought up the firecontrol module to program the Granat missile in tube five. Fortunately, programming the Granat was as simple as targeting the UGST, unlike the complex American systems. Vornado glanced over at the sonar module and mentally guessed the range to the sub, its bearing determined by the bearing in which the missile had emerged from the sea. The other sub had given himself away that instant, Vornado thought. Bad for him, good for the Lira. The captain of the sub would prudently have driven away from the launch point. Where would he have gone, Vornado thought, if it had been he who had launched it? His headache pounded as he tried to clear his head and think. East, he thought. He'd go east to get away from the blast zone. Vornado would aim west, he decided. If he could get the detonation to be thirty or forty miles from the other sub, it might shut down his reactor and open all the electrical breakers from the shock. He'd be stunned, but not dead, and Vornado would be able to get the hell out of the Barents.

He picked the location in the sea that he was aiming at, toggling the sonar module to display the navigation display, then putting it back on the sonar display, then turned to the firecontrol module and programmed in the detonation location.

"Attention, crew. In the time we have left I intend to power up the RK-55 Granat cruise missile and target the Western submarine. We will assume a range to the target and put the missile there. The warhead will detonate at slightly above sea level, but the shock wave will be enough to paralyze the attacker or make him think twice about shooting us again. If we can get the shot off, and if we escape this missile, this battle will be over."

Vornado shifted from the sonar console to the firecontrol console. He flooded and vented tube five while energizing the power circuits to the cruise missile. While it warmed up, he opened the outer door.

"Mr. Rusanov, pressurize the starboard bank torpedo tube flush tank with the ballast transfer pump."

"Yes, Captain. Pump energizing now."

Vornado put the tube in firecontrol automatic, then addressed the weapon and locked in his detonation point, checking it a second time. It made the assumption the other sub had withdrawn to the east, but that was solid. It was what B. K. Dillinger would have done.

Finally the RK-55 weapon was ready. He hesitated, realizing the ship was going too fast. If he launched the weapon at a speed of well over sixty knots, the missile would break into a thousand pieces from the fury of the water flow.

"Andrei, engine stop!"

"Engine stopped, sir."

"Engine astern, Andrei. Give it fifty percent reactor power!"

The ship shook like it had been grabbed by the hand of an angry god.

"We could shear the shaft off, Captain," Rusanov said.

"What's your speed?"

"Twenty knots."

"Keep it up, but tell me when we're at five knots!"

The ship trembled violently, the crew grabbing handholds in the shaking cabin.

"Five knots!"

"Now!" Vornado said to himself as he hit the launch fixed-function key, and the weapon was ejected from the tube. He listened, but the silent tube launch had ejected the canister of the cruise missile. Then he heard it clearly through the hull. The canister had breached the surface, and the sudden roar of the rocket launch was loud in the room, but quickly died to a whisper before it became quiet again.

"Andrei, engine ahead full, maximum rate of power increase! Take it to one hundred percent power!"

"Throttling up, sir."

The hull began to shake again, the feeling reassuring. Vornado considered launching a second Granat, but there would be no time to get a second missile loaded into a tube. He shifted over to the sonar console to see if the missile was going to work. As he watched, the bearing of the incoming missile changed from north-northwest all the way to south-southeast in a matter of a half second. The goddamned thing had just flown overhead at nearly supersonic speed.

The SUBROC flew on, hugging the waves, flying a mere thirty feet above the ocean, until the navigation unit indicated it was time. The winglets pulled the missile up into a steep climb, its altitude increasing as its speed decreased. At the top of the arc, the weapon again turned down toward the sea, but before it had a chance to accelerate the jet engine spun down as the fuel valve shut off. Six panels on the skin of the warhead section blew off under the force of explosive bolts and the depth charge separated from the jet engine. The missile body flew on and crashed down into the water. The depth charge ejected a small parachute, and for the next minute it sank to the Barents Sea below. Finally the waves grew closer and the depth charge hit the water.

A sensor on the unit's skin shorted out from the seawater, completing one interlock of the unit's safety circuit. A depth transmitter registered increasing depth as the unit sank deeper, the light from the surface vanishing, until it passed eight hundred feet. The final depth interlock cleared, and the unit began its final arming. At a depth of 990 feet, the weapon's computer ordered it to detonate.

There it was, Vornado thought, the noise to the southwest. It was the splash where the other sub's nuclear depth-bomb missile section had come to earth, directly astern of them. There were only a few seconds left before the depth charge hit the water in a second splash. He knew how frightened he was. By the expressions on the faces around him, the crew were terrified.

The sonar module registered the second splash, right on time. The depth charge was sinking now to its preset depth, which was programmed to be half the seawater depth for shallow water or a thousand feet for deeper water. Here it would sink to a thousand feet. The trip would take it about two minutes. Vornado looked at his gold Rolex one last time, watching the second hand make one graceful rotation around the beautiful azure dial.

"Attention, crew. In about twenty seconds you will be hearing the loudest bang you've ever heard in your lives. If we've been successful at putting distance between the splash and our position, we'll survive to continue the fight. Carry on."

Vornado barely shut his mouth after his speech when the shock wave hit them.

32

In the first half second of the blast, the low-explosive grain charges detonated at once, each one geometrically shaped to blow a section of bomb-grade uranium together into a precise sphere. Almost immediately the fission reactions multiplied until the heat was enough to raise the temperature of the uranium ball as hot as the surface of the sun, and when the fireball spread out it encountered the flasks of deuterium, or heavy water, that had been packed into the crowded warhead.

As the temperatures ascended to mind-boggling levels, the deuterium began to fuse, its protons coming together to form helium and giving off tremendous energy with each fusion. If the fireball from the uranium was big, after the fusion reactions had taken their course the fireball became the size of a small building.

Almost immediately the quenching action of the ocean absorbed the tremendous heat of the fireball, the gases blowing vertically out of the sea into a gigantic flare of steam and water. What was left of the fireball collapsed into a quintillion bubbles that rose slowly toward the surface, and a spherical shock wave reached out at sonic velocity, bounced off the bottom, and reflected off the surface, then reached out in an ever-expanding circle of a violent pressure wave. The shock wave moved outward, ready to pulverize anything in its path, and after it hit the bottom, the first thing it encountered was the aft port quarter of the Lira submarine as it raced northeast.

He began to fly in slow motion through the small control space, which had lit up in a million brilliant sparks and turned sideways and tipped slowly until it was completely vertical. As he fell, he wondered if he had already died. He slowly flew toward the aft consoles, but before he got there they disappeared in a huge fluffy cloud of gray smoke. He flew through it, the trip turbulent.

He spun through space in the dark smoke, the billowing dark mist around him moving rapidly past, and he could hear something. A voice, the voice of Rachel. Then he heard his children talking, their voices quiet, their words indistinct. Then Joe Kraft's voice started speaking, the sounds almost like what he would hear at a party if he had shut his eyes, their voices recognizable though their words were not. Then Hank Lewis spoke, then George Willey, his old executive officer, and his old crew on the *Hampton,* and then B. K. Dillinger. The voices of Dillinger's crew started speaking, and then Viktor Danalov, except it wasn't the Danalov of today; it was the Victor Kaminsky of two decades ago, talking to him in his midshipman's room, interrogating him about the raid on Whitehead, and then he heard the shrieking of Midshipman Whitehead himself. He could hear Yuri Belkov and the Kaznikovs, and then Abdas al-Sattar and his crazy brother Arsalaan. Strangely, the voices slowly died down, becoming lower-pitched, until all Vornado could hear was his father's voice, and then his mother's. It had been so long since he had listened to the sweet voice of his long-dead mother that he felt choked up, and yet there were no tears.

Because he had no eyes.

He tried to speak, but he had no mouth.

The man who had been Peter Vornado swirled, spiraling through the gray clouds at an incredible speed, until the light began to diminish, the gray becoming black, but feelings of warmth and euphoria came over him.

It was ended, he thought, but it was all right, because he was safe.

It was over. All of it. His Navy career, his time as a husband and father, his time as a contract agent to the Central Intelligence Agency, his time as the love interest of Svetlana Belkov, and his time as the captain of the Lira submarine. Before the grayness became completely black, a single voice spoke inside his head, saying something in a foreign tongue, but something he understood, the phrase repeated over and over again. As the voice spoke, lightning seemed to strike behind the curtain of smoke, briefly lighting up the mist, then the smoke became dark again.

Though he understood the meaning, it seemed like the voice was speaking to someone else, because the translation of the phrase was:

Would you go back?

Not *will you go back* but *would you*. There had to be meaning in the distinction, he thought. But if the question were for him, the answer came from his heart, and the answer was *no*. He saw all the pain of his life there in front of him—the pain of losing his mother, then the homesickness of being at the Naval Academy, barely mature enough to be away from home, and already in the first battle of his career with Whitehead, then the long, trouble-filled struggle for submarine command, with all its disappointments, the ache inside from burying his father, the terrible pain of being diagnosed with terminal cancer and having to let go of everything in his life, from his career to his wife and children, the pain of watching his struggles at the Terminal, the pain of watching his attack on the innocents on the *Kirovsky,* the pain of knowing he'd been disloyal to Rachel, and worst of all, the pain of his failure with the mission of the Lira, and how he was now responsible for the deaths of everyone on board, yet another group of innocent people who had trusted him with their lives and were now being punished for doing so.

Why, he asked wordlessly, would he ever want to return to that? No, he would turn his back on the idea. He wasn't sure what happened after life, but the way he felt now, there could be nothing worse than the hell he had just left, a miserable, broken failure of a life. He was done. It was over.

An image flashed in front of him then. Not just an image, but a reality, more real than any experience in his life. He had a body again, and he could feel the fabric of the jeans against his legs, the fabric of the T-shirt against the skin of his back, the hard tile of the floor on his knees, and the warm soapy bathwater on his hand. He looked in front of him, and in the bubble bath he saw two-year-old Erin, laughing and splashing, her platinum-blonde hair a halo around her beautiful head, her wide blue eyes—her mother's eyes—staring happily at him. She smiled and looked up at him and she spoke, saying only one word in her little-girl's voice:

Daddy.

He wept then, the tears soaking his T-shirt, his shoulders shuddering, his nose running.

And then he said the words that made all the difference.

Of course I'll go back.

Instantly Peter Vornado was back inside the vertical command post, flying through the air. In the next moment he smashed into the propulsion plant console, pain erupting around him, and the world faded at the edges, becoming black, the blackness growing toward the center, until there was only a small dot of light that slowly faded to nothingness.

The shock wave smashed the Lira submarine like a giant hammer, the sea an anvil, the outer steel of the hull deforming and rupturing. The wave reached out to torture the titanium metal of the inner pressure hull, but the inner hull was much more resistant and didn't rupture or tear apart. Still, the submarine was accelerated in a terrible jolt, with sufficient force to rip bulkheads off and send the heavy reactor off its foundations. Had it not been for the new sound mounts, the reactor vessel would have smashed through the hemispherical bulkhead of the third compartment and roared clear through the command post and on into the torpedo room, but the new foundation held against the terrible impact.

As the Lira submarine came to a halt from its high-speed retreat, it began to flood in the sixth compartment and take an up angle. The water flowing into the hull accelerated and gathered in the bilges. Every breaker had opened up, and the ship was completely dark. One motor generator had come off its bearings and punctured the first compartment bulkhead. Aft, in the fifth compartment, one of the turbine generators had experienced the same fate.

In the command post, the small six-member crew all lay on the aft consoles, their broken and shattered bodies lying in one large heap, covered with shattered glass from the flat-panel displays.

The ship's up angle began to become life-threatening. Up

to this moment, the ship's depth had been stable at two hundred meters, but as she began to get heavier, the Lira began to sink.

Ten seconds after the shock wave passed the Lira, a weaker version of it impacted the submerged USS *Tucson*. The *Tucson* shuddered in the rocking blast, half of its electrical breakers opening from the shock, but otherwise unharmed.

Within minutes, the *Tucson* began to recover from the shock wave. The battery breaker was reset by the crew, and the lights came back on. The motor generators were restarted, and power flowed to the AC electrical buses. The four-hundred-cycle electrical sets came on next, and in the control room the firecontrol technicians frantically tried to recover the firecontrol system.

In sonar, Senior Chief Keating worked to restart sonar. In the heat of a battle, there was no way he was going to allow the power outage to take down his equipment. When the ship was deaf, they could be killed in an instant. Sweat erupted from his forehead and his armpits seemed to melt as he labored to reconfigure the system. As he had hoped, within two minutes of restoring power, sonar was back on-line. Keating tried to use his most casual voice as he made the announcement to control.

"Conn, Sonar, sonar is back."

The ship still had no reactor power, since the reactor had scrammed when power was lost, and it would take at least ten minutes to restart the engineroom.

Keating set up the broadband sonar first, keeping an eye on the bearing to Master One. As he had expected, everything from the south to the west was "blued out" from the nuclear detonation. But what caught his eye was the rapidly approaching curve of sound, arcing over from the south and suddenly changing bearing from south to the north.

Either they'd just been flown over by a jet, or a missile had just flown overhead at low altitude.

"Conn, Sonar, aircraft mark on top," he said quickly.

In the control room, Dillinger's eyes grew wide as sudden fear gripped him.

The RK-55 Granat missile, called the SS-N-21 Sampson by NATO, had a proud history. It had been independently developed in a joint venture by several Russian design bureaus. It had anticipated most of the features of the American Tomahawk cruise missile, beating the Tomahawk to market by two years, but since the weapon had been shrouded in secrecy, the world never knew about it, and the Tomahawk became the darling of the world's militaries. But the missile didn't care about such matters. It merely waited, inert and sleeping, for its hour of need.

Late on this November morning, that hour arrived. Under the impulse of the flushing tank, the missile swiftly moved out of torpedo tube five of the Lira submarine. As soon as the rear of its watertight canister cleared the tube door, two fins snapped down, each fin angled downward to act as elevators to push the tail down and the nose up. It floated rapidly to the surface until its nosecone broached.

Two sensors in the skin of the nosecone sensed that they were no longer shorted by seawater. Thirty-six explosive bolts around the seam of the nosecone of the canister blew up at once, and the nosecone flew off into the night, tumbling slowly end over end. In the next five milliseconds the rocket motor ignited, the fury of the flames thrusting the missile out of the canister and pushing the canister underwater. The missile's needle-sharp nosecone came rapidly out of the canister, then the missile body, and finally its tail cleared the top of the cylinder. As the tail came free, four tail fins snapped outward and a NACA duct opened on the lower skin of the missile to suck in air for the compressor.

Under the thrust of the rocket the missile flew upward, tracing a large parabolic arc in the sky. As it flew over the surface of the sea, the underwater detonation of the SUBROC blew ten million gallons of seawater into the heavens, the plumes of steam and liquid almost reaching up to the missile's highest point on its trajectory.

The missile reached the height of its arc, its rocket fuel exhausted. The rocket stage separated, and the jet engine started. The missile dived down to the sea, flying toward its destination, its programming checking the stars above for a star fix, its inertial navigation system correcting itself from the fix on reality. Had the Granat been tasked to attack a city, it had the capability to follow the terrain, hugging the land a mere ten meters above the ground. Not even a sudden cliff could confuse the missile's guidance system. It could be programmed to go to waypoints, or to circle to the far side of its target and attack a city from the opposite direction from where the enemy suspected it to appear. It was ingenious, crafted with loving care by both scientists and engineers, groomed by technicians, and perfectly maintained. As it flew on, it eventually recognized the featureless spot ahead of it in the sea as the intended target.

The missile didn't care that the target was a spot on the ocean when it expected a city. It flew emotionlessly upward into the clouds, rotated its fins, and came back down again, checking the exact coordinates of the target. Satisfied that the target was correct, it armed its warhead and sailed rapidly downward. The radar altimeter came on, the detonation timed to coincide with the programming of the weapon's altitude setting. Tonight's setpoint was five meters above sea level. Even that low, the missile would be going nearly Mach 1 when it flew through the elevation of five meters, and before its needle nosecone even touched the ground, the warhead explosion would be fully executed.

The radar altimeter reeled downward. One hundred meters, eighty, sixty, forty. The final circuit aligned for warhead detonation. Twenty meters.

Fifteen.

The warhead's low explosive detonated, and before the missile traveled another meter the uranium-235 had been blown into a ball and exploded into a huge nuclear fireball, which consumed the heavy water canisters, and the fission temperatures provided the heat required for the fusion explosion. The fireball grew to a flattened spheroid over the water, the pressure wave blasting upward and sideways. At the surface of the water, almost a cubic mile of seawater was instantly vaporized. The shock wave reached down to pound the ocean floor, and outward seeking to hammer anything in its way.

For a fifty-mile radius the shock wave traveled, and as it passed it killed every single living marine organism in its path. One of the organisms was more resilient than the others, made of eighty-thousand-psi-yield strength steel. The shock wave reached out and smashed through the beast, rattling every solid thing inside it and rending the flesh of the organisms in its belly. As it passed, it sheared off the thing's top fin and its tail fins, even its front fins, then pulverized its nosecone, which was made of fiberglass rather than steel. The front of the shock wave kept on, uncaring, until eventually it encountered another steel mechanism like the first one, but this one it was gentler to, even though it wouldn't matter, because the second contraption was already busy dying. Finally the shock wave dissipated in the sea, the only thing left of it a cloud of bubbles the size of a small city where the weapon had first exploded.

For hours the ocean seethed with the fury of the rising angry bubbles from the two nuclear explosions. The only sounds that competed with the explosions were the sounds of groaning metal as bulkheads of the two machines in the sea bent from the pressure of the deep.

One second, Dillinger stood in the control room.

The next instant he was flattened on the deck as if by a giant hammering piston. His face throbbed against the hard, cold deck, in absolute blackness. Completely silent darkness.

Something flew down and hit him in the back of the head. He could feel the world begin to spin in dizziness. He could feel the gore at the back of his head. He felt his stomach contract. He felt himself vomiting from the pain, but he couldn't hear any sound. The horrible pain became something solid and heavy, crushing him, and he couldn't breathe.

Just as he thought it could get no worse, the spray of freezing arctic seawater hit him. The shock of it made his body convulse. He tried to lift his head off the deck, because the water was there, in his nostrils and pouring down his throat, and he remembered thinking how oddly salty it tasted.

Seawater.

Salty seawater at the beach.

His father in the sunshine, his arm extending slowly as the Frisbee soared over the flat sand, the disk coming closer to seven-year-old Burke Dillinger.

Don't call me Burke. My name is B.K.

"Fine, dear," his mother said, humoring him. "Come have lunch, B.K."

The world spun upside down, then right side up again. The air smelled salty; it smelled like the ocean. The fishy ocean scent he'd smelled when he got out of the car at Annapolis, a visceral reminder that he was near the water, no longer in northern Virginia.

Annapolis. Midshipmen in starched white uniforms. Reporting for duty in jeans and a short-sleeved shirt. *Put on the white works alpha with your gym gear underneath, scumbag . . . scumbag . . . scumbag.*

White works alpha with the gym gear underneath.

White works alpha.

Alpha.

Alfa.

Submarine.

Flooding.

Fire.

Sinking.

Drowning.

Dying.

Dead.

33

Sinking, Andrei Rusanov thought. His head pounded and there was a sticky liquid running down his face. He tried to touch his face with that arm, but a shooting pain thundered through it. He reached up with his right arm and felt his face. The right side of his face was a mess. His eye had swollen shut, and he must have broken the bones of his face. He could barely hold his head upright.

When he finally did, he realized he was tangled in a pile of bodies. He tried to push himself up, fighting the dizziness and the fear from being submerged in a completely dark room. He could smell blood. He could feel it as well. But it was the dark that frightened him more than that. It was darker than a mineshaft.

That wasn't completely true, he thought. He could see flickering dim light out of his left eye. He tried to look at it, but could only see a reflection in the broken glass of a console. He realized that the light was coming from the fires burning beneath them. When the word _fire_ went through his mind, the surge of adrenaline burst into him, and his mind seemed to clear. He coughed, the air heavy with the smell of burning insulation. The fire was a secondary problem, he realized. The bigger issue was the deck. Instead of being horizontal, it was inclined nearly straight up.

It was only his perspective that made it seem that way, he thought. It was more like a forty-five-degree angle, but on a submarine, that was a pitch high enough to be deadly.

What was he thinking? he wondered. There were far worse problems the ship was suffering than just its angle.

It was an emergency, and in an emergency on a submarine, one pushed the panic button. There was only one problem—the panic button was mounted above the ship

control console, which was now far over Rusanov's head.
He tried to get his footing, but the only thing that supported his weight was the pile of bodies. He was afraid he
was standing on someone's face, and if he pushed off, he
would paralyze someone, or worse.

A groaning boom resounded from the overhead,
screeching through the entire ship. Dear God, he thought,
the ship might be descending through creep depth. He had
to get to the switch. He should have had them mounted all
over the command post, but it would have delayed the
ship's mission. How odd that attitude seemed to him now,
he thought.

Another noise roared around him, the hull contracting
from the deep. This noise was frightening. The ship was
dying. He couldn't afford to avoid stepping on the flesh
beneath him.

"Sorry about this," he said aloud, realizing his voice
sounded odd. His mouth was full of the same sticky mess
that was on his face. He tried to spit and felt a half dozen
teeth leave his mouth. It didn't matter. He was alive and
breathing, and he had to help the dying ship. He lunged
for the bottom of the propulsion plant control seat. Using
his right arm, he struggled to climb up on the seat, feeling
winded already. His left arm throbbed. Gently he reached
out to feel it. It was swollen to twice its size, but the bones
hadn't come through the skin when they broke. He jumped
from there to the penetration for the radio mast, and from
there to the sonar control seat. He leaped from the seat to
the rails that surrounded the periscope, and crawled over
and through them to reach the port forward corner of the
command post. *Almost there,* he thought. He vaulted from
the periscope rails to the ship control seat, and heaved himself up over the leather surface of the seat until he could
stand on the back of it to reach the overhead above the
ship control console.

The panic panel was small, about the size of a shoebox.
There was a sturdy clear plastic cover, and below that five
identical toggle-switch protectors. The first switch would
shut all hydraulically controlled hull valves, using an ingenious air bottle and a small hydraulic accumulator mounted
near each valve, the emergency hydraulic actuators his own
idea, because if an emergency were severe enough to re-

quire that the panic panel be used, odds were that it would be severe enough to break the main hydraulic lines that ran like blood vessels throughout the ship. He pulled up the first protector and hit the switch. He could hear noises from above him—the first and second compartment valves shutting, he thought. That might stop any flooding through a piping system, but if the ship were flooding from the hull or the shaft seals, it was all over.

The second switch would blow the forward ballast using gas generator charges. With the ship's up angle, it would be better to blow the aft ballast volume first. Perhaps that would help level the ship. The gas generator charges the switches controlled were essentially hand grenades mounted throughout the forward ballast volume between the pressure hull and outer hull. They were a marginal system, because they had the capability to rupture the outer hull, and then they would be doing more harm than good, but they saved the space and weight of a high-pressure air system with all the compressors required. In normal operation, they used the emergency diesel to blow the water out of the ballast volume. Obviously that wasn't going to happen. Rusanov hit the switch for the after volume and heard an immediate detonation far below. He waited to see if the deck would level itself, and it slowly budged.

It had worked! The aft end was lifting slowly. The angle came off the deck, the deck finally stopping its imitation of a wall. As the deck began to tilt the opposite way, Rusanov hit the second switch, the forward ballast-volume gas generators. He could hear the crackling of the hand grenades going off above his head, the hot expanding gas forcing out the seawater. The ship would be tons lighter now. There was a free-flood area amidships that was also set up with emergency gas generators. Under normal circumstances it would be a terrible idea to use it, because it could give the ship so much buoyancy that it would roll over, but if the ship had been sinking by the stern, it was obvious that it had been taking on water far aft.

Rusanov lifted the protector off the amidships reserve buoyancy ballast volume, hoping he was doing the right thing. He coughed, the smoke beginning to fill the upper part of the room. He hit the switch, hearing the popping sounds of the gas generators exploding. No matter how badly they had flooded, they were rocketing to the surface now. That left the fire-suppression-system switch. That system was a halon system that would douse all the electronics rooms with halon, which would extinguish all electrical fires without killing human life. The trouble was, few of the electronics would survive being hit with the halon system, which meant the powerful distributed control system—all their displays and panels—would be dead forever. But if they were on fire, they were dead anyway, he reasoned. He lifted the protector over the halon switch and snapped it ruthlessly to the on position.

The room immediately filled with white vapor from the halon system activating at the aft end of the space. Rusanov worried for a long moment that the engineers were wrong, and that it would suffocate humans. He coughed, realizing that the atmosphere was contaminated. As soon as the ship surfaced, he needed to do what he could to open the hatch to the fin, the one that had gone to the escape vehicle and the bridge, and get some fresh air into the smoke-filled ship.

Fortunately there hadn't been a battery explosion. If there had been seawater anywhere near the lead-acid storage cells, the chlorine gas could kill them in minutes, and the explosion from the reaction would blast through the hull, even though it was made of titanium, and even though even a nuclear explosion hadn't breached it. An explosion like that was an even force over the entire hull. A battery explosion was like hitting an egg with a nail—it would punch a hole clear through it.

Rusanov was done with the panic panel. The fires aft had died, plunging the room back into total darkness, but the deck was level. And there was other good news—the hull was swaying. Waves! They had reached the surface. Rusanov found the switch of a battle lantern, the command post dimly illuminated by its lamp.

He turned to his injured shipmates. The first rule of first aid was not to move people, but there was no way to help them if they were all lying on top of each other. As gently as he could he separated the people from the tangle, his eyes drifting to Vornado.

"Captain Vornado," he said, his voice cracked and broken.

Vornado's face was covered with a thick coating of blood that had come from a head wound. There was so much blood Rusanov couldn't even tell where it came from. He reached down to Vornado's throat, looking at his body, which seemed whole otherwise. Vornado's flesh was still warm, but he wasn't breathing, and he had no pulse. Rusanov sighed. It was obvious.

Captain Vornado was dead.

Rusanov was not a religious man, nor was he a sentimental man. But as he saw Vornado's dead body lying there, he sobbed to himself, and then impulsively he threw himself across his chest. Vornado had elevated Rusanov from a lowly shipyard employee to his second-in-command, and had trusted him as no one else ever had. He was only ten years older than Rusanov, and yet was a father to him, the father he'd never experienced in his life. Though tears flooded his eyes, he knew the captain wouldn't want him to lie there crying like an idiot when the other crewmembers needed help. He tried to regain control and looked away from Vornado's lifeless body.

Beside Vornado was Dmitri Maslov. It wouldn't even make sense to reach for his throat. Maslov was almost completely decapitated, his head lying on his shoulders, only connected to his torso by thin filaments of bloody tissue.

Svetlana had a compound fracture of her thigh, a mass of blood and bones protruding through her coveralls. He felt her throat. She too was warm, and there was a slight pulse. He put his ear to her mouth. She was breathing—just barely.

Underneath what had once been the sonar console, Viktor Danalov lay. He was bloody, but his breathing could be heard clearly. He was wheezing and there was blood on his chest. Rusanov wasn't sure if it were his or someone else's. When he got closer, he saw the problem. There was a jagged piece of glass penetrating his chest. What was he supposed to do, pull it out, or leave him alone? He'd heard that pulling something out of a person who had been impaled was for the doctors to do. God alone knew if that glass was holding him together, and pulling it out could kill him. But they were here in the Barents Sea, a half continent away from a hospital. Eventually he'd have to pull out the shard.

There was coughing in the room, but Rusanov couldn't tell where it was coming from. He moved to the forward end of the room, where young Mikhail Maslov was collapsed. The kid had gone below when Vornado was about to torpedo the freighter. He must have returned to the room to help as the battle with the Western submarine started.

Maslov hadn't fared any better than his brother, Rusanov thought. His legs were covered in what seemed like gallons of blood. He must have suffered a severed artery and bled out. He felt Maslov's throat. It was cold and there was no sign of a pulse. Maslov's left eye was open, staring into the overhead. Rusanov reached out and shut it, the sound of coughing from aft making him turn.

The blackness eased. Around the edges it became a lighter shade of black. Still dark, but perceptibly lighter.

The lightness moved toward the center, and with it came awareness and thoughts. There were no sensations, only wakefulness. There were no memories. There was no self. Only the lightening universe and a wholeness, the emotion of being connected to an infinite meaning.

There was a thought coming from the distance. The thought could be perceived before it arrived. It was light on one side and dark on the other and it was wrapped around something vitally significant. It grew huge until it obscured the rest of reality. If the thought could be translated, the words would take away much of its true meaning, but it would come down to a single word. Not just a word, a commandment. The commandment was:

Live.

The smell came first.

Smoke.

Burned insulation. Burning electronics. Spilled amine chemicals.

Sight was denied him. He was in darkness.

It was silent.

Except for a distant bell tone. His ears were ringing. He could hear something sliding across a surface, and a human grunt.

He concentrated on trying to feel. At first there was nothing, as if he had no body, but the thought of that frightened him, and then he felt his heart racing in his chest.

His chest hurt. His arms ached. His pelvis throbbed in agony. His legs sent shooting pains up his spine. His back hurt more than the rest combined. And then the headache came, roaring between his temples and behind his eyes.

He felt the sensation of being underneath a sticky wetness. He reached up with one hand, slowly at first. It was in his mouth, a copper-tasting, choking mass. He coughed weakly, then tried to take a breath, the coppery thickness choking him. He coughed harder.

His hand reached his face, and it was a mass of blood and gore.

He tried to get the blood out of his eyes, finally able to blink. As he did, the blurry command post came into view. Someone was huddled over a body. He looked to the side and saw Svetlana.

She was dead.

He closed his eyes, coughing louder as the liquid came down his throat again.

He reopened his eyes and looked at her, realizing her chest rose, then fell. She was breathing.

He sighed in relief.

"Who is that?" Rusanov's voice called. "Captain!" He rushed to Vornado's side. "I thought you were dead!"

"I think you were right the first time," Vornado croaked. He turned on his side and vomited blood in a spreading pool on the deck. He pushed himself away from the blood and grabbed the lower pole of the radio mast, still lying prone on the deck. "Are we sinking?"

"Captain, the ship is steady. I activated the emergency deballasting switches at the panic panel. The electronics were on fire, so I used the halon."

"Are we on the surface?"

"Yes, Captain. The fin is gone, but the hatch functions. The hull was damaged badly, but we have watertight integrity."

"Battery. Did it explode?"

"It's fine."

Vornado smiled, just slightly. "Help me up."

Rusanov pulled Vornado up to a sitting position.

"Are you hurt?"

"Dizzy," Vornado said.

"Your head has a gash." Rusanov pulled out a long surgical dressing and wrapped Vornado's head with it, then wrapped him in a second bandage and then applied tape over that. "I could stitch it."

Vornado waved him away. "What about you? Your face isn't good."

"I think I may have lost an eye," Rusanov said. "My left arm is broken." He squinted at Vornado. "Sir, you promised me you'd keep me safe." He looked at the wreckage of the command post. "This isn't exactly what I had in mind."

Vornado tried to laugh, but it hurt. "I lied. What's the status of the crew?"

"The Maslovs are gone."

Vornado shut his eyes for a second, grief flooding him. "The others?"

"Svetlana and Viktor are alive but they're hurt badly."

Vornado looked at Svetlana's bleeding leg. "We need to put a dressing on that. And apply pressure." Vornado tried to move toward Svetlana but collapsed to the deck, vomiting again. There was even more blood this time.

"Sir, you worry me."

"Help me put a dressing on this." Vornado worked with Rusanov to bandage Svetlana's wound.

"Viktor?"

"He took that glass in the chest."

"Punctured his lung." Vornado moved closer. "What bandages do you have?"

Rusanov showed him the contents of the first-aid kit. He pulled Danalov's coverall zipper down and pulled the top of it off, exposing the wound. He wrapped some gauze around the glass fragment, took a breath, and pulled hard. The shard stuck at first, then came out, and with it a flow of blood. Danalov moaned. Vornado bandaged the wound, then pulled Danalov up to a sitting position and wrapped surgical gauze around his chest, then wrapped in several courses of surgical tape.

Vornado looked up. "We don't have a distress radio, do we?"

Rusanov shook his head.

"Radio circuits work?"

Rusanov vaulted to the aft electronics space, but came back with a drooping face. "Burned to hell."

"Help me up," Vornado said. Rusanov pulled him gently to his feet. They limped to the vertical accessway, where Vornado slowly climbed out of the hull. It was incredibly cold. There in the distance was a ship.

A submarine.

Its bow came out of the water, the hull at a severe incline. There was no fiberglass nosecone, only remnants of the wrecked BQQ-5 sphere. Aft of that the cylinder of the hull sloped down toward the water, meeting the waves halfway down. Something was missing, Vornado thought, then realized what it was. The ship's sail and bowplanes had been sheared off.

"We have to help them," Vornado said. "Get the inflatable life raft and find some parkas. And bring a toolkit."

The inflatable tossed in the swells of the Barents. The small two-cycle engine coughed to life, then steadied. Vornado throttled it up. The wind of the boat's passage blew the spray into the boat, soaking them with icy seawater. His fingers were incredibly numb. They got closer to the American submarine.

Vornado had been right. Though it was barely recognizable, the ship was a Los Angeles–class sub. Its paint had been blown off the entire starboard side, and it was so heavy aft that the bow had risen from the sea. Vornado guided the inflatable to the point where the hull met the waves. The hull's angle was about twenty degrees. Any more and climbing up on it would be impossible. The water on the hull was freezing already.

"Stay with the boat!" he shouted to Rusanov as he jumped onto the hull. He reached in and grabbed the heavy toolbox. He wasn't sure he'd be able to open a hatch even with the tools.

He climbed unsteadily up the hull to the wreckage of the sail. From a distance it had appeared to be sliced cleanly off, but up close he could see that the fracture was anything but clean. Remnants of masts and hydraulic lines and the structural steel of the sail protruded from the hull. He made his way through the mess until he reached what had once been the bridge access tunnel lower hatch, except that now there was nothing left of the tunnel structure. If he were lucky, he could do this with his bare hands. He grabbed the circular ring of the hatch dogs and rotated, but it was stuck. In the toolbox was a pipe wrench. He applied it to the ring and pulled as hard as he could, until the ring budged. He thought he would be able to weaken it and then open it by hand, but he had to use the pipe wrench to turn the ring through ten turns before he could open the hatch.

"Captain!" Rusanov shouted from the inflatable. "Hurry, sir! The sub is settling into the water!"

Vornado waved and pulled the hatch open. Immediately a blast of hot, broiling smoke came roaring up from the inside. It was as if Vornado had opened the gate of hell itself and peeked in. He should have brought one of the bottled air kits from the Lira, he berated himself, but there was no time to go back and get one and return before the submarine settled further into the water. He had ten minutes, maybe less.

The moment he stood on top of the hull seemed to expand to last an hour. The thought came to him that he should turn around and go back to the Lira and await help. This submarine was doomed, and in fact, it was already dead. He didn't need to do this, he told himself. He was no hero. His torpedoing the freighter testified to that. He should just return to the Lira. He was a husband and father. He had been spared up to now, but this terrible mission was over. The only responsible thing for him to do was save himself. Save himself and go home and allow this nightmare to fade. Grow old with Rachel and live a long and happy life.

Save yourself, he commanded himself. *It's the only responsible thing to do.*

Peter Vornado took a deep breath, clamped his eyes shut, and threw his legs down into the smoking hatch opening.

He promised himself he would find an emergency air mask as soon as he got inside. He knew exactly where the cubbyhole had been on the *Hampton* and the *Augusta,* and hoped it would be there on this ship. An eerie thought came to him—what if this ship were his old *Hampton,* and he was present for its funeral?

He pushed the thought aside and vaulted down the ladder, pushing his aching body, his heart hammering in his chest. If his view from topside had made this seem hellish, it was nothing compared to the interior of the submarine. The deck met his boots, but it was inclined steeply, too smooth and too wet for him to keep his footing. A momentary impression came to him in the darkness; that the slickness underfoot was blood.

He kept his eyes shut against the noxious smoke. Even if he'd had an air-fed mask, he wouldn't have seen anything. It was dark, and the black billowing hot smoke filled the space. He felt tears running down his cheeks beneath his clamped-shut eyes. This wasn't like hell, he thought; it *was* hell.

He forced himself to move to where the control room should be. There, in the overhead, starboard side, between the door to control and the door to sonar, there should be a cubbyhole, and in it about twenty emergency-air breathing masks. He reached up, but felt only the laminate of the wall. In fury he searched, cutting open his wrist on broken metal, but on the other side of it was something soft. Rubber! He pulled it and the mask came out of the overhead. He hoped he hadn't ripped the hose on the gashed metal. Quickly he strapped it on and tightened the straps, grabbed the regulator and snapped it to his belt, then found the free end of the high-pressure hose. He had known every manifold on the *Hampton,* each submarine-qualified crewmember required to find them blindfolded. He reached up, and the manifold was right where it should be. He stabbed the quick disconnect into the manifold, almost out of air.

This was it, he thought. If the emergency-air system had ruptured and depressurized in the explosions, he was a dead man. He was out of air and he'd never feel his way back to the hatchway again. The thought came to him that if he had to die in the tomb of a submarine, he'd rather it be an American submarine. At least then he'd feel closer to home.

Home, he thought. *Rachel. Marla. Peter. Erin.* The anger boiled up in him and he fought the morbid thoughts. There had to be air in the manifold. He had come too far to die here. He took the deepest breath he could, knowing that if the system had broken, he would be taking a puff of toxic fumes that would instantly drop him to the deck.

The air was foul, but it was air. Dry and coppery and smelling of something dead and fishy, but life-giving nonetheless. He hyperventilated in panic and a dawning awareness that this was the single most foolish thing he'd ever done in his life. He took another deep breath, reached up, and disconnected his hose from the manifold, his mind screaming at him to run back to the hatch and evacuate this burning inferno. No one would blame him, he knew. They would say he had done everything that he could.

But they would be wrong.

He was in the control room. During the battle, most of the ship's crew would have been here, and if not here, back in the propulsion plant.

Odds were, the people back aft couldn't be saved. The engineering spaces of the aft compartment were far underwater, and were probably flooding and about to take the ship down. But the crew here . . . There could be almost two dozen souls who could be saved right here, close to the forward hatch. All Vornado had to do was grab them and get them the few feet to the top of the hatch. As if possessed, he felt for a body nearby, the helmsman at the ship control panel. He unbuckled him and pulled him up, rushed him to the ladder, and with every ounce of strength pulled him up to the hatch.

Rusanov was right there to pull the man out. The sight out the hatch was alarming. Rusanov's inflatable was only ten feet down the hull from the hatch. The ship was sinking. Vornado let go of the helmsman and went back down for another body. He plugged his hose in, took three fast breaths, then grabbed another crewmember. He hurried him to the hatch, where Rusanov, broken arm notwithstanding, pulled the body to the boat. Vornado went back below. Three more pulls of air, and a third body.

Over five minutes, Vornado pulled every body he could find out of the hull.

"Captain Vornado!" he heard Rusanov through the roar of the fire. "Hurry! The hatch is almost to the water level!"

Vornado found another body, this one a woman. He pulled her out from under a bookshelf and muscled her to the hatch. There was no one left he could find in the dark and smoke. He was running to the hatch when he tripped and fell over one final body. He picked him up, the man's beard stubble rubbing Vornado's arm. He pulled the man to the hatch, where water started to come in.

The exertion had taken its toll on Vornado's muscles. He could barely move. He got the man's head out into the opening of the flooding hatch. Rusanov grabbed him as Vornado pushed him up. And then, of all the experiences in Vornado's life, perhaps the strangest happened right then as the unconscious man's body moved past Vornado up the hatch. Vornado caught a glimpse of embroidery at the man's pocket, right below his submarine dolphin emblem, barely visible through the smoke and rushing seawater.

The embroidery spelled something from a past that seemed so long ago as to be in another lifetime. The block lettering spelled: B. K. DILLINGER.

Just as Vornado's mouth came open in shock the explosion threw him into the ladder, and the world dissolved into bright flaming sparks.

The darkness came at the edges and moved rapidly to the center.

There was no tunnel, no dark mists, no voices, only deep blackness that absorbed his total consciousness.

This time it was truly over.

EPILOGUE

Rachel. The sound of her name was a moan. *I'm sorry.*

There was white light. Glaring in some places. Soft in others.

He could feel himself. A deep ache all over. His legs were hot. His arms were cold. His head throbbed.

The light was a blur, but he could sense someone close to him. He could smell perfume. It was *her.* He could see every moment they spent together. How wrong it was. How wonderful it was.

He blinked. There were long, cool fingers on his forehead. He could see the color yellow. The spun silk of her golden hair. It should have been short, but it came halfway down her forehead and had begun to cover her ears. At first he was frightened for her. The clients would see her. Then his alarm calmed as her fingers stroked his hair. The clients were no more.

He shut his eyes as it all came back to him. The battle raged behind his eyelids for some moments before he opened them again.

There were two people in the room. Svetlana Belkov, dressed in a formfitting business suit. And Burke Dillinger, dressed in Navy service dress blues. They stood close to the hospital bed and looked down at him. B.K. had that smirk he always wore when he had a secret. Svetlana's brows formed a frown of concern.

He tried to speak. Nothing came out at first, until finally he could croak out the words.

"How long?"

Svetlana spoke first. "Almost three weeks. You've been in a coma."

Something was wrong, he thought. She spoke *English.*

"Where?"

Dillinger took this question. "Bethesda Naval Hospital. Not far from home."

Home. Rachel. The children. He looked up. *And Svetlana.*

"B.K., could you give me a moment with Svetlana?"

Dillinger left the room and Svetlana sat on the bed.

"We can't be together," Vornado said slowly. They had to be the most painful words he had ever spoken. "Everything I told you about my marriage . . . it isn't true." He looked sadly at the sheets. "It was a cover story." How would she take this? he wondered, but when he looked up there was understanding in her eyes.

"I know," she said. "I was your controller."

He stared at her, his eyes widening. "What?"

"My boss wasn't Sergei Kaznikov. My boss was Hank Lewis."

"Oh," he moaned, sinking back to the pillow. He sighed as the sadness settled on his soul. None of it had been real. He had been worried that she would break apart his marriage, and now he found that she had been playing a role the entire time. "So all that was just acting?"

"No," she said quietly, her fingers reaching out to stroke his hair. He wanted to lift his hand and touch her, but he was too weak to move his arm. "I was living inside my cover, just as you lived inside yours. But I had to be closer to you than anyone else, and I had to be with you day and night. What better way to do that than to be your woman?"

It was all a lie. What a fool he'd been, he thought miserably. He looked away from her toward the wall. "Bring B.K. back in," he said hoarsely. He didn't want her to see his eyes. He'd gotten something in them, and they were watering.

She stood at the door. "Peter?"

He waved her away, but she spoke again anyway, her voice soft, the words of the English language as sensual as the Russian words she had spoken to him. "Sometimes, on movie sets, actresses genuinely fall in love with their leading men." She paused. "I know, because it happened to me this time."

He turned to look at her, but before he could say anything she was gone. He shut his eyes in shame and longing and bitterness and remorse.

Dillinger appeared above him. He could feel Dillinger's hand squeeze his shoulder.

"I heard about the whole thing from her," he said quietly. It seemed deliberate that he didn't say her name. His voice was solemn. "She told me all of it. You should let it go, Peter. You did what you had to do. It's over now. We'll all go back to the way it was."

"Except for the ones who died."

"I know, Peter. We lost the entire crew except for the ones you pulled out of the control room. You saved my life. You saved their lives."

"Who made it?" Vornado asked.

"You got all my battlestations junior officers except Fortunato and the ones standing watch aft. You rescued the helmsman, the COB, the chief of the watch, and the sternplanesman, my battlestations sonarmen, and the sonar chief. And my XO and me. From what I heard, that was a miracle. There was water pouring in the hatch when you pushed me out, and just then the battery exploded. Your guy pulled you out just before the hull—what was left of it—went down." Dillinger shook his head. "It was a bad day at sea, Peter."

Vornado reached out slowly and grabbed Dillinger's gold-striped sleeve. "I wasn't trying to hurt you, B.K. I just wanted to make a big bang so you'd be distracted and I could escape. I figured after we launched, you'd go east. What happened?"

Dillinger pursed his lips. "I went west."

Vornado sighed. "Christ. What a goddamned mission."

The two were silent for a long time. Vornado felt the room slowly start to spin. He was aware of his eyes blurring.

"Get some rest, Peter. I'll watch over you."

Vornado was going to protest, but he was asleep before he could find the words.

"Welcome, everyone. Come on in and have a seat at the conference table." Hank Lewis smiled at the three of them. "Coffee?"

Peter Vornado nodded. "American coffee." He took his seat at the large conference table. Through the window, the bare trees of the gray December afternoon swayed in the breeze. Beneath the trees, a week-old coating of snow lay on the grounds surrounding the new administration building of the Central Intelligence Agency.

Svetlana Belkov shook her head. Vornado stared at her CIA name badge, the tag identifying her as "Priscilla Whittaker," the name seeming more foreign than her Russian cover identity. Victor Kaminsky—formerly Viktor Danalov—accepted a steaming cup.

"Well," Lewis beamed. "I see you've all recovered quite nicely."

Priscilla Whittaker had undergone two surgical procedures for her left leg, and had spent the last weeks in physical therapy, though she still walked with a cane. Victor Kaminsky's punctured lung had healed, and otherwise he was in perfect health. The three of them had been picked up by the U.S. Navy destroyer that had been ordered north to the Barents Sea, with orders to tow the Lira out of Russian waters before the Russian Republic could investigate the explosions. Other than the fact that the *Tucson* had sunk in fifteen hundred fathoms of icy seawater after her battery exploded and ripped the hull in half, Vornado was still in the dark about the end of the mission.

"Physically recovered, maybe," Kaminsky said.

"How about you, Mr. Vornado? Headaches gone?"

Vornado rubbed his head. A scar from a twenty-stitch gash extended from his hairline down to his eye, but Dillinger said that it made him look like a pirate.

"The doctors gave me every scan known to medicine. They tell me I'm fine. No sign of any tumor recurrence either."

"Good, good. Let's begin. I just wanted to thank all of you for your inspired service, and distribute your bonuses with the thanks of a grateful country. And to convey the director's apologies for the mistake."

"What happened?" Vornado asked. He'd been promised that he would be told the whole story when he came for a debrief. "Why was the *Tucson* ordered to attack us?"

Lewis shook his head. "I've never seen the director more angry. Apparently the ops center uploaded the wrong orders. The *Tucson* got the contingency plan instead of the main orders. She was just supposed to linger there and make sure your mutiny went satisfactorily. If it seemed like you wouldn't prevail against the terrorists, the contingency plan was to put the Lira on the bottom. Obviously we couldn't have the Lira get away, loaded with nuclear cruise missiles, under the control of the Ahel al Beit." Lewis smiled. "Didn't make much of a difference, because when you torpedoed the freighter, the contingency plan would have come into play anyway. You surprised us. We never thought you'd attack the freighter, draw the *Tucson's* fire, and use the battle as a ruse to eject and kill the terrorists. Well done, but you should have told someone you were going to do all that."

"How the hell was I supposed to know it would play out that way?" Vornado said. "I suppose that means the CIA doesn't have a job for me?"

Lewis shook his head. "Sorry, Peter. Like I said, the director was furious. Part of the reason was that he thought you were impulsive. He thinks you can't be controlled."

Priscilla glanced over then, then turned back to Lewis.

"Anyway, please take this with the compliments of the agency." He handed across an envelope, then passed envelopes over to Priscilla and Kaminsky. Vornado opened his. It was a check for substantially more than the contract called for.

"Hank, what happened to the Lira?" Kaminsky asked.

"The destroyer was towing the Alfa to the Royal Navy Base at Faslane, Scotland, a relatively short hop of thirteen hundred miles from the sinking site of the *Tucson*. Unfortunately the tow line broke, and while they tried to reestablish the tow, the Alfa took on water and sank. She's at the bottom of the Norwegian Sea as we speak."

Peter Vornado looked down at the table, the news like a physical blow. He had worked so hard on that submarine, and it had been such a work of art in addition to being an achievement of mankind. He felt as if someone told him his own child had just died. *It was just a machine,* he told himself, but he couldn't help it. His voice trembled as he looked up at Lewis and spoke. "Did they at least get the notebook computer out of the captain's stateroom? It had every design drawing, every spec, every calculation of the Lira's design. We could build another one."

Lewis shook his head. "No one knew. It went down with the ship in a deep trench. The destroyer said they could hear it implode on the way down. There's probably nothing left of it bigger than a sheet of paper."

The rest of the debriefing went by uneventfully. At the door, Vornado shook Hank Lewis's hand.

"Thanks for the opportunity. I just wish I could go back to work."

"With that," Lewis said, pointing to the envelope, "you'll never have to work again."

That wasn't the point, Vornado thought. It was never about the money.

"One last thing," Lewis said, looking at Vornado's gold Rolex. "I'm afraid that stays with us. Agency policy—no trophies."

Vornado looked sadly at the watch, thinking about Yuri and Sergei and Leonov, all of whom had died in the explosion. Yuri, it turned out, wasn't "Svetlana's" father after all, but another of Lewis's agents. But it still hurt just as much that he was gone. And the Kaznikovs—international criminals though they were—were still human, and had both been decent to him. He missed them, even if they had been the CIA's enemies. Maybe the director was right, he thought. Maybe he had no business as a spy. He sighed, removing the watch and handing it to Lewis. Hank clapped him on the shoulder and left down the hall.

Victor Kaminsky came up, and Vornado shook his hand. "Thanks, Vic. It was great to meet you again. I didn't thank you twenty years ago, so let me thank you now for saving my midshipman career."

"You're welcome, Peter," Kaminsky said, smiling. "Amazing. I did a good thing that day. I wasn't sure I had at the time. Anyway, good luck." He left and walked down the hall.

Vornado turned to Priscilla. He put out his hand. She smiled and threw one arm around him, the other supporting herself on her cane. He could hear her sniff as she hugged him. She pulled back and looked in his eyes.

"Good-bye, Peter Vornado. I'll never forget you." She turned and walked slowly down the corridor.

Vornado watched her until she turned a distant corner. He went back into the conference room and stared out the window at the gray day. Finally he took his sport jacket and overcoat off the seat and headed for the exit. He turned in his visitor badge at the security enclosure, shrugged into his overcoat, and walked slowly out into the overcast, cold afternoon.

There on a park bench a man in a black overcoat sat, a white cap on his head. He stood as Vornado approached. It was a Navy commander, a head shorter than Vornado. He burst into a smile as Vornado came up to him. He held out both his fists, and Vornado smashed them with his own.

"B.K.," Vornado said. "What are you doing here?"

"Debriefing, just like you. The survivors have all been reprogrammed. Turns out we weren't in the Barents Sea after all. Just a milk run to the South Atlantic that turned bad with a defective battery. My crew didn't die fighting honorably in battle. They were killed by a stupid battery explosion." Dillinger sighed, his jaw clamping. He looked into Vornado's eyes. "Listen, I let your driver go. You can come with us. There's someone I want you to meet."

Inside Dillinger's limo was his executive officer, Lieutenant Commander Natalie D'Assault.

"I've already met your XO," Vornado said. "How are you, Natalie?"

"Hello, Peter." She shook his hand and smiled warmly.

"She's not my XO anymore," Dillinger said.

"Oh, until you get reassigned to another submarine."

"I got the news today. Smokin' Joe Kraft just assigned me to your old *Hampton,* Peter. I'm sorry. I know that's tough news. I know how you loved that ship. But at least it'll be me in command of the old girl, not someone who won't appreciate her."

"No, no, that's great, B.K. I'm happy for you." He meant it, Vornado thought, and though it still ached that he didn't command *Hampton* anymore, it would be better that B.K. would have the ship. "But Commander D'Assault won't be your XO?"

"No. You see, this isn't just Lieutenant Commander D'Assault. You're looking at the future Mrs. Burke Dillinger."

She punched him playfully. "Don't say it like that; it sounds like you own me. Just say, 'Peter, we're engaged.' "

"Look at this," Dillinger said. "Already she's the boss."

Vornado stared at the two of them. D'Assault looked

at Dillinger, obviously deeply in love with him. Dillinger just beamed.

"Congratulations," Vornado said. He was speechless for a moment. "I'll be damned, B.K. Leave it to you to find true love in the middle of a battle."

"Will you stand up for me, be my best man?"

"Of course." Vornado smiled.

"Speaking of battles, Peter," D'Assault said. "You put up one hell of a fight."

"You want to know what helped?" Vornado asked her. "I just kept asking myself, 'What would Dillinger do?' And I knew the answer. He'd fight to the death with no regrets."

Dillinger looked at him for a long moment. "Thanks, Peter. I like that."

In an abandoned section of the Royal Navy Base in Faslane, Scotland, the mothballed Royal Navy Fleet lay tied up to the rusting piers. Paint was flaking off the old destroyers and cruisers, the ancient vessels half a century old. Behind a long row of derelict destroyers a rusted hangar extended from far inland to the water's edge. Decades before, it had been converted from an airship hangar to serve as a pier facility where ships could be driven inside and worked on out of the rain and cold of northern Scotland. On the outside there were no lights and no sign of activity. The building had no windows, and the doors were all locked with heavy chains.

Inside, bright floodlamps illuminated the submarine lying in the slip of black water. The vessel had seen better days. Its hull had been compressed on one side, the flanks of the ship partially crushed. On top of the cylindrical hull, the place where the fin had been was now nothing more than steel struts and the remains of the masts and the periscope. A man climbed out of the forward hatch, which had once been under the front edge of the fin. He carried a notebook computer. He stood on the foredeck and handed the computer to his coworker.

"Incredible, isn't it?"

The second man nodded. "An automated submarine able to be operated by a few men in the control room. Unbelievable."

"So, how long to rebuild it?"

"It would take at least a year to understand the damned thing, much less start to refurbish it. The Yanks just want it watertight so it can make the trip across the pond to a secret shipyard on the East Coast."

"What do you think they're going to do with it?"

"I don't think even they know."

The lights of the living room were off, but the glow of the mellow Christmas tree lights lit the room. Peter Vornado threw the log on the fire and walked back to the couch, where he sat back down in Rachel's arms. He kissed her, softly at first, then more urgently.

Her eyes grew wide in mock alarm. "Peter, the children are still awake," she teased him. She snuggled into him. "I really missed you," she said. "Thank God you're not working in that old dusty shipyard in Peru. I'll bet you're glad to get away from the tropics, back to a nice cold Virginia winter."

"Definitely," he said.

"Do you still miss the Navy?" she asked.

He nodded solemnly.

"Well, I can't say I'm sorry about it. At least when you were in Peru, I knew you were safe in the drydock."

"Safe? That's where I got this gash in my head."

"I know, but it's not like you were in mortal peril. Not like B.K., who almost died in that freak accident. I never slept a night when you were at sea on the damned *Hampton*."

"You talk too much," he said. He leaned in to kiss her again when the doorbell rang.

"Who could that be?" she asked, wiping her mouth. She fished in her purse for a compact and expertly reapplied her makeup as Vornado went to the door.

Standing outside was Captain Joseph Kraft, wearing his black Navy overcoat, his hat under his arm, a huge smile on his face, and a bottle of champagne in his hand. Behind him, also dressed in Navy blues, were Commander Burke Dillinger and Lieutenant Commander Natalie D'Assault.

"Hi," Vornado said, not sure what to make of it.

"Sorry to crash in on you like this on a Friday night," Kraft said. "But the news is just too damned good for the telephone. I heard it when Commander Dillinger was in my office, and he asked if he could come along with his XO."

"Come on in, everyone."

Vornado introduced Rachel to Natalie, and the two women smiled and laughed.

"So what's the great news?" Vornado finally asked.

Kraft grinned. "You remember the medical board commander who kept turning down my requests to review your case? Turns out he's some passed-over lieutenant commander named Whitehead. Anyway, Whitehead gets relieved for cause. They found out he was having a torrid affair with his XO, even during office hours. Can you imagine? Anyway, after they fired him, the new commander came in. He called me personally, said he got a call from the Chief of Naval Operations himself. Not the CNO's chief of staff. Not the admiral-in-command of Navy medicine. The four-star Chief of Goddamned Naval Operations. He says to go back over Vornado's records while he waited on the phone. Peter, bottom line is, as of five o'clock this afternoon, you're requalified for submarine duty."

Vornado's face lit up. "Oh, my God, you're kidding." He looked at Rachel. She looked stunned.

"Oh, it gets better, Peter. The USS *Texas,* a brand-new Virginia class, has just been assigned to my squadron. It's yours, Peter. That is, if you want it. What do you say?"

For a long time Vornado looked at Kraft. He looked slowly over at Rachel, expecting her to shake her head, especially after what she had just said, but she finally nodded at him, tossing him a raised thumb before her face broke into a grin.

Peter Vornado smiled.

"Commodore, it would be an honor."

Kraft opened the champagne, and the future commanding officer of the submarine USS *Texas* tossed back the glass and smiled at his wife and his boss and his best friend.

Author's Note

The experimental vaccine program that cured Peter Vornado's glioblastoma is real. The program is being conducted under the inspired supervision of Dr. Allan Friedman at Duke University Comprehensive Cancer Center. Glioblastoma is the deadliest form of brain cancer and is a devastatingly swift killer of young adults. In the spring of 2002, one of our dearest friends was diagnosed with the disease. He was only thirty-seven years old and enjoying career success and a wonderful life alongside his wife and two young children. He was given only two weeks to live with conventional treatment. As a patient of the Duke experimental vaccination program, he experienced a miraculous albeit brief recovery. A few months later a new tumor appeared, complicated by hydrocephalus. The condition proved fatal within weeks. When our friend died, it had been a little over seven months from the initial glioblastoma diagnosis. With more research and funding, this terrible disease may be defeated. The Brad Kaminsky Foundation is devoted to the goal of finding a cure for glioblastoma and other brain cancers. To find out more about this worthy charity, visit www.tbkf.org.

The Alfa (Project 705 "Lira") Russian submarine described in this novel is real. The layout depicted in this book is accurate, as is the history of the submarine and the uproar it caused within the CIA and the Department of Defense. The declassified information available to the researcher of the open media misstates (perhaps deliberately) several facts about the Alfa, one of which is its speed, which is dramatically higher than reported. It could truly dive deeper and travel faster than the pre-ADCAP Mark 48 torpedoes, but was so loud as to make its utility questionable. Still, it remains one of the most innovative submarine ideas ever to submerge in the open seas, and were it to be resuscitated today with quieter machinery and modern technology, it would be formidable indeed. It could even cause yet another panic at the Pentagon and Langley.

In addition to being an engineering marvel, the Alfa is a monument to the failure of intelligence agencies on both sides of the Cold War, because the West failed to recognize it was an old idea that took decades to construct rather than a new thrust in submarine development. As the West reacted to an amazingly automated invincible submarine able to go faster and deeper than our torpedoes, the Russians were only beginning to realize the fact that the chief factor in submarine design is stealthy quiet, not raw speed. Either the misunderstandings revealed by this incident are typical of the struggle of intelligence agencies, or the agencies are deliberately publicizing their failures in a cunning attempt to make their enemies underestimate them, which could make true success more likely. In any case, it is altogether possible that the triumphs of the CIA will not be known until decades after they happen. We should be grateful that the men and women of the CIA are on our side.

For those interested in finding out more about the technology of modern submarines, from the physics of the nuclear reactor to the operation of the trash disposal unit, from acquiring a target to dispatching it with a torpedo, the best reference in print is *The Complete Idiot's Guide to Submarines,* by Michael DiMercurio and Michael Benson. While written in the enjoyable, easy-to-read style of a Complete Idiot's Guide, it is solid enough to be an official U.S. Navy Submarine School tech manual.

See you at test depth,

Michael DiMercurio
readermail@ussdevilfish.com
Princeton, New Jersey

About the Author

Michael DiMercurio was an honors graduate of the U.S. Naval Academy, a National Science Foundation scholar and graduate of MIT in mechanical engineering, a graduate of the Navy Nuclear Training Program, a Navy diver, and a chief nuclear engineer qualified officer and ship's diver on the USS *Hammerhead*, a Sturgeon-class fast attack nuclear submarine of the Atlantic Fleet. During the Reagan administration, DiMercurio and the *Hammerhead* spent over fifty days in trail of Russian nuclear submarines.

DiMercurio's Web site is www.ussdevilfish.com, and he can be reached at readermail@ussdevilfish.com. He lives in Princeton, New Jersey.